Class Letters

Class Letters

Instilling Intangible Lessons through Letters

Claire Chilton Lopez

SHE WRITES PRESS

Copyright © 2013 by Claire Chilton Lopez

All rights reserved. No part of this publication may be reproduced, distributed, or transmitted in any form or by any means, including photocopying, recording, digital scanning, or other electronic or mechanical methods, without the prior written permission of the publisher, except in the case of brief quotations embodied in critical reviews and certain other noncommercial uses permitted by copyright law. For permission requests, please address She Writes Press.

Published 2013
Printed in the United States of America
ISBN: 978-1-938314-28-5
Library of Congress Control Number: 2012922389

For information, address:
She Writes Press
1563 Solano Ave #546
Berkeley, CA 94707

This book is dedicated to all the students who connected with me through our monthly Class Letters. Your willingness to be honest and vulnerable inspired me to tell the world about our process. I'm especially grateful to the student who responded, "I never thought about it like this!" You started it all!

Foreword

I love English. Always have. It was my best subject in school, and always came quite easily for me. When I became a single mother, I wanted to find a profession that was aligned with my children's schedules. Teaching was a no-brainer.

I entered the teaching profession through an alternative certification program and spent my first year in a small town teaching 8th grade English. It was a difficult year for me, and I have often wanted to find my former students and apologize for their "learning experiences" in my classroom... or lack thereof.

The next year, I moved to a larger school and a higher grade. I enjoyed being with the older kids, but I soon became aware that they were unprepared for life after high school. I started to look for ways to help them understand that the choices they made today would affect the people they would become tomorrow.

After overhearing a plot to cheat on an assignment, I wrote my students a letter about cheating, asked lots of questions about their feelings on the subject, and asked for a thoughtful response.

I was amazed and pleased with the level of honesty in that first batch of letters. I realized that the kids not only needed but wanted an adult they could open up to. They appreciated my vulnerability and willingness to enumerate my own shortcomings. I wanted them to understand that adults have issues, challenges, doubts, and fears, just like they do. We make mistakes too, but most of my students didn't have adults in their lives who would admit to them.

That was the beginning of my monthly letters to my students. I touched on a variety of subjects throughout the year, including balance, motivation, and gratitude. I listed my struggles with the issue at hand, and I offered solutions that had worked for me. As an adult, I knew I had the wisdom that only comes with time and experience, but I thought it was important for the kids in my classes to think about the people they wanted to be, as well as the characteristics and skills that would help them make their transition into adulthood.

They grumbled about the letters, of course, as they did with most assignments, but many of them truly appreciated the opportunity to speak their mind on a subject. They wanted to be heard, so I "listened" via the written word.

The letters quickly became my favorite assignment; I couldn't wait to read what my students had written on a given subject. We were able to peek into each other's lives, relating to the commonalities we had. We shared problems and solutions, struggles and victories. The letters provided a means of communication and connection between my students and me that hadn't existed BCL: Before Class Letters.

I soon realized that these letters provided an amazing opportunity for teachers at almost any level to make meaningful connections with their students. Originally, I wanted to create a "how-to" book of the letters I had used in my classroom, along with examples of student responses. It quickly became clear, however, that copyright and privacy issues would not allow for that type of publication, so I wrote this fictional version instead.

I strongly encourage teachers to try connecting with students through the power of letters. Many times, the subject for my own letters grew out of an incident in our class or at school. Sometimes they related to issues outside of school or in the literature we were reading instead. Regardless of the origin of the idea, the intention of the letters was to examine a specific topic, often using examples from my own life, and to ask lots of questions to make my students think about that topic from different angles. I tried to be as objective as possible so that the kids could form their own opinions on the subject. The content for letters like these needs to be age-appropriate, obviously, but I believe this method could be just as helpful in the younger grades as it is in high school. And since the topics tend to be about intangibles, teachers in other disciplines besides English could also easily use this tool in their classrooms.

I also believe these letters could be used outside of the classroom. Coaches, counselors, and even parents could incorporate letters into their interactions with kids. I like letters as a communication tool because I can think about a subject ahead of time, and then craft and edit my words to ensure that my thoughts come across as intended. Letters can be re-read and digested in small pieces until a response is required. (I gave my students a week to read and consider the letter before writing their answers.)

I hope you enjoy *Class Letters*, but more importantly, I hope you incorporate letters into your classroom or pass the idea on to a teacher in your life. The results are amazing!

Happy writing,
Claire Chilton Lopez

Prologue

Anne rolled over as she rearranged her pillow. A glance toward the clock confirmed her suspicion: It was only 2:30 a.m.

2:30 a.m., and she was wide awake.

Ugh.

Rocky, her boxer, snored quietly in his bed on the floor. A police siren sounded faintly in the distance. Anne pulled on a robe, slipped on her flip-flops, and padded down the hall toward the kitchen. Hopefully some herbal tea would help. She flipped on the TV and surfed through fifteen weight-loss and work-from-home-and-earn-millions financial schemes before she snapped it off.

That's all I need. Who wants to be reminded that they are thirty-five pounds overweight and living with two kids on a teacher's salary?

Unfortunately, the restless evening was a typical one on this particular night. Tomorrow was the first day of school, and although Anne had spent the previous week preparing for the new school year, she battled nerves, excitement, and curiosity. What would this year's seniors be like? She had heard about the outgoing juniors. There were rumors about every class every year.

"This is the worst bunch of kids I've seen in years!"

Or, "What a great group of students—so diligent and respectful!"

Anne knew that, in reality, they were always a little bit of both.

She smiled as she padded back to her bedroom, hopeful for another few hours of rest.

In spite of her interrupted sleep, Anne awoke twenty minutes before the alarm. School mornings were always tough for Richard, her teenage son. He usually piddled around and required almost constant surveillance. Every year, Anne hoped that this would be the year he became more independent and had more initiative so that she wouldn't feel like she had to supervise him every step of the way. This morning was no different.

"Richard, are you dressed yet?"

"No."

"Get a move on, son."

"K."

"Maggie, how are you doing? We need to leave in fifteen minutes."

"I'm ready, Mom. Just waiting for the twerp—as usual."

Unlike Richard, Maggie loved everything about school: the learning, the challenge, and most of all, her friends. Getting Maggie to go to school was never a problem. Seeing her friends gave her life meaning and soothed her like an oasis in the desert.

Anne zipped her first-day-of-school dress, ran a brush through her hair, checked her makeup, rounded up the children, and hit the road for another school year.

When she entered the classroom, she looked around, confident in her preparations. Rows of desks stood at attention in straight lines, ready for the day. Posters adorned the walls, hoping to inspire onlookers. Papers lay stacked on a table, waiting to be distributed. Textbooks yearned to be read. Everything was ready.

At forty years old, Anne was only in her tenth year of teaching and her first year at Stephen F. Austin High, after working in a variety of other fields, from retail to restaurants. She had considered being a teacher in college but had graduated with a degree in English rather than education. When her two children had crossed over into adolescence, the single mom had decided it wouldn't be wise to leave them alone for extended breaks. As they were too old for a babysitter or day care but too young to be left completely to their own devices, teaching, and its vacation schedule, had become a viable solution. Besides, Anne enjoyed being with kids—teenagers specifically; she loved literature and writing, and hoped that she might make a difference in someone's life. So she'd signed up for an alternative teaching certification program, and voilà!—she was a secondary-level English teacher.

The butterflies were typical for her on the first day of school. She didn't worry about whether or not she could do the job anymore, like she had when she first started. But the usual questions had drifted through her mind as she tried to sleep the night before. What would the kids be like this year? Would she feel like she was impacting them? How would she keep them motivated and interested?

"Don't smile until Christmas" was the advice a veteran teacher had given her when she began, but that wasn't her style. She didn't want to be stern or intimidating; she wanted to connect with the students, and the connections she had felt with her own teachers had always begun with a smile.

Brrrring. Brrrring… the signal for class to begin.

Anne took her place by the door to greet her students as they entered the classroom. She enjoyed the ritual of shaking hands and greeting them. It proved to be a good barometer for many of the kids. Some would smile, some would grunt, some would simply walk past her with a "Bad day" or "Tired." Some devised their own version of a handshake—daps, high fives, or pound-its—but only after they felt comfortable with her.

The first week of school was simply a time to get to know the students and keep them busy until the counselors finished leveling the classes so she could begin the business of teaching. This was her third year of introducing British lit to seniors. She liked seniors; they were full of hopes and dreams, ready to take on the challenges of the world. Assuming they passed her class. Most did, but some just got too far behind, too wrapped up in their life outside of school.

The students filed in for their first-period class, took their seats, and waited for the day to begin. And then she heard it: "Hey, wait a minute. Your name is Mrs. English, and that's what you teach? Are you for reals?"

It always made her smile. She knew that the students who realized this coincidence were quick—and usually a handful.

"Yes, that's me. Mrs. English."

And with that, another school year began.

Chapter 1

With the preliminary class information out of the way—the rules and procedures, the dos and don'ts—Anne outlined the curriculum for the year. "As you may or may not know," she smiled, "English IV is British lit. We'll go through the literature book chronologically, beginning with *Beowulf* and ending with *Pygmalion,* by George Bernard Shaw. And, like every year in English, we'll do a research paper along the way."

A hand in the back.

"What's chrono-whatever?"

"*Chronologically* means we'll read it in sequence according to the time period in which it happened. *Chronos* is Greek for *time*. Does anyone know what *etymology* means?"

Blank stares everywhere.

"The etymology of a word refers to its root, prefix, and suffix. It helps you understand where a word comes from and its original meaning. Knowing the etymology of a word could help you dissect a word enough to understand the denotation, or dictionary definition, even if you've never seen or heard the word before."

Anne wrote the following words on the board: *chronometer, chronic, synchronicity*.

"Can anyone guess what these words mean?"

Another hand.

"Is a chronometer a time meter?"

"Very good—it measures time. What about *chronic*?"

"It's some badass weed, Miss," joked Ray, a Hispanic boy in the back row.

"I've heard that," Anne smiled. "What happens when you have a chronic disease or condition?"

"Isn't it when you have something that lasts for a long time?" asked Tiffany, a perky blonde in the front row.

"Yes, that's right. Good. Now, if I told you that the prefix *syn-* means *with* or *together*, what do you think *synchronicity* might mean?"

Tiffany raised her hand, "Something that happens at the same time as something else?"

"Right! We'll learn more about etymology as we go through the year. Like I said, it's a very handy thing to know. There are even times when I come across a word that I don't know, but if I know a piece of it, like the prefix or root, I can at least get an idea of the meaning. Then I usually get the rest from context clues. Now I want to explain your novel project. Each semester, I want you to read a novel outside of class that you choose on your own."

"What? I hate to read! I don't like reading nothing I *have* to read, so I know I don't wanna read extra stuff," said Ray.

"The good thing about this assignment is that you get to choose. You can read something from the *Twilight* series or a *Harry Potter* book. It can be one hundred pages or one thousand, and can be by any author you choose."

"It don't matter, Miss. I still hate to read. Do we have to?"

"Well, it's a test grade, and if you don't do it, you'll have a zero. A zero for a test grade almost guarantees you'll fail the six weeks. But it's ultimately up to you. Now, does anyone want to share what they did over the summer?"

"But, Miss, about the book thing," began Ray, "I don't know what to get or anything. And I was banned from the library last year 'cause that library lady hates me."

CLASS LETTERS

"I can help you choose something, and I can also talk to Mrs. Boyle to see about letting you check out a book for my class. Besides, you might actually like it."

As she turned her back to grab a stack of papers, she heard, "*Pssst.* You don't have to really read it, fool. Just look it up on the Internet. She'll never know."

Two of Anne's pet peeves were cheating and apathy, and this suggestion of using the Internet covered both. She would rather get one hundred mediocre honest projects than one stupendous dishonest one. She knew that reading was beneficial, fun, and a good escape. And, sadly, she was sure at least a few of her students could use a wholesome escape from their home life. Unfortunately, trying to convince a room full of teenagers was a difficult proposition. Rather than address the covert op during class, she wanted to sit on it for a while and determine a different tack. Besides, she was angry and needed time to think of an appropriate course of action.

Anne holed up in the teacher workroom during her conference period, sipping a diet cola and getting off her feet for the first time that day. The first day of school—the first week or two, really—was exhausting, especially after summer break. Her vacation days were generally unstructured. She might work in the yard, swim, go out to the nature center, or ride her motorcycle, and her summer attire was always comfortable: shorts, T-shirts, and flip-flops. Some days she was up at 7:00 a.m. to pull weeds before the heat of the day descended; some days she'd sleep until ten. Getting back into a regular schedule and school-appropriate attire was always a shock to her system.

"How are your classes?" asked Debra Carson, an algebra teacher.

"So far, so good. Just grabbing a little caffeine boost to get through the rest of the day," said Anne, raising the can. "Yours?"

"Pretty good, but it's just the first day. They're always good on the first day. Making it through next week will be more of a challenge."

"True. Just out of curiosity, do you think many kids around here cheat?"

"Cheat? Do I think *many* kids cheat? I think *all* kids cheat. Are you kidding? None of these kids is willing to work on their own."

"None? Really? I think there are plenty of kids who want to do their own work," said Anne.

"Maybe that's the case in English classes, but not in math. It's all just a cat-and-mouse game to see how many different ways they can find to cheat and how many we can actually catch 'em at."

"Isn't that just a little bit cynical?" teased Anne.

"Cynical? Nope, it's reality. I've been here thirty-five years, and trust me, they *all* cheat, the little shits. Well, have a great day!"

"Uh, yeah. See ya," said Anne. She knew Debra's reputation as a malcontent, but still hoped that Debra's attitude wasn't the pervasive one among the faculty.

Anne pondered her options about the potential cheating issue while stirring spaghetti sauce that night before dinner. Was there a game they could play or maybe a children's book that would get the message across? She didn't want to simply lecture the kids on the virtue of honesty. She wanted to do something that would bring the lesson home and make them think. She thought of her own children—her seventeen-year-old daughter, Maggie, and Richard, who was fourteen. She knew that she talked to her own children about such things, but how many of her students' parents did likewise? As a parent, what would she want a teacher to say to them? She knew she walked a fine line between being an instructor and taking on a more parental role—something that occasionally caused resentment with parents. Nevertheless, she felt a sense of urgency—most of these kids would be completely on their own in less than a year.

"What helps you internalize something you need to know?" she asked her children at dinner.

"Money," answered Richard quickly.

"How does that help?"

"I'll do just about anything for cold, hard cash, Mom," grinned Richard.

CLASS LETTERS

"Okay, but what about with my students? I can't pay all of them to learn something!"

"I like it when you write me letters, Mom. It's something I can read over again if I need to, and something I can look at and think about," Maggie said.

"Great idea, Maggie. I like writing you letters; it gives me a chance to say what I really want to say, because I can think about it and revise it. I'll consider that. Thanks."

"You're welcome, Mom. What are you trying to teach your students?"

"About the problems associated with cheating."

"Good luck," said Richard. "Everyone cheats, and no one wants to learn on their own."

"Does *everyone* include you?"

"Okay, Mom. Promise you won't get mad?"

"Here we go... okay, I promise."

"All right, every now and then I'll get answers for homework in algebra. But never on a test—homework only. You know I have a hard time with it, and Mr. Stemmons *always* grades the homework. I'd be failing right now if I didn't get some *help* with homework."

"How about getting some *help* from Mr. Stemmons? Or your sister? She's great at math."

"Ugh. I knew I shouldn't have told you."

"Just try it. You may actually get something out of it. Like knowledge."

"Yes, ma'am."

"A letter. Hmm... I like that. Who wants ice cream?"

After dinner, Anne sat in bed with a legal pad and a pen. She rarely typed things out on the computer. It seemed more personal to her to write things out longhand and transcribe into the laptop. And her bed was the most comfortable place in her home.

Once she began looking at cheating in general, she thought of all the different tangents she could travel along to make her point.

By the end of her two-page letter, she felt like she had covered the subject in a way that would make sense to teenagers. She would soon find out.

Chapter 2

A few days after the initial inspiration, Anne greeted her class. "Good morning! I have a surprise for you today."

"Yo, no work, right?" asked Ray.

"Actually, I do have some work for you, but there's no wrong answer, so whatever you do will be correct. All you have to do is read a letter, write a response, and turn it in."

"Reading *and* writing?"

"Ray, this is English class, so, yes, reading *and* writing. I have written you a letter. I want you to read it, consider what I have said, and write a page-long response. It's a quiz grade."

"You wrote each of us a letter?" asked Keosha, a beautiful black girl with almond-shaped eyes.

"No, it's to the entire class. All my classes, actually. Just see what you think and let me know. They are due a week from today," explained Anne as she passed out the papers. "Now let's move on to *Beowulf*."

After dinner that evening, Keosha read the letter.

"What's that?" her mother asked.

"Just some homework. My English teacher wrote us a letter and wants a reply sometime next week."

"Next week? And you're already reading it? That's a switch!"

"No big deal. I was just curious. 'Night, Mom."

"Okay. Well, time for job number two. See you in the morning. 'Night, honey."

Keosha finished the letter in her room. Considering she usually carried a C average in the classes she didn't fail, she didn't want her mother to think that doing homework would become a regular habit. But she liked Mrs. English. There was something approachable about her that piqued Keosha's interest.

September

Dear Class:

This is a first for me. I've never written a letter to my classes, but it seemed like a good time to start. Based on a recent conversation I overheard in one of my classes, I wanted to hear your thoughts on cheating.

First, what does cheating mean to you? Is it cheating on a test? Giving someone answers for their homework? I looked up the word on Dictionary.com, and here is a list of synonyms: mislead, defraud, hoax, victimize, deceive, and trick. Not a pretty list, is it?

You may consider some forms of cheating harmless, and you may even use another word for it, such as "helping" someone with their homework. And there are other words for cheating. If you cheat on your taxes, it's called tax fraud and you can pay a fine or go to prison. If you cheat on your spouse, it's called infidelity or adultery and can be grounds for divorce. If you do it in college, it might be called plagiarism and you could be expelled.

Look again at the list of synonyms. Several of them (mislead, trick, and deceive) also sound like lying. Defraud, hoax, and victimize sound like stealing.

Okay, let's say your best friend sucks at algebra, so you help her with her homework by giving her the answers. You probably don't think that's cheating, and you may be right. But one way to look at it is that you are cheating her out of an education. How is she going to understand Algebra I and move on to Algebra II (both are required classes here) if you give her the answers? Another definition of cheating is "to deprive of something expected." Your BFF might expect to understand algebra, or maybe she only expects to pass, but either way, who loses out?

I mentioned tax fraud and infidelity above. What if you (or your parents) did that—and got away with it? Is it still cheating? If no one knows, does it count? What if you cheated on a test just to pass? Whom does it hurt? Anyone? But what if you cheated, got an A, and bumped someone out of their rightful spot in the class rank, thereby depriving them of the scholarship they need because it's their only hope of going to college? Is there a line that you cross when "semicheating" becomes cheating, sort of like going from petty theft to grand larceny?

If you cheat, you may never get caught by a teacher, a spouse, or the government. But there's one person you can't hide from, and that's you. Even if no one ever knows, you will have to live with it. But what if cheating became easier every time you did it? What if it's so easy you move on to other forms of cheating, like lying or stealing? Can you live with that too?

You may think I'm making entirely too big a deal about this, but I want you to think about it. Think about the person you want to be. Every action you take today affects the person you become in the future.

You may want to know if I ever cheated. Yes, in high school I know I looked on other papers to get the answer. I didn't get caught. I don't lose sleep over an indiscretion that's twenty-five years old, but I don't cheat anymore either. It wasn't in line with the person I wanted to be then and want to be today.

Here's your assignment: Now that you have read the letter, think about cheating and its part in your life. What's your definition? Does cheating affect your life in any way? I want to assure you that your response will be between you and me. If, of course, you tell me that you're going to blow up the school or shoot a bunch of kids in the cafeteria, I'll have to tell someone. Otherwise, I want you to feel free to say what is on your mind and in your heart. I expect you to write a minimum of a page, and remember, it's a quiz grade. Enjoy!

Keosha was surprised at what she read. She had never had a teacher who admitted to cheating before. She had never had a teacher who seemed almost… human.

"But if that bitch thinks I'm gonna tell her 'bout all the times I cheated, she crazy."

The next day, replies to the letter began to trickle in. Anne couldn't wait to read them and see what her kids had to say on the subject. It was a full day; she gave her students a vocabulary test, they read a short story in class, and she was too busy making copies and preparing the next week's lesson during her conference period to read the letters, so she packed them up in her bag and took them home.

Evenings at home were always busy. Anne usually got home at about five thirty and immediately began preparing dinner. She believed in hot meals eaten together as a family. Sometimes the grunts, "yeahs," and "nothings" she received as answers to questions were the longest conversations she might have with one, or both, of her children, depending on their mood. After dinner was eaten and dishes done, it was time to straighten the house, do a load or two of laundry, nag at Richard to do his homework, and remind Maggie to get off the phone. There were days when her two teenagers were more challenging by themselves than her 175 students combined. Unfortunately, tonight was one of those nights.

CLASS LETTERS

"Do your homework *now!*" said Anne as she snapped off the TV.

"But, Mom, it's WWE," whined Richard.

"I'll WWE your behind if you don't do your homework."

"Okay."

"Maggie, off the phone."

"Five more minutes, Mom. I've done all my homework."

"Five minutes, then *off!*"

"Whatever," came Maggie's sarcastic reply across the hall.

"Watch your attitude, young lady, or that phone will be mine."

"Yes, *Mother.*"

Anne knew she had hit a nerve. Maggie only called her "Mother" when she was angry.

"Whatever," mumbled Anne. "Just four more years; they'll both be gone in just four more years…"

Across town, Ray read the letter about cheating. The response was due the next day. A quiz grade. He didn't want a zero for a quiz grade this early in the six weeks. Ray was a master at grade manipulation—he knew exactly how much he could blow off and still pass. Getting a zero so soon would mean that he would have to do some actual work later on. Ray knew he was smart; at least, he thought he was. He always knew the answers to the questions asked in class, but he never raised his hand. He had a tough-guy rep to protect, and answering questions made him look weak to his homies. Sometimes he even wanted to answer—wanted to do well in spite of his rep—but his ties to his friends were stronger than his desire to advance.

Still, he was intrigued by the letter and the teacher. Would his letter really be just between them? Would he get in trouble for the things he said in it? Could he turn it in without being seen? There was only one way to find out.

Ray dug through his little sister's backpack for some paper and a pencil. She was a good kid—only twelve years old and so smart. He had tried to protect her and keep her safe since their dad was sent to prison. Even with parole, Ray would be well into his twenties before his dad was released, and he took his job as man of the house very seriously.

Alone in his room, with hip-hop playing in the background, Ray sat on his bed wondering if he should tell the truth. He didn't trust many teachers—or adults, for that matter—but there was something about this one that made him want to try. He took a deep breath and started writing.

> *Your probably going to think I'm lying but I don't cheat. Ever. I always no the answer but I don't always say it. Why you ask? Cuz if I act as smart as I am, it makes my homies look bad and I can't do that to them. They are mi familia.*

Ray reread his answer. Satisfied with the content, he folded it up and stuck it in his pants pocket. He was supposed to meet up with Eddie and Mario. Time to blaze and cruise.

It was ten o'clock before Anne was able to sit down with the letters. Tomorrow was the due date, and she figured she would get an influx then, so she'd better knock out the few she already had. There would be some stragglers, the 25 percent or so who would turn the paper in late. And there would be some kids who wouldn't even bother with it.

The first one was from a girl. The handwriting and doodles gave that away before Anne began the letter. Typical of most girls, the letters were large, round, and printed rather than written in cursive. The doodles revealed the author: TW + DS = 4ever. Tiffany Wallace and David Spears were *the* couple of the senior class. They had been dating since spring break of their sophomore year and were about as popular a duo as any two students could be.

> *Dear Mrs. English:*
>
> *First I want to say that I'm really enjoying ur class so far. I think ur super nice and way cool. Now about cheating, I*

completely agree with u—cheating deprives you of a good education. So why cheat? Mostly it's laziness. Ppl don't want to work for nething. They just want everything handed to them on a silver platter. That's why they cheat. Me, I don't cheat accept for every once and the while when I have a lot of homework and I've been cheering at a game and it's really late and I'm really, really tired. But that's it. It's hard when the teachers pile on the work and I've got all my after school stuff—games, tumbling, dance and other stuff. In case you didn't know I'm on the competition cheer squad and it takes up a lot of time so, yes, I do cheat a little bit on homework and stuff but that's it. I hope ur not disappointed in me but I wanted to tell the truth. Thank you for reading my letter.

Sincerely,

Tiffany Wallace

PS Please don't tell my father.

Anne added her note to the PS:

I won't.

David's letter was also typical in handwriting for a boy—messy, small, and hard to read—but Anne managed with some extra light, much to her chagrin.

Mrs. English,

We learn in football about how not to cheat. If we cheat in a game, we might get a penalty or something which could cost us yards or even a down, sometimes points. Some things can lose a game. So I try hard not to cheat on the football field. But sometimes it's different in class. For example, if I don't understand something in math or science, I might have to cheat so I can keep my grades up. Cuz if I don't pass, I don't play and so it's really important to me to pass so yes, I cheat sometimes, because football is my life and I have to play or my dad will kill me. NO lie. He was a big deal when he went to school here. He was top rusher and receiver his senior year and he expects me to be as good or better. So, really, I don't cheat for me—I do it for my dad. But not all the time. Just when I have to.

David A. Spears III

Anne wondered, after reading Tiffany's and David's letters, how much pressure some of her students might be under to succeed. She wanted her own kids to succeed too, but she knew there were parents who were relentless when it came to pushing. Her stance was that, yes, they needed to succeed, but they also needed to balance it with some fun, and she felt sorry for the kids whose parents put constant pressure on them. She felt there was plenty of time in their lives to be completely focused on success and getting ahead, but high school should be a time for making memories. Maybe a subject for another letter?

Chapter 3

Anne had given the students a week to reply to the letter. During that time, she had waited to see how many would actually respond. A few had trickled in, but most were delivered on the appointed day. She could tell that some students had quickly scribbled their lines so that they wouldn't get a zero for the assignment. Most letters were about a page long and, hopefully, well thought out. She was anxious to see what new information and insight she could glean from the responses. In the meantime, she and her classes read through a few John Donne poems, discussing the similarities and differences between them, and she tried to relate the information to their everyday lives.

She had a faculty meeting after school that would prolong her wait. The principal, Mr. Hargrove, wasn't particularly long-winded, but there were always a couple of other teachers who tended to drag these meetings out. She knew she wouldn't make it home before five o'clock. Tonight was her son's night to cook, which for him meant frozen pizza, but it was one less thing for her to do.

Anne walked into her house after five, as predicted. She was tired, as usual, but she had piles of work to do at her second job—the one at home. She had gotten behind on the laundry, and her bathroom was a mess. Although she had worked in an office in the past, she couldn't remember what it was like to go home at the end of the day and simply relax, eat some dinner, and maybe do a little laundry or cleaning, without the addition of an hour or two of grading papers. Some days she longed for another job—one she could leave at the office. When those thoughts entered her mind, she remembered the vacation time—especially the trips in the summer with her children—and continued teaching. She wasn't even sure anymore what she could do in an office setting. Maybe she would look into it after they both graduated. But tonight she had letters to read.

With a load in the washer, the bathroom straight, and a belly full of pepperoni pizza, she sat down at the kitchen table and began reading. Many of the letters said essentially the same thing: yes, they copied homework but didn't consider it cheating; no, they didn't cheat on tests (most of the time). And when they did cheat on tests, it was because everyone else did it too or because the teacher's test was unreasonably hard and they had no choice. Then she came across one that surprised her. It was from Keosha:

> *At first I didn't want to answer this letter. I don't know you and I don't trust teachers because they have messed me around more than once. But I'm trying to be good this year and get all my work done. I don't want no trouble cuz I've already had plenty but I'm trying to turn things around. Last year a teacher got me in trouble and it wasn't my fault. I had to go to the alternative school for three months. Since then I don't trust teachers. But, like I said, I am trying to be good this year so I thought I'd write back anyways.*
>
> *I'll admit it. I have cheated in the past. I have copied homework and cheated on tests. I have never gotten caught. I won't tell you when or how, but I've done it. I wasn't going to tell you because I didn't think it was a big deal. But I have been thinking about it since I read your letter. Your letter was like that little angel and devil on my shoulder like you see in cartoons. The angel told me to tell you and the devil told me not to. I guess the angel won. But the other thing the angel told me was*

that you were right. To be honest, that kinda makes me mad. Because I used to be able to cheat without no problems in the past but now I'm not sure I can anymore. I'm not saying I'm going to quit cheating 100% but I'm going to think about it more now because of this letter. And part of me wants to tell you thank you and part of me is mad about it because sometimes cheating is the only way I pass. But, like I said before, I'm trying to turn over a new leaf and not do the things that get me in trouble. So maybe my cheating days are over.

Anne was hooked.

Chapter 4

September rolled into October, and the school year progressed on schedule with no problems. Anne was getting to know her students, and they were learning to trust her. She was a fallible human being, and when she made a mistake, she owned it. Her math skills were less than desirable, and she occasionally added up a test wrong. Or she might lose a paper in the black hole she called her desk. She didn't always know the answers to their questions, but she was always willing to do the research to find out. Whether it was to her children or to her students, she never held herself up as a perfect, holier-than-thou person. She felt like she always portrayed herself as *real*.

So it surprised her one day when a student challenged that.

That morning, Anne and Maggie had a fight on their way to school. Maggie was invited to a party and let it slip that there would be no adults in attendance.

"No parents, you don't go."

"But, Mom, everyone will be there. Only the real losers will miss it. Don't you trust me?"

"It's not about not trusting you. It's about your safety."

"I'll be fine."

"The answer is no, and that's final."

The rest of their trip was conducted in silence, Anne's hands gripped the steering wheel as she drove to school. Maggie tearfully delivered her final shot as she shut the car door: "I can't believe you won't let me go. You're such a bitch sometimes!"

Anne and Maggie rarely disagreed, and they never fought. Although she knew Maggie didn't mean it, hearing those words hurt, and it left Anne feeling sad, angry, and unsettled. She had a tendency to wear her heart on her sleeve, and the kids knew immediately when something was wrong. They might ask how she was feeling or if she was upset, but they would usually drop the subject quickly if Anne was vague or obviously distracted. But on this particular morning, Keosha wouldn't leave it alone.

"What's wrong, Miss?"

"Nothing."

"I know better than that. 'Sup?"

"Nothing. I'm fine."

"Okay, whatever. I guess since Halloween's coming up, you put on your mask early."

Whammo—out of the mouths of babes. Ouch!

Shortly thereafter, in spite of the no-phone rule, Maggie texted Anne: *I didn't mean what I said. Sorry Mom. ILY.*

Anne smiled, grateful for her daughter's loving heart, and sent a quick reply. *Me too. LU2.*

But the mask comment stayed with her as she watched her students interact. She saw Tiffany flirting with David between classes. Tiffany was currently all smiles and dimples, in spite of the foul mood she had exhibited in class two minutes before. She watched a girl she didn't know hug a boy and then make a face behind his back to her friend. She remembered a comment that a football player had made about putting on his game face. There were secrets hidden within her students, just below the surface. She knew that from experience, but she also felt it from a few of them. Secrets that ruled their lives and could put them on an unyielding course toward ruin if they didn't do something to help themselves. Letter number two coagulated in her mind.

CLASS LETTERS

The students were in Denmark with Grendel and Beowulf. She assigned a creative-writing exercise and allowed them to listen to their iPods and cell phones while they wrote. It helped them focus and kept them quiet. Most were writing; a few were sleeping. She allowed the sleeping ones to continue. For one thing, this was just a daily grade and she intentionally built so many of them into a six-week period that missing one or two was not a problem. Besides, several of her students worked full-time jobs to help support their families and didn't return home to sleep until well after midnight. She respected these kids—the ones who worked so hard outside of school but showed up for class the following day anyway.

"Time is almost up. Finish up your assignment and hand it in, but don't put all your things away yet. I have something else for you."

"More?" groaned Ray.

"Yep—another letter," smiled Anne.

"Like the one on cheating? I like those—I think they're cool," gushed Tiffany. "What's it about?"

"Read it and see! Remember, I need you to write a page. Some of your responses last month were just shy of a page—in some cases, a lot shy. And it's a quiz grade, so don't forget and don't blow it off."

Many of the papers were taken reluctantly, but she hoped that more students would enjoy the process of give-and-take that she was trying to establish.

October

Dear Class:

It's almost Halloween. Always a fun time—especially if you like candy (which I do!). Not too crazy about smashed pumpkins (as opposed to Smashing Pumpkins, whom I like) and egged houses, but I guess it's all in fun.

What else do you think of when you think of Halloween? Costumes and, specifically, masks. Right? First, a little history... Halloween itself has been around for many hundreds of years and is one of the world's oldest holidays. The name Halloween comes from an abbreviated version of All Hallows' Eve. Hallow is a word that means to make holy. All Hallows' Eve precedes All Saints' Day, which is a day when various religions remember the saints and their deceased family members and friends. The costume-and-mask part comes from Halloween's earliest origins, when the Celts would celebrate Samhain (the forerunner of Halloween). They were very superstitious and believed that Samhain was the night the ghosts appeared. The Celts wore masks and costumes when they went out at night in order to remain unrecognizable to the ghosts, and therefore safe. So, basically, the masks were used as a sort of physical and emotional shield against things that were perceived as fearful or threatening.

Now, on to the subject at hand. One of my students confronted me a week or two ago, which prompted this letter. I had a fight with my daughter on the way to school and was not myself when class started. This student asked me if I was all right. I told him/her (I want to protect the name of the guilty party—LOL!) that I was fine. It was a lie. I wasn't "fine." I was sad, upset, and distracted. Then he/she said something about it being almost time for Halloween and that I had my mask on early. Guys, I gotta tell you, that hurt a little. I try to be "real" with everyone all the time, but I guess that's not always the case. So I started to think about the different "masks" I have worn during my lifetime. There are a lot! Some are necessary, like in a job interview. I'm not talking about faking a resume, but you certainly want to be on your best behavior and present a positive picture of yourself to a possible future employer. But what about the ones that aren't necessary? The ones that are really fake? Like when you pretend to like someone because you think their brother is cute. Or maybe you suck up to a band geek because you want their "help" (i.e., notes or homework, etc.) in a particular subject?

CLASS LETTERS

Getting back to the history of masks when they were used as a protection, think about the masks you wear today. I know you wear them—I see them every day. For example, you may be cranky in class but magically turn into all sweetness and light when that special someone shows up during passing period. Or maybe you wear a tough-guy mask out on the football field because it's expected of you, but you don't really feel all that tough—and maybe you don't even like football. What do masks like these protect? How do they help you? How do they hurt you? What if you get so used to wearing a mask—maybe even different masks with different people—that you forget or completely lose who you are? What then?

You know the drill—one-page response between you and me (unless I have to take it to a higher authority), quiz grade, due in a week. Have fun out there on the 31st (but be safe). (And bring me all your leftover chocolate!)

Keosha let out a surprised gasp as she read Anne's letter. "Fuckin' A! She listened to me."

Tiffany read through the letter twice, allowing it to sink in. A single tear slipped down her cheek before she quickly wiped it away and shoved the letter into her bag.

Ray skimmed through the letter quickly, mumbling, "Mask? Bullshit. I am who I am. I don't put on no mask for nobody. Respect the man or move on."

"Did you have a question, Ray?" asked Anne.

"Uh, yeah. I don't wear no mask, Miss. I can't write this story… or whatever you call it."

"Take some time and think about it as you go through your day. Maybe you'll catch yourself with a mask on. Remember, there's no wrong answer, either, so you can always tell me how you make it through your day without a mask."

Anne could see that Ray was, as usual, flexing his machismo muscle.

She watched him during class: the way he scanned the room to see who was watching him, the way he would pay attention to her when no one was looking, and the way he feigned boredom when someone was watching—especially one of his buddies.

Although they were from completely different backgrounds, she felt she understood his insecurities and his combined desire and fear regarding success. Anne had struggled with her own issues, ones that had convinced her she wasn't good enough. Her answer for most of her life: Why try? She had worked hard to overcome the negativity and self-loathing that had filled her mind for so many years, but it wasn't an overnight, or easy, proposition. She knew that if Ray could overcome his shortcomings, it probably wouldn't be anytime soon, but she hoped that maybe something she said or did would impact him. All he needed was to crack that door open just a little and allow some light into his life.

Kim Le had been in the United States for only a few years. One of her fondest memories was attending Buddha's birthday party each May. The festivals always included warm spring breezes and picnics. Kim's favorite part was the mask dance. The masks in this traditional form of Korean theater represented people, deities, and animals. By the end of the dance, even the audience was participating. It was a time of joy and celebration. She wasn't clear about these masks, though. At the end of class, she timidly and respectfully approached Anne for clarification.

"I don't understand these masks, Mrs. English. I know a little about the Korean masks we use in dances, but this kind confuses me."

"Hmm... well, Kim, masks like these are all about pretending to be something you're not. The problem with the masks in the letter is that sometimes people use masks all the time. The biggest problem with this is that if people pretend for too long, they forget who they really are. For example, what if you're sad? Do you pretend to act happy?"

"Sometimes."

CLASS LETTERS

"Sometimes I do too. I think that's pretty normal. Most people will do that from time to time. But how would you feel if you *always* had to act happy when you were sad? I think it would be a really hard thing to do. Does that make sense?"

"Yes, ma'am. Thank you."

"You're welcome. Have a good evening."

"You too."

Kim pondered her newfound knowledge. Her English was good—especially compared with her parents—but she missed the subtler concepts that had no literal translation. She was a shy child and had a difficult time asking for help, but it seemed easier with certain teachers, like Mrs. English.

Keosha's evening routine was predictable and consistent, and tonight was no different. Her mother came home from her first job at about 5:00 p.m. and left for job number two at about 8:00 p.m. to return around 1:00 a.m. Keosha's time frame at home was from 4:55 p.m. to just after 8:00p.m., then back home at 12:55 a.m.. During her at-home hours, Keosha was friendly, helpful, and loving; once she was out on the street, life became chaotic and unpredictable. She never knew what to expect. She hung out with street thugs, crackheads, and thieves. Sometimes it was exciting; sometimes it was scary. The only place where she was truly able to relax was at home with her mother. It had been just the two of them throughout Keosha's life. She knew there had to be a guy somewhere in the past, but she had no idea who her father was, and her mother refused to discuss it. When she was a small child, her favorite game to play had been "family" with her few dolls. Disco Barbie was the mommy, a one-eyed teddy bear was the daddy, and she was portrayed by a little white doll baby in a diaper. It was already 8:15 a.m., so Keosha quickly scribbled a reply:

Dear Mrs. English, I can't believe you wrote about masks. I saw dat and was like wow, she listens. I think we all got masks. I got one. Sometimes it protects me, sometimes it protects my moms. That one is the good li'l girl mask. My moms she works two jobs. She tries real hard to take care of me. It's just the two of us—no dad, no brother or sister. I know she wears a mask sometimes 2. Sometimes she pretends she don't mind working so much. She pretends she ain't tired all the time but I know the truth. I help out where I can but I don't see her much except for a couple hours at night. The rest of the time it's just me. Sometimes I don't always hang out wid the best people. I have to wear a mask wid them 2. But I do what I have to do to help out. It ain't no big deal but sometimes I get scared. That's when I really have to put on a mask. But it's all good. I deal.

Satisfied with her response, Keosha left the apartment to see what was happening in the streets. It was one of those wonderful fall nights—crisp but not yet cold. Still, she zipped her hoodie as she headed toward the park a couple of blocks from her apartment. During the day, it was a haven for young children swinging and climbing on the equipment. At night, the dealers and thugs moved in and set up shop. The park "belonged" to the BADs—the Bad Ass Dawgs—a local street gang with no national affiliation. Their primary enterprise was drug dealing, with some robbery and auto theft thrown in for good measure. They weren't as violent or deadly as some gangs, but their numbers were rising and their reputation was growing. Keosha scanned the crowd nervously as she walked up.

"'Sup, li'l mama?" asked BD, aka Big Dawg, the leader of the gang.

"Nuttin', jus' chillin'," she replied.

"Lookin' fine tonight," added LD, aka Li'l Dawg, BD's younger brother. He was always hitting on Keosha.

Keosha ignored him and joined Tamika and LaQuandra, her best friends.

"That boy's been after you since ninth grade!" chuckled Tamika.

"No shit!" said Keosha, shaking her head.

Tamika and LaQuandra were part of the BADs. Tamika, newly

pregnant, and BD had hooked up over the summer; LaQuandra was three months pregnant by Rollo, BD's second-in-command. So far, Keosha had stayed on the fringe—not in but not really out, either. She liked the camaraderie and feeling of belonging. Part of her knew that this wasn't the best environment for her, but she stubbornly followed her friends in spite of it. She knew that Tamika would shoplift and LaQuandra was an accomplished pickpocket, but Keosha had yet to participate in any kind of criminal activity. She knew it was just a matter of time.

Throughout dinner, Tiffany gushed to her parents about how well things were going at school.

"We're playing Central this Friday. Of course we'll win. They pretty much suck at football. And David's…"

"Don't say 'suck,' Tiffany. It's not ladylike," admonished Tom Wallace, her father, sipping his nightly scotch.

"Uh, okay. Sorry. David's all excited because they say there will be some college scouts there. David says that even though he still has another year, he wants to make a good impression. They remember that stuff, you know."

"David doesn't have to worry—he'll get picked up for sure. Does he still want to go to UT?" he asked.

"Oh, yes! He's not even going to consider anyplace else. He's going to major in business and take over his father's car dealership. He has everything mapped out."

"Is that his plan or his father's plan?" asked Tonya Wallace, Tiffany's mother.

"It's both. David's father has always dreamed of David going into business with him. And David is okay with it too."

"Just okay?" asked Tonya.

"Well, you know how Mr. Spears is. He's always had lots of plans for David."

"But what does David want to do?"

"Tonya, Spears Motors is the biggest dealership in town. Why wouldn't he want to work there—and own it someday? Seems like a good future and great job security to me. And if he and Tiffany continue dating, it'll be good for her too," said Tom.

"You know how David's dad is. Always pushing, always demanding more out of David. I think it's a lot of pressure for a kid," said Tonya.

"Boys need pressure. It's good for them."

"Glad I'm not a boy!" smiled Tiffany.

"I have expectations for you too, young lady. National Honor Society, top 10 percent, and a good college."

"Daddy, I'm going to UT with David. UT is a great college."

"And a good law school. You want to follow in your old man's footsteps, don't you?"

"Of course, Daddy." Tiffany knew her dad's dream had always been to put up a sign one day: Wallace and Wallace, Attorneys at Law. Of course, that dream had also meant that Wallace #2 was a son, but Tiffany tried to fulfill her father's vision, nonetheless.

"That's my girl! Better get cracking on that homework."

"Yes, Daddy."

Tiffany sat on her bed after dinner and reread the letter. Tears again filled her eyes as she thought about the two masks she wore. They were in opposition to each other, and the stress was becoming more difficult every day. She thought of them as her "good-girl mask" and her "David mask." The good-girl mask was the one her parents and teachers saw: the pretty head cheerleader, the A student, the popular girl. It was the mask she was born to wear. She knew her parents' expectations were high, and she would have been surprised if it had been any different. She was their only child and had been pushed and prodded all her life. The David mask was tougher to wear these days, but she was terrified to take it off.

Tiffany had known David since elementary school and had been thrilled when he finally noticed her during their sophomore year.

After manipulating every situation possible (as only high school girls can), she had won his heart. It was a logical match—both were athletic, good-looking, smart, and popular. His jealousy had been flattering at first; she'd enjoyed feeling like she "belonged" to someone. However, it had mutated into something more confining. He began controlling who her friends were, what she did in her spare time, and even what she wore. His reasoning was that he loved her and wanted the best for her, but sometimes it was too much for Tiffany. Especially when he became angry. It didn't feel loving then—it felt scary.

David had begun to pressure Tiffany into having sex during their junior year, but she had held out until last summer. They waited until Tiffany's parents were guaranteed to be out of the house for an extended period of time. He brought a rose and a bottle of cheap champagne. They drank out of cartoon paper cups from Tiffany's bathroom and listened to music. It was the most romantic day of Tiffany's life. She didn't like sex as much as David did, but she wanted to make him happy, so she put on her David mask and did whatever he asked, as often as he required. Still, Tiffany knew that soon her perfect little world would be turned upside down.

Kim Le had pondered the idea of masks since her conversation with Mrs. English. She understood how people could put on different masks in different situations. And she understood, as Mrs. English had suggested, that it wasn't good to pretend to be one thing all the time, especially if it was a lie, such as acting happy when you're sad. But her mask was much more important than just acting a certain way: she had to hide her secret.

Chapter 5

"Kill the Hornets!"

"Spray the Hornets!"

"Splat the Hornets!"

Anne smiled as she watched her second-period homeroom brainstorm ideas for their spirit door. It was homecoming week—the equivalent of race week for NASCAR fans, crammed into five short days. Football players had that extra strut in their walk, cheerleaders and drill team members practiced their halftime moves, and everyone wanted to win the coveted Spirit Stick for the best classroom-door decoration. Anne sweetened the pot by dangling a pizza party as incentive, in addition to spending $40 she didn't have on streamers, balloons, poster board, markers, and glitter. She didn't mind losing a class period (or two, or three) to plan and implement what was destined to be an award-winning door. Besides, sports always took precedence over academics during football season. Tiffany organized her collaborators, barking orders like a general.

"C'mon, people, we *have* to make a decision! I say we make a giant flyswatter and can of bug spray, with 'Kill the Hornets' as our cheer. Kristen, you and Jeanie start cutting and twisting the streamers so we can frame the door. Ashley, you get the poster boards and start on the flyswatter and spray can. Mrs. English has markers and glitter, so make 'em sparkle! Robert, you help Ashley. Ask Kim if she wants to help—she has great handwriting and can make the letters. Jason, you and Stephen and John start blowing up balloons."

While half the class helped with the door, the rest of the class took advantage of the downtime. Some slept, some chatted with friends, some listened to music. Surprised, Anne noticed that Ray was over in the corner, writing quietly. She considered taking a stroll around the class and praising Ray for his effort but decided against it. She didn't want to interrupt him, and she certainly didn't want to draw attention to him. Although he had his moments as class clown, she knew he preferred fading into the background.

Tiffany supervised the workers closely. Chasing perfection was her constant goal, whether on the cheer squad, in the classroom, or creating a winning spirit door. David strolled by with two of his teammates, perusing their efforts.

"Hi, David!" beamed Tiffany.

"Hey, Tiff. What are you doing on your door?"

"It's going to be so cool. We're making a huge flyswatter and can of bug spray so we can kill the Hornets! We're using streamers and balloons too."

"Balloons? What do balloons have to do with killing Hornets? That's lame," he laughed.

"Really? Do you really think so?"

"Uh, yeah," he said sarcastically. "Joe, isn't that about the dumbest thing you've ever seen?"

"Yeah, dude, can't say that I disagree with that."

"But they add to the decorations. We were going to attach them to the ceiling above the door. Sort of like drops of bug spray…" explained Tiffany.

"Seriously, Tiff? Balloons don't look like bug spray," David scoffed as he walked away.

"I guess not," she sighed, as she deflated. "Okay, people, forget the balloons."

"Forget the balloons? I just spent the last fifteen minutes blowing these up. I think we should use them anyway," said Jason.

"But David thinks it's stupid."

"Who cares what David thinks? It's not his door," said Ashley.

"I care what David thinks! He's my boyfriend!"

"But this is for *our* class. We decide, not David," added Kristen. "Do you really take that crap from him?"

"Crap? What crap?"

"The way he orders you around. And especially the way you do exactly what he says," said Ashley.

"He doesn't order me around. And I don't do exactly what he says, either."

"Sure you do. I've seen it. I'm your best friend, remember?" said Ashley.

"I can't talk about this now. We've got to work on this door. Besides, everything's fine with me and David."

"Whatever," sighed Ashley.

Kim listened to this exchange, marveling at the way kids her age focused on trivial matters. If they lived the life she had, they would understand how truly insignificant such things were. Life in North Korea had been quite different from here. Korean citizens were constantly bombarded with songs and propaganda about the government. Her parents knew people who had mysteriously disappeared, never to be seen or heard from again. Her own father had been watched for months, as if he were a criminal instead of an engineer. Kim's family was never certain why "they" were watching him—but "they" didn't need a reason. Finally, a few years ago, a friend had informed Kim's father that "they" were coming for him. The fear of unjust imprisonment, torture, or death, along with the famine and starvation that affected everyone, had convinced him that it was time to leave. Their town was near the Chinese border, but it was a risky venture: If they were caught by the Chinese, they would be returned to North Korea for imprisonment. Some refugees were shot on sight. But Kim's parents felt it was worth the risk. It took three long months to get to America.

Once they were settled, her parents worked in a convenience store. Although he was a brilliant engineer, Mr. Le's grasp of English was minimal, and he couldn't find a job in his field. Three years later, they had saved enough money for a down payment on the store. Kim and her parents were the sole employees.

It had been a long day, as usual, and Anne was tired, as usual. But within her school bag, she had the responses to the October letter and was anxious to read them. This process of give-and-take with her students had quickly become her favorite part of the job. Luckily, it was Maggie's turn to cook—fish sticks were on the menu—and Anne found time to read a few letters before dinner. One was from David.

> *Dear Mrs. English,*
>
> *Masks are really important. Like you said in your letter, when I play football, I have to put on my game face. For me, that means turning on a switch in my brain that is all about winning—no matter what. I have to be focused, alert, and tough. I can't let anything distract me. The same is true with baseball (even though I don't have on a helmet, which is kinda like a mask). Because if I mess up on the field, I hear about it from my coaches but mostly from my dad. He expects me to be perfect out there like he was. And I try my hardest. Most of the time I can do it but sometimes I am playing against someone who is better than me. My dad never wears a mask. I know exactly how he's feeling whenever I look at him—especially when I miss a tackle or a pass. I know he's mad then. I can see it from 20 yards away. But it's all good because it makes me work harder. I have to do good in sports so I can play college football like he did (hopefully at UT like he did), get a business degree, and work at the dealership that my dad has. That's my plan. If I have to wear a mask all the time to do it, I will. Hey,*

CLASS LETTERS

if you need a new car, I bet my dad would cut you a deal. I know teachers don't make much money.

Sincerely,

David A. Spears III

Anne smiled at the last comment. "He's right about that," she muttered. She had seen his father's reaction to David's mistakes on the field. David was right—anyone could see his dad's displeasure a mile away. Anne usually added a note at the end of their letters. To this one, she wrote: *I think you are a gifted athlete.*

"Dinner!" called Maggie from the kitchen. Reluctantly, Anne put her papers away until later.

"Cool! Fish sticks!" smiled Richard. "Why'd ya hafta cook broccoli to go with 'em?"

"Because you need to eat your vegetables," said Maggie. Ever since Richard was born, Maggie had competed with Anne over mothering him. As Richard got older, he acted resentful of Maggie's "mothering," but Anne always felt like he enjoyed the attention, in spite of his outward reaction.

"Yes, *Mother*," he retorted.

"Maggie, dinner looks great. Thank you for cooking tonight. Isn't it nice to have Maggie cook dinner, Richard?" said Anne.

"I guess."

"Well, I'm starving! Let's eat!" said Maggie.

After dinner, Anne eagerly returned to the letters. Most of them were similar: yes, they had worn a mask, depending on the situation; no, they didn't wear one all the time; no, the mask didn't take over their personality. Anne's primary purpose was always to make the kids think, but sometimes they also confessed.

Dear Mrs. English:

It took me awhile to understand the meaning of masks that

you wrote about. I understand now that you don't mean a real mask to wear but one that you make up. I wear that kind of mask all the time because I have to. It can be hard sometimes because it's like lying every day of your life. But it's necessary for me. And my family. I know this is too short for the assignment, but that's all I can say about the subject. I'm sorry.

Kim Le

Tiffany's letter was also surprising. One question: *Can I come tell you about my mask in person and still get a grade?*

The secrecy concerned Anne, but she felt like it must be something important. At the end of Tiffany's "letter," she wrote, *Yes, you may.*

The following day at school, Anne returned the graded papers. Tiffany sighed, relieved by Anne's response. She quietly approached Anne's desk after class.

"Can I come by after school?" she asked.

"Of course," Anne replied.

Chapter 6

Carry on my wayward son… There'll be peace when you are done…

Anne listened to the Kansas song, one of her favorites, playing quietly on the radio as she entered grades into the computer. The song always made her think of Richard, so much so that she used it as his ringtone on her cell phone. He seemed mighty "wayward" at this point in his life—not much direction, drive, or discipline—but he was still young, and she was hopeful. It was 4:15 p.m.; school had been out for forty-five minutes and no sign of Tiffany.

I'll give her another fifteen minutes, and then I'm heading home, Anne thought.

Not long after, she heard her classroom door open.

"Mrs. English? Can I still talk to you?" asked Tiffany.

"Absolutely," answered Anne.

Tiffany sat gingerly on the chair next to the desk. She looked around the classroom and attempted to make small talk.

"Those projects are really cool," she said, pointing to some posters on the wall.

"Those are from fifth period. Your class is over there," gestured Anne.

"Oh, yeah. I can see mine from here."

"I really liked the art on yours. You're quite talented."

"Not according to my dad."

"Really? I'm sorry to hear that. Have you ever talked to Mrs. Henderson?"

"The art teacher? Oh, sure. She thinks I could major in art in college. Become a real artist. Maybe teach."

"Excellent!"

"Yeah, well, my dad's dream is for me to be a lawyer like him."

"What about *your* dream?"

Tiffany studied an invisible spot on the desk, her eyes filling with tears.

"My dreams don't matter. Nothing matters anymore."

"What's going on? Wanna talk about it?"

Tiffany slowly raised her gaze, and the profound sadness within it, to meet Anne's.

"I'm pregnant."

"Are you sure?"

"Oh, I'm sure. Did you see the movie *Juno*? That was me a couple of days ago—drinking SunnyD and taking pregnancy tests."

As a mother, Anne knew the kind of commitment that was required to raise children. As a teacher, she knew that most of her students were totally unprepared to make that kind of commitment. There were single moms at her high school; there were single moms at every high school that she knew of. And this kind of confession was one she hated to hear. She often wondered how they made it—or if they made it. Many lived with their families. Most never went to college. A handful stayed with the fathers. Anne took a deep breath.

"How are you doing?"

"Hmm... well, David dumped me. The minute I told him. He thinks it would hurt his chances to get into UT." She paused, remembering the conversation. "Can you believe it? Can you fucking believe it?" she raged. "Oh, sorry."

"Lord, Tiffany! You have more to worry about than cussing in front of a teacher!"

"I guess you're right," she chuckled.

"Have you told your parents?"

"Ohmygod no! And you can't, either. Please, Mrs. English?" Fear sprang from her eyes like she was a gazelle being chased by a tiger.

"I wouldn't dream of it. Have you thought about what you're going to do?"

"David wants me to get rid of it. I don't know if I could, though. I think it would be really hard."

"It would take some serious thought," Anne advised.

She knew she frequently walked a thin line with her students concerning personal issues. She cared for these kids and hated seeing them in pain. She herself had gone through a challenging, rebellious phase in high school and college where she had done things she wasn't necessarily proud of. She often wanted to share her experience with her students—especially the ones who were facing similar issues. She wanted to help and comfort them, to let them know that it would all be all right. They could learn from these experiences and use their new insights to grow and change. She tried to remain detached.

"What would you do, Mrs. English?"

"Oh, honey, I can't tell you what to do. It's your life, and your circumstances are very different from mine. You have to make those choices for yourself, see what happens, and hope for the best. You already know where David stands, so at least you have that piece of the puzzle."

"I guess."

Lynyrd Skynyrd's "Free Bird" filled the silence.

"Is there anything I can do for you, Tiffany?"

"Nah. Thanks for listening. You're right—it's my choice. David can go to hell! So, that's my mask: seventeen, pregnant, hiding it as best I can for now, and trying to figure out what to do next."

"I see. I can understand why you wouldn't want to share that news on paper. Let me know if you need anything. And keep me posted about your decision, if you want to."

"Thanks, Mrs. English. I really appreciate it."

"Happy to help. See you tomorrow."

"See ya! Oh yeah—will I still get a grade for this?"

"Yes, ma'am. Written responses are preferable, but I'll take your oral 'letter' just this once."

"Cool. Thanks! Bye!"

Tiffany almost seemed like she was back to her perky self. Still, Anne hated hearing the news, and she whispered a brief prayer for her. *Her life's really gonna change*, she thought, picking up her purse. *Regardless of what she decides, her life is definitely gonna change. God love her!*

Anne sifted through the rest of the letters in her school bag—the ones that were turned in late—and approximated the number remaining. It was already ten o'clock, but since she had only about ten and wanted to hand them back the next day, she continued. The first letter was from Ray.

> *I will tell you the truth. I didn't like this letter when I got it. But you said there's no right answer so I guess the point is to just answer it. So here goes.*
>
> *Like I said, I didn't like this letter. I didn't see that I wore a mask. But I wear a mask every day of my life. It's hard to explain. I never saw it before now. You told me to look for it. And I did. And now I see it all the time.*
>
> *Here's the deal. I know I'm smart. I told you that in my last letter. I do all my work. I just don't turn it in. So I get the knowledge. But I don't get the grade. I don't let my homies see me doing good. I can't. I have to be a certain way. They expect me to. I gotta be the tough guy who don't care about school because that's how they are. But I never saw how much I did it before now. I even do it when I don't have to like when I'm at home with my mom and my li'l sister. I guess it's a habit. But I tell you what else I don't like about this letter. Like I said, I see*

> it all the time and I wish I didn't. Cuz it's like I can't go back now. I can't go back to not seeing it and I don't know what to do. So I'm kinda mad about this letter. Not at you. Just at the letter.
>
> You prolly don't believe this but I have dreams. I love working on cars. I'm good at it too. I used to help my grandpa work on his. We would talk about stuff and listen to Tejano music while we worked. Until he died. When I was 12. Since then I don't have no one to talk to. If I could I would open a mechanic shop and do good work, and make good money so I can help my mom and li'l sister. My girlfriend's dad is a mechanic and I help him sometimes. But you have to be smart to do that. I mean, you have to really be smart and act like it. Get good grades and stuff. So you can get into trade school. Not just know your smart and not do anything about it.
>
> Your student
>
> Ray

Anne reread the letter. She was amazed at the insight and honesty. She'd known he had it in him, but she'd feared that it was all buried too deeply for him to access it in so short a time.

"Wow," she breathed. She wanted to add the right note at the end. Something that honored the risk he took and the insight he had gained. She wrote:

> I'm so proud of you for seeing this and admitting it. It's even more impressive since you didn't like the topic to begin with. But instead of blowing it off, you dug deep and got some amazing insight. Good job!
>
> PS. I think you'd make a great mechanic, and I would definitely bring my car to you! Don't give up on your dream just because getting there is hard and maybe a little scary. Everything worth having is worth working for. You can do it!!

Chapter 7

Light streamed in through the window. Saturday morning, and her house was peaceful and quiet, except for the song of the mourning dove outside: *oo-wah-hooo, hoo-hoo*. Anne smiled and whispered a soft thank-you to her little sister, as she did every first Saturday morning, when Karen had "custody" of Maggie and Richard. Karen and Anne had always been close, but ever since Anne's husband had left, ten years ago, Karen had taken on more responsibility with her niece and nephew. Karen also knew that as much as Anne loved her children, she needed some time to herself. Karen had devised the plan and made the offer: She would love to have Maggie and Richard spend the weekend with her once a month. At first, Anne was speechless. Their dad had left with no forwarding address or phone number. Anne didn't know where he was, or even if he was still alive. Charlie (or Chaz, as he called himself) was a self-centered, self-indulgent singer-songwriter. The only problem was that when Anne met him and fell instantly in love with him, she only saw the singer-songwriter aspect of his personality. The self-centered indulgence came in the form of an addiction to crack. One Saturday while she and the kids were at Maggie's soccer game, he took everything out of their joint checking and savings accounts, stole her grandmother's diamond ring, and took off.

Anne couldn't have gotten by without Karen; their parents lived several hours away, Anne's bank accounts were depleted, her home was in foreclosure, and she had two small children. Karen, who was a dedicated hematology/oncology nurse at the children's hospital, took them in for a year, until they could get back on their feet.

Maggie and Richard knew her only as their crazy Aunt Karen, because she was so much fun. When they were with Karen, they might go on an imaginary boat trip through the Amazon, create beautiful art, or head out to the nature center. Often, they spent the morning making sack lunches for the homeless and then delivered them around lunchtime. Karen sang in her church choir and was an active member, so she "volunteered" them to help with church projects. Even if it was work, it never seemed like it when Aunt Karen was around. Anyone could spot her curly red hair and freckles a mile away, but her brilliant smile was her true beacon. She exuded love wherever she went, and Anne often wished she was more like her sister.

Once Anne was able to buy a small house in her school district, they moved out. She had been accustomed to Karen's help and input while they were living together, so the transition back to full-time single mom was difficult for Anne. That was when Karen devised the plan. Of course, she phrased it as if Anne were doing her a favor, but Anne knew the truth and was so very grateful.

Anne cherished her solo weekends. They were her saving grace. Teaching was hard by itself; parenting was hard by itself. Together… well, together, she knew, they could be her undoing if she didn't take advantage of the offer. In the end, it took only about six months for her to release the guilt she had experienced whenever her kids went with Karen on "their" weekend. Now, she looked forward to the weekends, planned for them, and enjoyed every single second.

Over the years, she had gotten into a routine. First, she and the children got the house spotless on Thursday night so she could enjoy a clean house all weekend. Then she resolved never to bring work home on *her* weekend. The hardest time was during the time of year students worked on their biggest research paper, because she read every rough draft, made comments, and took notes. She could read about four per hour, times about 150 students... equaled... ? She was hopeless at math, but she knew it took a long time to get through those papers. Still, she had always managed to keep *her* weekends work-free. On Friday night, she might call a friend for dinner or a movie or to listen to music. At some point during her once-a-month Saturday, Anne treated herself to a pedicure or a massage, and sometimes both if it was a special occasion, like her birthday. She might rent a movie, read a book, take a nap, check out garage sales, take a day trip... the list was endless. Sometimes she found a friend to accompany her, and sometimes she didn't. One thing that singlehood had taught her was to be comfortable in her own skin, all by herself. It was awful at first. Anne didn't know what to do and found herself pacing, zoning out to TV, or sleeping all weekend under the guise of "needing the rest." Anne had never truly been alone until those weekends. She had gone from her parents' home to a college dorm to an apartment with roommates and, finally, to a husband.

Karen always asked about her activities when she returned the kids on Sunday night, and she quickly noticed a pattern. She finally had a talk with Anne.

"Annie," she said firmly, "you can't stay holed up in this house all weekend. It's not healthy. Remember what Mom said? All day long you are emptying your bucket, a drop at a time, with all you do for other people—your students, your kids, your friends and family. If you don't take time to fill up your own bucket every now and then, you won't have anything left for anyone else."

When Karen stood up, wagging her finger at Anne, the resemblance to their mother was unmistakable. In her best "Mom" voice, Karen instructed her: "Anne—go fill your bucket!"

They had a good laugh, and Anne got the message. Ever since then she had been determined to get out and truly enjoy this gift from her sister.

She knew one thing on her agenda this morning: her guilty

pleasure. Karen was a Trekkie to the core. She had tried to get Anne interested but with little success. Then, for her birthday, Karen had given Anne the series *Starship Enterprise*. She knew the story well—she had watched the entire series twice herself—and felt this was a good way to introduce Anne to the *Star Trek* phenomenon. Once Anne got to know the characters, she was hooked. She admired Captain Archer's integrity, Phlox's humorous bedside manner, and T'Pol's very scientific brain, and that Trip was just flat-out cute! Since then, during her once-a-month Saturday she poured a cup of her favorite coffee, crawled back into bed with Rocky by her side, and watched three episodes. No matter how badly she was left hanging and wanted to go on, three was her limit.

Today was a particularly lovely early-November day. Gorgeous riding weather! Last June, Anne had taken a motorcycle safety course. One thing she missed about Charlie—the only thing she missed about Charlie—was riding on the back of a motorcycle with him. The motorcycle itself was long gone to Charlie's dealer in lieu of payment for crack, but Anne had been saving for a motorcycle of her own ever since she had taken the class. After the last of her three *Starship Enterprise* episodes ended, Anne went motorcycle shopping. She had been looking online and planned to meet a seller at her home at 11:00 a.m.

The 750 Honda Shadow was a gorgeous blue, complete with saddlebags, a great set of pipes, and power that wouldn't quit. Susan was a diminutive woman who looked more like a Sunday-school teacher than a biker: Soft gray curls framed her face, and bright blue eyes sparkled along with her welcoming smile. The motorcycle had forty-five thousand miles on it; it was well ridden and well loved. Susan thrilled at the idea of Anne's purchasing her beloved bike.

"I've had the brakes replaced, there are new tires, and the clutch was rebuilt just last month. The saddlebags are practically new—I bought them in July."

"Wow. With all the work you've done, why are you selling it?"

"I had a feeling I was preparing Old Blue for someone special. I guess it's silly, but I always name my bikes. And, now that my husband has retired, we want to take some long road trips, and I'd like a bigger touring bike. What do you think?"

"It's great. Honestly, compared to similar bikes, your price seems kind of low. Are you sure about it?"

"Absolutely! She'll be a wonderful bike for you, and I would feel so much better about selling her to you. I have a good feeling about you. You said on the phone that you learned to ride last summer?"

"Yes, my ex-husband had a bike, and I always enjoyed riding. I decided to take the bull by the horns and learn how to ride myself. I had no idea how empowering it would be!"

"Ah, yes! I think men take motorcycles and riding a little for granted. It's predominately a man's world, after all. But it's different for a woman. To feel that strength and accomplishment, it's wonderful! I remember when I first started to ride. I was terrified but determined. Now I can't imagine living any other way. I bet it'll be the same for you."

"I hope so. I'll admit, it makes me a little nervous to try to handle this bike all by myself, but it's something I really want to do—for me."

"That's all I needed to hear. Sold!" exclaimed Susan. "Why don't you ride it home, I'll follow in your car, and then you can bring me back?"

"Perfect! Thank you so much."

"It's my pleasure," smiled Susan.

Anne spent the rest of the day with the wind in her face. She took her time and grew more comfortable as she rode out by the lake and off in the hills. It was exhilarating, and she laughed out loud in response to the joy and freedom she felt. As she rode along the twists and turns, savoring every second, a deep and immense gratitude filled her heart. She became acutely aware of the amazing blessings that had been bestowed on her. Even in her darkest times, good always prevailed. She didn't necessarily want to repeat some of her past and its accompanying lessons, but she could see how everything had fallen together just as it was destined to do. She could see that without her disastrous marriage, there would be no children, and that was something she couldn't imagine. She had gone from being the scared, hopeless wife of a crack addict to a self-sufficient, self-supporting, happy, independent woman. And not just any woman—a biker babe! The idea made her giddy with joy and appreciation. Everything from her past prepared her for this moment. Life was good, and she wanted to share her gratitude with the world.

Maybe the November letter would be a good place to start, she thought.

Chapter 8

Anne's attitude of gratitude dissipated Monday morning. It was research paper time—one of the hardest times of the school year for her students and for her. This group was no different from any others she had taught: they hated the research process. Because of this, teaching it was like pulling a 747 uphill in the sand. Daily. Groans permeated the classroom. Anne clenched her jaw, bracing for the inevitable complaints and whining.

"Aw, Miss, do we hafta?"

"I hate doing research papers!"

"We just did one last year!"

"Guys, c'mon. You're seniors. You wrote one last year, the year before that, *and* the year before that. Besides, these are skills you'll use throughout high school, college, and graduate school and in your workplace. I've used my research skills in other jobs."

Anne walked up and down the aisles, passing out a packet of information.

"Ohmygod—it's like a book!"

"Do we hafta read all this?"

Anne continued, "This packet explains everything you'll need for your paper. It includes information on taking notes, citing sources, embedding quotes, and writing the paper. This is the only packet you'll get, so don't lose it. Remember, writing a research paper is like eating an elephant—we'll do it one bite at a time! If you put in consistent effort and stick to the schedule, you'll be fine. But if you procrastinate or fall behind, this can be a rough assignment. And remember, it's a requirement of the department here, so if you don't complete the process successfully, you won't pass the semester. You don't pass the semester, you don't graduate."

"Just like last year, guys. We might as well just do it and get it over with," advised Tiffany.

"I know it's a lot of work, but I have taught this class for several years now, and I promise we'll get through it together. Now, let's go through the packet," said Anne.

The reaction was the same in all her classes, just as it had been last year and the year before that. Anne knew it was a challenge for them—especially since it was like giving them completely new information, in spite of the fact that they had all written one before. This was their last big project of the fall semester, and the next six weeks would test them all. Luckily, Thanksgiving break would give them some much-needed respite, but it was still three weeks away. Anne carefully scheduled the research paper each year so that there was plenty of time to complete each section, as long as they worked consistently. She also considered herself in the schedule—no papers to grade over Thanksgiving break, if at all possible. Their rough drafts were due the week prior to the break, and if she worked consistently too, she would have them all graded in time for the break.

That night, Maggie and Richard were bickering, the dishwasher refused to work, and Rocky had gotten into the trash, again, eaten something he shouldn't have, again, and thrown up on the living room carpet. Anne's attitude of gratitude from the weekend flew out the window. She felt cranky too, just like the kids here and at school. Life had suddenly become overwhelming. And it was only Monday.

"Maggie and Richard, come here, please," Anne called from the kitchen.

"Mom, Maggie won't leave me alone," whined Richard.

"He went into my room again. I've told him a million times to stay out of my room!"

"You went into my room without asking. Mom, she took my Cowboys jersey without asking!"

"I needed it for a pep rally, brat."

"Enough!" said Anne, losing her patience. "Maggie, give Richard his jersey, and Richard, stay out of Maggie's room. And apologize to each other while you do the dishes."

"By hand? What about the dishwasher?" asked Maggie.

"It appears to be broken. I've called the repairman; he'll be here on Saturday."

"Saturday? Do we have to wash them all until then?" groaned Richard.

"Yes, sir. Now get to it. I need to soak in the tub for a while. No more fighting or complaining tonight. Got it?"

"Yes, ma'am," they said simultaneously.

"I'll wash and you dry," said Maggie.

"No, I'll wash and you dry," countered Richard.

"You two get to work that one out yourselves. Please don't kill each other in the process. I'll be in my room. And please don't disturb me unless the house is on fire or someone is trying to kill you."

"Does that include Maggie? She told me she was going to slit my throat in my sleep tonight."

"I'm pretty sure you don't have to worry about that, Richard. Now get to work on those dishes, and I'm going to sit and soak."

The master bathroom was one of the reasons why Anne had bought this house. The previous owners had reconfigured it to include a jetted tub—Anne's saving grace on more than once occasion. She carefully chose the bath salts she wanted to use, smelling each one to see which would calm her the most.

"Lavender, that's the ticket," she said softly.

Anne lit the candles, turned off the light, put a Billie Holiday CD into the clock radio, and slid into the comfort of the warm water.

"Ahhhhhhh... that's more like it." Serenity washed over her as soon as the water did. She thought back to the weekend and the joy and gratitude she had felt then. How had it disappeared so quickly? Why couldn't she hang on to it?

So much for writing a letter extolling the virtues of gratitude, she thought. *Until I got into the tub, I didn't have an iota of gratitude in me. Who could be grateful? Kids griping at me all day at school, kids fighting when I get home, broken dishwasher, damn dog.*

Anne closed her eyes and sank more deeply into the warmth. Billie's signature song was playing.

Lady sings the blues
I'm telling you

"Sing it, Sister," Anne sighed. She didn't have the blues about a man, but that dishwasher sure had her down. And the kids, and the gift from Rocky... Geez, her life would be *so* much easier without all this stress. But she didn't really want Rocky to go away. He provided good protection and affection for her and the kids. And, of course, she loved her children. And she generally enjoyed her job—in spite of the dreaded research paper.

Anne sat up in the tub. She remembered getting an email recently from a friend about gratitude. Something about being grateful in spite of your circumstances. She tried to recall the wording. Something about having to wake up early because it means you have a job, being grateful for being overweight because it means you have food on the table...

The words began to come together in her mind. She quickly got out of the tub and dried off—she didn't want to lose the inspiration for this letter. Sitting in her robe on her bed, she scribbled the letter she would give her students the next day.

"Good morning! Today we're going to talk about taking notes and citing sources. Remember, we will be in the library gathering information by the end of the week, so I need to make sure you remember how to do these skills. But first, your November letter!"

CLASS LETTERS

"A letter *and* a research paper? I figured we'd skip the letter this month," came a voice from the back.

"No such luck!" laughed Anne.

"Lemme guess. This letter is about the virtues of research," teased Amber.

"Hmm… sort of, Amber," smiled Anne.

"Letter? What letter?" asked Tony Rogers, who had recently transferred into Anne's class.

"I write the class a letter each month about a subject that has nothing to do with English, but you do have to write a response. There's no right answer, and your answers will be between us, but it is a quiz grade, so don't forget about it! You have a week to turn it in."

"At least it isn't due tomorrow," sighed Tony. "We're still unpacking from the move."

"I know you have a lot on your plate, but you can get it all done," encouraged Anne.

"Oh, it'll be okay. I'm just grateful to be settled."

"Grateful to be settled, huh? In spite of having to move and do all that work? Sounds like you're already on the right track for this letter. It's about gratitude."

"Gratitude? You're right—it has nothing to do with English! It's my worst subject," said Tony.

"Stick with me, kid, and you'll do fine!" said Anne with a wink. "That reminds me—do your parents have an email address you could give me? I write emails to all my parents letting them know what we're doing in class. I also attach these letters so they can read them too."

"My dad has one. Here you go," Tony said, handing Anne a slip of paper.

"Wonderful! Thanks, Tony! Now, let's go over your note-taking skills. Get out your packets, please."

Later that evening, Tony maneuvered his way through the boxes in the living room, past the boxes in the kitchen, and into his bedroom, where a few more boxes could be found. He knew they would all be unpacked eventually, but right now it felt like they would never be settled. He and his dad had moved around a lot in the past couple of years, but this was the last time. Tony's dad, John, was the new owner of the local motorcycle shop. Things were finally looking up.

Tony was intrigued by the letter Mrs. English had passed out in class, even if he wasn't all that great at English.

November

Dear Class:

Wow! I had the best time last weekend! I have been saving my pennies for quite some time, and I bought a motorcycle Saturday morning. I'm so excited! I spent the rest of the weekend enjoying my new bike and the gorgeous weather! Then Monday hit. Broken dishwasher, gripey kids (at home and at school, thank you very much), sick dog… UGH! Talk about going from one extreme to the other—complete bliss to total depression in no time flat!

After reading about the change in my life from the weekend to Monday, you may be surprised to discover that this particular letter is about gratitude.

Sometimes things don't go our way. Sometimes there are people or circumstances that seem to overshadow all the good in our lives. Sometimes it's really hard to be grateful. But here's a secret: The more gratitude you have in your life, in spite of your circumstances, the happier you'll be. There is good in every situation—even the really tough ones. Sometimes you have to look really hard to see it, but it's there. This is how I turned my attitude around:

As I mentioned, Monday was not a good start to the week, especially after such a wonderful weekend. The broken dishwasher means that someone has to wash the dishes by hand until we can get it fixed. It also means I have to pay a repairman to fix it, since I know nothing about dishwashers. But, in spite of all that, I AM glad to have a dishwasher. It is a wonderful, time-saving, work-saving appliance, and I am grateful for it.

On Monday, I had two kids at home who couldn't seem to get along. They were fussing and bickering and making everyone's life miserable. But in spite of all that, I AM grateful for my children. Most of the time, they get along well (it would be unreasonable to expect them to be perfect angels 24/7!). Most of the time, they bring much joy to my life. I wouldn't trade them for anything!

On Monday, Rocky, my boxer, got into the trash, made a huge mess, and then got sick all over my living room carpet. But, in spite of all that, I AM grateful for his love, companionship, and protection.

And, finally, on Monday, I had to deal with whining and complaints from all of you about this research paper. I know that these are good skills for you to practice. I know that this will all be beneficial in the long run. And I know you will fight me every step of the way! But, in spite of all that, I AM grateful for my job and for the opportunity to share my days with you! My job helps me pay for that repairman. And all of you, even when you're unhappy with me and/or your assignments, make my life richer.

This letter is about gratitude—especially about the gratitude you can have in spite of your circumstances. First of all, circumstances change. The dishwasher will be fixed. Rocky will feel better. My kids will get along again (someday!). And you will live through the research paper process (I promise!). The other aspect about gratitude is that there is always something to be grateful for. You can start with the basics: air, water, food, clothing, and shelter. Some things are harder to see, and you *may have to be really willing and open-minded enough to see them, but they're there. ALWAYS!*

So, what do you have to be grateful for, in spite of appearances or circumstances? Is there something in your life that seems awful but has a little kernel of gratitude hidden within it? I bet you can find it.

You know the drill: one page, quiz grade, due next Tuesday, don't threaten to blow up the school or I'll have to tell someone! Maybe you will find inspiration in the following quote by Henry Ward Beecher: "The unthankful heart... discovers no mercies; but let the thankful heart sweep through the day and, as the magnet finds the iron, so it will find, in every hour, some heavenly blessings!"

If nothing else, if you do this assignment, you can be thankful for the grade, even if the message escapes you! LOL.

"Dinner's ready," called John from the kitchen.

"Be right there!"

"Hey, son. Whatcha been doing?"

"Reading a letter my English teacher wrote the class. It's about gratitude."

"Gratitude, huh? I know you don't have anything to be grateful for," teased John, handing Tony a paper plate.

"You got that right! Wait'll I tell her about my abusive father and my sad home life!"

"Uh-oh—CPS should be knocking any minute!" laughed John. "I'd better hide! Wait a minute—do I hear tires squealing outside? They must be here already! Gotta go!"

They both laughed at the joke, and then paused, lost in their own thoughts, and continued the meal in silence. After a few minutes, John continued the conversation.

"How are you liking all your classes?"

"Not too bad. I think chemistry will be okay. And, of course, math. I hope I do okay in English. I really like the teacher."

"What's her name?"

"Mrs. English—can you believe it?"

"That's kinda weird! Do you have a Mrs. Math or Mrs. Chemistry teaching you too?"

"I know, right? Mrs. English is really cool, though, and I like the letter she wrote us. It's all about how you can be grateful on the inside in spite of what's going on in your life on the outside. Oh, I almost forgot. I gave her your email address. She says she likes to send updates and stuff to the parents. Oh, and guess what?"

"What?"

"She rides a motorcycle."

"Cool! I'll look forward to hearing from her. She sounds like a good one! How's football practice?"

Chapter 9

Most of the students were diligently looking for information about their research topic. A couple of them tried to get in a game of chess before getting to work.

"Jason and Stephen, no chess till you're done," said Anne as she swept the library, looking for stragglers. "Janie—you're in the fiction section! Get over to bios, please."

"But, Miss, I haven't checked out a book for the novel project for this semester."

"You'll need to do that on your own time. We're only in the library for five days, and you'll need every bit of that time to get your research done. Now, get to work, please."

"Whatever," Janie grumbled as she moved to a different section.

After making another pass through the library, answering questions, and encouraging the dawdlers, Anne situated herself in a central location. As the students gathered the necessary information, they reported to Anne that they had met their quota for the day.

"We got our three sources—can me and Jason play chess now?" asked Stephen.

"Jason's not mean," replied Anne with a smile.

"Huh? I didn't say he was mean. I said can me and Jason play chess now?"

"Jason, did you hear Stephen say you were mean?" teased Anne.

"Miss, I didn't say he was mean!" said Stephen.

"You're supposed to say 'Jason and I,' dipwad," sighed Jason.

"Oh, I get it. So, can Jason and I play chess?" asked Stephen.

"And you have all your work done?" quizzed Anne.

"Yes, ma'am, we do."

"All right, then. But remember, you have to get another three sources tomorrow—and you want to make sure they are good ones. You could spend time getting ahead," suggested Anne.

"Naw, we're good. We'd rather play chess," answered Jason.

"Okay. Just remember that this paper is a—" Anne began.

"Requirement of the department. If we don't pass, we fail the semester. Got it," parroted Jason.

"At least you've been listening!" smiled Anne. "Go ahead and play."

As Jason and Stephen walked toward the chess table, Tiffany approached, smiling.

"Mrs. English? Is it okay if I write more than a page for the November letter?"

"Absolutely! There's no limit on how long it can be. You must have a lot to be grateful for."

"I'll tell you all about it."

"Can't wait to read it!"

Anne had noticed that Tiffany had an extra bounce in her step. Whatever was going on with her must be good. Anne let out a sigh of relief.

Keosha was preparing for her nightly rendezvous with the BADs. Something was brewing with BD; Tamika was on edge but wouldn't talk about it, and Keosha knew not to ask BD directly. When she arrived at the park, Keosha saw BD and Rollo talking intensely to an unfamiliar face. He was tall, with Denzel-good looks. He had a swagger and air of confidence about him that Keosha found attractive.

"Who's that?" she whispered to Tamika.

"That's Benny. BD and him are talking about doing business together."

Keosha knew that whatever the "business" was, it was illegal. She also knew not to press for more information. If she was told anything, it was on a need-to-know basis. Although Keosha was still considered something of an outsider, she found the intrigue and risk exciting. Part of her wanted more of it, but she was also afraid of it. Tamika, on the other hand, had pushed her way into the BADs via pregnancy. She had told BD that she was on the Pill, hoping to get pregnant and become part of his life. She got her wish and began shoplifting and carrying drugs and money for him. He had resisted her involvement at first, but once she was pregnant he had decided that she might become useful. The bigger she got, the more ingenious he became in using her pregnancy to his advantage.

BD called Tamika over to him. "T, c'mere," he barked.

The four of them talked among themselves for a bit, glancing at Keosha periodically, and then Tamika motioned for Keosha to join them.

BD made the introductions.

"Benny, this is my homegirl Keosha."

"'Sup, Keosha," said Benny.

"'Sup," answered Keosha with a nod.

"My boy here tells me you want to move up in the world. Maybe get more involved in some business," said Benny. "You might say that BD and me, we're expanding and need some good workers."

"Sure," said Keosha, feigning courage. "What you want me to do?"

"I got a delivery for you to make tomorrow night, k? We'll see how you do wid dat and then decide what else we want," said BD.

"I'm down," agreed Keosha.

"Aight. Be here, ten o'clock," said Benny. "That's it. Go on home, now."

Keosha did as she was told.

Kim was still up doing homework. It was late, and she had spent too much time on the computer. Her parents were old-school and didn't like the way Kim had changed since they had come to America. She was still shy and quiet, but they didn't approve of her clothes, hair, and makeup. Kim had strict rules to follow, so she spent as much time with friends as possible.

"All that black," her father would say to her. "You look like you go to funeral."

Kim's rebellion was purely exterior to her parents. The real rebel lived inside.

Dear Mrs. English,

Gratitude is something I'm very familiar with and I try to look for gratitude in everything. Sometimes things aren't all that great on the outside but I have to remember where I came from. This is what I'm grateful for. I'm grateful that my family and I are living in America, even though we live in a small apartment. I'm also grateful that my parents and I have jobs here so we can get food and pay rent, even though we work long hours to do so. I'm grateful I can go to school and learn better English. And even though I can't tell you more than that, I'm grateful I have you to talk to in these letters. Thank you.

Kim

Kim wanted to talk to Mrs. English about her situation, but her few friends warned her to keep quiet. So, for now, her secret remained just that.

In the frilly pink bedroom of a large house on the other side of town, Tiffany thought back over the events of the previous evening. She had had a long talk with her parents. Yes, there had been tears and disappointment, but there had also been understanding and communication. She couldn't wait to tell Mrs. English about it. Although she would have preferred another oral letter, she knew that the first one was an exception.

> *Dear Mrs. English,*
>
> *So much has happened since we talked a few weeks ago. It's hard to know where to begin. I told you that David broke up with me after I told him about the baby. He's still being a jerk and I can see now that he wasn't the great guy I thought he was. So I'm grateful for that. I don't want to be in a relationship with someone who breaks up with me when things get rough. I'm glad I could finally see that. But the biggest thing I'm grateful for is my parents. I had a long talk with them and told them everything. I mean everything! The last letter really got me thinking about how much I keep from them and how much I wear a mask with them. After reading it, I really wanted to tell them everything but I was afraid of what they would say. I finally got up the courage and this is what happened.*
>
> *I told them about the baby. At first they were shocked, to say the least. They didn't know David and I were having sex, much less that I was pregnant. So I told them. It was hard to do. My mom and I cried and my dad got real quiet. Then he surprised me. He said, Okay, let's talk about it and figure things out. I couldn't believe it. I thought he would kill me (literally). But he was way more understanding than I thought he would be. I think he'd like to beat up David (and I'd like to watch). LOL. They wanted to talk to David's parents but I told them how David acted when I told him and I said I'd rather just do this alone. They think he should pay child support but I don't want anything from him. Not after he dumped me in my time of need. We talked about my options. I told them no way would I get an abortion. They still want me to look into*

adoption and I said I would. I know having a baby would be hard but I also think it would be fun. I'm sure I could finish high school and go to college even if I have a baby to take care of.

I can't say that I'm really grateful to be pregnant right now. I mean, part of me is excited and stuff but part of me is really scared. But I am grateful that me and my parents are talking about it and that everything is out in the open. I don't know all that I'm going to do yet about the baby or school or anything but at least my secret is out. No more mask for me. LOL. And that's what I'm really grateful for the most. And I'm also grateful for you, Mrs. English. Thanks for listening and talking to me. It really helps.

Tiffany

David lay on his bed, tossing a football into the air and grumbling about the recent events in his life. *How could Tiffany do this to me? This could wreck my whole life. All I want to do is finish high school, get a scholarship to UT, and play with the NFL, preferably the Cowboys. Is that too much to ask? What a bitch!*

"David, have you finished your homework?" asked his mom as she tapped on his door.

"Almost."

"Better get to work, son. It's getting late."

"Okay."

David took the November letter out of his backpack and read it.

Grateful? What do I have to be grateful for? God, she's a bitch!

He could feel the anger rising in him. It was getting harder to control. He had heard that about steroids, but they had never affected him like this before.

"C'mon, get a grip. Gotta do this damn letter and then bed. Early day tomorrow," he reminded himself. He gripped the pen and began to write.

CLASS LETTERS

I'm grateful most of all for football. I spend most of my time outside of school on football. It starts in the summer before school starts. We have two a days and they are a killer! We also have weight training all summer. We have to come into the gym at least three times a week. Then there's football season—the best time of the year. During the winter there's more weight training and in the spring there's spring training (for football). And then it starts all over again. Why would I be grateful for all this hard work? One, I love it and have been playing since I was six. Two, it's going to be my ticket to college (UT) and then to the NFL (Cowboys). I'm also grateful for my dad. He has supported me throughout my whole football career. And life. So that's what I'm grateful for.

David A. Spears III

David had found it more difficult to sleep lately, and tonight was no exception. He knew he had to get some good sleep tonight—the big game was tomorrow. Luckily, he was prepared: he had bought a couple sleeping pills off a guy in third period. Hopefully one would do the trick and he could save the other one. He downed the pill with the rest of his protein shake and eventually drifted off to sleep.

Ray washed the dishes and cleaned the kitchen. His mother had pulled a double shift and left him in charge of dinner. Hamburger Helper was his specialty—nothing fancy, but it got the job done. He checked on Maribel and found her sleeping soundly in her tiny room, underneath a Hannah Montana bedspread. It was his Christmas present for her; he had picked it up at a garage sale for $2. She loved it like it cost $200. He had already done the rest of his homework. All that was left was the letter for Mrs. English. He looked forward to writing it. He dug out a pencil and piece of paper from his backpack.

You ain't gonna believe this. I been doing a lot of thinking since that last letter. Sometimes I still think about it. But mainly I decided I don't want to wear the mask that makes me look dumb anymore. So I been trying. I even turn in my homework now. I asked my teachers about my grades n I got all Cs and a B. I haven't had a B since elementary school. That's what I'm grateful for...

Keosha missed the last two days of the week—her first two absences of the school year. Anne assumed she was sick until she heard some whispers in the stacks at the library.

"... hear about Keosha?"

"... hanging out... BD and Rollo... "

"... drugs... jail... "

Anne held out hope that the rumors were false—or at least about someone other than Keosha. She went about the rest of her day, working with her students and ready for the weekend, but Keosha stayed in the back of her mind. Anne's weekend passed quickly—Maggie and Richard both had soccer games, and there was the usual housecleaning and other chores to keep her body busy and her mind occupied. Still, she thought of Keosha often and was anxious for the school week to begin again. She breathed a sigh of relief when Keosha walked into the classroom Monday morning, smiling.

"Here's the November letter, Miss. I hope it's not late."

"No, Keosha, it's not due till tomorrow. But you missed two days in the library last week—you have some catching up to do."

"Yes, ma'am. I can take care of that for homework."

As Keosha almost skipped out of the room, Anne watched, baffled but smiling.

Anne's day was full—Mondays usually were. She spent her class periods teaching and her conference period getting ready for the rest of the week. And because of the pace during the research project, she felt she had to get graded assignments back to the kids as soon as possible—even if they turned the work in late. She finally made it home about six, later than usual.

"Hi, Mom. Didya get the stuff?" asked Richard.

"What stuff?"

"The stuff for school tomorrow."

"What stuff for school tomorrow?" Anne was losing patience at the lack of pertinent information.

"The stuff for Spanish class. I texted you. Didn't you get it?"

Anne checked her phone. There was a text from Richard, just as he had said, but her phone had been on vibrate and she had missed it.

"Avocados and chips, huh?"

"Yeah, I figure we'll need about twenty or twenty-five avocados and two or three bags of chips."

"That's a lot of guacamole, Richard. How about half that amount?"

Richard shrugged. "I guess."

"Okay, wanna come with me?" asked Anne.

Before he could answer, Maggie called from the living room.

"Mom? Is that you?"

"Yes, Maggie, I'm home."

"Ohmygod, Mom, we have to go get a pink feather boa," Maggie said breathlessly.

"A *what?*"

"A pink feather boa. It's for History. I'm in a group and we're putting on a skit tomorrow, and I need a pink feather boa."

"What period of history featured a pink feather boa?" quizzed Anne.

"It's sort of a modern version of ancient Egypt and Cleopatra," explained Maggie.

"I see," sighed Anne, as she calculated a plan of action. "All right, well, hmm... How about this? I think the three of us should get the avocados and chips, find a pink boa *somewhere,* and stop in at Sonic for burgers and shakes while we're out. What do you think?"

"Cool! I didn't want that chicken or whatever it was that you thawed for dinner anyway," said Richard.

"It's pork," Anne corrected.

"Well, whatever it is, I like burgers better."

"That sounds good, Mom, but I also have a ton of homework," said Maggie.

"We should be home by eight or so," said Anne. "That should give you plenty of time."

"I guess," said Maggie, contemplating her options. "Okay, let's go."

It was closer to eight thirty when they finally arrived back home after what had turned into much more of a shopping trip than Anne had anticipated: socks and underwear for Richard; tights and a sweater for Maggie, who also needed bras and panties but refused to buy them whenever Richard was around, because of his merciless teasing.

Anne was exhausted. It felt more like a Friday than a Monday. She sat down on the sofa, took off her shoes, propped her feet up on the coffee table, and absentmindedly flipped on the TV. It felt good to finally relax a little. She sat up quickly, remembering.

"I have Keosha's letter in my bag! I sure want to see what she has to say!"

Anne retrieved the letter, resumed her comfortable position, and began to read.

Miss—I am grateful like I ain't never been grateful before. I almost made a bad mistake but something happened that stopped it. I got with some bad people and I was gonna do something they wanted me to do so I could fit in better. I was scared but I was gonna do it anyway. So, I was going over to the park last week to meet up with them people I was gonna do something for. I had just gotten to the park and was talking to my homegirls. Then all of a sudden, there were cops everywhere. They picked us all up and took us to jail. I was so scared. But I didn't have nothing on me, like I would have a little while later, and so they just talked to me. They had to call my mom to come down cuz I'm a minor. She had to leave work. She was so mad. But she was also scared. I could see it in her eyes and it woke me up. It was like I could see my whole future in her eyes in that minute—or at least the future I would have if I had made that bad mistake. They kept me till late which is why I missed that one day. Then they called and wanted to talk to me again. My mom went with me. That's why I missed that other day. Then my mom and I had long talks over the weekend about me and my future. I could see how taking one wrong turn can affect my whole life. So that's what I'm grateful for—not taking that wrong turn. And I'm grateful for my mom for sticking by me and helping me.

"That was a close one," said Anne softly. "Thank you, God, for protecting Keosha. She's such a good girl, and I, too, am grateful she didn't take that wrong road."

Chapter 10

During research paper time, the days flew by quickly for Anne and the students. After gathering information in the library and organizing thoughts into an outline, they spent the week in the computer lab, typing rough drafts.

"Miss, how do I save?"

"I can't find the work I did yesterday! Help!"

"Where's the word count thingy?"

"Would you explain again how to do quotes?"

"Citations? What's a citation?"

The questions were endless, and Anne always felt as if she had run several miles by the end of the day. Rough drafts were due on Monday, giving them an additional weekend to work if they needed it, but she offered bonus points for anyone who turned it in early. This year's crop of kids operated just about like every other class she had taught: About 10 percent turned their papers in early, 70 percent turned them in on time, another 10 percent got them in late, and the rest never bothered.

Times had certainly changed since Anne wrote a research paper—there had been no Internet or computers for her. She remembered hours at the library and looking through a pile of books she had checked out or magazine articles she had copied. She marveled at how easy it was to use computers now compared with the IBM Selectrics and other "advanced" typewriters from her day. No more correction tape or cartridges. Revision and editing were a breeze on the computer, versus completely retyping each draft on a typewriter.

Thanksgiving break was peeking around the corner, and not a minute too soon. She needed some time off, even though she would most likely spend part of it grading rough drafts. Thanksgiving break was also the time when she and Karen packed the kids and dog in the car and headed north to Missouri for their annual obligatory visit with their parents. Prior to their father's heart attack a few years earlier, Fred and Jane had always made the drive to Texas and stayed with Anne. Now, although Fred was in good health, Jane fussed over him like a mother hen and rarely allowed him to spend that much time on the road.

Karen and Anne tried to make the car trip fun for the kids. They bought puzzles and games to play on the road, snacks to munch on, and a couple of new CDs to listen to. As Maggie and Richard grew older, they became more preoccupied with iPods and cell phones than with Mad Libs and crossword puzzles. Still, Karen and Anne stocked up and took advantage of the diversions, even when Maggie and Richard refused to participate.

The days prior to the break were always busy. Grading took priority, but there were bags to pack and last-minute errands to run as well. This year, in spite of their mother's disappointment and chiding, Karen and Anne were reducing the length of their trip by a few days. The two sisters had made a pact that *this* would be the year they would begin to cut their visits short. Anne recalled the conversation she had had with Karen in early October.

"Anne, you know what it's like when we go. You're stressed, I'm stressed. It's just not worth all that stress for either one of us. Besides, you're the one who really needs a break, and you know you won't get one up there."

Anne eventually agreed to the shorter visit; her need for some real time off took precedence over any guilt she might carry. Their plan was to leave on Monday morning, get in Monday night, and leave Friday morning after Thanksgiving rather than stay through the weekend as they had in years past.

"Mom, it's just a couple of days shorter. We'll be there for almost a week," reasoned Anne in October when she broke the news to her mother. After an hour's worth of "discussion" about the whys and wherefores of this trip, Jane relented.

"Okay, you can cut the trip short this year, but next year, you're staying the whole time," Jane warned. "And you'll have to go see Aunt Martha while you're here. I told her you all were coming."

"Okay, Mom," said Anne, relieved that it was settled.

By the time the last bell rang on the Friday before the break, Anne was mentally, physically, and emotionally exhausted. She had been grading rough drafts every night from the minute she returned home from school until midnight, when she could barely keep her eyes open. All her hard work had paid off, though—she had only twenty papers left to grade over the break. She decided to treat herself to a long motorcycle ride on Saturday. She had seen a flyer posted in the local motorcycle shop that mentioned a group ride that began Saturday morning and would continue into the afternoon. This would be her first group ride, and she was nervous, but she decided to bite the bullet and give it a try. It was sunny but chilly, so she bundled up in her leather chaps and jacket to ward off the cold wind as she rode.

She pulled into the parking lot of the motorcycle shop at around nine forty-five to sign up for the ten o'clock start time. There were a few women in attendance, but most of them were riding behind husbands or boyfriends. Across the crowd, she spotted Susan standing next to her shiny new cruiser.

"Susan! Hi!" Anne called.

"Anne! How wonderful to see you! How are you enjoying your bike?"

"I love it! I hope you don't miss it too much, because you can't have it back! Besides, your new one is gorgeous. I'm really excited about doing this ride today, but also a little nervous. It's my first time," confided Anne.

"Wooohooo! A virgin!" Susan laughed. "You'll do fine. Yes, I miss Old Blue, but I gotta tell ya, I am in love with this new bike. It's so comfortable for long rides—and Herb and I have been going on lots of them now that he's retired."

"What did you name this one?" smiled Anne.

"Lightning! What do you think?"

"That's a great name. I guess that's why you have lightning bolts on the tank."

"Actually, it was the other way around. They came with the bike and inspired the name. Have you named your bike? You should, you know. Really personalize it and make it your own."

"I'll see what I can come up with. Maybe I'll be inspired on this trip."

"Well, here's someone that can inspire you: meet John, the owner of the shop. John, this is Anne. She's taken the motorcycle safety course, so she's a fairly new rider and it's her first group ride. Not only that," said Susan, leaning toward John menacingly, "but she bought Old Blue from me, which makes her a very special friend, and I expect you to take good care of her!"

"Yes, ma'am," agreed John, in mock fear. "Anything you say, Miss Susan! You got me shaking in my boots! C'mon, Anne, I'll get you all set up, introduce you around, and give you some pointers about group riding."

"Awesome! Thank you," said Anne.

"Hey, I'm not about to go up against Susan. She might beat me up," John laughed. "Actually, she and Herb have been friends of mine a long time. They helped me get this shop up and running when I moved here."

"The only time I've met Susan was when I bought the bike from her, but I feel like I've known her forever."

"Yep, they have that effect on people. Both of 'em. Let's get you checked in. It's about time to hit the road!"

Anne was welcomed readily into the group, and she enjoyed the ride immensely. John, Susan, and Herb kept an eye on her throughout the ride, answering her questions and noting points of interest along the route. The group rode for a couple of hours, stopped at a great, out-of-the-way hamburger joint to eat and unkink for an hour or so, then continued on their journey until they returned to the shop around three o'clock.

"How'd you like your first group ride?" asked Susan.

"Frankly, I'm a little sore, but other than that, I had a great time. Thanks for all your help."

"Get in a tub with lots of hot water and soak for a while when you get home. That should help. There are different seat pads for your bike too. You can get a bead pad for next to nothing, or you can spend two hundred for a really good gel pad. If you are serious about making a lot of long rides, you might want to spring for the gel pad. It makes riding so much more enjoyable. Your bum will thank you. And, Anne," Susan pulled her close, whispering, "that John is a good one. I'm just sayin'."

"Good to know! Thanks again. I think I'll get in that tub as soon as I get home." Anne gave Susan and Herb each a hug and mounted the bike for the ride home.

"Bye, Anne!" waved John. "Come ride with us again soon."

"Will do. See ya!" smiled Anne, and she roared out of the parking lot.

The rest of the weekend was spent in preparation for the trip to Missouri, which they were leaving for first thing Monday morning. In spite of the relaxation she had felt on the ride two days before, tension wormed its way into Anne's neck and shoulders in anticipation of seeing her parents. These trips had never been pleasant. Actually, Karen and Anne's entire upbringing hadn't been pleasant, but once the sisters had moved to Texas, they had learned ways to recognize and combat their parents' manipulative behavior.

Once they were solidly on the road, Maggie and Richard snoozed in the backseat, using Rocky as their pillow. Etta James sang quietly in the background.

"Do you think this trip will be different from the others?" asked Karen while Anne steered behind the wheel.

"What do *you* think?" asked Anne wryly.

"Naw, just wishful thinking. I know the minute we walk in, the griping will start. Ugh!"

"Remember our pact. We stick together in a united front. And if one of 'em starts in, we set our boundaries and stick to 'em!"

"Well, you know Dad won't stick up for us as long as she's around."

"I know. At least we can see the pattern now. God, when I think of all those years that I bought into their crap!"

"And to think, it only took us two years of therapy to get to this point!" laughed Karen. "Really and truly, sis, it helped me so much to see that therapist with you. It answered so many questions and made so many things clear. I always thought we were close before, but after sitting in that office with you for all those appointments—hearing your side, comparing notes, and having Kris explain the intricacies of our family dysfunction—I swear, I couldn't have done it without you."

"I know, Karen. I feel the same way. There are so many reasons I'm grateful for you, but working out our family stuff together has to top the list."

"Our parents always knew how to put the *fun* in *dysfunction!* But seriously, I have always admired how well you've raised your kids, in spite of Charlie *and* the shitty upbringing we had. You've had your hands full, but I think you've done a terrific job with Maggie and Richard, raising them on your own after their asshole of a father abandoned you like he did."

"Shh… the kids might hear you. In spite of what Charlie did or didn't do, he's still their father, and I try to speak respectfully about him. Not that they even ask much anymore."

"I say you're better off without him," said Karen.

"There's no doubt about that! Hey, how long do you think it'll be before Mom reminds me that I'm still overweight? Or that neither of us is married?" speculated Anne.

"And no prospects for either of us, don't forget about that!" laughed Karen. "Hmm, let me see… I don't know. She might wait 'til dinner."

"Let's make a bet. I bet you a pedicure she starts in on us within an hour of our arrival."

"I'll take that bet. But I think she'll at least wait until dinner. She might even put it off 'til Tuesday."

"There's no way she's waiting *that* long! You're on!" said Anne. "Now, let's look for a gas station. We're almost to empty—and I gotta pee!"

Anne pulled her SUV into their parents' driveway as the sun sank below the horizon. The two-story colonial hadn't changed since they'd left home—inside or out. The lawn and flower beds were perfectly manicured by their father, while the inside was a perfect example of 1980s interior design, completely unchanged since the girls were in high school. The pastel paint-splash wallpaper was the same, and the overstuffed furniture still looked completely comfortable on the parquet flooring. Hunter green was the predominant color in the den. And the mirrored wall in the dining room still reflected the brass-and-glass dining room table. The girls had chosen the decor for their bedrooms: Karen had gone with a Southwestern theme—turquoise walls, multicolored drapes, and a matching bedspread that included the iconic howling wolf—while Anne's room was salmon pink and seafoam green, with poufy floral window valances and matching silk-flower arrangements. Walking into their respective rooms was like becoming a teenager all over again. Anne could practically feel the zits popping out on her forehead.

After unpacking the car and depositing their bags, Karen, Anne, and the children greeted and hugged Fred and Jane amid the usual questions and comments:

"How was the trip?"

"Look how you've grown!"

"We've missed you!"

"Oh, you brought that dog, too? How nice."

"Who's hungry? Dinner's all ready," said Jane, giving the group a new focus. "Oh, and Anne," her mother added in a hushed tone, "I made a special low-cal dinner, just for you."

"Thanks, Mom, but that really wasn't necessary."

"Aw, honey, it's no trouble. Besides, how do you expect to find a man when you're carrying around all that extra baggage?"

And, just like that, Anne was once again that awkward teenager who felt like nothing she did was ever good enough.

Chapter 11

"Did you hear her telling me about the low-cal dinner she made for me?" Anne asked Karen as they were unpacking and getting settled after dinner.

"I didn't hear her, but I saw the dinner—grilled fish and steamed veggies, while the rest of us had fried fish and mac and cheese. I mean, it's a healthy dinner, but to make yours different and to make it all so obvious is stretching it a bit, even for her. But at least you won the bet!" said Karen, trying to cheer Anne up.

"How is it that I can work so hard in therapy, become this happy, confident woman who is comfortable in her own skin, and then show up here, and within thirty minutes all that confidence is out the window? It's weird—I expect her to act this way, but when she does, it always surprises me."

"I think we both need to sit down with her and tell her what we talked about in therapy—that we are both happy with our lives, that we don't want or appreciate her interference, and that our relationship with her suffers because of it. Do you think she would stop if we asked her?" wondered Karen.

"We'd probably have to set that boundary over and over and over again, just like Kris said we would. But I think she'd listen eventually. Remember, it's just like a mobile—if one part of it moves, the other parts *have* to move. So long as we keep that mobile moving, she'll follow suit."

"I hope so! When do you want to talk to her?" asked Karen.

"The sooner, the better," said Anne.

Fred and Richard sat on the sofa, watching one of the many football games that hijacked the TV this time of year. Maggie sat sideways in an overstuffed chair, legs dangling over the side and totally engrossed in texting her friends. Jane had been a football widow for over forty years and found other ways to occupy her time. Tonight's outlet included scrapbooking, a newly acquired hobby. Anne and Karen found her carefully measuring and cutting at the dining room table.

"Hey, Mom. Whatcha doin'?" asked Karen.

"Oh, girls, look! I'm putting together a scrapbook of your high school years. At first I couldn't decide whether to do a separate book for each of you or one with both of you in it. I finally decided on two separate books. See? Anne, yours is the one with the pink stripes, since you've always been so girlie, and Karen, yours has animals on it, since you were always bringing home strays. Aren't they cute?"

"They're great, Mom. Can we talk to you about something?" asked Anne.

"Of course! Anne, look how skinny you were in this picture! It must have been the angle, because I don't remember you looking like that."

"No, Mom. It's not the angle. That's how I looked in high school."

"No, I don't think so. I specifically remember taking you to the doctor in your junior year, and you were definitely twenty pounds overweight—at least. Oh, Karen! Here's a picture of you with that cute Jimmy Ayers! You should have married him! I hear he's doing quite well, and Lord knows, you could use the help. I know nursing is a noble profession, like teaching, but you girls are so smart! Surely you could have found higher-paying jobs."

"We like what we do, Mom," said Karen.

"You could like something with more money, too. How about med school?"

"Mom, I don't want to be a doctor. I love being a nurse—it's what I'm meant to do."

"Maybe, but—" Jane began.

"No 'buts' about it, Mom. I'm happy in my career."

"Mom," began Anne, "we really need to talk about something with you."

"Sure, honey, anything."

"We know you love us, and we appreciate all the help and guidance and support you've given us over the years. But, Mom, you have to stop criticizing everything we do. We like our lives just the way they are—careers, being single, and, in my case, even being a little overweight," said Anne.

"Criticize? I don't criticize! I only want to help."

"You may call it helping, but to us, it feels like criticism," said Karen.

"But you *know* you'd make more money as a doctor. And Anne *could* stand to lose a few pounds. And you would both be so much happier with a man in your life. See how happy your father and I are? It takes two to tango!"

"All those things may be true," began Anne, "but the fact of the matter is that Karen's a nurse, and she loves it. Sure, I could stand to lose some weight, but, really and truly, I'm happy with my body and comfortable in my skin. And, as far as needing a man, well… maybe someday. But right now, I have my kids to focus on and a job to do that takes up lots of time. If a good man shows up someday, I'll give him a chance, but until then I'm going to enjoy my life, regardless of my marital status."

"But all I ever wanted was for you girls to be happy."

"That's the thing, Mom—we are!" Karen continued. "We are both very happy with our lives. We have good lives. Yes, there have been some bumps along the way, but we've learned and grown from them. Are our lives perfect? Of course not! We both work hard, but we also find it satisfying and fulfilling. We may not be married, but we both have lots of friends and plenty of outside interests. Anne just bought a motorcycle and has had a blast riding it!"

"A motorcycle? Oh my goodness—they're so dangerous!"

"I took a motorcycle safety class, and I'm very careful. But Karen's right—I love it."

"Okay, girls, you promise you're happy?"

"Yes, Mom, we are," answered Karen.

"We promise," agreed Anne.

"Well, I'll try not to 'criticize,' as you call it. Really, I was just trying to help."

"I know, Mom, but it comes across as criticism. We love you and we love visiting you, but, honestly, it's very stressful to see you because of your nagging," said Karen.

"Oh, so now I'm a nag?" sniffed Jane.

"Okay, maybe that was the wrong word," said Anne, glancing at Karen. "We don't want to hurt your feelings, but we also just want to be free to live our lives as we see fit, without interference or suggestions on how we can do it better. As long as we're happy—"

"And we are," interrupted Karen.

"As long as we're happy," continued Anne, "why not just be happy for us?"

"But what if I feel like it's necessary to help you or give you advice?" asked Jane.

"How about this? Wait until we ask for your help," suggested Anne.

"Oh, I don't know about that! Isn't it part of my job as your mother to help you make better choices and live happier lives?"

"Sure it was—when we were children. But we're adults now and capable of making our own choices—and our own mistakes. Your job as a mom was to prepare us for adulthood, and you did a great job at that. Now, trust that you raised us well and that we are fully prepared for any challenge that comes our way. And if we need help, we'll ask for it," said Karen.

"But your father is always watching TV or tinkering in his workshop. He doesn't need me anymore. You girls are all I have left."

"Find some volunteer work to do. You could help out at a senior center or maybe at a day care or school—you were always great at playing games and making arts and crafts when we were little. Focus your talents where they can really be used. You have so much to give! We'll even help you find someplace while we're here, if you want," said Anne.

"I'll try," sighed Jane. "But please don't get mad at me if I slip every now and then. Old habits are hard to break!"

"Not a problem! We love you, Mom," said Anne.

"Love you, Mom," said Karen, hugging Jane.

"And, Mom, no more 'special' dinners, please! It's too much work for you, and it just makes me feel bad."

"It's really no trouble, I just wanted to—"

"Help. I know. No more, okay?"

"Okay. I'll try. How about some ice cream? Anne, you can even have two scoops!"

"Balance, Mom. It's all about balance. No need to swing from one extreme to the other!" laughed Anne.

"Whew! We lived through another visit!" sighed Karen as they pulled away from their parents' home.

"I'm so glad we had that talk with Mom at the beginning of the trip. It made things so much easier this time."

"Did you see how many times Mom stopped herself from 'helping' during breakfast this morning?" asked Karen.

"I know! She went from offering me low-calorie syrup to piling extra pancakes on my plate. She's so funny! At least she's trying."

"Do you think she'll drive all those old people crazy at the senior center?"

"I doubt it. The director said they really need volunteers. I'm so proud of her for volunteering. I think she'll do a great job," said Anne.

"What are you going to do the rest of the break after we get home?" asked Karen, changing subjects.

"The good news is that I finished grading the rough drafts last night, so that's out of the way. I'll check the weather and maybe do some riding. And, of course, there will be piles of laundry to do! At least we cleaned house before we left, so it's in good shape. What about you?"

"I dunno. I may just find a trashy book and curl up in my pj's in front of a fire if it's cold enough. Besides, I have to rest up for next weekend, when your two brats—I mean, precious children—come to stay," teased Karen.

"Hey, I heard that!" said Maggie. "Richard's the only brat in our family."

"Am not!"

"Are too!"

"I am not!"

"You are too!"

"Enough!" said Anne. "Or I'll find a dark place back in the woods to bury your bodies so that only the maggots and wolves can find you."

"Ewwww, gross, Mom!" scowled Maggie.

"Yeah, and the bugs will crawl into your nose and mouth and eat you from the inside out," added Richard.

"Mom! Make him stop!"

"And your eyeballs will get mushy and fall out, and your fingernails will grow three inches, and spiders and cockroaches will crawl all over you and bite you!"

"Mo-o-om!" whined Maggie, stretching the word to three syllables.

"Okay, I goofed! I should have known that Richard would take that ball and run with it!" Anne laughed. "Let's just all relax and enjoy the ride home, shall we? Who wants to play Mad Libs?"

Chapter 12

Anne stood at the window, watching the cold drizzle outside. As she sipped her coffee, she reviewed the events of their trip, still amazed at the results. Once Karen and Anne sat down with their mother, the tone of the visit flew off in a new direction. It was obvious to Karen and Anne that Jane was giving it her best effort. She had her slips every now and then, but overall she did a great job. Right before they left for their return trip, their dad hugged them both and said with a wink, "I don't know what you said to your mother, but the difference is remarkable. Just hope she keeps it up!"

Anne thought about the little mobile that was her family. Kris was right: when one element changed, the whole dynamic changed. Anne was especially proud of herself about speaking up to their mother; she was always the one who took the criticism to heart, while Karen had found ways over the years to slough it off. For her, it was simply a constant annoyance, like a gnat buzzing in her face. Anne, on the other hand, internalized the messages, owned them, and lived her life as if they were true. The sessions with Kris had been particularly helpful for her, but it took a long time to undo the damage, and Anne had to do much of the work on her own, combating the demons in her head that told her she wasn't good enough. Taking the motorcycle safety course and buying the bike had been part of that. She felt a sense of empowerment and accomplishment at having tackled this feat in spite of the voices in her head that told her she would never ride.

On the drive back, Anne flipped through a magazine she had bought on the road. In it was an article on goddesses and the description of their traits. Once she read that the Egyptian goddess Isis was the goddess of empowerment and femininity, she knew that she should name her bike Isis. Isis was the complete female, known as The One Who Is All. She taught her earthly sisters how to grow crops, spin fabric, and tame men enough that the women could live with them. That was Anne's favorite part, and she giggled to herself at the image. A "new" mom and a great name for her bike—it had been the best trip ever!

Both kids made a hasty exit in search of friends after spending so much time with adults, and Anne received calls from them asking if they could spend the night out. Anne was ready for some separation herself and agreed to both requests. After loading and reloading the washing machine three times, she took a break to check her email. Her cousin in California had sent his typical assortment of blanket emails: a few jokes, some phenomenal pictures, and a couple of emails blasting the president. Another friend was circulating a petition to change a ruling in Congress. The email from the woman who had walked the globe in an effort to eradicate breast cancer showed up again. But there was one that caught her attention.

It was sent by a colleague, and it included a video of another teacher who made her students feel special by giving them a ribbon that said Who I Am Makes a Difference. The teacher gave each of her students one and told them, specifically, how they had made a difference in her life.

"Brilliant!" Anne whispered to herself. Immediately, the wheels in her mind began turning as she thought of the December letter.

Anne returned to school refreshed after the break. This week, the revision and editing process on the research papers began. Once again, the students rebelled.

"I used spell-check and the grammar checker—isn't that enough?"

"I don't know what else to say!"

"What am I supposed to do?"

Anne stressed the importance of editing and rewriting: "Editing and rewriting are important parts of the process—maybe *the* most important parts. It is the time in the process where you make sure that you are getting your message across so that the reader will understand exactly what you are trying to say. Ernest Hemingway was said to have revised the ending of *A Farewell to Arms* thirty-nine times before he was satisfied. His reason was that he wanted to get the words right. If revision was good enough for Hemingway, it's good enough for you. Get to work. Final drafts are due Monday."

Anne watched her students through new eyes that week. She wanted to make their December letters as personal as possible, and she paid close attention to each student and his or her gifts. She watched Amber, a popular drill team dancer, explain the citation process to a quiet, mousey band member. She saw Hank, the top point guard on the basketball team, school a special ed student on the finer points of organization. Anne realized how many gifts her kids had—and she couldn't wait to tell them about them!

Anne walked back to her classroom after a visit to the office during her conference period. She hadn't checked her mailbox since the day before, and there was bound to be a pile of things in there. Today there were several flyers—the band members were selling chocolate bars, the choir was selling candles—and the upcoming exam schedule. Anne had a strict rule: she bought whatever overpriced item whichever group was selling, but only one, and from the first kid who asked her. It never took very long before someone hit her up.

"Mrs. English! Would you please buy a candle from me?" asked Tara, an alto in her sixth period.

"Sure, Tara. Give me the order form during class, and I'll look it over while you're working."

"Thanks, Mrs. English—you're the best!"

Personally, I think we should get a $50 monthly stipend for all the crap we buy from these kids during fundraising season, Anne thought. "You're welcome, dear. See you in class" was what came out of her mouth.

Like mothers and *Madeline*'s Miss Clavel, teachers have a sixth sense when something isn't right. At first Anne could feel it, and then, as she rounded the corner, she could hear it. Tiffany and David were on the landing of the staircase to the second floor, arguing.

"I can't believe you're just going to give our baby away!" David shouted, throwing down his backpack.

"I didn't say I was going to give it away. I said I talked to an adoption agency. I haven't decided yet."

"You fucking bitch! You're ruining my life!"

"You said you didn't want anything to do with the baby!" yelled Tiffany, crying.

"You're ruining my life! Can't you see that? You're ruining my life!" David's voice grew louder as he became more agitated. He paced back and forth on the landing, fists clenched, jaws locked in place. He punched a wall on the far side of the landing and came back toward Tiffany in a blind rage.

"David, stop!" yelled Anne. "Quick, someone—call an AP from the office. Call two!"

David lunged at Tiffany, tripping on his backpack. He fell into Tiffany, sending her down the stairs.

"Oh, dear God!" cried Anne. "Someone get the nurse—and hurry!"

Tiffany was conscious but in pain, with a cut on her forehead that left a stream of blood by her eye. David had collapsed in a corner of the landing, repeating, "Ohmygod, ohmygod, what have I done?" Teachers, administrators, and the nurse rushed from all sides, clearing the halls, attending to Tiffany, and taking David to the office.

Any kind of fight was unsettling, but this altercation left Anne shaky. She had never seen David like that. She wondered if anyone had. She had heard the kids say that some of the football players used steroids, but she didn't know which ones. She assumed they would get caught in a random drug test eventually. But at this point she was more concerned about Tiffany.

The fight between David and Tiffany was the topic of conversation for the rest of the day, in spite of Anne's attempts to keep the students on task.

"Did you hear about the fight?"

"I heard he hit her."

"No, dude, he pushed her down the stairs."

"Did you know she was pregnant?"

"No, did you?"

Anne finally had to threaten the class.

"No one is going to talk about David and Tiffany. It's inappropriate to discuss it. It's called gossip, and we're not doing that in this classroom. Next one who talks about this incident is going to the office."

After school was out for the day, Anne stopped by to speak with Terry Ryan, the school nurse. She and Anne had worked together for a while now, and Terry had been particularly encouraging when Anne told her about the motorcycle class. Terry had ridden for years and had given Anne lots of pointers when it was time to buy. Sometimes when Anne had a light workload, she'd hang out in the nurse's office and listen to Terry's biker stories.

"Hey, Anne. Been riding lately?"

"No, we went out of town over the break, and it was too yucky when we got back. I wanted to check on Tiffany. How is she?"

"Bless her heart. They took her to the children's hospital for observation, but she had quite a fall. I know she told you she was pregnant. I just hope the baby's okay."

"Do you think it would be all right if I stopped by on my way home?"

"Sure. She'll be sore for a while, but I think that's about it."

Anne walked down the colorful corridor of the children's hospital. She hated it whenever a child was hurt and needed hospitalization, but they had certainly done their best to make the experience as friendly and safe as possible. Four-foot-tall cutouts of children gave directions throughout the hospital. Tanks with neon fish adorned the common areas, and there were murals on the walls of lakes and mountains, castles and fairylands. Tiffany's room was in a hall with circus animals, just past the dancing bear.

Anne poked her head in the door and found Tiffany there with her parents.

"Hi, Tiffany. May I come in?"

"Sure, Mrs. English. I can't believe you came!" answered Tiffany.

"We'll just step out for a cup of coffee and let you two visit," said Tiffany's mother.

"Thank you, Mrs. Wallace," said Anne.

"Please, call me Tonya. Tiffany talks about you all the time. You're one of her favorites."

"She's a great gal. I wish I had a hundred just like her!" answered Anne.

"We'll be down in the cafeteria, honey," said Tom Wallace, kissing her forehead.

"Thanks, Dad."

Anne noticed the sweet smell of scotch as Tiffany's father breezed past. She sat on the chair next to the bed.

"How are you feeling?"

"Okay, I guess. Sore. The doctor days I can go home tomorrow but that I shouldn't go back to school till next Wednesday." She paused. "Mrs. English?"

"Yes, dear?"

"I lost the baby." A single tear rolled down her cheek.

"I'm so sorry, Tiffany."

"I know it's probably for the best, and all, but it still makes me really sad. I mean, it was a person. A real person, growing inside me."

"I know. I'm sure it doesn't help right now, but time is a mighty healer. You'll get through this."

"David really scared me. I've never seen him like that. I heard he started taking steroids after we broke up, but I didn't believe it. My dad called his dad and they talked about it. I think they're going to have David tested or something. I hope he's okay."

"I'm sure he will be. They'll get him checked out and find him help if he needs it. I'd better let you get some rest. I just wanted to stop by and see how you were doing."

"I'm okay. Thanks for coming by. I guess I'll see you next week. Hey, wait! Our final draft is due Monday, right? Will mine be late?"

"Yes, it's due Monday, but yours won't be late. Looks to me like there are extenuating circumstances. Don't worry about it. Get some rest. I know you'll get it in; I'm not worried. Besides, I know where you live!" teased Anne.

"How? You've never been to my house! Oh, I get it—the school records. You're funny, Mrs. English!"

"You get some rest now. See you next week. Bye, Tiffany," Anne said with a wave.

"Bye, Mrs. English. Thanks again."

Anne slept late the following Saturday. Easy to do, since the kids were with Karen. It had been a long, exhausting week, more so than usual. The weeks between Thanksgiving and Christmas were always busy with choir concerts, papers, exams, plays, and the kids who were spending extra time before and after school to catch up enough to pass the semester. But that was just at school—her children had their own end-of-semester, pre-Christmas projects and activities as well. Just this past week, Anne had baked cookies, made a costume for a play, and cheered at a soccer game.

None of that mattered today.

The kids were occupied with Aunt Karen, and one of their special "adventures" (as she called them) was to visit the Angel Tree at the local mall. The ritual had been in place for a couple of years now: Maggie and Richard each chose a needy child to buy gifts for, Karen gave them $50 apiece, and the three of them ate lunch while discussing their strategy.

"My girl's name is Annabelle. She's five years old and loves dolls. Aunt Karen, what would be a good doll for a five-year-old? Or maybe a dollhouse instead for the dolls she probably already has. Or do you think a pretty coat would be better? She might need a coat."

"Maggie, those are all good ideas! If you were five, would you rather have a doll or a coat?" asked Karen.

"A doll, of course! Duh! Who's your guy, Richard?"

"His name is Eric, and he's ten. Maybe a video game! That new war game is supposed to be really cool!"

"You don't know if he has a system, dummy. And, besides, he's probably too young for one of those war games. I wouldn't let *my* ten-year-old play 'em," said Maggie.

"You're not a mom—you don't know what your imaginary kids might want to play."

"Well, nothing *that* violent, that's for sure," retorted Maggie.

"How about a board game or a race track with cars?" suggested Karen.

"Board game? Are you kidding? He'd be bored stiff!"

"You like board games. In fact, you were the one who suggested we play that word game last night," Karen reminded him.

"Yes, but I'm not a kid like Eric is. I'm way more mature."

"Mature, my ass!" laughed Maggie.

"Am too!"

"Okay, guys, we are not having a repeat performance of the car trip. Let's finish lunch and go shopping!"

Back at home, Anne sipped coffee while checking the weather reports. The forecast was clear skies, a slight breeze, and cool temperatures—perfect riding weather! Anne put on her gear and zipped over to the shop to buy some riding sunglasses.

"Be right with you," came a voice from the back.

CLASS LETTERS

"No rush," called Anne.

John appeared from the back room.

"Well, hey there! Great day for riding!"

"That's why I'm here," answered Anne. "I need some riding sunglasses. My regular ones don't work too well."

"Sure, I have some right over here. These are great for the price—they're on sale," he said, handing her a pair.

"I think these will work just fine. Do you have any suggestions for a good route? Maybe one with some fall colors? It's been so pretty lately!"

"Yes, it has. I took a great ride the other day: I went south on Route 6, west on 71, and then back north on Farm Road 1145. There's a great burger joint right there at the junction of 71 and 1145. And they have the best apple pie in the county. You can sit outside on the patio and eat lunch. But you *gotta* get the pie! It makes my mouth water just thinking about it."

"How long a ride is it?" Anne asked.

"Not bad. Probably an hour down there, an hour fifteen, maybe thirty minutes coming back."

"That sounds perfect! Thanks for the information."

"Anytime! Stop back by sometime and tell me how you liked it."

"Will do," called Anne. "See ya!"

As promised, the ride was gorgeous. Red and gold leaves danced against the blue sky in a wondrous ballet. A dog, enclosed by a fence, kept pace with Anne, jumping and barking as if to share in her exhilaration. A flock of geese flew overhead, honking their salutations. Anne felt at one with her bike, the road, the animals, and all the beauty surrounding her.

She found John's lunch recommendation, the Junction Grill. She sipped sweet tea on the patio, watching dragonflies dart around the stream. Sunlight filtered through the leaves of the giant oak tree that shaded the patio, casting soft shadows. The cheeseburger, juicy, flavorful, and hot off the grill, was accompanied by thick, crispy fries. After lunch, Anne savored every bite of the apple pie—flaky crust with a cinnamon-butter richness engulfing the apples. Before she left, she ordered a piece of pie to go—a thank-you present to John for the wonderful suggestion.

In the midst of all the beauty and joy she was experiencing, Anne had a momentary pang of sadness, wishing she had someone to share it all with. These feelings didn't come along often for her, and they were usually fleeting, but they came nonetheless.

The ride back was as wonderful as the ride down, and Anne didn't want it to end. She stopped back by the shop on her way home to drop off the pie.

"Hey! How was the ride?" John greeted her with a smile.

"It was everything you said it would be. I had the best time! And I brought you a little something to say thank you," Anne said, handing him the to-go box.

"You didn't have to do that, but I'm glad you did!" said John, peeking in the box. "Mind if I dig in? I'm starved!"

"Go ahead. Enjoy! I'd better get home anyway."

"Don't run off. Tell me about the ride. What was your favorite part?" asked John, taking a big bite.

"That's a tough question to answer. This may sound weird, but I guess my favorite part was when I was riding along and I felt like I was a part of it all—the trees, the animals, the road, the sun, the breeze—everything. Like we were all one, y'know?"

"I know exactly what you mean. That's probably my favorite thing about riding too, but I had never thought of it quite like that. But, yeah, that's it. Feeling like everything is connected," agreed John. "Would you like something to drink? I've got some soft drinks in the back."

"I don't want to keep you from your work."

"What work?" John laughed. "This is probably the slowest time of the week for me. All my customers came in early and are now out enjoying the day, just like you. I doubt if anyone else will come in until closing time."

CLASS LETTERS

Anne hesitated momentarily and then sat down. It had been a while since she had spent time, one-on-one, with a man. She rarely dated—all the men at the school were either married or too young—and she was never one for the bar scene. But John's crooked smile and dancing green eyes were comforting and inviting. They talked like old friends. They compared notes about this route, and John shared stories of other experiences he had had during his riding career. No talk of work or spouses, ex or otherwise, or kids—just motorcycles, new experiences, hopes, and dreams. Time passed quickly, and soon John began the process of closing up for the day.

"Thanks for spending the rest of the afternoon with me. It would have been boring around here without you. And thanks again for the pie! It hit the spot," said John.

"I enjoyed it, too. And thank *you* for the route, the lunch spot, and the soda! It's been a great day."

John hesitated. "Would it be okay if I call you sometime?"

"You mean, like, for a date?" asked Anne.

"Yes, for a date, silly," laughed John. "As pretty as you are, you must have lots of guys asking you out."

Anne blushed. "Nope. No guys. No dates. You must have me confused with someone who has a social life."

"Well, maybe we can remedy that. What do you say?"

"All right. That would be fun," agreed Anne.

"Great! I'll call you this week and we can set something up."

"Okay, bye."

"Talk to you soon!"

Anne climbed on her bike, incredulous but smiling at the turn of events that day.

Chapter 13

Monday morning, and final drafts were due. Anne needed to send a parent email before class started. One of the things she prided herself on was her communication with parents. At the beginning of the year, she asked for parents' email addresses so she could keep them up-to-date with the class. It was a tedious task inputting all the information, but it paid off after that. She also attached the monthly letters in addition to catching parents up on due dates, projects, and other reminders that they probably never heard from their child. As a parent herself, Anne knew the value of communication with the school and her own children's teachers—especially Richard's. Anne often became great pals with his teachers each year because of their almost constant communication, and the ones who were less than prompt in answering emails (or didn't answer them at all) frustrated her, so she was determined to keep *her* parents well informed.

Some months required more than a single email—like November. Because the research paper was such a large project, Anne sent emails almost once a week, instead of once a month. And, as she had experienced with some of Richard's teachers, she became pals with some of her parents, even though she had never met most of them in person except on Meet the Teacher Night at the beginning of school, when she barely knew all of her students. Putting a name, face, and email address together happened occasionally, but most of her parents remained simply a name and email address.

> *Hi, Parents! If your child is still alive at this point, that's a good sign. That means that he/she has survived the research process. As a reminder, final drafts are due today. I know this has been a long, arduous task for the kids, for me(!), and maybe even for you, but it's almost over, and, trust me, we are all grateful. Please make sure that your student doesn't drop the ball this late in the game and that he/she gets this final paper in this week. We will read a few short stories this week and next, discuss the elements of a short story, and then prepare for finals. After that—winter break! Time is running short!*
>
> *It's also time for the December letter (see below). I stole the idea from another teacher, and I love it—I hope you do too. As always, if you have any comments, questions, or concerns, feel free to write or call. Thanks for all you do!*
>
> *Anne English*

December

Dear Class:

I'm a thief! Yep, I stole this idea, so I can't take any credit for it, but I thought it was so cool, I wanted to do it too.

Inside this envelope, you will find three ribbons that say Who I Am Makes a Difference. One is for you, and two are for you to give away. First, let me tell you about the one for you. This letter is a little different from the others because it is personalized. At the bottom, you will see a handwritten note from me about how you make a difference in my life. Did you know you could make a difference in a teacher's life? You can! Sometimes it's something small (but still very important!), like the way

CLASS LETTERS

you greet me when you come to class. Sometimes it may be something bigger, like when I see you helping one of your peers. Sometimes it may be huge, like courage you exhibited during a difficult time. Regardless of what it is, you have still made a difference in my life... and I am so grateful for that! I hope you will remember how special you are, and how many gifts you possess, when you look at the ribbon.

Now, for the other two: I want you to give each of them away to someone else, and tell them why they make a difference to you. It could be your parents or a sibling. It could be the guy who gives you water at soccer practice or the girl who listened to you when you were upset. It could be a teacher, a minister, a small child, an adult, or anyone in between.

Your assignment: I want to know how you liked the letter and getting the ribbon, and who you gave your ribbons to and why. Simple, huh? And fun! I have had a great time personalizing these letters. I hope you enjoy reading them.

You make a difference to me because _____

_____

_____

_____

Have a great break! See you next year!

Anne reread the email, satisfied that she hadn't left anything out, and hit send at 7:55 a.m.

Only a few parents actually responded. Usually they wanted to know how their child was doing in class, and a few thanked Anne for the updates. But there were always one or two who enjoyed carrying on more of a conversation with her, sometimes sending along items of interest or commenting on the email or monthly letter. Tony's father, John, was one of those.

She had never met him—Tony had joined her class during the

second six weeks, long after Meet the Teacher Night—but his emails made her smile. He was one of those parents who forwarded other emails, commented on hers, *and* wanted to know how Tony was doing in class. Luckily, he wasn't a "high-maintenance" parent who wrote if their child made an eighty-nine or below, distraught and demanding an immediate answer.

At 8:02 a.m.:

Great letter! Love the idea. I can't wait to see what Tony's personalized message is. Care to give me a sneak peek? LOL! I asked him about his final draft and he swore he would have it in today. Please let me know if he doesn't so I can beat him when he gets home! LOL! Hope you're having a great day!

John

At 8:05 a.m.:

John—I don't have Tony until fifth period (after lunch), but I will let you know. Happy Monday!

Anne

At 10:23 a.m.:

Q: What does a fish say when it hits a wall?

A: Dam!

A customer just told me that one and it cracked me up. Thought I'd share.

John

At 12:01 p.m.:

That's one of my favorite jokes! It cracks me up every time. Thanks for the laugh.

Anne

CLASS LETTERS

At 1:05 p.m.:

Success! Tony just turned in his paper. Sadly, no beating today. Maybe he'll do something at home and you'll get lucky! ; o)

Anne

At 4:03 p.m.:

Tony showed me his December letter and gave me a ribbon. I am so touched. What an amazing gift. Thank you for inspiring him. I feel he's very lucky to have you for a teacher. Have a great evening.

John

At 5:19 p.m.:

I feel equally lucky to have him as a student! Hope you have a good evening too.

Anne

Dewayne Johnson was a tall, good-looking guy who caught everyone's attention: male, female, student, and teacher. From his first day on campus in early December, he strutted around with an air of confidence as if he owned the school. Girls found him irresistible, boys found him threatening, and teachers didn't quite trust him. *Too smooth.* Although she tried to act cool around him, Keosha was particularly smitten.

A new student at the end of the semester was a challenge for any teacher. Almost invariably, the student hadn't read any of the literature that was on the SFA reading list for the semester, and special assignments had to be created so that the teacher could a) give him some grades for the rest of the semester and b) give him a final exam. Anne scurried around to find enough work for Dewayne so that he would stay occupied but not disadvantage the rest of the class.

Anne always tried to give her students the benefit of the doubt, but a glimpse at Dewayne's ankle monitor hinted at a different story. She watched Keosha flirt with him, giggling at his jokes. She knew Keosha was vulnerable to his type, and Anne felt protective, as if it were Maggie doing the flirting. Once again, Anne had to tread that line carefully.

Anne had spent most of her spare time working on the individual letters. She made a conscious effort to make them special—a difficult task with some students. There were always a few out of her 150 she didn't know well. Usually it was because they were so quiet; they came to class, participated when asked, and did all their work, but kept to themselves the rest of the time. And, on the opposite end of the spectrum, there were always one or two who had a way of pushing her buttons. These she knew *too* well—and not in a positive way. Anne had to dig deep to find something positive to say beyond "you have a nice smile" or something equally vague and impersonal. Finally, there were the ones she had really formed a bond with. Their letters were usually easy to write, and with some, like Ray, she really hoped they soaked it all in. She enjoyed telling her kids how proud she was of them, pinpointing a special talent they had, or recognizing an achievement; she watched these kids closely as they opened their letters. Ray and Keosha both read their letters and then shoved them in their backpacks. Tiffany smiled through glistening eyes. A whisper of a smile crossed Kim's face as she read her letter. Tony sat back at his desk as if to say, *I haven't even been here that long, but she's got me pegged.*

Apparently they enjoyed reading these tributes as well. Anne was surprised at how quiet the students were when they first opened the letters and read the contents, and then at the comments she heard:

"Look! She wrote something to me at the bottom!"

"What does yours say?"

"Cool!"

CLASS LETTERS

"Awwww... thanks, Mrs. English!"

Then, as the responses trickled in, she was able to relive it all over again. Most of the students gave their ribbons to their parents or best friends. Some students even passed a ribbon back to her, appreciative of her part in their lives.

Dear Mrs. English,

Thank you so much for the ribbon. And I really liked what you said about me—that I was courageous. It doesn't seem all that courageous to me. I've just had a lot of stuff happen lately and all I've really done is walk through it. But I've also had a lot of help. That's where the rest of my letter comes in. First I gave one ribbon to my parents. They were so supportive when I told them I was pregnant. And then, I wasn't pregnant anymore. But I guess that everything happens for a reason. It's been kinda sad but I'm getting through it okay, especially with my mom and dad's help. It was also kinda hard when David went to rehab cuz I know that when he gets out, he'll be going to the alternative school for the rest of the year. I mean, I don't want to date him but I still care about what happens to him. Mom and Dad have helped me see that this is all for the best.

The other ribbon goes to you (duh—I taped it to the letter! LOL). Seriously, I couldn't have gotten through any of this without you. First you let me talk to you, then you helped me, then you visited me in the hospital. I don't know any other teachers who would do that. Well, Coach Watson, my cheer coach, came by the hospital but I was asleep. Anyway, that's why you make a difference to me. Thanks for everything, Mrs. English!

Tony's letter was written in a similar vein:

I was so surprised when I read what you wrote on my letter about how I'm a good son and that I have such a good relationship with my dad. I don't know how you know this stuff, but you're absolutely right! LOL.

My dad is my hero and my best friend. He's the best guy I know. I haven't told you much about me but the last few years have been kinda tough. But my dad has been there every step of the way. First back in the spring of 2005 my mom decided she didn't want to be with my dad anymore and she ran off with some other guy. We were living in Louisiana at the time. Then Katrina hit and we lost everything. We never heard from my mom again after Katrina. I heard she was killed but I don't know for sure. We came to this area and moved around some before we settled here. My dad's a mechanic and we've met some great people along the way. He's got a shop now and is doing okay. But he's been there for me the whole time. We've stuck together and grown closer because of all of this stuff. So, I guess it's no surprise that I gave him a ribbon. I gave the other ribbon to Jake. He's a great guy and was really nice to me when I first came to this school. We hang out a lot and have become good friends.

If I had another ribbon, I'd give it to you. You really helped me feel at home when I first got here. And I really think these letters are cool. They give us kids a way to talk to a grown-up without really talking to a grown-up, if you know what I mean. My dad's always telling me how lucky I am to have you as a teacher. I guess he's right! ;o)

Tony

Chapter 14

The rest of the fall semester was a blur for Anne. The end of the semester was always a challenge: many students tried to play catch-up and turn things in late so they would pass, novel projects were due, final drafts were all in, and, of course, final exams were happening. This was exacerbated by the fact that the kids—and teachers—were *all* ready for the winter break. Students were distracted and off task more often than not these days; class time was generally chaotic and frustrating for teachers and students alike. It was the time in the semester when teachers lost patience and began to plead, bargain, and threaten:

"Just cooperate for a few more days; then we'll all get a break."

"If you get this work done in class today, you can play cards."

"I know you're ready for a break, but we still have to go over this exam review—unless you'd rather take the test without the review."

"C'mon, guys! Get to work!"

"The next person who talks to their neighbor instead of working is going to the office!"

Responses to the December letter were still trickling in, and, in spite of the other demands on her time, Anne read each one. The students were always surprised when she told them she read them all. But Anne felt that if they had invested the time to write them, she should reciprocate when they were turned in. Ray's letter was succinct, as usual.

I felt great when I got the letter from you. I didn't know you were proud of me for my grades. I'm pretty proud of me too. I guess it helps to turn stuff in! LOL. I gave my ribbons to my mom and my girlfriend. Both of them are there for me, no matter what. My girlfriend's dad is a mechanic and he's letting me work in his shop so I can make some money and help out my mom. Everything's going real good for me.

Anne smiled as she read his reply. She had watched him throughout the semester. His grades had risen dramatically, he participated more in class, and he seemed happier. Anne was thrilled at the rapid transformation, although she took no credit for it. She recognized his potential and encouraged him, but he had done the work and was reaping the benefits.

Keosha's letter was equally short, but also disturbing:

I felt good getting the letter. Thanks for writing what you did. I don't think that going to the police station was all that brave. I didn't do nothing. Anyway, thanks.

I gave my ribbons to my moms and my boyfriend. My moms she's always working. She has two jobs. I'll probably have to get one soon too. Anyway, she works hard and I wanted to tell her thanx. The other ribbon was for my new boyfriend, Dewayne. He's had kinda a rough past but he made it through and I'm proud of him. He's the best thing that's ever happened to me.

Surprisingly, Kim's letter was also short—and late. Both were unusual for Kim, and it concerned Anne.

Dear Mrs. English:

I gave my ribbons to my parents for their hard work. I appreciate the one you gave to me. Thank you.

Anne arrived at school earlier than usual the next day. With only one week left in the semester, she had an especially heavy workload. She tapped her pencil on the desk.

"Okay, final-exam review. Let's see… we need to address *Beowulf*, Chaucer, uh… Oh! poetry up to the 1800s…" Anne mumbled as she made a list of items for the final review.

Kim poked her head in the classroom.

"Mrs. English? May I speak with you?"

"Kim! Come on in," Anne answered. "Are you okay? You look… upset."

Kim's face was streaked with dirt and tears. Her rumpled clothes hung on her, and Anne noticed for the first time that she was losing weight she didn't have to lose. Dark circles under her eyes emphasized the lack of sleep.

"Everything is terrible. I'm so scared. I don't know what to do."

"My goodness! What's going on, Kim?"

"You know how I tell you in my letters that I sort of have a secret but I can't tell you?"

"Yes."

"Okay, here's the deal: I'm gay. I've kept it a secret because my friends tell me that gays here get bullied. And I didn't want my parents to know—they'd freak."

"I can understand that. But what's wrong now?"

"I've been getting anonymous notes about how I'm gay and how whoever it is is going to hurt me. I get phone calls all night long from a private number. They call me names and hang up. I can't eat or sleep. And just now…" Kim put her head in her hands and began to cry.

"Take your time," soothed Anne, handing her a tissue.

"Just now, before school, some guy came up behind me and pushed me down in the dirt outside and called me names."

"Oh my God! Who was it?"

"I don't know. I didn't recognize his voice, and by the time I got up, he was gone."

"Kim, I'm so sorry this happened to you. You have every right to feel safe at school. I'll let the APs and your counselor know."

"No! I don't want this getting all over school and then get really hurt. And I've heard that sometimes even the parents of gays are threatened. It scares me, Mrs. English. But I can't help what I am, can I?"

"In my opinion, no, you can't, but I know there are others who don't agree with me."

"Isn't there some kind of way all the gay kids at school could work together to stop all of us from being bullied?"

"I know there are clubs like the Gay-Straight Alliance. Have you ever thought about starting one here?" asked Anne.

"But then everyone would know about me. What if it all got worse?"

"*Or* what if you banded together with your friends and educated the kids here? Let them know that bullying is wrong, that gay kids are just like everyone else? You could make a difference," suggested Anne. "In any case, you need to let the administration know about what's happened to you. You deserve respect. You deserve to feel safe."

"Would you come with me to talk to the office?"

"Absolutely! I'd suggest that you make an appointment with the principal. My conference is fourth period, so it would be easier for me during that time or after school. But you need to tell someone. If you don't, I will."

"I know you're right," said Kim with a sigh. "I'll stop by the office on the way to class. Fourth period, right?"

"Yes, fourth period. I'm proud of you. It takes a lot of courage to stand up to a bully."

"It helps having you on my side."

"It would be an honor," said Anne.

Kim popped her head in Anne's door between first and second period.

"The meeting is set for fourth period."

CLASS LETTERS

"Wow! That was fast! Good for you! I'll see you there," said Anne. She could already see the light returning to Kim's eyes.

Anne went straight to the office after third period. She had no idea what would come out of this meeting. This was the first year for the new principal, Mr. Henderson, and Anne didn't know him well. She had heard he was fair and open-minded, but she hadn't had any direct dealings with him—until now. She was willing to take the risk for the sake of her student. Kim was in the waiting area.

"Ready?" asked Anne.

"Ready as I'll ever be!" said Kim.

"Let's do it!" smiled Anne.

Anne began the conversation to break the ice.

"Mr. Henderson, my student, Kim Le, came to me earlier to tell me about some bullying she has experienced."

"I'm sorry to hear that, Kim. What happened?" asked Mr. Henderson.

Kim cast a wary glance at Anne. Anne nodded her encouragement.

"Well, uh… I've gotten some threatening notes and phone calls. And someone pushed me in the dirt this morning before school."

"Why would anyone want to do that to you?"

"Well… uh… it's because… uh… " stammered Kim.

"Go on, Kim. It's okay," said Anne.

"I'm gay, Mr. Henderson. My parents don't know. And I don't do anything at school—or at least I didn't think I did—that would make people think I'm gay. But I hang out with people who are, and I guess other people assumed I was too. I don't care if anyone knows anymore. I just don't want to be afraid here at school. I like school and I like coming here—or at least I used to."

"Do you know who is making these threats or who pushed you today?"

"No, sir."

"Hmm… without a name or an idea of who it might be, it's going to be hard to catch this person or persons. I do have an idea, though."

"What's that?" asked Kim.

"We had a Gay-Straight Alliance at my previous school. I wasn't sure how it would work at first, but it was a great addition to our campus. Both gay and straight kids attended meetings, so no one could pinpoint who was gay and who wasn't. That helped encourage people to come. They passed out pamphlets about bullying and had a day of silence to protest the problems that gay students face. They helped educate the kids and made it a safer school. How would you like to start one here?"

"You'd let us do that here?" asked Kim.

"You betcha!" smiled Mr. Henderson. "As long as someone agrees to sponsor it," he said, looking at Anne.

"Why not?" Anne smiled. "Count me in."

"Really, Mrs. English? You'd do that?" asked Kim.

"If it's a way to give our gay students a safe school, I'm all for it."

"Wow! Thanks, Mrs. English. When do we start?" asked Kim.

"I love your enthusiasm, Kim!" said Mr. Henderson.

"Let me do some research and put together a plan. I doubt we could do anything this semester, but we can get things in place for the spring," said Anne.

"I'll see if I can dig up some funds if you need them to get started," offered Mr. Henderson.

"I'll take it!" laughed Anne. "Looks like we're in business, Kim!"

"Kim, please let me or one of the assistant principals know if you experience any more bullying. And if you remember something that could help us figure out who has been hurting you, let us know. I think you're doing a very brave thing by starting the club. But the main thing is to keep you safe, so let us know."

"Yes, sir, I will."

Mr. Henderson continued, "Mrs. English, thank you for your help here—and for agreeing to sponsor the club. I think it will be a great addition to our school."

CLASS LETTERS

"I'm happy to help," smiled Anne. "Kim, we can both do a little research to figure out our next move. Let me know what you find out."

Anne and Kim walked out of the office and headed off in different directions.

"Hey, Mrs. English. Thanks again!" called Kim.

"You're more than welcome," answered Anne with a wave.

Chapter 15

Although grades weren't due until after Christmas break, Anne spent the Saturday after exams reconciling her grade book so she could relax until January, when school resumed. It had been a hectic semester, but most of her students were keeping up. And Ray was doing more than just keeping up—he was excelling in all his classes. Anne had talked with some of his other teachers, and the report was unanimous: Ray was turning in all his work, and his grades climbed higher with each six-week period. She knew he was helping out at a nearby mechanic's shop. The inspection on her car would expire at the end of the month—just over a week away—and she thought it was a great opportunity to pay Ray a visit at work. As soon as she finished grading, she drove to the shop.

"Hey, Ray! Long time no see!" Anne laughed as she pulled up.

"Gosh, Mrs. English, it's just the first day of vacation and you're already checking up on me?" joked Ray.

"I had to make sure you were behaving! Besides, I need to have my car inspected."

"We're running a special on oil changes, and it looks like you're due for one. How about it?"

"A mechanic *and* a salesman? You're a very talented guy! Sure, Ray, fix me up."

"Will do, Mrs. English. There's a waiting room inside. I'll let you know when your car is ready."

"I sure hope there's more to read besides *Popular Mechanics* in there!"

"Not sure about that. I don't spend much time in the waiting room. But this won't take long."

"Okay, Ray. Thanks."

Anne sat down and rifled through a six-month-old *People* magazine. She spied Ray's boss, Jessie, talking to the receptionist.

"Excuse me," Anne said.

"Yes, ma'am, can I help you?" asked Jessie.

"I wondered if I could speak to you about Ray."

"Is there a problem?"

"Oh, no, not at all!" Anne answered quickly. "I'm his English teacher, Anne English. I just wanted to say that Ray has let me know how much he enjoys this job. You have had a very positive impact on his life."

"His English teacher? He talks about you all the time! He really likes you. I'm Jessie."

"Nice to meet you, Jessie. He's such a good guy. His grades have been climbing, and he's turning out to be quite a leader in my class. I think his relationship with Isabel and you has been part of that change."

"I see so much of myself in Ray. I was just like him at that age. My road took me to gangs and prison. I don't want that for him. I was raised by a single mom too. A boy needs a strong male influence in his life, and when he doesn't have one, he'll go looking for it—even if that means blowing off school and getting into a gang. He was headed down that path, but I think he's turning that around. I'm very proud of him. Like he was my own son."

"I just wanted to say thank you—and keep up the good work!" said Anne.

"I plan to, but it's really pretty easy. For one thing, he's my best mechanic. He has a real natural ability for working on cars. And, of course, there's Isabel. She loves him, and I want the best for my daughter, so I try to help him stay in line."

"You're doing a great job," smiled Anne.

"Your car's ready, Mrs. English," called Ray.

"Wow! That was fast," said Anne. "It was nice meeting you, Jessie."

"Likewise," Jessie said, shaking her hand.

"Have a great break, Ray. See you in January!"

"Bye, Mrs. English. You too!"

Anne left the shop, driving toward home. As she approached the motorcycle shop, she found herself pulling in for no particular reason. An internal argument began:

What am I doing here? I don't need anything at the shop. There's that vest I've been wanting. But it's too close to Christmas—I don't have any extra money for that. Maybe I could get something small. No that's silly. I don't need to buy anything.

Anne sat, frozen with indecision.

But now I've been sitting here forever, and it looks weird. I guess I could just go in and poke around, not buy anything. I have to do something. I can't just sit here. C'mon, admit it—the only reason I'm here is to see John. Oh my goodness—what am I doing? He said he'd call, but it's been almost a month.

Anne dug around in her purse for a mint.

And the last thing I need is a man. Geez—I must be crazy. Okay, so now I've been here for, like, ever. I have to do something! *He is cute, though, and so nice…*

A knock on the driver's-side window startled her.

"Coming in?" asked John, smiling.

"Of course," said Anne. "I was just looking for something. See? Here it is," she said, blushing and holding up a ballpoint pen.

"I can see why that would take such diligence," teased John, opening her car door. "C'mon in!"

"Right behind you," said Anne cheerfully. "How embarrassing," she muttered, chastising herself.

"What's that?" asked John.

"Um… looks like a nice day to ride."

"It is right now, but it's supposed to rain later."

"I heard that."

"So, what have you been up to?" asked John. "Oh, hey! Just so you know, I tried to call, but I got a recording that your phone was disconnected. Did you give me the wrong number so you wouldn't have to talk to me?" John asked with a wink.

"Of course not! What number did you dial?"

"Uh, let me check my log.… It was… eight one seven, five five five, three two oh four."

"Ohhhh, no. It's *eight* four, not oh four," Anne corrected.

"Crap! I'm sorry. You probably thought I was one of those guys who says he'll call and never does. That's not me. Promise. So, where were we? Do you have kids? The last time you were here, we decided not to talk about our personal lives. But, honestly, I'd like to get to know you better, so tell me everything."

"Now?" asked Anne.

"Why not? Maybe you haven't noticed, but I don't have any customers at the moment."

"Yeah, but…"

"Okay, how about this? I'll do this the right way. Miss Anne, would you like to have dinner with me tonight?"

"Dinner? I don't even know your last name," she laughed.

"That's an easy fix. It's Rogers. Now will you have dinner with me?"

"Wait a minute. Did you say Rogers?"

"Yes. Is there a problem?"

"Your name is John Rogers?" she asked.

"Yes."

"Do you by any chance have a son named Tony?"

"Yes. How did you know that? Are you working for the FBI?" John teased.

"Does Tony go to Stephen F. Austin?"

"Yes. Okay, now this is getting weird."

"Oh my God. You're *that* John?" she gasped.

"Which John? Don't confuse an old man!"

"I'm Anne English, Tony's teacher."

"Tony's teacher? Are you kidding me? You're the one who writes the letters and sends me emails all the time?"

"Yup, that's me."

"Small world, huh? Well, that's just one more reason—how about dinner?"

"I guess," Anne gulped.

"You don't have to make it sound like a death sentence!" laughed John.

"I've never been on a date with a parent before. I don't even know anyone who has been on a date with a parent."

"Is there some kind of rule against it?"

"Not that I know of. It's just never come up."

Anne's mind raced through all the possibilities and problems that could arise.

"Tony wouldn't care—he thinks you're great," said John.

"He's such a good kid. I know you're proud of him. He's shared some of his experiences with me in his letters. It sounds like you two have had a tough time in the past few years."

"Nothing we couldn't handle. But I couldn't have done it without him, either. You know what they say: If God brings you to it, He'll bring you through it."

Anne paused. "John, I would love to go out with you, but I think we should wait until after school's out—just to be on the safe side."

"I sure don't want to get you in any trouble. Could I call you at home? We could just talk and get to know each other."

"I think that would be all right."

"When's school out?"

"June 1st," said Anne.

"Okay, we'll just talk for now, but we have a date on June 2nd. Deal?"

"Better get to know me first. You might change your mind, ya know."

Just then, as if waiting for the conversation to end, four customers walked into the shop.

"I'd better let you get back to work," said Anne.

"Before you go, would you please write your number down so I can call—and actually get through?" John laughed.

"Sure thing. I'll look forward to it."

"Me too," said John. "Talk to you soon. Bye."

"See ya," said Anne with a wave.

As soon as she got into the car, she called Karen.

"You're not going to believe what just happened," said Anne.

"Are the kids okay?"

"Yes, the kids are fine. Guess what? You know how I've told you about that cute guy John who runs the motorcycle shop? I met him through Susan and Herb—the people who sold me the bike. Remember? I went on that long ride?"

"Oh, yeah. Cute, green eyes, nice smile, got it."

"And you know how I've told you that one of my parents, named John, writes me and is so cute and funny in his emails?"

"Yeah. You've called them Email John and Biker John so that I'd know the difference."

"It's the same John! I couldn't believe it. I stopped by the shop on my way home, and we got to talking, and lo and behold, it's the same guy. *And* he asked me out!"

"You said yes, right?"

"Nah. Not now, anyway. Not while Tony is still my student. That could get weird."

"I can see that. Bummer! So you're just going to forget about him?"

"No, we decided it would be okay to talk on the phone some. Then maybe we can go out during the summer." Anne paused for a moment, letting it all sink in. "I still can't believe it's the same guy. Small world. So, what are you doing?"

"Putting groceries away. Nothing exciting. What are you up to?" asked Karen.

"Almost home. Ready to start my vacation."

"I bet you are! Hey, I almost forgot. I talked to Maggie earlier, and they want to go to the mall tonight. Is that all right with you?"

"Absolutely! I know how much they look forward to doing that with you. What time?"

"I thought I'd pick them up about four-ish, maybe shop first, then eat at the mall. And we might even do a little shopping for you know who," hinted Karen with a lilt.

"Do you mean little ol' me?" Anne asked in her best Southern-belle accent.

"Yes, little ol' you. I'm not even going to ask you what you want, because the three of us have already decided. It was the kids' idea. You're gonna die!"

"Oooooh! Sounds exciting! Hey, I'm home. I'll see you when you get the kids. Love you!" said Anne.

"Love you too. See ya!"

Anne pulled into the garage and sat for a minute before going in. She remembered the conversation with John, and her mind whirled. *He really called? He seemed interested. So weird that it's the same guy. He's so cute. And I knew that Email John* had *to be cute. What a strange day this has been. I wonder what tomorrow will bring.*

Chapter 16

Anne had always enjoyed the Christmas season. She delighted in the decorations in the stores, downtown, and throughout the neighborhoods, and was frequently heard humming Christmas songs as she went about her day. Because the research paper required so much time at the end of the semester, Anne had no energy left for a Christmas tree until the break began. Heading to the tree lot was her first order of business Saturday morning.

"Who wants to get a tree?" she asked Maggie and Richard while they crunched on cereal.

"Imdom," said Richard with his mouth full.

"Excuse me? I didn't quite catch that," said Anne with a smile.

"I do!" reiterated Richard after finishing his bite.

"That's one! How about you, Maggie?"

"Duh! You know I love to go shopping for a Christmas tree! And our special ornaments!"

"Wonderful! Let's make a day of it! We can have some lunch, go to the ornament store, and pick out a tree. Let's get the other decorations out before we go, so we can start decorating right when we get home."

The Christmas after Charlie disappeared, Anne thought the children needed something special, but money was tight. She hit on the idea of taking them to the Christmas store and having them pick out one ornament apiece to hang on the tree. Since then it had become a family tradition, and the children looked forward to that part almost as much as anything else during the season. They even wrote their age somewhere on the ornament, turning each into a window to the past. Some ornaments were tied to bittersweet memories, like that first one, but decorating the tree and talking about the years that the ornaments represented was a magical experience for Anne. She usually just listened to Maggie and Richard as they put each ornament on the tree. She marveled at how they had grown and matured, and invariably learned something new about each child in the process. Richard peeked into the box that held their ornaments.

"Wow, Maggie, look! I was only five when I got this truck ornament. Just a little kid," Richard said wistfully.

"Here's the snowman from when I was thirteen," said Maggie. "That's the Christmas I had a crush on Timmy Kramer. He's such a goofball now!"

"Everybody ready? Let's hit the road!" said Anne.

They finally returned home after spending an hour at the ornament store and another hour at the tree lot, in addition to having lunch. Next they had to reposition the furniture to accommodate the tree and string the tree with lights before putting on the ornaments. Anne put a Christmas CD in the player and made hot chocolate. She eavesdropped as they reminisced, overcome with gratitude and love at the people they were becoming.

"Hey, here's the one I got after I had the chicken pops," said Richard.

"That's pox, silly," said Maggie. "Yeah, I remember. You had them first, and then I got them right after Christmas. It was awful! I even had to go back to school with those red dots after the scabs fell off. It was so gross, and Jared Thomas made fun of me. He called me Polka Dot for a month!"

"Cool! This is the one from our white Christmas! Remember when it snowed so much that we made that huge snowman? Man, that was a blast!" said Richard.

"Yeah, and we snuck up on Mom and pounded her with snowballs!" laughed Maggie.

"I remember! Two against one! No fair!" laughed Anne. "But just you wait. Ever since then I've been practicing, improving my aim, and devising a plan of attack so that you two will never do that to me again." Anne voiced her "evil" laugh: "Mwahahahaha!"

"Yeah, right, Mom," said Richard sarcastically. "You couldn't hit the side of a barn."

"Hey, don't count your old mom out of any fight, young man. There's still a lot of spunk left in this old gal."

"You're not old, Mom," said Maggie. "In fact, you're beautiful!"

"Yeah, Mom, you really are. You should date," said Richard matter-of-factly.

"Oh, Mom, you should! You really should," encouraged Maggie.

"Date? *Me?* I wouldn't know what to do on a date."

"It's easy. Just talk about him—guys like that. Ask him about stuff he likes to do. We can go shopping, and I can do your hair and makeup. It'll be fun!" said Maggie.

"You two really wouldn't mind if I dated?"

"No way! Besides, Maggie's graduating and I'll be next, and you'll be here all alone. Except for Rocky, of course." Richard scratched the top of the boxer's head.

"Mom, you deserve to have someone who makes you happy," said Maggie. "God knows our dad didn't."

"Aw, honey, your dad has… issues. He can't really help it. It's who he is." Anne hesitated. "Do you miss him?" she asked tentatively.

Maggie and Richard were quiet for a minute and then looked at each other.

"No, Mom, we don't miss him," said Maggie quietly. "We did when we were little, but we know more now about who he really was and what he did. Aunt Karen's sorta filled us in."

"But she—" Anne began.

"It's okay, Mom. It's good that we know," Richard continued.

"Sometimes, I'll admit, I'd like to have *a* dad, but not *my* dad. But whether we have a real dad or not, you are the greatest mom in the world, and I love you," he said, hugging her.

"Me too, Mom," said Maggie, completing the group hug. "I love you soooo much!"

"You two, look what you've made me do! I'm all drippy and sniffly and weepy! Oh, I love you two so much. I am so very blessed!"

"Okay, let's get back to work," said Richard, clearing his throat. Anne noticed a quick swipe at his eyes as he turned the other way to get an ornament. She smiled at her man-child, wistful about the days past and excited about the future. He had always had a sweet and gentle heart, but he had also learned to stay strong in his convictions. She had raised him well, albeit without a partner, and was proud of her role as a parent so far.

Maggie, too, was a loving soul. She was always the first one to volunteer when it helped people in need. This had also translated into poor boyfriend choices when she was younger, but, luckily, she seemed to have outgrown that particular defect. She was a writer, like her mother, and dreamed of becoming a novelist, also like her mother. Richard's future plans tended to be vague but profitable. His interests lay in building things. His favorite toys were blocks and Legos, and his constructions grew more complicated and interesting as he aged. Anne thought he would make a terrific architect or engineer someday, but she kept her visions to herself, waiting to see what he would become naturally.

The banter and memories continued through the tree-trimming process, until they turned off the interior lights, lit the tree, and stood back to admire their work.

"I think this is the prettiest tree we've ever had," said Anne.

"Mom, you say that every year," said Richard.

"Do I? Well, then, I guess each tree has been the prettiest up to that point—or something like that," laughed Anne.

"It's gorgeous!" exclaimed Maggie. "Oh, Mom, Lauren just texted me and wants me to spend the night. Can I?"

"May I?" corrected Anne.

"May I?" asked Maggie.

"Sure, honey, have a good time."

"Mom, since Maggie's going to Lauren's, can she drop me off at Joe's on the way? He wants me to spend the night too."

"And leave me here all alone?"

"You'll have Rocky. Besides, you have to practice for when we're both gone," said Richard, raising an eyebrow.

"Oh, goody," said Anne flatly. Quickly changing her tune, she said, "Yes, yes, go ahead. Have fun. Call me in the morning, please."

"Thanks, Mom!" said Richard.

"Bye, Mom! Love you!" called Maggie.

"Love you too!" Anne replied to the two car-door slams. She looked at Rocky, "Well, buster, it's just you and me."

Anne had loved writing as long as she could remember. She had written illustrated stories about fairies and horses when she was a child, and maudlin poetry as a teenager, and now had been working on a novel for two years and had finally completed a rough draft. She was going back through it, hoping the revision process wouldn't be quite as lengthy. Between the kids, school, and a bike ride every now and then, there was little time for writing, but it made her feel alive.

She arranged a place at the dining table—the laptop, a thesaurus, a glass of tea, her cell phone, some notes she had taken, some tissues—and began to read. She had read through three chapters when the phone startled her to alertness. An unfamiliar number appeared on the caller ID.

"Hello?"

"Hey, Anne, this is John—Tony's dad, from the motorcycle shop."

"Hi, John. How are you?"

"Just fine. I figured you were off for your break. Am I interrupting anything?"

"Not at all. I need to stop anyway."

"Stop? What were you doing?"

"Oh, I wrote a novel, and now I'm revising it."

"A novel? Wow! That's impressive."

"Maybe after it's published, but so far, no luck."

"What's it about?" he asked.

"Four women who are friends and support each other through good times and bad. Your basic chick lit."

"It sounds good! Maybe I can say I knew you when you were a struggling writer. Anne English? The famous novelist and Oscar-winning screenwriter? Oh, yes, I know her. We're like two peas in a pod, best buds, BFFs."

Anne laughed. "That's a very optimistic vision of the future."

"Aren't we going to be best buds? I'm hurt!"

"Best buds, *maybe*. It was the bestseller/Oscar-winner thing that seemed a tad bit optimistic, in my opinion. What about you? What do you like to do?"

"The shop takes up a lot of time. Tony takes up most of the rest. And whatever's left is usually spent on my bike. My life is pretty simple these days. I like to camp out and tinker in my wood shop. Helps me relax."

"What kind of things do you build?"

"Furniture, mostly. So far I've made all the furniture in my house except the sofa and chair."

"Now *that's* impressive!" said Anne.

"Aw, I don't know about that. But I enjoy it, and that's really all that matters." John paused. "I don't want to overstay my welcome on our first phone date, so I'll let you get back to your book. Maybe you could stop by the shop sometime over the break and we could have a shop date. There's also another group ride next weekend, weather permitting. I guess that would be a group date."

"That sounds like a lot of dating, considering we're not dating," Anne laughed.

"It's not *dating* dating, it's quasi-dating… only not."

"Clear as mud! I'll stop by soon for a shop date, and maybe the group date. Weather permitting, of course."

"Of course. Good night, Anne."

"'Night, John. Thanks for calling."

Anne found it difficult to focus on revisions after that.

Chapter 17

Anne strolled down the aisle of the store, enthralled by all it had to offer. Beautiful clothes swirled on carousels, fresh flowers beckoned her to come near, and delicious aromas floated in from the distance. She fingered a soft blouse of beige silk before holding it up in front of a mirror. A dress composed of blue, purple, and green swirling fabric caught her eye. She examined it carefully before trying it on. The fabric felt like the softest of cashmeres. She tried it on: a perfect fit! *I believe this is something John would like,* she thought as she twirled in the oversize dressing room. She walked over to the flower stall to find hundreds of gorgeous flowers waving in the breeze, as if in a meadow. She chose a large, multicolored bouquet and buried her nose in the delightful fragrance. In the distance, she heard a ringing sound. It stopped and then began again. The noise confused her, and she looked around for a salesperson, but there were none to be found.

Again the ringing, closer this time. And again, until…

Anne awoke with a start. Her body seemed to work, but her head was fuzzy. A glance at the clock told her it was the middle of the night.

Rrriinnnnnnggggg!

Anne snapped awake—it was the phone. She quickly turned on the light, spilling a glass of water on her bedside table in the process.

"Damn!"

She grabbed the phone quickly, but she missed the call. She

checked the caller ID: Mercy Hospital. A few seconds later, the voicemail arrived and Anne dialed the access number.

"Hello, I'm Linda, a nurse in the emergency room at Mercy Hospital. Please return my call as soon as possible."

Anne's heart raced as she dialed the number for the ER.

What could have happened? Is it Karen?

She waited for someone to pick up, for what seemed like an hour.

"C'mon… pick up… pick up, please," she pleaded with the ringing phone.

"ER, Sharon speaking."

"A nurse named Linda called and left a message. I'm Anne English."

"Just a minute. I'll get her."

Again, an interminable wait.

"This is Linda."

"Linda, this is Anne English. You called my house a minute ago, but I didn't get to the phone in time. What's happened?"

"Mrs. English, your daughter, Maggie, has been in an accident and is currently in the emergency room."

"Oh my God! Is she okay?"

"She's talking. We'd like you to come down to the hospital. Do you have anyone to drive you?"

"Uh, no. It's just me. I'll be right there."

"Drive carefully. Good-bye."

"Uh, okay. Be there as soon as I can."

Anne grabbed the sweats and T-shirt that she had worn cleaning the house that day. Her hair went back in a ponytail while she slipped her feet into flip-flops. She grabbed her purse and dug through it, looking for her keys. Frustrated, she dumped the contents on the bed. She grabbed the keys and her wallet from the pile.

Her mind raced with possibilities as she drove to the hospital. Rain had made the roads slick, and she wondered if the weather had had anything to do with the accident. She took a deep breath, calming herself, and began to pray out loud:

"God, thank you for my precious daughter. I don't know what I'm going to find when I reach the hospital, but I know you are with me as well as with her. And, God, even if she leaves me now, I know she'll be with you. And I know that, with your help, I can get through anything. Thank you for the last seventeen years. You gave me such a gift when she was born. Thank you, thank you, thank you. May your will be done."

Anne focused all her attention on getting to the hospital as quickly and safely as possible. She parked her car and ran in through the ER doors as they opened automatically for her. As she reached the check-in counter, she said, "Maggie English. Margaret. I'm her mother. They called and told me she was here."

"Trauma room twelve, Mrs. English. Follow the red line through the doors, and it will be at the end of the hall on the right."

"Thank you."

Anne found the room and peeked through the curtain. Maggie lay in the bed, unconscious, tubes running everywhere, head bandaged. Anne's eyes filled with tears as she watched her daughter breathe.

"Are you the mother?" asked a voice behind her.

"Yes, yes, I am," she replied.

"I'm Linda. We talked on the phone."

"Yes, how is she? What happened?"

"She was awake for a little while. She said that she and her friend were driving home and someone ran a light and hit them. The doctor will be in soon to talk to you."

"What about her friend? Is she here?"

"No one was brought in except your daughter. I'm assuming her friend was all right."

"Okay, thank you." Relieved, Anne pulled a chair close to the hospital bed and stroked Maggie's arm.

A few minutes later, the doctor appeared, stethoscope around his neck, chart in hand.

"Mrs. English? I'm Dr. Herrera. Your daughter is a lucky young lady. According to the police report, the car was hit on the left side, just behind the driver's door. Any closer to your daughter and we would be having a very different conversation. She has a broken arm, a broken leg, some broken ribs, cuts from the glass, contusions. She's got a bad cut on her head that needed stitching, and a possible head injury. We'll need to run more tests to be sure. We'd like to keep her in ICU for a few days to make sure she's all right. Brain injuries can be tricky."

"*Brain injuries?* She has a brain injury?"

"We found a small spot on her brain. It could be nothing, but we'll need to watch it and see if it changes."

"How long will she be in the hospital?"

"About three or four days. It all depends on how she does and if we see any changes."

"But Christmas is in two days!"

"I'm sorry, Mrs. English, but Maggie needs to stay here."

"I understand. Of course I want to do what's best for her."

"We should be moving her to the ICU in the next thirty minutes or so. If all goes well over the next few days, she can go home after that."

"Thank you, Doctor. I appreciate everything you've done for her."

"Not a problem," said Dr. Herrera, as he shook her hand and ducked out.

Anne turned her attention to Maggie. Once again, tears filled her eyes as she watched her daughter. Anne closed her eyes and whispered a prayer of thanks for Maggie's spared life. Just then, Maggie opened her eyes.

"Mom?"

"Yes, baby, I'm here."

"What happened?"

"You were in an accident. Don't you remember?"

"The last thing I remember was driving to Lauren's house after a late movie. Where's Lauren? Is she okay?"

"You were the only one brought into the hospital. I'm sure she's fine."

"When can I go home?"

"In a few days, honey. They want to be sure you're okay."

"But it's almost Christmas! Am I going to be here for Christmas?"

"Yes, sweetheart, that's what the doctor said. They want you to stay in the ICU for a couple of days to make sure you're all right. Apparently you got a pretty good bump on your head."

"I'm so sorry, Mom. I didn't mean to get into a wreck and ruin Christmas."

"First of all, it wasn't your fault. Someone ran a light and hit you, so you just get that out of your head right now. Second, no one's Christmas is ruined. It will simply be postponed until you come home."

Maggie tried to shift positions in the bed.

"Ow! I hurt all over!"

"I know. You're pretty banged up, but you're going to be fine."

"I guess I have a broken arm," Maggie said, holding up her left arm. "Did I break my leg too?"

"Yep, and a couple of ribs. You also have some stitches on your forehead."

Maggie felt around gently to find the spot. Her fingers found the bandage covering the stitches.

"Oh my God—it's huge. Am I going to have a scar?"

"I don't know. They're pretty good at stitching people up. I'm sure you won't even be able to see it when it heals."

"I'm going to look like Frankenstein," Maggie pouted.

"I doubt that. Maybe the Bride of Frankenstein, though," teased Anne, hoping to elicit a smile.

"Not funny, Mom," Maggie frowned.

"I'm sorry. I just wanted to see your beautiful smile. But I've changed my mind. Don't smile. Whatever you do, don't smile. Wait, I think I see one coming. Don't you do it!" Anne used the trick that had worked wonders when Maggie was a little girl.

"Okay, Mom. Your strategy worked again. I'm smiling, see?" Maggie produced an exaggerated smile.

"Well, it's better than nothing!"

The nurse reappeared.

"Someone will be in shortly to take you to the ICU. They'll give you something to help you sleep when you get there. You need your rest. It probably wouldn't hurt you to get some rest either, Mrs. English. She'll be out for a while."

"Yeah, Mom. Go home. I'll be fine. After they knock me out I won't know if you're even there, so you might as well go home."

Anne paused, torn between her maternal instincts and common sense.

"All right," she relented, "but only after you get settled and fall asleep."

"You know that's what you'd tell me to do if you were lying here."

"Yeah, yeah, I know. But—"

"No 'buts' about it, Mom—you're going home, and that's final."

Anne smiled at her daughter's insistence.

"Yes, ma'am," she replied, "as soon as you're asleep."

"That's better!" Maggie smiled.

"There's that smile I've been waiting for!" exclaimed Anne.

A handsome orderly poked his head around the curtain.

"Anyone here need a ride to the ICU?" he asked, smiling.

"That would be me," Maggie raised the arm with the bright pink cast on it.

"Cool. Pretty girls get a discount. C'mon, let's go! My name's Jake, by the way."

"Maggie."

"Nice to meet you, Maggie. I hear you tried to wrestle another car."

"That's what they tell me. I don't remember a thing."

"Well, that's probably a good thing. Now, let's get you to the ICU so you can get some sleep."

"Sounds good."

Anne picked up their belongings and followed Jake to the elevator.

Once they reached the ICU, it didn't take long before Maggie was sleeping soundly. Although Anne was reluctant to leave, she knew that she needed her rest too. She gently kissed Maggie on the forehead.

"I love you, sweet daughter," she whispered, and headed toward the elevator.

Anne walked to her car as if in a fog. She sat in the car for a moment, letting it all sink in. Her mind whirled as she pictured Maggie in the hospital bed. At first a few tears fell, followed by deep, racking sobs and a flood of opposing feelings: gratitude that Maggie was alive, horror at the near miss, and fear of the implications of a brain injury. Wiping her eyes and nose on the sleeve of her hoodie, Anne started the car for the drive home.

Still shaky, she stopped at a convenience store for a snack and a drink. She grabbed a diet soda and a package of powdered donuts and stood in line at the counter.

"Three oh two," said the clerk.

"And a pack of Marlboro 100s, and a lighter," Anne said quickly.

"Ten fifty-three."

Anne pulled out $11, pocketed the change, and left the store. She hadn't smoked since Charlie left, but she decided the stress of the situation called for a pack of cigarettes. Once back inside the car, she quickly opened the pack, lit a cigarette, and inhaled deeply. It did the trick, and she felt the tension abate.

Back at home, Anne felt like she had been gone for a week instead of a couple of hours. She heard a sound coming from the kitchen and realized the coffeemaker was beginning to perc. Too wired to sleep, Anne went back outside for the morning paper and poured herself a cup of coffee. She held the mug in both hands and took a sip. The warmth of the coffee soothed her, and she could feel a little more tension leave her body. She sat down on the sofa, flipped through the paper without reading anything, then turned on the TV. Nothing was on except an old war movie and infomercials. She snapped the TV off and paced, looking for something to do. For the next hour, Anne piddled around the house, unloading the dishwasher, sorting laundry, and straightening the bathroom. The sun was beginning its ascent as Anne ran out of unfinished chores. She tried to read, but found herself reading the same page over and over because she couldn't retain the information. Exhaustion overcame her, and it wasn't long before she could barely keep her eyes open. She crawled back into the bed she had left just a few hours ago, before her world was turned upside down. She was asleep within minutes.

Once again, the phone awakened her.

"Hello?" she said groggily.

"Anne, it's Susan. It's ten o'clock, girl! Get up!"

"Susan. Hi. It's been a long night."

"What happened?"

"Maggie was in an accident last night. She's in the hospital with some broken bones and a possible head injury."

"Oh my God! I'm so sorry. Is there anything I can do?"

"No, I've got it covered. Thank you, though."

"I'm so sorry I woke you. I'm sure you're exhausted. I was just calling to see if you were going on the group ride today. I guess I got my answer."

"No ride for me. I'll be heading back to the hospital soon."

"Will you promise to call if you need anything?"

"I promise. Thank you so much."

"How about this? After the ride today, I'll make a batch of my famous chicken spaghetti and bring it over so you don't have to cook," Susan offered.

"How sweet! Thank you. That would really be a big help. Richard spent the night out last night, but he'll be home later and I know he'll be hungry. He's *always* hungry!"

"He's a growing boy! That's about all they do at that age—eat, sleep, and grow!"

Anne chuckled. "You have him pegged!"

"I'll be over about five this afternoon with casserole in hand. I may be able to scrounge up a chocolate cake while I'm at it."

"Please don't go to a lot of trouble."

"Absolutely no trouble at all. I'm happy to help. I'll call before I come to make sure you're home. See you later!"

"See ya! And thanks again, Susan. You have no idea how much it means to me."

"You're welcome. Bye!"

"Bye!"

Anne showered and dressed. Eleven o'clock—Richard might be awake by now.

"Hi, Mom," he answered.

"Hi, sweetheart. Are you up and dressed?"

"Yeah, just eating some cereal."

"I'll be leaving here soon to pick you up, okay?"

"Aw, Mom, I was going to hang out with Joe all day. He's got the new video game I've been wanting to play."

"Not right now, son. I'll be there in a few minutes, and I need you to be ready."

"All right," said Richard reluctantly, recognizing that the tone in her voice meant business.

"Thank you. I'll see you in a minute. Bye."

Anne drove to Joe's house, picked up Richard, and explained the situation as they drove to the hospital. He was his usual no-big-deal self until he saw Maggie in the hospital bed. He gasped slightly, and his eyes widened at the sight of her in the bed. But he quickly recovered his cool, calm exterior.

"She looks okay to me. Except for the cast and bandage and stuff. Why can't she come home?"

"They want to be sure she's okay, that's all. It'll just be a couple of days."

"What about Christmas?"

"We'll have to postpone it for a little while this year."

"Aw, man," Richard whined. "I know you got me that game I've been wanting. Can I just open that one present?"

"How do you know that?"

Richard looked down at his feet. "I poked around in the hall closet a couple of weeks ago and found it."

"Oh, Richard," said Anne, exasperated.

"I'm sorry, Mom. Besides, you're a terrible hider. It was easy to find."

"Of course it was when you're poking all through everything. We'll discuss this later, okay? I want to talk to the nurses and see how Maggie's doing."

Anne stepped over to the nurses' station. Maggie yawned and opened her eyes.

"Hi, Squirt," she said, smiling at Richard.

"Hey. How are you feeling?" asked Richard.

"Sore, mostly, but okay."

"Why do you have to stay here so long?"

"'Cause they want to be sure my brain's okay, I guess."

"Your brain's never been okay," joked Richard.

Maggie smiled. "Well, maybe they just want to see if I still have one."

"Doubtful, but I guess only the doctors can tell us that for sure."

"Very funny. Where's Mom?"

"Talking to the nurses."

"Will you ask her to come in here, please?"

"Sure," said Richard, poking his head out into the hall. "I see her. She's coming back this way."

"Well, you seem to be doing just fine," Anne reported.

"I'm still really sleepy. And I have a headache. And my body is so sore," said Maggie.

"I'm sure you will be sore for a little while. The nurse said she would be here in a minute with pain medication."

"K. I think I'm just going to sleep today, Mom. You and Richard should go home."

"Why do you keep trying to send me home?" teased Anne. "Are you hoping that cute orderly will come by?"

"The nurse said he stopped in earlier. He left a note. It's over there," she pointed to the bedside table.

"Hmm, let's see… 'Maggie, I hope you feel better soon. Jake,'" Anne read aloud. "That was sweet."

"Yeah, it was. Mom, I'm really tired. I just want to sleep. Go home. I can't sleep with you watching me. It makes me nervous."

"If you insist."

"I do. Come back later, okay? And would you bring my cell phone?"

"Well, first, you're not supposed to even have it on in the ICU, so it wouldn't do you much good. And like you said, you need your sleep."

"Would you at least call Lauren for me and see how she's doing?"

Anne smiled at her daughter's selflessness. "I've already talked to her. She's fine. Of course she's worried about you, but I told her you were going to be all right. She wanted to see you, but ICU is just for immediate family. I told her you'd be home in a couple of days."

"Okay. Love you, Mom."

"Love you too, baby. See you later."

"Later, sis."

"Bye, Richard. Make Mom get some rest."

Anne and Richard left ICU and walked toward the elevator. As the doors opened, Anne was surprised to see John standing there, holding some roses.

"John! What are you doing here?"

"Hi, Anne. How's Maggie?"

"She's going to be okay. How did you know she was here?"

"Susan told me before the ride today. I got someone to watch the shop so I could see how you two were doing."

"It was a long night, and it's been a long day today. Richard and I are going home to get some rest."

"I got these flowers," said John, handing Anne the vase.

"Maggie can't have flowers in ICU."

"I know that. I didn't get them for Maggie; I got them for you. I figured you needed a little pick-me-up."

"That was very thoughtful of you. Thank you."

"You're welcome. Can I walk you to your car?"

"Sure, thanks."

Anne filled him in on the details as they walked to the garage. Once she let her guard down, she could feel the exhaustion creeping over her again. She turned to John as they reached her car.

"Thanks again for the flowers. I really appreciate it."

"I'll give you a call later to check on you. Get some rest," said John, squeezing her hand and lingering a moment or two longer than he intended. He could see the worry in her eyes and empathized. He had been in the same situation once, a few years ago. He held the vase of roses for Anne while she and Richard got in the car. The memories of that awful time flooded over him, and he found himself wanting to be the shoulder he knew Anne would need. He also knew that this instinct to protect and support her could mean only one thing: he cared for Anne more than he had realized.

Chapter 18

Tiffany's winter break was filled with all the things she loved: sleeping late, time with girlfriends, and, of course, trips to the mall for the post-Christmas sales. She always received a generous amount of Christmas money; her grandparents and father found it much easier to augment her bank account than to try to ascertain the preferences of a teenage girl. December 26 was her favorite day of the year; she and Ashley were the first ones at the mall. Hours later, lugging bags full of incredible deals, they headed for home. Next on the agenda was the rest of their December 26 tradition: snacks, drinks, and going up to Tiffany's room to listen to music and bask in their purchases.

"Ooooh! Look at how great these pants go with this shirt!" exclaimed Ashley.

"Too cute! My boots would work with them too. I love that we're the same size. It's like having twice the clothes!"

"I know! Wait! I think I have a purse that will go with that too. Do you hear something? Is that your cell?"

"Gotta be yours. I have mine right here," said Ashley, holding up the latest model.

By the time Tiffany found her phone in her purse, the ringing stopped.

"It's David," she said, checking caller ID. "Think I should call him back?"

"Yeah, why don't you do that? That way you two can get together and he can shove you down the stairs again and maybe kill you this time instead of just sending you to the hospital."

"Ash, we've been over that. He tripped. He didn't mean to. He *has* apologized."

"Whatev. It's your life."

"C'mon, Ashley, don't be like that. I mean, it's not like I want to date him again, but I don't want to be mean to him, either. I still care about what happens to him."

"Okay, 'scuse me for worrying about you. I just don't want you to get hurt again—physically or emotionally."

"Me neither. Trust me. Let's just see what happens. If he gets weird, I'll get off, okay?"

"Okay. Let's see what happens."

Tiffany locked eyes with Ashley as the phone dialed David's number.

"Hey, David. I saw you called. How are you?"

"I'm good. You?"

"I'm doing fine. Did you have a good Christmas?"

"Yeah. What about you? Did you get your usual pile of cash?" he joked nervously.

"Yeah, Ashley and I just got back from the mall. Did you want something in particular?"

"Well… um… I, uh… I heard about the baby. Tiffany, I am so sorry."

Tiffany lowered her eyes and straightened the bedspread. "Oh. Uh, yeah, it's okay. I'm doing okay."

"I'm glad to hear it. I never intended to hurt you."

"Yeah, I know."

They both paused, unsure of what to say next.

"Well, I gotta go," Tiffany broke the silence. "Ashley's here and we have plans."

"Oh, okay. Sorry if I bothered you. See ya," said David.

"See ya," replied Tiffany, and snapped her cell phone shut.

"See? No big deal." She turned to Ashley. "He just wanted to see how I was."

"We'll see," answered Ashley, a skeptical frown on her face.

Later, after the thrill of the new toys had worn off, Tiffany and Ashley settled into a romantic comedy. Sitting on the sofa with a big bowl of popcorn between them, they lounged in their sweats and slippers.

Ding-dong.

"Wonder who that is," said Tiffany, rising toward the door.

Ding-dong.

"Coming," she called. "Geez, hang on a minute," she muttered.

Tiffany opened the door to find David standing there, holding a bouquet of flowers.

"I brought you these," he said, holding the bouquet in front of him.

"Thanks, David. That was sweet."

Ashley walked up behind Tiffany, looking over her shoulder.

"What're you doing here?" she asked.

"Hi, Ashley. I'm just dropping off some flowers for Tiff."

"Okay, you've done that," she replied.

"Ash, don't be rude," admonished Tiffany.

"Sorry."

"It's okay. I've got to go anyway," said David. "Bye Tiff. See ya, Ashley."

"Bye," answered Tiffany. She turned to go into the living room. "God, Ashley. Can you just chill?"

"I can see I'm not going to win this one. That's okay. He'll show his true colors eventually."

"Cynic," teased Tiffany.

"Realist," answered Ashley.

"We'll see."

"Yes, we will."

Anne awoke early, ready for the day to begin. Maggie would be checked out of the hospital around noon, and Anne couldn't wait to have her back home, where she could look after her. She had a short list of things to get today: a shower seat so that Maggie could bathe without standing up, a few of her favorite snacks from the grocery store, and some fresh flowers for her room. Not a big bouquet, just two perfect buds in a small vase that could sit by her bed. They planned to celebrate Christmas tonight. Anne had the extravagant meal ready to go: beef tenderloin, twice-baked potatoes, broccoli, and, for dessert, the maple mousse that all of them craved. Anne's mother had picked the recipe up many years ago at a restaurant in San Francisco during her honeymoon, and it had quickly become a popular tradition in the Roberts household.

Anne sat at the dining room table, absentmindedly flipping through the newspaper and sipping coffee. She studied the vase of flowers John had brought her. Many of them were still gorgeous; just a few needed to be removed. Anne had worked in a flower shop in high school and had always enjoyed arranging fresh flowers. She carried the vase to the kitchen to begin the remodeling process. The dead and mostly dead were the first to go. Next, she pared down the rest of the bouquet, examining the state of the flowers, taking away dead leaves, and trimming the ends of the stems. The "new" bouquet was placed back in the center of the dining room table until the next session. Anne would trim away at a large vase of flowers until only a few blossoms were left, but she was often able to stretch the life of the flowers, and her enjoyment of them, into at least two weeks, sometimes longer.

She smiled at her handiwork and thought of John. She had been surprised, and pleased, to see him at the hospital. The fact that he was obviously interested in her made her giddy; that he was willing to wait made her grateful for two reasons: it reinforced his interest, and it showed his respect for her wishes. A thought struck her: it must also mean that he wasn't going anywhere, literally or figuratively. Anne had never known when Charlie would show up. Sometimes he would stay gone for days "at a gig," but he never returned with the money he made. Sometimes he would hang around the house for days, sleeping till noon, waiting for the next gig. When they were first together, the chaos brought excitement to Anne's ordered life. But by the time she realized that all the "excitement" was irresponsibility in disguise, they were married and she was pregnant with Maggie.

Anne had spent the last ten years as a single mother focused on her children. She didn't date, although there were times when she missed the company of a man. She enjoyed her friends, and she occasionally called on the husbands of close friends if she really needed a man's physical strength or expertise, but over the years she had grown more independent, self-sufficient, and brave. She bought books on home repair and car maintenance at a half-priced bookstore. She learned how to change her own oil, fix a toilet, and wire a lamp. And, although these simple tasks took her twice as long as they would have taken someone more knowledgeable and experienced, she relished the empowerment and accomplishment she felt when the job was complete.

Anne arrived at the hospital anxious to retrieve her daughter. While they waited for Maggie to be released, Jake stopped by the room.

"Hey, Maggie! I'll bet you're ready to go home."

"I sure am! I want to sleep in my own bed without the nurses coming in to check on me every thirty minutes!"

"Bet you won't miss me beating you in gin rummy!"

"I won more games than you did. You still owe me a soda, Buster," teased Maggie.

"I thought you forgot about that."

"No way, Jose! I fully expect you to pay your gambling debts."

"All right, you got me," Jake laughed. "I've gotta run, but I'll call you in a few days to see when I can win that soda back."

"You're on! Thanks for everything, Jake. Talk to you soon."

"See ya, Mags!"

"Mags?" Anne raised an eyebrow.

"That's what he calls me. I think it's cute."

"Isn't he a little old for you?"

"Not really, Mom. He's a sophomore at the university—just two years older than me. He's pre-med and wants to be a pediatrician."

"That's very admirable. I guess if he's just a sophomore…"

"Geez, Mom, it's not like we're getting married or anything. We're just friends."

"Okay, okay," said Anne, holding her hands up in surrender. "You win. Just friends? I can deal with that."

"Good, because he's a really nice guy. I promise you'll like him. Can we go home now?"

The nurse walked in with discharge papers.

"Let's go over a few things before you leave. Here is a prescription for pain medication. You need to see Dr. Fredricks, the orthopedist, in three weeks. Until then, stay in bed as much as possible with your leg elevated. And she will need to be in a wheelchair to get around until he puts her in a walking cast, Mrs. English. You've already rented one, right?"

"Yes, it's at home," answered Anne.

"Good. Keep the casts dry when you bathe. You'll probably want to rent or buy a shower chair."

"It's at home too."

"Great! Looks like you have everything you need. Any questions?"

"No, I think we're good. Thanks for everything," replied Anne.

"All right, Miss Maggie, you're free to go. Take care of yourself," said the nurse.

"Will do! Bye," answered Maggie. "C'mon, Mom, let's go home!"

Maggie's first duty was to inform her friends she was home again via Facebook. Then she sent out a text to her entire contact list, just to be sure. After that, it was time for Christmas.

"Mom, when are we going to open presents?" she asked.

"I thought we'd have a nice family dinner, light a fire, play some Christmas music, and then open presents."

"Aw, Mom, do we have to go through all that? Can't we just dig in and do all that now?"

"We can do everything but the dinner—that's going to take time to cook. Sure, why not? Let's have Christmas."

"All right! It's about time! Because of you, I've had to look at all these presents for days, waiting to open them!" teased Richard.

"It's good for you to wait," said Maggie. "Builds character!"

"I don't want to build character; I want to open presents!"

"Then let's open some presents!" agreed Anne. "Here, Richard, hand this to your sister, please. And I believe this one is for you."

Maggie and Richard tore into their gifts, emitting appropriate "oohs," "aahs," and "thank-yous" as needed. Each Christmas, Anne worked hard to ensure that both children received at least one gift they really wanted amid the socks, underwear, and other necessities. As the children aged, they put more thought into her gifts, beyond the traditional perfume and costume jewelry. This year, they surprised her with a leather vest to wear while riding her motorcycle.

"Oh my goodness! It's wonderful!" Anne exclaimed.

"Look on the back, Mom," said Richard.

Anne turned the vest over to see a large patch of silver angel wings and red roses, with the words Lady Biker beneath them.

"I wanted to get a patch that said Biker Bitch, but Maggie said no," said Richard.

"Richard!" exclaimed Anne.

"No, Mom, it doesn't mean you're a *bitch*. It's sort of like saying you're a biker babe, except you're probably too old to be a babe."

"I get it, son. Thanks," Anne said wryly.

"The angel wings are there to protect you, Mom," said Maggie. "And the roses are 'cause you like fresh flowers. We were not going to get you a Biker Bitch patch under any circumstances," she added, shooting a look at Richard.

"I appreciate that. It's beautiful. I will wear it with pride. Thank you so much."

"We think it's cool that you ride," said Richard.

"Maybe you should wear it today and take a ride over to that motorcycle shop and show it off to that guy that works there," Maggie hinted.

"How do you know about *him*?"

"I'm not an idiot, Mom. Go for a ride. You've been cooped up either here or at the hospital ever since the accident. Don't worry about me. I can get the twerp to help me if I need anything."

"Well, it *is* a gorgeous day today…"

"Go ahead, Mom, I'll just be playing my new game, and Maggie'll be either on the phone or on the computer, as usual."

"If you're sure…"

"Yes! Go! Be free! Have fun!" encouraged Maggie.

Anne hurried off to change into riding clothes. She turned to admire the vest in the bathroom mirror, so grateful for her children. In a flash, she was out the door and on the road.

Chapter 19

As Anne neared the motorcycle shop, an epic battle raged within her that sounded more like a discussion between Maggie and Lauren than the ramblings of a woman in her forties: *Should I go to the shop? Maybe he's busy. I don't want to appear too interested. But you* are *interested, silly. What's wrong with his knowing that? But you said you were just going to be friends. Going by the shop doesn't mean you're dating. You're just stopping by to say thanks for the flowers and show off your vest. C'mon, what's the big deal? Don't be such a chicken! For crying out loud, Anne, just do it!*

Anne coasted into the parking lot, stopped, and sat there for a moment as the argument continued: *You're here—just go in. But what if…? No more butts! Get your ass in there.*

Anne laughed out loud at the pun.

"What's so funny?" asked John.

"John! I didn't see you walk up. Oh, nothing. I was just thinking about something funny Richard said," Anne smiled.

"I'm glad to see you. How's Maggie? I figured you wouldn't leave her and venture out for a while."

"She insisted. She thinks I need a break. Besides, Richard is there if she needs anything. She's doing fine. Still a little sore and uncomfortable, but healing."

"I'm glad to hear that! Cool vest. Turn around and let me see the back."

"Isn't it great? The kids got it for me for Christmas," said Anne.

"Very nice. So, what are you doing today? Got any plans, or just going for a ride?"

"No plans. I just wanted to get out of the house for a while. Correction: the kids wanted me to get out of the house for a while. I guess they're right—I haven't done anything except shuttle between home and the hospital for days. It does feel good to have a little freedom."

"Freedom's just another word for nothing left to lose."

"Nothing don't mean nothing if it ain't free," added Anne.

"Sing it, sister!"

"Feeling good was easy, Lord, when he sang the blues. Feeling good was good enough for me," sang Anne.

"Good enough for me and Bobby McGee," John joined in off-key.

Anne and John laughed at their impromptu duet.

"You are a terrible singer," laughed Anne. "Good thing you're cute!"

"So, you think I'm cute?"

"Well, yeah. You're a very nice-looking man."

"From cute to nice-looking—that sounds like a demotion in girl-speak."

"And you sound like you're fishing for compliments!" teased Anne.

"Okay, you got me. Cut me some slack! It's been a long time since anyone thought I was cute or nice-looking… or anything, for that matter."

"Surely you've had your pick of women—cute guy, nice bike, business owner…"

"You know how women are. They want only one thing, and I will *not* be used as a sex slave," said John in mock protest. "Seriously, I just haven't met anyone who interested me. Until you, that is."

Anne blushed. "I've been out of the loop so long, I hardly know how to act around a man anymore."

"I think you're doing just fine. In fact, you are doing a superb job. You've certainly made an impression on me."

"You're easy!"

"But I'm not cheap," joked John. "Anne, I really like you. A lot. And I don't want to be just friends. In fact, I want to be way more than friends. And, to take it one step further, I've wanted to do this since I read your first email."

John leaned in, placing his hand on Anne's cheek. She closed her eyes and could feel the warmth of his breath close to her face.

Buzz!

The front door alerted them to the presence of a customer.

They both jumped back like children caught in the act.

Susan walked in, smiling.

"Hey, you two. What are you up to, as if I didn't know?"

John cleared his throat. "Just talking. How are you, Susan? Out for a ride?"

"Yep, Herb and I are going to ride that pretty loop north of town, but my puppy used my goggles for a chew toy."

"That's too bad. You know, Susan, they sell things like that at the pet store. You don't have to donate your goggles. Isn't this the kind you bought last time?" asked John, handing her a pair.

"You have a good memory, John. Must be the reason your shop is doing well. Customer service at its finest!"

"Not so much a good memory. More like it's the third set of goggles that that behemoth you call a puppy has destroyed!"

"Tiny is the sweetest Great Dane you'll ever meet," said Susan. "And he's only a little over a year old, so technically he's still a puppy."

"I stand corrected," John bowed.

"Don't you talk bad about Tiny," said Susan, wagging a finger at him.

"Yes ma'am. I mean, no ma'am… ma'am," stuttered John.

"Look who's frazzled!" joked Susan, elbowing Anne in the ribs. "Hey, what are you up to, Anne? Wanna come with us?"

"You really should, if you have the time. It's a beautiful ride," added John.

"Let me check on Maggie first, just to be on the safe side." Anne moved to a display case on the other side of the store.

"And what were you two up to? Did I interrupt anything, I hope?" asked Susan.

"Nope, just talking," said John, glancing at Anne.

"You're a terrible liar! For what it's worth, I think you make a great couple," Susan hinted.

Anne returned from her phone call. "Everything's fine. Richard's even being nice. I'd hate to go home and mess that up! I'd love to go, Susan. I think it would be good for me to get out of town for a little while. How long a ride is it?"

"Not long. One and a half, maybe two, hours. We haven't ridden it in a while. What do you think, John?"

"That's about right. Probably closer to two, but it's worth it."

"Sounds perfect! Let's go," said Anne. "Bye, John. See ya later!"

"Bye. Have fun and ride safe!"

Herb led the procession, with Susan and Anne side by side behind him. Anne had always loved the winter landscape. It had its own brand of stark, monochromatic beauty, especially true on cloudy gray days. But today's landscape seemed alive. Wispy white clouds raced across sapphire skies. Recent rains supplied the missing ingredient for new growth in the fields. The air was crisp and clean, with an occasional whiff of sweetness from a passing elaeagnus or honeysuckle.

After about forty-five minutes, Herb waved them to exit up ahead at a café popular with bikers. It was a small wooden building that leaned slightly to the left. A large covered patio surrounded the entire restaurant and provided the only seating. A long row of motorcycles surrounded the patio like sentries at their post. The smell of grilled burgers wafted on the breeze, reminding Anne that she was hungry.

"This joint has the best burgers in the state," said Herb, choosing a table.

CLASS LETTERS

"And fries," added Susan.

"And chocolate malts," they said together, laughing.

Anne joined in, "Chocolate malts? I love chocolate malts! When I was little, there was a drive-in named Virgil's. They had the best chocolate malts ever, and my grandmother would take me there for a special treat. Good times." She smiled as she sat down, reminiscing.

"Y'all sound like a commercial," said the waitress. "What'll ya have?"

"I believe we are all in agreement," said Herb. "Three cheeseburgers, all the way, three fries, three chocolate malts. Is that correct, ladies?"

"Sounds good," replied Anne.

"Absolutely!" said Susan.

"Got it. Back in a few with the malts."

"So, Anne, how are you liking the ride?" asked Susan.

"It's wonderful. I'm so blown away by the gorgeous weather, the clean air, the sun…"

"Great. So, Anne, how are you liking John?" she continued, glancing at Herb.

"Susan," admonished Herb, "that's none of your business."

"I'm nosy. So sue me! C'mon, spill it!" said Susan, turning to Anne.

Anne blushed, smiling. "We're just friends. He's nice. I like him. That's all there is to tell."

"All right, Ms. Coy. Actually, the truth is, you're the first person he's been interested in since all that mess in Louisiana."

"What mess in Louisiana?" asked Anne.

"See what happens when you stick your nose in where it don't belong?" asked Herb. "Listen, Anne, we need to let John tell you about that, don't we, Susan?"

"Uh, yeah, we do. Anne, I'm so sorry. I was sure he would have told you by now," said Susan. "I feel terrible. John really is a good guy. He's just had a tough time. It's not like he's some serial killer or something."

"Oh, yeah, now I feel better," said Anne.

"Really, Anne. I'm asking you to trust me on this. I'm sure he'll tell you all about it when the time is right. I really didn't mean to spill any beans."

"I know. It's okay. Mmm, here come the malts!" said Anne, grateful for the distraction.

The rest of the afternoon was light and fun. Anne returned home uplifted and smiling.

"Hi, Mom," said Richard without looking away from his video game.

"Hey, son. How's your sister?"

"She's okay. I made lunch and pushed her to the bathroom a couple of times. She wanted Jell-O. And I put oil in it."

Anne was practiced at Richard's disjointed comments, but this was a little confusing, even for her. "Oil? In the Jell-O?"

"No, in her hair… and wrapped it in plastic wrap. It stinks. Girls are weird. There! Blew you outta the water!" he yelled at the TV.

"Sometimes we are, son, and you'll be much better off if you just learn to deal with it. See? You're getting a head start."

"Lucky me. Oh, man! Where'd that guy come from?"

"Did you clean the kitchen?"

"Not exactly. I've had to take care of Maggie," he protested.

"Yeah, I can see that."

"No, really, Mom, I just started playing a little while ago. Lauren's here."

"Well, why didn't you say so, silly?"

"Uh-uh-oh."

"Never mind. I appreciate all you've done, sweet boy."

"You're welcome, Mom. But don't call me 'sweet boy' anywhere but here, okay? It sounds kinda babyish."

"Sure thing, sweet boy," smiled Anne.

She found Lauren sitting on Maggie's bed next to her, looking at the computer. Maggie's head was wrapped in plastic wrap, just as Richard had said. Anne could smell the olive oil from the doorway.

"Can you believe what Lady Gaga wore in her new video?" asked Lauren.

"I know! She looked like a fish caught in a net. It was weird, even for her. Oh, hi, Mom. How was the ride?"

"It was lovely. How are you? And why in the world do you have olive oil in your hair?"

"It's a natural deep conditioner. You should try it."

"I'm good, thanks. Has Richard been helpful?"

"Yeah, the twerp has actually been nice. Maybe you need to have his brain checked!"

"Aw, now, isn't it nice to have a civil relationship with him instead of bickering all the time?"

"I guess, even if I almost had to die first," said Maggie.

"Well, you didn't die, thank God, and I think you should enjoy it and cultivate it. Who knows, maybe you'll even like each other."

"Richard's not so bad… for a little brother."

"Not too bad at all. I'm going to clean the kitchen. You two enjoy whatever you're doing. Do you want to stay for dinner, Lauren?"

"Can she spend the night, Mom?" asked Maggie.

"Sure. Want me to call your mom and let her know?"

"Sure, Mrs. English. Thanks."

Anne busied herself with the kitchen. Not only had Richard "not exactly" cleaned, but there were still dishes from last night to do. Anne contemplated her options: she could call Richard into the kitchen and stand over him while he cleaned like he was supposed to, or she could let it slide and simply mention it to him later. Option B won out. Anne was too preoccupied at the moment with Susan's earlier comment to deal with Richard. She was debating whether or not to confront John. After all, she had her children to think about. And herself. She didn't want to get involved with John and then have to end it after his secrets were revealed. And she certainly didn't want another relationship based on dishonesty. Asking for details seemed the only way to go.

Chapter 20

For the past dozen years or so, Anne had believed that two holidays should be stricken from the calendar because of the lies and pain they caused their participants: New Year's Eve and Valentine's Day. The lies about Valentine's Day were obvious: the idea that everyone should be in love, and if you weren't in love—and extraordinarily happy—then you weren't really a whole, complete human being. Anne resisted this unrealistic view, but the ad execs in New York made it difficult with all their propaganda. New Year's Eve held a similar deception: that you'd wake up to find a new year, and all your problems from the previous year would somehow magically disappear while you were sleeping. Not only that, but the hope that came with making a few empty promises was usually dashed by mid-January. It reminded Anne of the women who visited their stylist with a picture of the latest starlet's new haircut and were so disappointed when they still looked like themselves after spending fifty dollars to look like someone else. Anne's cynicism was due largely to her relationship with Charlie. There had always been a gig on New Year's Eve, complete with the drunk female partiers Charlie found irresistible. Of course, if he didn't find any willing partners, he came home and demanded sex from Anne. She always felt it was safer to simply give in. She had yet to call it rape. Then there was that Valentine's Day when Charlie gave her a card and some candy. She was thrilled until she opened the card. Charlie had mixed up the envelopes; Anne received the card (which gushed about her "awesome body" and their "mind-blowing sex") meant for his girlfriend. It was their last Valentine's Day together.

This year, it looked like Anne would be flying solo on New Year's Eve. Richard was going to Joe's house. Maggie had begged to spend a couple of nights at Lauren's house, and, after a talk with Lauren's mother, Anne had agreed. Maggie had been cooped up in the house since she had returned from the hospital, and she needed a change of scenery. Even Karen had plans—some doctor who was new to the hospital and to town. He was taking her to one of those fancy parties at the new hotel downtown that featured a five-star restaurant and dancing to a jazz band Karen loved. Karen was thrilled, and who could blame her? She told Anne all about the guy, emailed her pictures of the new dress, shoes, and accessories that had cost her two weeks' salary, and was spending the day getting ready. Karen had appointments for a new hairstyle, a massage, and a mani-pedi. Anne had never seen Karen so excited about any date—or any guy, for that matter—and, although it was momentary, she felt a pang of jealousy.

If she was going to be alone, at least she could pamper herself a little bit. She made a short grocery list—fresh flowers, candles, diet sodas, frozen mini-quiches ("fancy food," as Richard called them), a split of cheap champagne, and black-eyed peas for luck—and drove to the store after dropping Richard off at Joe's. Her plan for the evening included a bubble bath, complete with candles, a mani-pedi of her own, a movie (or two), and champagne for the ball drop at midnight.

Anne lay in the bathtub, radio playing, candles burning, and reviewed the last couple of weeks. She thought of the fear she had felt the night of Maggie's wreck and her ensuing relief a few days later when the neurologist cleared Maggie and her undamaged brain. She thought of John, the flowers and conversations, and the almost-kiss. She smiled at Richard's kindness toward his sister. Both her children were growing up, maturing, and, in small but steady ways, readying themselves to leave her. The thought excited and saddened her at the same time. What would her world be like without the children in her daily life? Where would they go to college? What kind of adults would they become? She saw glimpses of it periodically, when Richard stepped up to accomplish a difficult task, or when Maggie and Anne discussed a novel on a deep literary level. Anne knew they acted more like Karen's peers than like her niece and nephew. And yet at times, she couldn't help but see the snaggle-toothed smiles or skinned knees they had left behind years ago.

Anne pulled on the warm, fluffy, cotton candy-pink robe and slippers her parents had given her for Christmas. Underneath, her soft skin slid against a silky black chemise she had received from Karen. *Gotta love sisters! At least they don't pretend you're a nun!* Anne thought with a smile.

She collected her mani-pedi bag, full of all the files, clippers, lotions, and polish she needed, and placed it on the coffee table in the living room alongside the flowers. After the timer rang in the kitchen, she arranged the treats on her best china, grabbed a step stool to help her reach the crystal champagne flute on the top shelf of the cupboard, and pulled a real cloth napkin from the bottom of the linen closet. She arranged the table to her satisfaction and sat down. Once she did, Rocky laid his head in Anne's lap in a combination of extreme devotion to Anne and desperate hope that she would drop one of those delectable-smelling treats.

"This is nice," she said aloud to herself. "I should do this more often. What do you think, Rocky?" He raised his eyes toward hers without moving his head an inch and smiled.

"Yeah, I know, you're only here for the food. But surely you must care about me a little bit, don't you, Mr. Rocky Boxer? After all, you share my bed"—Anne's voice lowered, and she paused as she looked Rocky in the eyes—"if you know what I mean."

Another statue-stiff grin. Anne gave his head a good rub.

"Okay, Rocky, love of my life, let's see what movies are on. Here, have a treat!" Anne tossed a morsel to Rocky, who snatched it out of the air with ease. She flipped on the TV and tuned to the movie channel. Then her phone began to ring. It was John.

"Hey there!" she answered.

"Hi. I wasn't sure if you'd be home or not. I thought you'd probably have a hot date or something, but then I figured you'd be home taking care of Maggie. Am I interrupting anything?"

"Nope, and you're wrong on both counts. No hot date for me, and Maggie's at Lauren's for the night. I figured she could use some girl time. It's just good old Rocky and me. What about you? You could have a hot date too, you know."

"Aw, now, you know that's not true. Besides, I have a date and I'm talking to her. That is, if you're not too busy. Got time for another phone date?"

"Actually, there is something I'd like to discuss with you."

"Uh-oh. That sounds serious."

"I don't mean to pry, but Susan mentioned something the other day."

"Oh, that. Yeah, she called me and told me what happened. She's right—I'm not some serial killer, I promise!" he joked.

"Is it too much for me to ask what she meant? Like I said, I don't want to pry, and I don't want to make assumptions, either, but you were going to kiss me, right? And it just seems like if kissing is in our future, I'd like to know more about you."

"Well, I hope kissing is in our future. Actually, I wish kissing was in our past. I really wanted to kiss you the other day. I was disappointed when it didn't happen." John paused. "You have every right to ask for whatever you need. Ask me anything you want. I'll tell you the truth."

"The main thing is whatever trouble you had in Louisiana."

"Yeah, lots of trouble there. Okay, here goes: I was married to a woman named Crystal. And, unfortunately, she also liked crystal. Crystal meth, that is. And crack. That was really her downfall, crack was. At first she just used on the weekends or when we'd go out. And she didn't use at all when she was pregnant with Tony. Anyway, she started using more and more. She'd stay gone for days, or she'd call for me to pick her up from some sleazy motel. It made me sick to watch her spiral downward. She was such a talented artist. That's why we moved to New Orleans: we thought her art would sell better there. And she did good for a while. But, like I said, she started using more and more. I had to ask her to leave. I had to think of Tony. It nearly killed him to see his mother like that."

"I can imagine. Crack was my ex-husband's downfall too. He left ten years ago, and we haven't heard from him since. I have no idea if he's dead or alive."

"I'm sorry to hear that. How have the kids handled it?"

"Maggie remembers more than Richard, but they've both seen more than their share of abuse. It was more emotional than physical, but they both take their toll on everyone. Maggie wants nothing to do with him; Richard just wants to protect me."

"Yeah, that emotional abuse sneaks up on you. Crystal did a lot of that too. It's weird how you can start to believe it. Anyway, she left and things got better for Tony and me. He started doing better in school, and he wasn't so angry all the time. Then Katrina hit and turned our world upside down. We lost everything. That's when we came to Texas. I got in touch with Susan and Herb. They put us up until we could find a place. It took us a little time to get settled. We moved around a little. I did odd jobs. It was like we had lost our bearings. Then Herb loaned me the money I needed to start the shop. It turned everything around for us."

"You're kidding. That's amazing!"

"Yeah, they broke the mold when they made those two." John took a deep breath. "Finally, a few months ago, we heard Crystal was dead. They found her body in some abandoned warehouse after Katrina. No ID. It took them a long time to identify her from dental records. By then we had moved to Texas and they had to track us down. We're all the family she had left, so they kept looking till they found us. So, that's me in a nutshell. Or at least the last few years. It's just Tony and me. My parents are gone. Her parents were gone before we met. We were both only children. That's my story, and I'm sticking with it."

"I'm sorry you had to go through all that. But I am grateful you told me."

"Are you still seeing red flags?"

"Nah. I guess you're a good guy, like Susan says you are."

"I'd like to think so. I'm good to my kid, I make a decent living, I'm good at what I do, and I love to spoil women. Well, maybe 'women' isn't quite right. I love to spoil the woman I'm involved with. The problem is, I haven't been involved with anyone in a really long time. I hope I haven't forgotten how! Any chance I could practice on you?"

"You've got the charm part of it down!"

"Oh, really? So m'lady is pleased?"

"Yeah, I'm a sucker for all that charm and romance and stuff. I'm kinda girlie that way. Actually, I think most women like it, whether they'll admit to it or not."

"Hmm… now I have a plan of attack. I must go forth and… uh, plan! Prepare to be charmed, m'lady."

"I look forward to it, m'lord."

"Good night and adieu. Parting is such sweet sorrow… or something like that. Shakespeare and I did not get along in high school!"

"Not a problem. I know someone who might tutor you. And John…" Anne began.

"Yes?"

"Thanks again for sharing your story with me."

"It was my pleasure. Anything to make you feel more comfortable. I'll let you get on with your evening. You and Rocky have fun!"

"Night, John. And happy New Year!"

"It certainly is. Night."

Chapter 21

Tiffany stood in front of the mirror, next to the pile of clothes she had been trying on. She couldn't decide between a coy and demure I-think-we-should-take-it-slow outfit, or a come-and-get-me ensemble. It was her first real date with David since his time in rehab. Actually, it wasn't going to be a "real" date; her parents had forbidden her from seeing him, so she was meeting him at a party.

"This is it!" she exclaimed. It was perfect: her skinny jeans, the high-heeled boots she had gotten for Christmas, and a slinky, shimmery, low-cut top that fit her like her skin. Luckily, it was cold enough for a coat—her father didn't approve of anything that made Tiffany look the least bit womanish. She gave her head another toss as she spritzed on some perfume.

"Leaving!" Tiffany called from the front door.

"Have fun!" her mother answered from the kitchen.

"And be careful!" added her father.

"I will. See ya next year!"

Tiffany hopped into her Neon and sped toward the party.

Ray had been looking forward to New Year's Eve for months. It was Isabel's favorite holiday. She always said that no matter what happened in the previous year, you could always start fresh at New Year's. Ray's plan was to take her to the big New Year's Eve party at the park and take her away from the others at midnight to shoot off some fireworks. After their kiss at midnight, he would propose.

Ray loved Isabel's optimism. She lifted him up when he was down. She never saw the bad side of a situation, only good. That was Isabel through and through—only good. He had been saving for a ring ever since he had started working for Jesse. He didn't have as much as he had wanted, but he had responsibilities at home, too. Maribel's school had initiated a new dress code this year, and she had needed new school clothes—an unexpected expense. And then his mom had gotten that late-summer cold and had been out of work for two weeks. Everything fell on Ray during that time—bills, rent, food, and gas. Still, he was proud of what he had been able to save. Living within a budget, balancing a checking account, and having a savings account were all foreign concepts to him, but Jesse had insisted that Ray become responsible with his money.

"Dude, you're a grown man. You have responsibilities, a mom and sister. And I know you got your eye on my daughter. I'm not blind. You gotta take care of your shit. If you don't know how, I'll teach you. I didn't know how either, till I went to prison. They had classes on social skills and practical living skills and shit. I thought it was bullshit at first, but I learned a lot. That's how come my business is successful. I take care of my shit."

After that, every payday, Jesse and Ray sat down together and talked about where the money should be spent and how that worked within Ray's budget. But Jesse made Ray put 10 percent in savings off the top.

"Man, you gotta pay yourself first. That's the smart thing to do. Then you always got a reserve in case the shit hits the fan. And once you get used to it, you won't even miss it, I promise."

Ray had been a diligent saver, usually adding 5 to 10 percent over Jesse's recommendation for the ring, although he had been tempted at times to empty the account. People from the neighborhood knew he had been working steadily, and they constantly approached him about the next get-rich-quick scheme. Sometimes it was merchandise that "fell off a truck" that he could resell. Every now and then, his homies got into a tight spot and needed a tough guy who knew his way around a gun, and they called Ray. The money and excitement were a temptation, but Ray liked the direction in which his life was headed. He had met the woman of his dreams, he had a great job and was learning mechanic skills from a master, and his life at home with his mother and sister was much less chaotic. They finally knew they could depend on him.

Once Ray was satisfied that he looked as good as possible, he pulled the small black box out of his pocket and flipped the lid open. Nestled inside, surrounded by velvet and satin, was a one-quarter-carat diamond solitaire. Ray had never been so proud of anything in his life. When he had "officially" talked to Jesse about marrying Isabel, Ray had asked about his pride in the ring.

"How come I feel so proud that I bought this for her? It seems like she should be the important one, but I feel like I'm more excited about the ring than the proposal. But you know I love her, right, Jesse? I mean, this don't mean I don't love her."

"I know, son. The pride you feel is about your accomplishment. The ring is just a symbol. You're doing things you've never done before—and liking it. You got a good steady job, a great girl, if I do say so myself, and you're good to your mama and sister. All that stuff's important—and you're doing it, man, you're doing it!"

Ray smiled as he remembered the conversation. Ray's father had been in prison since he was five; Jesse was the closest thing to a dad Ray had ever known. He took the time to teach Ray things he needed to know. Not just about fixing a motor, but about being a good man. Ray was an apt pupil, and Jesse looked forward to adding a son to his family.

Ray checked his hair once more in the mirror before slipping the box back into his pocket. No one was at home; Maribel was spending the night with a friend, and his mother was pulling a double shift. She said it was to give the people who had someplace to go a night off, but

Ray knew it was about the money. Ray hated that she worked so hard, and he looked forward to the day he could be the sole breadwinner.

"I guess I *am* doing it," Ray said as he locked the front door.

Kim had mixed feelings about going to the party at the park. The Gay-Straight Alliance she had helped start at school had gotten off to a rocky start: Kim had received prank phone calls and other calls from a blocked number with the voice on the other end berating her for her preferences, and, worst of all, the classroom they met in had been vandalized. Someone had spray-painted crosses, scriptures, and admonitions about going to hell across the whiteboard and wall. Administrators found out who was responsible: a couple of redneck football players who had been tackled one too many times. They were sent to the alternative school and banned from the high school campus for the remainder of their high school career. Still, it took a while for the club members to feel safe again. Hoping to encourage the club members, Principal Henderson had supplied paint, brushes, and drop cloths and allowed club members to decorate the room in their own fashion. They had created beautiful murals espousing love, peace, and tolerance. They'd even held an open house for all students to see their artwork and learn more about the Alliance. It didn't hurt that popular kids like Tiffany Wallace were involved, or that Mrs. English was the sponsor.

Kim was never much for dressing in roles, like some gays. She wasn't the "butch" one, nor was she the "femme." She dressed simply and comfortably, usually in jeans, flip-flops, and a T-shirt. Since it was chilly out tonight, she wore a sweater and athletic shoes along with the jeans.

Her parents had already left for the Korean American New Year's Eve party at the cultural center. Although the traditional Korean New Year was celebrated on January 1 and lasted for three days, this was an attempt to join the Korean and American traditions. The American portion was the date and the celebration at midnight, complete with confetti and noisemakers. The Korean additions included traditional

Korean games and food, generally soup and rice. It was expected to be a fun party, and Kim's parents were looking forward to a little taste of home.

Kim was meeting friends at the park. They had all agreed ahead of time to leave if there was any hint of the two vandals. The word through the grapevine was that the two boys were angry and looking for revenge. Kim had contemplated skipping the party altogether, but Mrs. English had pointed out that the boys would win if she stayed away when they spoke one day after a meeting.

"Don't give them your power or allow them to determine how you will run your life. That's how they win. It takes courage, which you obviously have in spades. You can do it. Go in a group; there's safety in numbers. Be proud of who you are, because you are precious!"

Mrs. English always helped Kim stay on track. She was proud of who she was, and of the impact she was having around school concerning gay rights and attitudes of tolerance. Membership had risen by 40 percent since the open house—and most of those members were straight. Of course, she wanted the GSA to be a supportive and fun place for gays and straights, as well as a safe haven for gays struggling with acceptance, but she also knew that the straight students were a great endorsement. Other straight students were more likely to join once they saw their friends hadn't "caught" homosexuality. Even though a few close-minded individuals were still sure that gays and lesbians were the spawn of Satan, on the whole, life was simpler and safer for gays and lesbians on the SFA campus these days.

Kim snatched her keys and bag off the bed and headed out to the party.

Keosha swirled and turned in front of the mirror. She looked fly in her new jeans and a hot shirt Tamika had given her, and she knew it. Tamika was almost four months pregnant with BD's baby, conceived shortly before school started. Since she was already showing a little, she had given Keosha all the clothes that reminded her of her "skinny days."

Keosha did not want to go the way of her friends, pregnant and not even out of high school, so she had resisted Dewayne's requests for sex—until now. She had decided that tonight was "the" night, and she'd made sure she was prepared: she had bought a box of Trojans in case Dewayne didn't have any. "No glove, no love" was her motto, and she was determined to stick with it, in spite of the opposition he might give her.

Yes, he could be stubborn, but he had many other qualities that appealed to Keosha. He had provided for his mama since her heart attack through his job at Walmart. She knew he was restless—she could feel it—but she didn't know if it was attributable to her or to his job. He had never worked a real job before. Previously, his only means of making money had been illegal—running drugs and even guns for some gangsters in the next town. That's why they had moved and he had changed schools. Since then he had cleaned up his act, and he had some pride about the changes he had made. At least, that's what Keosha thought. That's what everyone thought, but Dewayne had quickly reverted to his old ways, just more cautiously.

People see what they want to see. Keosha had noticed that Dewayne had become increasingly impatient and irritable lately. She attributed it to his schedule of working almost forty hours a week, plus finishing up his senior year. But his schedule also included late-night runs to other areas in the city, sometimes in the next county. He was ambitious and wanted to move up in the organization; his ridiculous excuse for a job was simply a ruse to placate his mother until he finished high school. She had raised him, on her own, all his life, giving him every advantage she could. Her dream was to see him graduate; he figured he could give her that, but he also wanted to provide for her in a way Walmart would never allow him to.

Keosha tugged on the front of her tight knit shirt to expose just a little more cleavage.

"There's no way he can resist these tits," she said to herself in the mirror before leaving for the party.

Chapter 22

The place everyone called a park was more of a field with a grove of trees around the edge, ancient soccer posts, a pair of squeaky swings, and an old concrete-block concession stand in the back. Boys played impromptu touch-football games or soccer games on the field and kids smoked their first cigarette in the grove, after-school fights usually took place there, and the concession stand was a notorious make-out spot. Tonight it was the location of the big New Year's Eve party. Word had gotten out, so there would be recent alumni from SFA there, as well as kids from other schools. There would be beer, weed, and music—and a rotation crew of stakeouts to warn of any incoming police cars. The stakeouts had to be eighteen or over so that they didn't have to adhere to a curfew, and they went in pairs so as not to draw suspicion. Some kids walked; most came in carloads of people ready to party. The cars were parked as close to the concession stand as possible for light, as well as shelter from patrolling eyes. They knew the cops would stop by periodically; they just wanted to be sure the weed and beer were cached so that no one went to jail and the party didn't get shut down.

When Tiffany met David by the concession stand, there were already about forty kids there. Tiffany could smell the marijuana in the air. She had never tried it, but she knew its distinctive aroma.

"Want a beer?" asked David.

"Okay, but just one. I'm driving, remember."

"Geez, Tiff, don't be such a pussy. It's just one beer."

"I said I'd have *one*," said Tiffany.

"Here's your *one*," said David, handing her a beer. "Let's check out who's here."

David and Tiffany strolled through the groups of teenagers. Kim was there with several members of the Gay-Straight Alliance; Keosha was hanging out with BD and the rest of the Dawgs. Ray and Isabel were off by themselves, holding hands and talking quietly, as usual. David steered Tiffany over to a dark corner to check out the party.

"Why did you want to stand over here?" asked Tiffany.

"Watch the crowd at the picnic table," suggested David.

Tiffany watched as Keosha sat on the picnic table with a steady stream of "clients" stopping by to make an exchange.

"Ohmygod! Did you know Keosha was dealing?" Tiffany asked David.

"Yeah. Ever since she started dating Dewayne. I hear he's a bad motherfucker. She better be careful. Someone told me she carries a gun on her at all times—even at school."

"You're kidding! She's so nice. How could she get mixed up with those thugs?"

"I dunno. I guess some girls will do anything for their guy." David paused and looked at Tiffany. "What about you? Will you do anything for your guy?"

"What do you mean?" asked Tiffany.

"You know."

"No, I don't. What are you talking about?"

"C'mon, baby. When are we gonna have sex again?"

"Are you kidding me? After last time? No way, David. Sorry," said Tiffany.

"You can get on the Pill. You don't even have to have your mom go with you. Just go to one of those clinics."

"No, David. It's not gonna happen. We're not even dating anymore."

"Oh, baby, you know you want to. Those clothes you're wearing are an open invitation." David pulled her close and started kissing her.

"No means no, David. Stop it!"

"Come *on*, Tiffany. You've made me wait long enough." David had a tight grip on her arms.

"David, stop it. You're hurting me."

"You wanna give me blue balls? Huh? You think you're gonna make me wait some more? We'll see about that," he growled as he pushed her to the ground.

He held his hand over her mouth to prevent her cries for help. Although she struggled, he was much stronger than her, and he had her arms pinned down. Tiffany could hear his pants unzip, and she tried to kick her way free. Just then, a dark figure loomed over David and yanked him up by his collar.

"I believe the lady said no," said Ray, holding David by the front of his jacket.

"Hey, buddy, this is none of your business," said David.

"I'm making it my business. Now get your punk ass outta here."

"Try and make me, motherfucker," said David.

"If you say so," said Ray as he punched David in the face, knocking him to the ground as Tiffany watched. Isabel helped Tiffany up.

David got up and made a run at Ray, who quickly stepped aside, tripping David. Ray pulled him up by the collar again and pushed him against a tree.

"Listen to me very carefully, *puto*. First, you're going to apologize to Tiffany. No woman deserves the way you have treated her tonight. Next, you are going to leave this party."

"But Tiffany's my date," protested David.

"Not anymore. We will take her home safely. As I said, you are leaving this party. And from now on, you will also stay away from Tiffany."

"That's for her to decide."

"Oh, I've decided, all right," said Tiffany. "I never want to see you again. Ever."

"You heard the lady. Now apologize."

"Sorry, Tiff. You're right—no means no. I'll go, but this isn't over," said David, glaring at Ray.

"If you say so, man. I'll be waiting."

David brushed off his clothes and walked away. "This isn't over," he yelled over his shoulder.

Ray ignored the threat and turned his attention to Tiffany. "Are you okay?"

"Yes, thank you so much. I don't know what would have happened if you hadn't come along."

"My pleasure. You know he's back on steroids, right?"

"I heard that, but I didn't believe it. I guess they were right."

"We're going to be leaving soon. Do you want a ride home?"

"Yeah, I guess so. Some New Year's Eve this turned out to be."

"At least you're safe," said Isabel.

After dropping Tiffany off at her house, Ray and Isabel drove over to the Point, a small city park that overlooked the lake. Although most teenagers were there to neck, it was Ray and Isabel's favorite place to sit and talk. It was here that he had first told her he loved her, so it was fitting that he had chosen this spot to propose.

They sat close together, his arm around her and her head on his shoulder, with the radio playing softly in the background.

"It was wonderful the way you helped Tiffany tonight," said Isabel.

"No woman deserves to be treated like that," said Ray. "If anyone tried to hurt you like that…" His voice drifted off as he considered his words.

He continued, "I don't know what I would do if anything ever happened to you."

"We will never know, because that will never happen."

"I love you so much, Isabel. I can't imagine my life without you."

Isabel took his face in her hands. "*Querido*, we will live a long and happy life together. Nothing can tear us apart, I swear. You are doing a great job at the shop. We're almost out of high school. And, best of all, my dad already loves you like a son."

Ray kissed her softly. "You're right. We have our whole lives ahead of us. And there is only one person I want to spend the rest of my life with—and that's you. You are my strength, my hope, and my promise of a good future. You are the best thing that's ever happened to me. I know I don't have much right now, but I will someday, and I'll be able to get you really nice things."

He paused, uncertain of how to continue in spite of all the practice.

"You told me that New Year's Eve is your favorite holiday because it means we can let the past go and look toward the future. I want to be with you in my future—forever. Isabel, would you do me the great honor of becoming my wife?" Ray pulled the ring out of his pocket and slipped it on her finger.

"*Querido*, yes, yes, yes! It's beautiful. You can't afford this."

"Yes, I can. I've been saving. But I wish it was nicer. You deserve better."

"It's the most wonderful ring ever made, and I will never take it off. I don't want another one—this is the only ring I want, because you are the only man I will marry."

Ray gently pulled her close and kissed her. "Thank you," he whispered.

"For what?"

"For saying yes."

Chapter 23

"Wakey, wakey! Eggs and bac-y!" Anne's lyrical voice floated through the house. Three hundred and sixty-three mornings a year, breakfast consisted of the highly processed, oversugared cereal that her children loved, but she always made eggs and bacon for the first day of each semester.

Richard groaned, "I don't wanna go back to school."

"I know, honey, but spring semester starts today; baseball is on the horizon!"

"That's the only thing that'll make me get outta bed. That and maybe some bacon," Richard smiled.

"That's more like it! Better hurry—you don't want your breakfast to get cold. Maggie, are you up?"

"Yes, Mom—just putting on my makeup."

"Give it up, Mags. There's not enough makeup on the planet to help your mug," teased Richard as he strolled by her bedroom.

"Bite me, bro."

Anne sighed. She loved her children beyond measure, but two weeks with them—and their normal sibling bickering—always eliminated any reluctance she harbored about going back to school.

As Anne dressed, she thought about her students, hoping they had had a good break and were ready to get back to work. Her plan was to dive into a poetry unit first, then a novel, and finally a play. Anne found that students liked reading plays aloud, claiming the parts they wanted. It was a good way to end the year because she encountered little resistance. And the spring semester was generally chock-full of resistance. "Senioritis" could get pretty bad after spring break.

Anne was stuck regarding her January letter. She had tried writing it over the break, but nothing had come to her. She had continued to wait for inspiration, certain that something would come to her when the time was right. She considered a number of topics—new beginnings, motivation, starting over—but they all seemed so trite. Her cell phone interrupted her ruminations.

She smiled as she recognized the caller ID.

"Hi, John!"

"Hey! I just wanted to wish you a happy first day back. Are you ready for the hordes that will descend today?"

"I think so," she laughed. "I'm stuck on a topic for my January letter. Any ideas?"

"Hmm… how about a long dissertation about how you can't wait for summer so you can date this great catch you've been talking to?"

"Down, boy! I bet this semester flies by."

"I hope so. I'm ready to spend some good, quality, one-on-one time with you."

"No worries. It'll happen."

"I guess I'd better let you go. We can't have a tardy teacher!"

"No, sir, we cannot! Thanks for calling. Have a great day!"

"I'm glad I caught you before you left. Make it a good one! Bye!"

"Bye, John."

Anne flipped on the radio for the drive to school. She had grown up during the rock-and-roll era, and it continued to be her favorite genre. Mick Jagger serenaded her:

You can't always get what you want
You can't always get what you want

Anne smiled as the topic for the January letter congealed.

CLASS LETTERS

January

Dear Class:

I love old rock and roll, and one of my favorite songs inspired this letter. There's a lot of wisdom in those old songs, if you listen closely.

"You can't always get what you want..."

Everybody has hopes and dreams, regardless of their age. An eight-year-old hopes for a puppy, a sixteen-year-old wants a car, and a fortysomething teacher may dream of riding her motorcycle around the Hill Country near Austin.

What do seniors hope for? Graduation? A college acceptance letter? A $20-an-hour job? Let's face it—pretty soon, one phase of your life will end and another will begin. It's an exciting adventure to see how your life will unfold. There are a few things you can do to help yourself realize your dreams.

First, I think it helps to spend some time in preparation. How specific are your hopes and dreams? If they are just sort of nebulous ("I think I want to go to UT"), you should probably spend some time zeroing in on what you really want. You don't want to spend a lot of time or money in a situation you don't like ("UT is toooooo big!") when a little research would have helped ("Tarleton fits my personality sooooo much better!"). The more prepared you are, the easier it is to achieve your dreams.

Some aspects of preparation take a while, so you also need to allow enough time. For example, you can't decide to go to UT and then just show up on the first day of class. You have to apply, maybe write an essay, put together a schedule, or apply for grants and scholarships. And, just in case, it's always a good idea to have a backup plan. Sometimes, regardless of your preparation, things don't work out and you have no control over the outcome.

So what happens if you do extensive preparation but it doesn't work out? The college acceptance letter doesn't come, or that hot job prospect is filled by another applicant? It happens. Everyone gets disappointed at times. E-V-E-R-Y-O-N-E. I've had lots of jobs and plans that haven't worked out. What do you do then? Fortunately, you always have a choice. You could 1) focus on your plan B (if you have one) or 2) continue pursuing your original dream—either in a new form or by coming at it from a different angle. If it's important to you, persevere! For example, I wrote a novel a few years ago and tried to get published. I sent millions of letters (seemed like it, anyway) to literary agents and publishers. I am still unpublished, but my plan is to do a major revision this summer and try again.

Another thing to consider is that you may have to grieve your dream. If you absolutely, positively have to go to UT and no other school will do, you're going to be very disappointed if you don't get in. Your dream will have become a fantasy that's out of reach. Believe it or not, you have to go through some (if not all) of the stages of grief so that you can move on from anger to acceptance.

Hopes and dreams are great! They give us something to work toward and exciting experiences to look forward to. I may not always get what I want (sometimes that's a good thing!)—but I always get what I need.

"Your responses are due in a week," said Anne to the class. "Please turn to page three sixty-four. Tiffany, would you read the poem?"

"Sure," said Tiffany. "'Stopping by Woods on a Snowy Evening,' by Robert Frost. *Whose woods these are, I think I know...*"

Anne's attention drifted to her morning phone call from John. He had captured more of her attention lately.

"*And miles to go before I sleep / And miles to go before I sleep.*"

"Thanks, Tiffany," said Anne. "Who can explain those last two lines?"

Ray raised his hand. "The first one is talking about how far he has to go on his horse to get home or wherever he's going. The second one is about his life and how far he has to go before he dies."

"Excellent, Ray! Now, what does that mean to you personally? One of the joys of poetry is that we can each take the poet's words and see how they apply to our own life."

"To me, it means that I have lots of time in front of me and lots of stuff I want to do. And I have promises to keep too. Me and Isabel are engaged, and I need to make sure that I am the best husband I can be."

"Engaged? When did this happen?" asked Anne.

Ray blushed. "New Year's Eve. She even said yes!"

"Of course she said yes. You are a great guy, and she's a very lucky gal. Congratulations!"

"Thanks, Mrs. English. I'm pretty stoked about it."

Tiffany raised her hand. "I think that the fact that the woods are 'lovely, dark, and deep' shows that even though the future is unknown, we don't have to be afraid of it. We just have to walk through it."

"Great insight, Tiffany. You will get to expand on that idea in your January letter. It's about planning for the future—and all of you will need to start doing some of that planning sooner rather than later. Now let's look at another one of my favorite Robert Frost poems, 'The Road Less Traveled.' What's this poem about?"

"Doin' yo own thang, Miss," said Keosha.

"That's right, Keosha. Which part of the poem shows you that?"

"The part about the two paths. One path is the one er'body think you should take. The other is the one you want, even though not as many people have been on it."

"Very good. Is one better than the other?"

"I guess that depend on the person takin' the path. It's up to your own—what do you call it?—discretion. You gotta be true to you."

"Right! What are some of the paths that people might not understand?" Anne asked the class.

"You can't choose who you are or who you love, and some people don't understand that," said Kim.

"That's a good one. Sometimes people judge others out of their own ignorance or fear. What's another one?"

"Well, not doing what everyone expects you to. Like in your job. Maybe you want to do one thing and your parents want you to do something else," said Tiffany.

"Another good one. Our parents can have hopes and dreams for us that we may not agree with. For example, my sister always wanted to be a nurse. My parents thought she should be a doctor, which she could have easily done. But she felt that nurses had more hands-on contact with the patients, so that's what she's doing. Now, of course, my parents see how happy she is and how good she is at her job, and they are glad she went in that direction. But I remember some pretty intense discussions about her career choice when she was in college. Good job, guys! Tonight, for homework, I want you to read the three poems by Maya Angelou: 'Alone,' 'I Know Why the Caged Bird Sings,' and 'Still I Rise.' Choose the one you like best, and write a paragraph about what it means to you. See you tomorrow!"

Ray glanced at Keosha as they each gathered their belongings. Her face seemed harder, her eyes less trusting. He knew that look because he had seen it in his own reflection. He felt that she was making choices she would come to regret, and decided to take some action.

"Keosha, wait up."

"'Sup, Ray?"

"Listen, I know what you're doing, and I think it's the wrong way to go."

"Doing? I'm not doin' nuthin.'"

"C'mon, Keosha. I've known you since elementary school. Don't lie to me. Besides, everyone knows."

"Knows what?"

"That you're dealing for BD. It'll come back and bite you in the ass, K. For reals."

"Nah, bro. It's all good."

"I know what I'm talking about. I spent six months in juvie, remember?"

"Yeah, whatever."

"Okay, Keosha. Do what you want. But if things get tough and you want out, lemme know."

Keosha hesitated. "Why you wanna help me?"

"Just payin' it forward," said Ray as he walked to his next class.

Chapter 24

Ray's words bounced around in Keosha's brain the rest of the day. She had known him a long time, had seen him spiral downward into gang life throughout middle school and most of high school. Early indications that things were turning around for him were the smiles he wore more frequently. By October he was working a steady job at Jessie's garage. She saw him participate in class and make good grades, but it was that sparkle in his eye and his peaceful countenance that made a real impression on her. Although she hadn't realized it yet, Keosha wanted that deep, sparkly peace for herself more than anything else in the world.

"What's the matter, baby?" asked her mother, Minnie, before she walked out the door for her second shift. "You look like you're far, far away. Anything I can do to help?"

"No, Mama. I'm okay. Jus' a lot on my min.'"

Because it had always been just the two of them, Keosha and her mother had always been close—until Keosha got into high school. Minnie had passed it off as typical teenage rebellion at first, but Keosha had pulled further and further away from Minnie during her high school career.

Minnie was frightened for her daughter but felt powerless to stop her. It was as if Keosha had fallen down a dark hole and was just out of reach. Minnie had watched her grades drop from A's to C's in the last three years, but it was hard to monitor Keosha's progress while working two jobs. She did the only thing she could: pray.

BD's ringtone interrupted their conversationless moment.

"'Sup," said Keosha as her mother waved good-bye and walked out the door.

"Where you at, girl?"

"Eating."

"Come over after you done, aight? You got work to do."

"Aight."

As soon as she ate her last bite, she was out the door. Keosha pulled her hoodie closer to her body. It was a typical January evening—about forty degrees, with a north wind blowing, bringing the temperature down around thirty. Too cold for a simple hoodie, but it was all she had. She thought again about Ray's offer to help, but she wasn't ready yet. The lure of the money was an ever-present motivator, but she was a soft touch and gave much of it away to "friends." She also passed as much money to her mother as she could without arousing suspicion. It grew into a game for Keosha to see how much money she could give her mother and still fly below the radar. Keosha would add a $20 bill to Minnie's wallet, hide a five or two in a pants pocket, or stick some extra groceries in the back of the pantry. Keosha smiled at the little dances and whoops of excitement when Minnie came across one of Keosha's hidden treasures.

Keosha knocked on BD's apartment door. Dewayne answered.

"Hey, baby," said Dewayne.

"'Sup," said Keosha.

"Jus' chillin' wid my homies."

"BD around?"

"Yeah, he in da kitchen, cuttin' and weighin'."

BD, ever the businessman, usually cut some cornstarch, baking powder, or baby powder into the cocaine. He was much more interested in making a profit than he was in customer relations. As Keosha walked in, he was beginning to slip the powder into tiny plastic bags.

"Here, K. Take these to da park and get to sellin', girl. You was a li'l light las' week. And take Li'l Joe wid ya. He can do your runnin.'"

Most street dealers had a runner who retrieved the drugs from a secret stash after a customer paid so that the dealer didn't get caught holding. Runners were always underage so that, as minors, their sentence would be short and kept off their record.

"Li'l Joe? Ain't he jus' eight years old?"

"So? Nuthin' wrong wid starting young."

"That's not right, BD," objected Keosha.

"You tryin' to tell me how to run my business, bitch?"

"No way, BD. It ain't like dat. He jus' young, that's all," answered Keosha timidly.

"He doin' jus' fin', ain't ya, li'l man?"

"Yessir," said Li'l Joe.

"I think you could take a lesson from Li'l Joe and be a li'l more cooperative. You feel me?"

"I feel ya," said Keosha. "I'm gonna pee 'fore I head out."

"You know where it's at. Help y'self," said BD.

"Be right back," Keosha said to Li'l Joe.

Keosha stepped into the small bathroom and locked the door. She studied her face in the mirror for a minute, wondering what had happened to that A student she used to be. Although uncomfortable with the whole idea, Keosha hoped she could talk some sense into Li'l Joe while they were at the park. Eight was too young to get involved in this life. She would encourage him to wait until he was at least twelve.

Suddenly, Keosha heard someone bust through the front door. She quickly snapped off the light and hid in the bathtub behind the shower curtain. She heard muffled shouting from the other room, probably a drug deal gone bad or an assault by a rival gang. The shouting escalated until she heard several shots in a row—*pow, pow, pow, pow*. She heard people running, doors slamming. Then silence.

Keosha waited several minutes to see if it was safe before she slowly came out of the bathroom. The living room looked nothing like it had prior to her trip to the bathroom. A chair was on its side, and a lamp was broken in pieces on the floor. All the dope was gone. So was the cash BD kept in rubber-banded rolls in a cigar box. A table was upturned, along with the beer bottles and full ashtrays that had been on top. Everyone had scattered. Keosha studied the room for a minute.

"Living the dream," she said to herself.

As she walked toward the open door, she heard a groan and some movement behind the couch.

"Oh my God!" she exclaimed.

Li'l Joe was lying in a pool of blood. Keosha quickly dialed 911.

"There's a li'l boy here. He been shot."

"Where are you?" asked the dispatcher.

"Bonnieview Apartments on Oak. I don't know the address. Apartment two fifty-six. Hurry!"

"Police and paramedics are on the way. Stay with me until they get there, okay? How's the boy doing?"

"Okay, I guess. He's still breathing."

"Good. Stay with him. Help will be there shortly."

Keosha moved the couch away from the boy so the paramedics could see him. She rolled her hoodie into a ball and placed it gently behind Joe's head. She could hear sirens in the distance.

"Doin' okay?" she asked.

Joe nodded, eyes closed.

"No names, aight? Jus' say you was here borrowing a cup a sugar or sumthin'. Got it? Wrong place, wrong time."

Joe nodded. The sirens were very close.

"Gotta go 'fore the cops get here, k? You jus' stay here—they'll take good care a ya. See ya, li'l man."

Keosha slipped out of the back door and into the night as the police and paramedics pulled up.

Chapter 25

Keosha took alleys and side streets back to her apartment. Li'l Joe's face—eyes closed, forehead bathed in sweat—remained embedded in her mind.

"Eight years old? Are you fucking kidding me?" she murmured, shaking her head.

The more deeply she delved into this world, the more it horrified her. At first it was a daring and lucrative adventure. Illegal, certainly, but enticing. While she "worked," she wore her "tough girl" persona like a cloak she could shed once she returned to the safety of her home. But this... this was different... and *real*. Keosha hadn't felt tough as she knelt over the bleeding child.

Keosha mindlessly pulled her English binder out of her backpack. She skimmed the new letter, reading without comprehending. She flipped on the radio, leaned back on her bed, and reviewed the events of the evening. Although she knew it was a possibility, she had never been involved in any altercations with a rival gang. She thought about how a gang was supposed to be a family that looked out for each other, and yet BD and his buddies had all run off, with no concern for her or Li'l Joe. Keosha desperately wanted to talk to her mother when she returned home from work, but she was afraid that the distance between them was too great. Nevertheless, she missed the closeness they had had just a couple of years ago. What had happened to them? What had happened to *her*?

As she sat there pondering her recent past, the song playing in the background became clearer:

You can't always get what you want
You can't always get what you want

She picked up the letter in a flash of recognition and read it more carefully. Hopes and dreams? She used to have them. When she was little, she had dreamed of a pony. When she got a little older (and a little more hormonal), she had dreamed of Domino, the coolest rapper around. But lately, her dreams consisted of not getting caught and going to jail. *Eighteen-year-old girls don't normally worry about going to jail*, she reasoned. *Eighteen-year-old girls should be looking toward college or a good job, not watching eight-year-old boys getting shot up.*

The reality of her current situation and her prospects for the future clarified in her mind, flashing like the neon sign in front of a cheap motel: *Loser. Loser. Loser.* Keosha collapsed into a pile of tears, frustration, confusion, and fear.

Later, when Keosha heard the sound of her mother's key jangling in the door, for the first time in several hours she could breathe again. She could hear her mother in the kitchen, washing the dirty dishes in the sink. Although this was Keosha's responsibility, Minnie was too tired to reprimand her. The microwave dinged the dinner bell, and Minnie sat at the kitchen table, eating in silence.

When the noises subsided, Keosha stepped quietly to the kitchen doorway and studied her mother's profile as she ate dinner and flipped through yesterday's newspaper. Keosha noticed the wisps of gray in her hair, the creases on her forehead, the slump of her shoulders. Keosha felt a pang of guilt; her mother had worked two jobs as long as she could remember, and they had aged her.

"Hey, Mama," said Keosha timidly.

"Hey, baby," her mother smiled. "C'mere and gimme some sugar.

I've missed you! I swear it seems like weeks since I seen you. How's school? How's Tamika? Gettin' big, I bet. Now, when's she due?" Her mother chattered on, touching on all aspects of Keosha's life.

"School's okay; Tamika's huge and due any day," she paused. "Uh, Mama... um..."

Minnie looked up to see the worry in her daughter's eyes.

"What's wrong, baby?"

"Everything!"

"Can we narrow that down a bit?"

"I been makin' bad choices, Mama."

"What kind of bad choices?"

Keosha looked straight at her mother and blurted it out as fast as she could, "I been selling weed and stuff for BD an' I was over there tonight to pick up my stuff so I could go out an' I went in the bathroom an' heard shots an' came out an' Li'l Joe was on the floor an', Mama, he had been shot. Oh my God, Mama, I'm so sorry an' I'm so worried about Li'l Joe an' I don't want no more of that life. I know it was wrong and I'm so sorry."

"Baby, is that where you was getting money to help out? Have I done such a bad job of takin' care of you?"

"Oh, no, Mama! You've done a great job. But you work two jobs and I know it's hard on you and I never see you anymore. I thought if I helped out, you could cut back on one."

"I appreciate the thought, but there's better ways to help out. Thank God you never got in no trouble. That could ruin your life."

"I know, Mama," said Keosha, looking down, crying. Her mother took Keosha in her arms and held her as she sobbed.

Keosha looked up. "What do I do now, Mama?"

"Well, the first thing is that you will have no more 'business' with BD, understand?"

"Yes, ma'am."

"We are doing just fine, baby girl. It's not a palace, but we have a roof over our heads, food in our bellies, and clothes on our back.

That's more than a lot of folks can say. So we need to be grateful for all our blessings, instead of runnin' out and gettin' in trouble 'cause we want more. If you want extra spending money, I know the grocery store is hiring, and so is the dollar store. I bet they'd work with your school schedule."

"Probably."

"Yes, ma'am, I believe they would. And another thing I'd change is your friends. It's too easy to get tempted into doin' wrong if you're with people who are doin' wrong."

"But Tamika's my best friend!"

"Is Tamika dealing too?"

"No, but BD is the baby daddy an' she hangs with him most of the time."

"Well, baby girl, you jus' need to hang with her the other times. Don't let nobody influence you to do things you know are bad."

"She never liked that I was selling. She thought it was dumb. And she don't even like BD all that much, but she's stuck with him. Baby's gotta have a daddy."

"You didn't, and you are doin' jus' fine. Most of the time, anyhow," Minnie said.

"I'm gonna do better, Mama. I promise."

"I know you will, baby."

"Can we go to the hospital to see how Li'l Joe is doing?"

"Sure, we'll go tomorrow. It's late. School tomorrow. Time for bed."

"Yes, ma'am."

"One more thing. Keosha, I love you more than anything on this earth. I'm so grateful you didn't get hurt tonight, and I'm so glad you got out of this situation without doing some kinda long-term damage to yourself, like prison or addiction. I'm so proud of you for telling me. You know we gotta talk to the police, right?"

"Yes, ma'am."

"Now, before you go to bed, ask God for forgiveness and tell Him how grateful you are for all He's done for you, k?"

"Yes, ma'am. I thought you'd hate me."

"No way! Now scoot!"

"I love you, Mama. 'Night."

"'Night, baby."

Alone in her room, Keosha sat on her bed for a minute before slowly going to her knees.

"God, I figure you're pretty mad at me right now, but I want you to know I'm really sorry. I know it was wrong an' I won't do it no more. Please make Li'l Joe okay. He's jus' a kid and doesn't deserve to be hurt. Thank you that I got out of that bullsh—I mean, crap—before I got in real trouble. But mostly, thank you for my mama. I don't know where I'd be without her. I guess that's all I gotta say. 'Night! I mean, amen."

Chapter 26

Once she made the decision to come out, Kim became an outspoken and visible advocate for gay rights. She moved into action quickly after getting the go-ahead from the principal to start the Gay-Straight Alliance at school. She approached other GLBT students, prompting a flurry of phone calls and texts. Their first goal was to plaster the school walls with colorful posters espousing positive relationships between gays and straights. The poster party would be held at Kim's house the following Saturday.

Kim and her mother made a trip to the dollar store for poster boards, markers, snacks, and drinks. The ride was a quiet one; Kim was reflecting on the conversation she had had with her parents barely a month before.

It was a cold rainy night, and Kim and her parents were finishing up their dinner of rice and soybean soup. Conversation was minimal during dinner, allowing Kim time to screw up her courage. Homosexuality, like most everything else, was a taboo subject in North Korea. Although her parents were open-minded in some areas, Kim was uncertain how they would feel about the unconventional sexual orientation of their only child.

Speaking in Korean, as they always did at home, Kim began the conversation, addressing her father as head of the household.

"Father and Mother, I have something to tell you."

"Yes, my daughter, what is it?" asked her father.

"I have become involved in a new club at school."

"What kind of club?" her father asked.

"It's a club that helps homosexual and heterosexual students get along better. Mrs. English is the sponsor."

"That sounds like an admirable club to join," said her father.

"Yes, I believe it is. I joined it because it's where I belong."

"Belong?" asked her father.

"Yes, Father. I belong there because I'm gay."

It was out. Her secret was revealed. She watched her parents' reaction, waiting for a response. They simply looked at each other with the silent communication that comes after years of marriage. Kim couldn't breathe. Finally, her father spoke.

"Kim, we came to this country in search of the freedom we couldn't find in our homeland. You would not be permitted to have this kind of relationship there, so this is simply another reason why coming to America was a good choice. Your mother and I only want to see happiness in your heart. That is all that matters."

"Really? You don't hate me?"

"How could we? You are our daughter."

Kim's eyes filled with tears. "Thank you for understanding. I didn't want to disappoint you."

"That is something you could never do," replied her father. "What are your plans with this club?"

"We want to raise awareness about gays in our school and promote cooperation between gay and straight kids."

"Very admirable. How can we help?"

"Could I bring some friends over sometime?"

"Of course. All are welcome here."

Kim smiled now as she recalled the conversation. She glanced at her mother, wondering if she felt the same as her father or had simply acquiesced because of her submissive role in the family. Kim had become much braver in recent months and decided to ask her.

"Mother, I would like to know how you feel about me and the club."

"I think you are very brave."

"Brave? Really?"

"Oh, yes. Many years ago, I had a cousin in a nearby village who was gay. She kept it inside, confiding only in me. She was very unhappy because she was not free to be who she really was. It was prohibited by law. When we were seventeen, she took her own life. I was very sad for a long time afterward. I do not want to see that happen to you. I believe this club can help people like my cousin so they don't feel so alone, and I am proud of you for your courage. She was too afraid to speak out, and she died because of it."

Kim sat in silence for the remainder of the trip, absorbing this new information. She was grateful that her mother didn't disapprove of her or her lifestyle. After relating the story of her childhood, Kim's mother was suddenly much more "human" and approachable. Kim sighed in relief and gratitude with the knowledge that she had the support of both parents. She knew other kids whose parents were either in denial or homophobic, so her parents' acceptance meant that much more.

The poster party was a big success. Ten kids arrived and spent the afternoon painting posters, discussing ideas for other projects and fundraisers, and laughing. For Kim, it was gratifying to see the group interact in such a positive way. She saw kids who were normally shy and quiet at school open up among their "true" peers, reinforcing Kim's determination to get more kids involved, enjoying their lives, and feeling safe. Membership was slowly growing, and more students were becoming aware of the club's existence, but it still had a way to go.

Sunday night after dinner, Kim busied herself with the next week's assignments. Chemistry was her biggest challenge, so she tackled that first. Once those problems were out of the way, she could relax and work on English. Twenty vocabulary words and a chapter out of her literature book later, she was ready to write her January response. This was her favorite assignment. Mrs. English had proved to be a wise and supportive confidant, and these letters almost seemed like a one-on-one conversation with her.

> Dear Mrs. English,
>
> I like the song you picked for this month's letter. I had never heard of the Rolling Stones or that song before, so I looked it up online. I know I can't always get what I want. If I could, I'd get us a larger apartment and I'd get my parents better jobs. Back in Korea, my father was an engineer, but he doesn't speak English very well so my parents just work in a store. But I also know that I have what I need in the form of food, clothes, and shelter.
>
> I got something else I need a few weeks ago too. I told my parents about me. I was afraid of what they would say. This is something that is never discussed in Korea. Both my parents are okay with it. My mom even told me about her cousin who was gay and killed herself because of it. And she doesn't want that to happen to me.
>
> There's another thing I want too. Remember that we were going to make posters for the Gay-Straight Alliance this weekend? Well, we had about ten kids show up—most of them gay, but there were a couple of straight kids too. Anyway, I had a great time. It was so much fun to feel free to be me. I saw one girl who's really quiet at school, but she was laughing and having fun. I believe it was because she felt free too. So, what do I really want? I want everyone to get along, no matter what color you are, what race, what sexual orientation, no matter what. I don't want to feel afraid or ashamed just because I'm different from some people. I know it won't be easy and it probably won't even happen in my lifetime, but I hope that some day, differences won't matter.

CLASS LETTERS

But even if I can't get what I want right now, I know I have what I need. Parents who love and support me, and teachers who listen and support me (you!). I'm really grateful for these letters. It was easier for me to come out to you in a letter. And I knew you wouldn't make fun of me. So thanks for the letter and thanks for listening.

Your student,

Kim

Chapter 27

Anne pulled her coat closer to her as she walked quickly to her car. It was one of those cold, gray, January days that was better spent curled up in front of a fire than going to work. It had already been a long week in the classroom, and Anne could feel the early stages of a cold—sneezes, sniffles, and a scratchy throat had plagued her since last night.

"I'd cut off my right arm to stay home today," she grumbled as she waited for the car to warm up. But since staying home meant twice as much work as actually going to school, she rarely took sick days. There was a flu bug going around, and the sub list was already too short.

"Thank God it's Friday," she sighed as she walked into her classroom.

The January class letters were due, and although Anne loved reading them, she would relish a weekend in bed. The day progressed without incident—approximately a quarter of each class was out sick, and the rest were tired and ready for the weekend. Classes were cut short by a few minutes each so that the school could have its winter pep rally. During football season, there was a weekly pep rally before each game. This was Texas, after all. But the winter sports—basketball and soccer—had one combined pep rally in January. There would be another one in March for the spring sports: tennis, track, and cross country.

The noise in the gym sounded muffled to Anne—a sure sign that she was more congested than she thought. At the conclusion of the school day, she dragged her weary body and stuffed-up head home—along with a satchel full of papers to grade.

As she opened the front door and smelled the aroma of pot roast, she remembered the Crock-Pot she had thrown together that morning and smiled at her own genius.

"Whew! I was wondering what we'd have for dinner tonight!" Anne chuckled to herself.

"Maggie! Richard!" she called.

"In my room, Mom!" answered Maggie. Anne peeked in the door to find her daughter trying on clothes in front of the mirror.

"I decided to clean out my closet," Maggie announced. "It's pretty crowded in there after my post-Christmas shopping extravaganza. I've been putting it off and am finally sick of it. How was your day?"

"Why are you walking around without your cast on?" asked Anne. Maggie had been in a walking cast for the past month and still had a week to go.

"I'm fine. It's a walking cast. I've been walking in it, and now I'm walking without it."

"You still have another week to go."

"I'm fine, Mom, I swear. Besides, I'm sick of it."

"I want you to leave your cast on for another week, per doctor's orders."

"Mom, I'm fine. Really."

"Well, congratulations on your medical degree. I had no idea you were a licensed doctor," said Anne, slipping into sarcasm.

"But, Mom…"

"Do it now."

"Okay."

Anne heard additional grumbling but was too exhausted to discuss it. "There's pot roast in the Crock-Pot. Help yourself when you get hungry. I'm going to bed."

"Whatever."

Anne ignored the insolence and looked for her son.

"Richard?"

No answer.

"Richard?"

No answer.

Anne knocked on his door. Still no answer.

She opened the door and found Richard fully engrossed in his Xbox.

"Richard! I've been trying to get your attention forever."

"Sorry, Mom. I've been trying to beat this level for days. There! Take that, you miserable Nazi!"

"Richard, stop playing and look at me, please."

One exasperated sigh later, Richard paused the game.

"What?" he demanded.

"Don't you use that tone with me, young man, or that Xbox will live in the top of my closet for a week."

"Sorry, Mom. I'm listening."

"Thank you. Your sister is in her room, there's a pot roast in the Crock-Pot, and I'm going to bed."

"K."

Anne shook her head as she plodded to her bedroom. Apparently neither of them thought it was unusual for her to go to bed so early… or they were just too wrapped up in their own lives to care.

Anne muttered under her breath. "Teenagers. Sheesh! Could they be any more self-absorbed? I swear, if I dropped dead today, they probably wouldn't even notice."

Anne peeled off her coat, dropped her satchel, kicked off her shoes, crawled into bed, and fell into a deep sleep.

She awoke the next morning, surprised to find herself still dressed. It took a minute or two to piece the past eighteen hours together. She tried to get up and felt her head spin.

"Ohhhh… that's not good."

Anne stumbled into the kitchen to find Maggie—sans cast—spreading peanut butter on a waffle.

"Hi, Mom. You look terrible."

"Gee, thanks, Maggie! Love you too," Anne chuckled. "Actually, I feel terrible. I'm going to get *un*dressed now and put on some sweats. Would you please fix me one of those waffles? I don't have much appetite, but I need to eat something. Your brother up yet?"

"Mom, it's not even ten. He won't be up for another hour, at least."

"That's true. I'll be in my room. And Maggie…"

"Yes, Mom?"

Anne clutched the doorway to steady herself. Her first impulse was to say, "Put that cast on!" but instead, "I love you" came out of her mouth.

"Love you too, Mom. Now get into bed! I'll bring you some chamomile tea too."

"That would be lovely. Thank you, sweetheart."

Anne slowly returned to her bedroom. Every muscle ached, her head felt like it was going to explode, and her nose was beginning a steady drip.

A long-sleeved T-shirt and baggy sweatpants were the perfect ensemble for such a day. She rustled through the medicine cabinet for an unexpired cold remedy, snatched the box of tissues from the counter, and paused to look at herself in the mirror.

"Ugh. Puffy, bloodshot eyes, messy hair, and a red nose. If John could see me now, he'd run as far away as possible!"

Anne slipped back into the bed she had vacated less than an hour earlier, along with her school satchel, and started reading the latest collection of letters. The first one was from Ray.

Hey Miss!

The Rolling Stones is one old school band, but it's pretty good. I listened to some over at Jessie's one night. He used to listen to them all the time way back when he was a kid. Were you a kid then too? Never mind, I know it's not polite to ask a lady her age. LOL.

I like that idea about getting what you need. I heard once that you better watch what you ask for cuz you might get it. I'm not exactly sure what that means cuz I really want Isabel to marry me and she is. I know that I want her AND need her. I want her cuz I love her and I want to spend the rest of my life with her. She's the best thing that ever happened to me. She helps me with school, she helps me stay on the right track, and she even loves me back. I guess I need her for all those reasons too. I'm not sure where I'd be today if it weren't for her. Probably in jail.

And I need Jessie in my life too. My dad has been in prison since I was five years old and he's not getting out anytime soon. And I don't know if I want to see him even when he does get out. My mom used to take me to see him when I was little and then it just stopped. I don't know why but I don't care. I don't even know him. So it was really cool when I met Jessie and he gave me a job and kinda took me under his wing. He's taught me the things that a dad is supposed to teach his son, like how to work on cars and how to be a man—things my mom can't really teach me. She's great, but she's just a mom (if you know what I mean, no offense, cuz I know you're a mom too). And now, since I'm gonna marry Isabel, it's like he's going to really be my dad. He helps me in lots of ways, and that's why I need him in my life.

Ray

Anne always looked forward to Ray's letters because they were so full of honesty and hope. She wrote a little note at the end: *I'm so grateful you and Jessie (and Isabel) found each other. I think they are blessed to have you in their life too.*

Maggie popped her head in, carrying a tray. It was beautifully arranged with a peanut butter waffle and some sliced strawberries on a plate, a cup of fragrant tea, and a hand-drawn get-well card.

"Here you go! Waffle, strawberries, and tea."

"Thanks, hon. I don't remember ordering strawberries," she teased.

"You didn't, but they have lots of vitamin C, and since we don't have orange juice, the strawberries will have to do. I want to see this plate clean, young lady," admonished Maggie.

"Yes, ma'am. I'll do my best."

"And don't you even think about grading all day. You need your rest!"

"Aye, aye, Captain," saluted Anne.

"I'm not kidding, Mom. You can't get sick, because that means I'll probably get sick, and I can't get sick because the Winter Snow Ball is next weekend and I already have my dress and it's my first real date with Jake. Now, eat up and get some rest."

As usual, there was more going on than just the sweet concern of a child for her mother. Nevertheless, Anne did the best she could and left only a few bites on the plate.

As she sipped her tea, Anne moved on to the next letter in the pile.

Dear Mrs. English,

Anne recognized the flowery handwriting as Tiffany's.

Wow. This letter really hit home for me because sometimes it's hard for me to tell the difference between my wants and my needs. For example, I didn't really need to be a mom at 17, but part of me wanted to. I was glad and sad all at the same time after my miscarriage. I know it would have made my life really hard, so I'm grateful that I miscarried, but it would have been cool to have a baby. And not because it was David's but because it was half mine. I can't imagine what it must be like to see a little "mini-me" walking around. I hope I get another chance at having a baby when I'm older and can handle it better.

I have another situation in my life now that concerns wants and needs (but please don't tell my father). I'm pretty sure my dad is an alcoholic. He drinks Scotch every night after work and after dinner too. I'm afraid that he drinks too much. He's a great guy when he's sober, but my mom and I are never sure what will happen when he's drunk. Sometimes he passes out and sometimes he gets really mad about stuff. He's never hit me or my mom but he can still be pretty scary. I really want AND need him to quit drinking. Or at least not drink so much. I'm a growing teenager and I need my dad. I've tried talking to my mom about it but she doesn't want to listen. I know everything looks pretty good on the outside. People think I come from such a nice family, that we've got money, and that I'm so lucky, but it's really not like that. I never have friends over because I don't know what he'll do. I have to make up excuses why he can't come to stuff. But it's because I don't tell him (on purpose) or he forgets if Mom tells him. It's been going on for a long time, but it seems to be getting worse. What can I do to make my dad stop drinking?

Tiffany

Anne sighed. Boy, could she relate! She remembered how lost and alone she felt when Charlie was at the height of his addiction, how scared and uncertain her life was. Although Charlie's primary obsession was crack, a friend had suggested Al-Anon, the group for families and friends of alcoholics. Anne hated going to the meetings at first. Slogans like "Live and let live," "How important is it?" and "One day at a time" had made no sense to her. There were steps and suggestions for living with an alcoholic. Anne didn't want to live like *that* with Charlie—she wanted him to quit! They told her to worry about herself, not Charlie. They told her to take care of herself instead of always taking care of Charlie (which they termed "enabling"). Slowly their loving messages sank into Anne's consciousness and she learned how to live with active addiction by setting boundaries and detaching with love instead of anger. She learned how to separate Charlie from his disease (after learning that it *was* a disease). Over a period of several months, Al-Anon saved her life and her sanity. Even after Charlie left, she continued to attend meetings because they helped her in *all* her relationships—with her children, her students, her family, and her friends. Although it was difficult for her to make regular meetings during the school year, she went to one or two a week, coupled with an online "meeting" where a topic was presented and group members shared via email.

Anne took another sip of tea and considered her reply.

Tiffany—I'm so sorry that you are having these issues at home. I know, from experience, how difficult that situation can be. You can find help in Al-Anon and Alateen. They are both groups for families of alcoholics, and they will give you lots of tools to help you cope. Living with an alcoholic can be hard, but it's not impossible. I would encourage you to check out Alateen. Here is a website to get you started: www.al-anon.alateen.org. I hope it helps. Let me know if there's anything I can do for you.

Anne knew that some of her replies to the letters could potentially cross a line if a parent found out and wanted to make it an issue, but she also felt that for some of her students, she had an obligation to help, even if it cost her her job. Some kids needed help and hope, and she felt strongly about providing them, especially when they asked.

Five letters later, she was exhausted. She closed her eyes halfway through the sixth and was asleep within seconds.

Off in the distance, Anne heard a song playing over and over. When she was awake enough to determine that it was her ringtone, it stopped. She rolled over to look at the clock through a half-opened eye. Four o'clock! She had been asleep for five hours. Even though the missed call was from John, which usually stirred up the butterflies in her stomach, Anne groaned, rolled over, and went back to sleep without listening to the message.

A nanosecond later, Maggie knocked quietly on the bedroom door.

"Mom? It's almost eight. Don't you want some dinner?"

"*Eight?* I've slept all day!"

"I'm sure you needed it. How are you feeling? Can I get you anything?"

"Some water would be nice. Is it hot in here to you?"

"Not really." Maggie felt her mother's forehead. "You're burning up! I'm getting the thermometer."

Maggie returned, thermometer in hand and concern on her face.

"Open up, missy," ordered Maggie.

Anne might have enjoyed the role reversal if she hadn't felt so sick, but she could barely sit up.

"OMG, Mom! It's one hundred and three! Okay, no more grading for you! I'm going to make you some tomato soup and get you some aspirin. You just stay put."

"I'm not going anywhere, I promise!"

Anne looked at the blinking light on her phone and took the opportunity to listen to John's message.

"Hey there, little lady. Just wondering how your Saturday was going. It's supposed to warm up a little bit tomorrow. Maybe you and me and Susan and Herb could go for a ride. Well, let me know if you're interested. See ya!"

They had used Susan and Herb as "chaperones" once or twice before. Since Anne didn't think it was appropriate for them to date until after the school year, John had hit on the idea of a sort of double date that consisted of friendly rides with Susan and Herb. It gave him a chance to be with Anne and still honor her request in a way that

Anne found acceptable. But riding tomorrow? It wasn't supposed to get above fifty degrees outside. John's zealous ability to hop on his motorcycle and go for a ride, regardless of the temperature, amazed Anne. She could hear his voice in her head: *"That's why you have leather chaps, gloves, and a jacket—you get to ride toasty warm no matter what!"*

"Not happening," Anne said to herself as she dialed his number.

"Well, hello! I'm glad you called back!"

"Hey, John. I'm not going to be able to make it tomorrow. I'm sick as a dog."

"Oh no! Tell Dr. John all about it."

"Fever, chills, runny nose, body aches, headache… all the fun symptoms!"

"I am sorry to hear that! What can I do for you?"

"Nothing. I'm sleeping most of the time, and Maggie is taking good care of me."

"Are you going to school on Monday?"

"I'll have to see how I feel tomorrow. Hopefully the worst of it will be over by then."

"I know it's twice as much work to get a sub, but you need to take care of yourself."

"I will. Maggie's making me some soup and has banned me from grading. I'll probably just go back to sleep and see how the world looks in the morning."

"Okay. I'll check back with you tomorrow. Hope you feel better!"

"I'm working on it! Thanks!"

"Good night, Anne."

"'Night, John."

Anne slept until noon the following day, but awoke feeling like the storm had passed.

"Hi, Mom!" said Maggie from the living room sofa. "It's good to see you up and around. Feeling better?"

"Much! Thanks for taking such good care of me."

CLASS LETTERS

"Anytime!"

"Where did those come from?" asked Anne, motioning to the vase filled with yellow roses.

"I'm not sure. You must have a secret admirer. I found them on the doorstep when I went to church. I've been dying to know who they're from. I bet it's John."

Anne smelled the roses before opening the card.

"Oh, they're heavenly!"

"Mom," whined Maggie, "open the card!"

"Okay, okay," laughed Anne. She had already recognized the handwriting, so the sender was no mystery, but she was anxious to see what the card said. The outside had a picture of a monkey in a nurse's uniform. The inside said, "Stop monkeying around and get well!" John's handwritten message was simple but enough to start the butterflies swirling: *Take good care of yourself until I can. Love, John*

"Read it!"

"'Stop monkeying around and get well!'"

"No, the part from *him*. The gushy part!"

"There is no gushy part. Just a sweet note. And it's private," said Anne with a wink.

"Hmph," said Maggie. "No fair, but that's okay. I'm just glad you're better! And, Mom, no grading!"

"I am better, but I'm still going to take it easy today. Don't want a relapse! I need to grade, but I promise I'll stop if I need to."

"I'll be watching."

"And I'll be good," answered Anne, kissing Maggie on the forehead.

The letter on the top of the pile was from David, who now attended the alternative school because of his continued harassment of Tiffany. Although he was on a different campus, he was still considered Anne's student.

Mrs. English:

I can see how I got my wants and needs all messed up. I've been seeing a counselor since I've been at the alternative school and he's really helped me see some things better. He says that I take one thing and focus on it and obsess on it because I think I need it in my life, but really, I don't. Like with the steroids. I thought I needed them to be a better football player, so I could live up to my dad's dream of me going All-State. All they did was mess me up. Then I focused on Tiffany. I thought I needed her too, but what I really need to do is focus on me and get myself straight so I can go to college. I won't get a scholarship now so I'm going to start out at the community college and try to get into UT after I get my basics out of the way. I'm getting clearer about what it is that I really do need besides just what I want. I need an education… I just want football. I don't know. It's hard sometimes to figure stuff out but I feel like I'm at least on my way.

It's not too bad being over here. It's quieter and I get out before the rest of the high school since it's self-paced. I miss my friends and being at the real school. I'm getting used to it. And, honestly, I don't know that I need to be here but I guess I don't have a choice. Anyway, I'm glad you're still my teacher. I always liked your class.

Sincerely,

David

The next letter was Keosha's. Anne had heard about Li'l Joe through the grapevine and was afraid for her student. She had followed Keosha's year with great interest. Anne knew Keosha was smart and hoped she was too smart to do something really dumb.

CLASS LETTERS

Dear Ms. E:

I had lots of experience lately with needs and wants. I been having some issues outside of school that have been hard and I have to look at myself and my future.

I was at an apartment where a little boy was shot. No one knew I was there cuz I was in the bathroom. When I came out, I saw Li'l Joe lying in a pool of blood. It scared me bad. I was worried for him but scared for me too. I didn't do it, but I had to go tell the police about it. All I could tell 'em was who was there before I went to the bathroom, and what I heard while I was there. I recognized some voices. I know that telling is the right thing to do but it still scares me. What if they try to hurt me or my mama? I heard that the police rounded all them boys up, so maybe we be okay. But the important thing is that I needed to tell the truth. First my mama made me, but once I got talking about it, I could see that this all needs to stop—the violence, the drugs, all of it. I mean, if someone innocent like Li'l Joe can get hurt, then it could happen to me too, even though I'm not as innocent as he is.

Anyway, the doctors say he gonna be okay, and the police say I'm gonna be okay too so I guess it's all good. Have a good weekend.

Keosha

Anne wrote: *I'm so proud of you!*

And she was.

Chapter 28

Ray paced nervously outside the bathroom door. It seemed like Isabel had been in there for twenty minutes, but only two or three had passed. She had missed her January period and was on the other side of the door, taking a pregnancy test. Thoughts swirled through Ray's head like leaves tossed around in a winter wind. How would he support them? What about school? Where would they live? Should they get married now? He loved Isabel—there was no doubt about that—but the thought of a responsibility like a baby was scary. They were careful, but some babies just need to be born.

The toilet flushed… and the door opened slowly.

"Five minutes," said Isabel, setting the timer on her phone. "Then we'll know for sure."

"Want a soda?" asked Ray, searching for something to do during their wait.

"Sure. Thanks."

The trip to the kitchen and back used up a whopping thirty seconds. Four minutes to go.

"What are we going to do if I am?" asked Isabel slowly.

"Let's see what the test says first."

They glanced at each other, and Isabel quickly looked away. Ray studied her face: the beautiful curve of her neck, her glistening hair, the long lashes that hid her lovely doe eyes. He knew she would be a wonderful mother, but how would he do as a father? Until Jessie had come along, Ray's parental influence had been minimal. With his father in prison, Ray was considered the man of the house but had rarely performed these duties throughout most of his life. He did what he wanted, when he wanted. While his mother worked, he ran the streets and flirted with criminal behavior, generally shoplifting and petty theft. He tried to take care of things at home for his mother and sister, but he simply didn't know how. When Ray began dating Isabel, Jessie sat him down for a long talk about life and responsibilities. Jessie recognized the lost boy inside the young man and provided the insight and direction Ray needed. Once he began working for Jessie, Ray's attitude, work ethic, and focus changed. He found someone to look up to, emulate, and talk to—someone who understood his plight and was willing to guide him.

Some of the lessons were tough and involved hard work on Ray's part. Jessie took pride in his mechanic work and expected the same from Ray. In the beginning, Ray would look for shortcuts when working on a car. Once, a man came in with a slow leak in his tire. Although Jessie had shown him how to properly patch a tire, Ray was running late for a date with Isabel and simply plugged it. But the plug didn't hold, and when the man returned to complain, Jessie realized what Ray had done. Jessie apologized, gave the man a new tire, and took the money out of Ray's paycheck. On payday, Jessie explained why quality work was so important.

"When people come to me to work on their cars, they trust me to do the right thing. My reputation as a mechanic determines my income and the quality of my life. If I don't give them the service they expect—and deserve—they will go somewhere else and I've lost at least one customer, and probably a lot more."

"How can one guy make you lose other customers?" asked Ray.

"They tell everyone I'm a bad mechanic. Word of mouth is my best or worst advertising. If I do a good job, not only will I have them for a customer, but they will recommend me to their friends too. I will not accept crappy work from you, because it's my reputation and integrity on the line. These things didn't mean much to me when I was your age, but, trust me, they are your most precious possessions. Think about it."

Integrity was first and foremost in his mind at the moment. Integrity and a pregnancy test, that is.

"It's time," said Isabel softly.

They held hands and walked into the bathroom together. Before they reached the test, Ray stopped and looked into Isabel's eyes.

"I love you, *mi vida*. I promise to take care of you and stand by you, no matter what happens. You are already my wife in my heart, and nothing would make me happier than to have a child with you, whether it's now or later. I'm here for you, Isa, and nothing will make me leave."

Isabel looked deeply into his eyes for a moment. "I believe you. Are you ready?"

"Yes."

Both of them looked at the stick in her hand and smiled at the sight of a plus sign.

Chapter 29

The winter months were exceptionally frigid this year. Anne's motorcycle stayed in the garage, longing for adventure. Even with all the gear she had acquired, she was not interested in riding—or turning into an icicle.

She was, however, interested in John. Since they spent the majority of their time together either on the phone or riding with Susan and Herb, this winter seemed interminable. Anne found herself looking for excuses to call or stop by the store, but resisted the urge. He occupied more of her thoughts than she had anticipated, and it concerned her. She called her objective confidant to talk over her fears.

"Hey, Karen," she said, trying to sound chipper.

"What's wrong?" Karen sighed.

"Wrong? Nothing's wrong."

"Anne, gimme a break. What is it? School? The kids? John?"

"It's John. Well… it's really more me. I get so confused! I really like him and think about him all the time. And with the weather the way it's been, we haven't been on any rides with Susan and Herb."

"You know, I never did understand that," said Karen. "Seems to me like you two are consenting adults who really don't need a chaperone."

"I know. It sounds dumb, doesn't it?"

"It's dumber than dumb! I *think* you have enough self-control to avoid ripping his clothes off every time you see him, don't you?"

"Of course," laughed Anne. "I guess it seemed like less of a 'date' if they came along. Once the school year is over and Tony is no longer my student, I think it'll be okay to venture out on our own, just the two of us. But, Karen, the closer June gets, the more nervous and confused I become."

"Why? You just mentioned how much you like him. I'd think you'd be thrilled to be able to date him."

"I start thinking about the 'what ifs': What if we really hit it off? What if we fall in love? What if we break up? What if the kids don't like him? What if, what if, what if…"

"What if you just chill and take this thing one day at a time? That's what I'm doing with Lorenzo. There are so many 'what ifs' connected to that relationship, I'd go crazy if I tried to figure them all out."

Dr. Lorenzo Lombardi had arrived at Mercy Hospital and in Karen's life only a few weeks earlier. All the females in the medical complex smiled a little more brightly and swished their hips just a little bit more when he appeared on the scene. He could have modeled for Michelangelo's *David*—especially if *David* had striking blue eyes and dark, wavy hair. But the moment he saw Karen, rushing around with her stethoscope hanging from her neck and her hair frantically positioned in a loose ponytail, no other woman existed for him. He'd tried to charm her, but she was suspicious of his good looks and suave accent. Lorenzo finally persuaded her to go out on New Year's Eve to hear some jazz. Karen became convinced of his sincere attraction, relaxed, and had a great time. They had been an item ever since.

"How is Lorenzo?" asked Anne.

"Wonderful. Amazing. Magnificent."

"I think I get the idea," laughed Anne. "I'm so glad you're happy! It's about time you found someone wonderful who deserves you."

"Tell me about it! And you deserve someone wonderful too. Relax. Don't worry about tomorrow. Enjoy today."

"One day at a time, huh? I guess I can do that. Thanks, Karen. You always know how to talk me down."

CLASS LETTERS

"That's what sisters are for, my dear! And remember, he doesn't have to make all the first moves. Give him a call or stop by the store. You don't need any other excuse except that you wanted to say hi."

"Yeah… maybe… we'll see," sighed Anne.

"Hey, is it five already? Omygosh—Lorenzo is picking me up at six. Gotta fly!"

"Have fun, sis! Love you!"

"Love you too, Anne. See ya!"

Anne stared at her phone for a minute, shrugged her shoulders, and mumbled, "Oh, what the hell!" and dialed.

"Hi gorgeous! Are you keeping warm on this blustery day?" answered John.

"I'm trying! I miss riding, though."

"Lightweight!" he teased. "All you gotta do is gear up, and you're warm as toast."

"There's not enough leather at the rodeo to get me on a bike when it's thirtysomething degrees out!"

John laughed. "You're not alone! Susan and Herb don't go riding unless it's above sixty. I guess it's just crazies like me who are willing to go out when it's cold. No worries! It'll warm up again eventually. How's school?"

"It's good. The kids keep hoping for a snow day."

"They may get it. The weatherman says we've got that norther coming this week."

"Well, you know what they say: only fools and foreigners predict the weather in Texas! Even still, I'll probably go to the grocery store and stock up on staples, just in case," said Anne.

"And firewood! You'll want to have a nice fire going. That's one thing I miss by living in an apartment—a big fire to warm things up. We had a big stone fireplace when I was growing up. My dad and I would go out and find a dead tree to chop up. We always had a great time. We'd spend hours talking about things while we cut up those trees."

"What kinds of things did you talk about?" asked Anne.

"Football, hunting… guy stuff. But he also found ways to teach me about life and love at the same time, without being too mushy. My dad was a true man's man, but he was a real softie underneath." John paused. "He was passionately in love with my mother. Everyone could see it. The way he talked about her, the way he treated her, the way he simply looked at her… I've always wanted a relationship like theirs. I still do."

"I'm sure you will find that, John. You're a great guy. Any woman would be lucky to have you in her life."

"What about you, Anne? Are you feeling lucky?"

"I always feel lucky when I'm talking to you."

"Is it June yet?" John asked.

"Not yet, but it'll get here, I promise."

"It can't get here soon enough for me. Look, Anne, I know that in some ways we hardly know each other. I mean, we haven't even been out on a real date yet. But I also know that there is something very special about you—about us. Something that only comes along once in a lifetime. Do you feel it too, or am I just fooling myself?"

"No, John, I feel it too. It's exciting and scary all at the same time."

"Yes, it is, but it's more exciting than scary. I know you don't want to get hurt again. Me either. But I don't see that happening with us. I think we're going to be okay."

"I think so too," smiled Anne. "I'd better get dinner started. Richard will be reduced to skin and bones if I don't feed him soon."

"We can't have that! I'm glad you called. You know, you can call anytime you want. Day or night. I'm always happy to talk to you."

"Thanks, John. Enjoy your evening."

"It's already wonderful after talking to you. 'Night."

"'Night," sighed Anne.

Chapter 30

Once Kim acknowledged and shared her homosexuality with her family and friends, her entire demeanor changed. Instead of the shy, quiet girl she had been most of her life, she became an outspoken activist for gay rights. The turnaround was obvious and inspiring. She started a blog called *Come Out, Come Out, Wherever You Are*, encouraging other teens to come out of the closet, sharing her experiences, and linking gay teens from all over the world. She already had around one hundred followers. She had learned to ask thought-provoking questions, like Mrs. English's monthly letters did, in order to get kids thinking and talking about themselves and their challenges. When she wasn't blogging, Kim spent her time arranging meetings and activities for the Gay-Straight Alliance, in addition to maintaining its Facebook page. The next big event for the club was the Valentine's dance, which she aptly named Hearts United. A local band agreed to play for free, and the GSA would provide refreshments and decorations. It was a big step for the school, and certainly not without controversy, but Kim and Mrs. English were determined to make it a success.

Kim sat before her computer, sending emails and updating the GSA page for the high school. It seemed like years since she had come out at school and to her parents. Aside from the one attack at school, Kim's life as an uncloseted homosexual had been relatively uneventful. She was grateful for that, but others weren't always as lucky. Her greatest wish was to have others accept *all* students and their relationships, regardless of orientation. To this end, she worked diligently within her club and the community at large.

Anne thought about the dance and Kim's courage as she pondered her February letter. She wanted it to be about love—all kinds of love—but she always walked that fine line, unsure of how far to go. Although it was 2011, Anne knew she still lived and worked in the Bible Belt and that some subjects were still considered taboo. But she also felt that it was an important message—to love others regardless of race, religion, or sexual orientation.

After several attempts, she composed a letter in which she was able to express her thoughts with only a few concessions in its content.

February

Dear Class:

It's that time of year when hearts, flowers, Cupids, and chocolate abound! Everywhere you turn, you see ads and other reminders that February is all about LOVE. Traditionally, the relationship portrayed by the media blitz is between a man and a woman, but there are others that are just as loving and appropriate. I hope this letter will help you see love in another way.

There are many kinds of love. There are romantic relationships, the love of family and friends, love for church or country, or the love of an ideal. The word love itself is used in a variety of ways. I love my children, but I also looooooove chocolate! Obviously not the same kind of love. ;)

Have you thought about what love means to you? I believe that the word itself is overused. I have heard kids in the halls talking about love: they love their teacher or class, they love an outfit someone is wearing, or they make a joke at someone's expense, followed up with "Just kidding—love ya." Or I see comments on social media sites where one student messages another, "We never talk but I love you!" What kind of love is that?

I've heard it said that the opposite of love isn't hate, it's indifference. Love itself, and the use of the word, should be anything but indifferent; however, when it is used in every situation to express every emotion, it loses its meaning and sincerity. Words are powerful, and when we use them haphazardly or without thinking of their meaning, their power can be ignored or misconstrued.

So why do students especially, and people in general, use the word love in so many situations? Is it laziness? Maybe. I suppose it's easier to tell your friend, "I love you" instead of, "I care about you and appreciate our friendship," but isn't that really what you mean?

Words can be powerful manipulators. If you walk into a room set up for a party and say, "Oh, I just love cake!" aren't you really trying to snag a piece? Or when you suck up to your mom or dad (or teacher!), telling them how much you love them, but you really want money or a good grade or to be ungrounded, aren't you using words such as love to get your way?

So we've looked at the language of love. Now let's look at different love relationships. What constitutes a loving relationship? Spouses, and parents and their children, are the earliest love relationships we see. As we mature, we find others we love, such as friends, extended family, and other significant people in our lives. Sometimes others don't understand the feelings we have for our beloved because they may not understand the relationship, but does that mean our feelings aren't valid?

So there are two aspects of love I want you to consider. First, are you true with your words? Do you say what you mean and mean what you say? Do you really love that person, or do you simply appreciate their place in your life? If it's a matter of appreciation, try to express that thought as best you can without simply tossing them a ubiquitous "Love ya!" Don't be lazy with your words. Use them with integrity and truly consider the message you're trying to get across.

Next, I want you to consider the love relationships you see around you. Even if it's a relationship you don't understand or agree with, is their love any less worthy than one you approve of? Don't let judgment or ignorance color how you see others. Live and let live—or, in this case, love and let love!

Think about love, how you express it, and how you view it. Just don't forget the chocolate!

Anne reread the letter, hoping that it expressed what she truly believed. Her greatest love, before her children, sister, and parents, was her love of God, but according to the school board and the First Amendment, she was unable to go into personal detail. And she was probably pushing the envelope with the allusion to those "other" relationships, but she felt it was important to mention. As she made the required number of copies of the letter for all her classes, she hoped they would understand all the messages contained within it.

Chapter 31

Around eleven o'clock, Tiffany heard her father's car pull into the garage and knew what to expect. The pattern had been set for several years now: if Dad didn't come home by six or seven, he would be drunk when he eventually arrived. True to form, she heard him downstairs in the kitchen, bumping into things, opening cabinets, and looking for leftovers. She had learned to ascertain his mood by the sounds he made. If the commotion was minimal, he generally ate something, maybe drank some more, and passed out in front of the TV. If she heard glass breaking and cabinet doors slamming, it could be one of his scary drunks.

"So far, so good," she muttered. Of course, she never knew for sure. Sometimes things set him off and he became very angry. Little things, like dishes in the sink or something out of place in the micromanaged world he ruled.

Tiffany thought about the last letter she had written for Mrs. English. She was still surprised that she had told her family's secret, but she was tired of the lies. When she was young, his drinking wasn't bad. In fact, the Wallace home was a fun place to be. Her parents had dinner parties, barbecues, and pool parties. Tom Wallace was always the life of the party and the center of attention. Everyone loved him, and life was good. But when Tiffany was about ten, his drinking grew out of control. There were no more parties, no more friends over to spend the night, no more laughter. Tiffany remembered asking her mother, "Why is Dad so upset all the time?" Her mother told her that he was fine. Their life was fine, their family was fine, everything was fine. It didn't seem "fine" to Tiffany, but she was too young to understand, and, as children will, she assumed that she was the problem. If she behaved well, or made better grades, or was prettier or more athletic, maybe her dad wouldn't drink so much. She didn't know that alcoholism was a disease and that she wasn't the cause of her father's unhappiness.

Tiffany tracked the muffled noises. The deep *thud* was the refrigerator door, the wooden *thwack* was the cabinet door, the tinkling sound was more ice, and the *clinks* came from the flatware. The TV blared. Why did he always become deaf when he was drunk? She sighed. All was well.

"Tonya!" he roared.

Uh-oh, thought Tiffany.

She heard her mother's feet pad down the hall past her door. She called from the top of the stairs, "Yes, Tom?"

"Get down here!"

"Is there something you need, dear?" called her mother in that syrupy-sweet voice she had when she was afraid.

"Get your ass down here!"

Her mother moved halfway down the stairs. "Yes, dear?"

"Get your goddamned ass down here *now*!"

Tiffany knew what that meant, and it wasn't good. He was mad about something, and yelling at his wife was his coping mechanism. Tiffany was so tired of the fighting, name calling, and yelling, but she was also afraid. Her mother always made excuses for him, called the firm when he was "sick" (with a hangover), and then pretended like everything was, well, "fine."

"Why haven't you paid these goddamn bills?"

"They only came a few days ago, dear. I was going to pay them tomorrow."

CLASS LETTERS

"What's this bill from Kohl's? Three hundred and fifty goddamn dollars?"

"Tiffany needed some new clothes and a dress for the Valentine's dance. They were all on sale."

"She doesn't need any clothes. Have you seen her closet? Take them back."

"But, Tom, she's already worn some of them and they look really cute on her."

"Are you arguing with me?"

"No, dear, of course not, but…"

Tiffany heard her mother scream and she raced to the top of the stairs. She saw her mother lying on the floor, holding her cheek, as her father stood over her. Although he had come close, he never hit her before tonight. She ran downstairs to her mother's side.

She looked at her father in disbelief. "You *hit* her?" she asked.

"I'll hit you too if you don't move."

Tiffany found a courage within her that had been long buried. She stood up to face him.

"You've gone too far this time, Dad. I'm not going to let you hurt her again."

Tom laughed. "And what are you going to do, Little Miss Cheerleader? A cartwheel?"

"Dad, all I'm asking is that you not hurt Mom anymore," she said evenly.

Tom looked from Tiffany to his wife and back to Tiffany. The desperation and determination in Tiffany's eyes, and the fear on Tonya's face, seeped into his booze-soaked brain.

"Fucking cunts. Going to bed," he slurred, and stumbled upstairs.

Tiffany helped her mother off the floor. "C'mon, Mom, let's get some ice on that."

Tonya sat at the kitchen table while Tiffany filled a baggie with ice.

"Why do you put up with it, Mom?"

"It's not his fault; I shouldn't have left that bill lying around. I knew it would make him angry."

"Not his fault? Are you kidding me? He's the one who drinks. He's the one who starts the fights. And tonight, he's the one who hit you."

"I'm sure that was a one-time thing. He's never done it before, and I'm sure it'll never happen again. He'll apologize tomorrow, like he always does."

"What part of that scenario is okay, Mom? He. Hit. You."

"Like I said, it was a one-time thing. Drop it, okay, sweetie?"

"Mom, I need to tell you something."

"What is it, honey?"

"I told Mrs. English that Dad was an alcoholic."

"What? He's not an alcoholic. He just overindulges sometimes."

"*Overindulges?* Is that what you call it?" Tiffany paused, considering her next words. "Mom, Mrs. English told me about Al-Anon. It's a program for families of alcoholics. I checked out their website, and there's a meeting at the Methodist church tomorrow night. Let's go together and see what it's about."

"Tomorrow night? I can't go to any meetings at night. I have to cook dinner for your father."

"Okay, there are some meetings during the day too. Maybe you could go to one of those instead."

"I'm not going to any meetings. How embarrassing! What if I saw someone I know? They'd think your father was an alcoholic. Besides, he'd be very upset if he knew I was doing something like that."

"So it's okay for you to be upset, but not Dad?"

"That's right. I can handle it better than your father. I just don't want to add fuel to the fire, so to speak."

"Mom, that's bullshit!"

"Tiffany! Such language!"

"Oh my God, Mom! Can you hear yourself?"

Her mother became very serious. "Tiffany Renee Wallace, listen to me. Everything is fine. I don't want to hear another word about it. Do you understand?"

"Fine. Whatever. G'night."

Tiffany had never felt so alone in her life.

Chapter 32

Keosha's life centered on police interviews and photo lineups following Li'l Joe's shooting. Her insight and information were invaluable to the narcotics officers. Not only were the officers able to pick up BD and his gang, they also apprehended BD's supplier. They were able to keep Keosha's identity a secret so there would be no retaliation, and Keosha simply played dumb whenever the subject was brought up at school. Her biggest concern was Tamika, who was ready to give birth to BD's baby at any time. She knew that BD wouldn't be a good father to the baby or partner to Tamika, but she felt guilty about her part in his absence. As a result, Keosha touched base with Tamika daily, hoping to help her friend during this time.

"Hey, T. How you doin'?"

"Girl, this baby is ready and so am I! I feel like the Goodyear blimp!" laughed Tamika.

"You look beautiful."

"Damn, girl, you need glasses. I talked to BD's mama last night. Looks like BD's gonna cop a plea and go down for a coupla years. Probably be out in twelve to eighteen months."

"That's not that long, T. You can do it."

"Thing is, Keosha, I'm not sure I want to. I mean, who wants a criminal for a daddy? An' maybe it's not right to do that to the baby. I seen how you been doing things different, and I'm prouda ya. Maybe I can change too. For the baby."

"Tamika, you can do anything you want. BD didn't do nothing but knock you up. He ain't helped in no way during your whole pregnancy. An' remember how he wanted you to do a DNA test to be sure it was his? Personally, I think you're better off without him."

"You know how Granny hates BD? She told me she'd pay for me to go to cosmetology school if I'd keep the baby but get rid of BD. I'm thinkin' 'bout takin' her up on the offer."

"For reals? Ooh, Tamika, you gotta do it! Think about it. You could have a trade, make your own money, build up a clientele… You'd be great at it, too. You been messin' with everybody's hair since you was a kid. Do it, girl!"

"It kinda scares me, Keosha, all of it… bein' a mama, leavin' BD and bein' alone, and tryin' to get ahead in life."

"You're not alone, Tamika. You got me and LaQuandra and your granny. That's enough to get started. Then, once you're working, you'll get lots of new friends that aren't always in trouble and bringing drama into your life. Maybe a boyfriend…"

"Who gonna wanna date me and raise some other dude's baby?"

"Look, Tamika, I don't know all the answers, but I do know that you got some decisions to make. Think about them from your point of view—no one else's, okay?"

"K."

"K. Now, is your life better with BD or without him? All of it, not just the sex or the occasional attention, but all of it."

Tamika pondered for a moment.

"It's better without him. I know I can't trust him, and I know that he don't care 'bout me like I care 'bout him. An' I *know* he don't want no baby."

"Good. You're thinking about what's best for you *and* the baby. Now, with BD outta the way, you can go to school, and you don't even have to pay for it."

"But that's my granny's retirement. I don't wanna take that from her."

"Okay, then how 'bout this? You take the money up front, and when you got a good business going, you can pay her back."

"I hadn't thought of that. That's a good idea. I can get my education and not feel guilty 'bout it all the time. And when Granny's gone, I can support myself and the baby. I don't need no man!" This was an eye-opening concept for Tamika, and her awareness gave her a taste of the freedom she could have.

"You go, girl! That's the spirit. And I'll be there every step of the way, quizzing you 'bout color and cuts."

"My own private tutor?" Tamika laughed.

"Only if you need help, but I bet you won't. You already know a ton about hair, and it comes real natural to you too."

"You know, I'm feelin' better 'bout all this stuff. Thanks, Keosha. I knew I could count on you."

"Anytime, T. I'll always be here for ya. Talk to you soon, k?"

"K. Bye."

Two hours later, Keosha received a text from Tamika: *Baby coming, going to hospital.* Keosha grabbed her purse and headed out to the bus stop. The number 4 went right by the hospital, and it came past her stop every fifteen minutes, so she wouldn't have long to wait.

Tamika was already assigned to a room when Keosha arrived. She peeked her head in to see how her friend was faring.

"Hey, girl. How you doin'?"

"Whew! Once this baby decided to come, it's coming fast. These contractions are badass. It's like someone is... *ooohhhhhhhh!*" Tamika cried out in pain.

"Would you please go to the waiting room? Tamika needs her space," said the nurse.

"No problem. Good luck, T! You can do it." Keosha sat next to Tamika's grandmother to wait for the new arrival. Once again, she didn't have to wait long. Barely an hour had passed when the nurse came to tell Tamika's grandmother that mother and daughter were fine. Seven pounds, three ounces, nineteen inches long.

Keosha said a quick prayer, something she had found herself doing more and more lately. "Thank you, God, that Tamika and the baby are okay. And thanks about the BD thing and the money from her granny. I don't know how you work things all out the way you do, but it's pretty cool." Keosha sat for a minute to reflect on all the grace and goodness in their lives before seeing her friend. She stopped, afraid she had made a mistake, and added a hasty "Amen!"

Chapter 33

Tiffany sat in her car in the parking lot before entering the building. She felt like a traitor but had nowhere else to turn. She witnessed teenagers like her hugging, greeting each other, laughing together in shared camaraderie. How could they be happy? How could they *laugh*? Life was grim for Tiffany, and she couldn't imagine anything different. It was 5:52. The meeting would start in eight minutes. She screwed up her courage, opened the car door, and walked toward the building.

Inside she noticed small posters on the wall with different mottoes: Live and Let Live, One Day at a Time, and Think. Two larger posters had something to do with steps and traditions. A cute redhead greeted her.

"Hi, I'm Nicole. Is this your first time?"

Tiffany nodded.

"That's what I thought. This is a great place. I'm really glad you're here."

"Thanks," said Tiffany quietly.

"The meeting's about to start, but we can talk more afterward if you want."

"K."

The chairperson was a woman in her thirties with smiling eyes and a kind face. She opened a well-worn notebook and began the meeting with the Serenity Prayer.

The hour-long meeting was a blur for Tiffany. They were talking about things she didn't understand, such as boundaries and sponsors. The kids talked and laughed about their lives and trials with an honesty that surprised Tiffany. When it was her turn to speak, she simply said, "I pass," unable to talk about the horrors at home. The meeting ended with everyone holding hands in a circle, reciting the Lord's Prayer.

Nicole turned to Tiffany at the conclusion of the prayer.

"Well, what did you think? Do you have any questions? Duh—everyone has questions! I know it's all pretty confusing at first, but it'll make sense after you've been here for a while."

"I guess," said Tiffany. "I don't get why people are laughing at some of this stuff. It's really not funny."

"Laughter is part of our healing. Usually by the time we get to Alateen, we're not laughing much. In fact, most of us are pretty angry, hurt, and confused. I know I was. I mean, parents are supposed to take care of their children, not spend all their time drinking. It's pretty sick when you think about it. Some of us have it pretty bad, others not so much, but we're all still affected by alcoholism. It's a disease. Did you know that? Even the AMA says so. But knowing that doesn't make things easier at home, does it?"

"Not really," answered Tiffany.

"I get that," said Nicole. "But we learn ways to cope with the drinking, ways to protect ourselves. We can't help the alcoholic unless they want help—and mine never have. Both my parents drink. All day, every day. I thought it was normal. I thought everyone's family was like that. My mom's sister brought me to my first meeting a couple of years ago. She started going to Al-Anon and heard that there was a program for kids. Going to meetings doesn't mean that everything will be okay at home, or that your parents will quit drinking."

"It's just my dad," said Tiffany.

CLASS LETTERS

"It doesn't really matter who it is, just that there's a problem. Anyway, like I was saying, Alateen doesn't fix everything, but the best part is that you learn you're not alone. Other kids have been through what you've been through—or something like it."

"So I can't learn how to make my dad stop drinking? I thought that's what this was for."

"Nope. Sorry. But you will find help—and hope. And you may even laugh again," said Nicole with a wink.

Tiffany's eyes blurred, and she stammered a quick "Thanks. I gotta get home."

Nicole looked into her eyes. "I know it's hard, but it gets better, I promise. Take my number and call anytime, day or night, okay? And come back. It really helps. You'll see."

Tiffany hugged her and whispered, "Thank you. I'll be back. I promise," and walked quickly to her car, hands shoved in her pockets.

Chapter 34

Ray and Isabel sat quietly in the waiting room, holding hands. They had filled out all the paperwork. It would cost $1,000 for approximately eight months of doctor visits, prenatal vitamins, labor and delivery, and postnatal care for Isabel and the baby. It sounded like a lot all at once, but Ray was able to make payment arrangements. Of course, there would be other charges, such as anesthesia if she needed it. That was, if everything went well… Ray felt the familiar punch in his stomach that had begun when he had learned Isabel was pregnant.

He was happy about the baby, and he adored Isabel, but he had grown and changed so much over the past year, and he felt a great weight of responsibility on his shoulders. The "old" Ray would have denied fatherhood and abandoned Isabel and the baby. But the "new" Ray had gained a self-confidence and sense of integrity he hadn't known before. Jessie's tutelage and hard-earned wisdom, along with Isabel's encouragement and belief in his abilities, contributed to Ray's elevated self-esteem. And, surprisingly, Mrs. English's letters made him think about the man he wanted to be. He had never thought he would have a life like this. He was scared, excited, and calm all at the same time. Still, things were moving pretty quickly. He had already moved into Jessie's house, and he and Isabel were getting married in two weeks. Even with all the things that were up in the air, the one thing he knew, the one thing that kept him grounded, was his love for Isabel.

"Isabel Perez?" called the nurse.

"Here I am," said Isabel, grabbing her purse and standing up.

After the preliminary assessments were made—weight, blood pressure, pulse—the doctor came in for the sonogram.

"All right, Miss Isabel, let's take a look."

The doctor pulled back her shirt and squirted gel on Isabel's belly. Isabel flinched.

"It's cold. Sorry! Okay… let's see what's going on here," she said as she moved the probe over Isabel's belly.

"There's the heart. See it beating?"

Ray and Isabel looked at the shape on the screen in amazement. This was something they had created out of their love for each other. It was love at first sight.

"Wait a minute," Dr. Rios said.

"Is everything all right?" asked Ray.

"Yes, everything's fine. I just want to confirm… yes, there it is… a second heart!"

"Our baby has two hearts?" asked Isabel.

"No, Isabel, you're having twins!"

"Twins?" asked Isabel.

"Twins?" Ray repeated.

"Twins. And, since you're about eleven weeks along, I'd say they will arrive in early August."

Ray and Isabel looked at each other, incredulous, and smiled. As if on cue, they both said "Twins" and laughed.

Chapter 35

The Hearts United dance was only days away, and Anne was busier than ever. The February letters were due, as were the essays on the novel they were reading, so most of her "spare" time was spent grading. And she was staying later at school to help Kim and the rest of the GSA prepare for the dance. They were painting posters, verifying assignments, and polishing last-minute details in her classroom after school. This was the first dance of its kind at the high school, and they all felt the same unspoken pressure to make sure it went off without a hitch.

"Aaron, you, Becky, James, and Owen are responsible for decorations. You'll need to start by five at the latest if it's going to be done by seven. Do you have enough help?" asked Kim.

"Yeah, we've got another five or six kids coming to help," answered Aaron.

"Great. Uh… Sally. You and Angela are in charge of refreshments. How's that going?"

"It's going well," said Sally. "I've got five people bringing three dozen cookies each, and another five making punch. We'll get the serving trays and punch bowl from the cafeteria and be all set up by six. Oh! Trey and Jordan are bringing plates, cups, and napkins. We should be all set."

"Cool," said Kim. "Last but not least, Tony, is your band ready to rock?"

"Absolutely!" said Tony. "We'll begin setting up around four thirty, do our sound checks, and grab a bite to eat before we play."

"Just be sure that we have music going at seven o'clock sharp!"

"Will do!"

"Listen, guys," said Kim, "I really appreciate all the hard work you've put into this dance. I think it's going to be so much fun! Your last challenge is to get all your friends to come. Bribe them, threaten them, do whatever you have to do to get them there. It's important that we have a good turnout. Thanks again for everything! See you tomorrow."

Anne gathered up her satchel and purse and prepared to go. "Great job organizing this dance, Kim. I think it's going to be a hit."

"I hope so! I wanted to thank you too, Mrs. English."

"What for, Kim?"

"Everything! Your letters, sponsoring the club, and just generally being so supportive."

"My letters?"

"Yeah, it was the October letter—the one about masks—that started me thinking about me and how I lived my life, afraid to show anyone who I really was. Then I came out to you in December, and you didn't even flinch. You gave me the courage to be me. You changed my life, Mrs. English."

"Oh, Kim, honey," said Anne, tearing up, "you always had that courage within you. I'm glad something I said helped bring it out."

Kim gave her a quick hug. "You're awesome. See you tomorrow!"

"Bye," said Anne, wiping her eyes. "Such a sweet girl. I'm so glad she's happy. Thank you, God!"

Just then, her phone rang.

"Will this day ever end?" she sighed. Her face brightened when she read the caller ID.

"Hi, John!"

CLASS LETTERS

"Hey there. I wanted to run something by you."

"Shoot."

"Well, I guess you know that Tony is playing at the dance Friday night. I haven't seen the band play in quite a while, and I was wondering if it would be okay for me to come to the dance. I can help out too—make sure the punch isn't spiked, run kids out of the broom closet, that sort of thing."

"What a great idea! We can always use an extra pair of eyes."

"And, luckily for me, I know that there's a cute little English teacher who'll be there too. Maybe I could get her to dance with me," hinted John.

"Hmm... maybe. We'll see. In any case, it'll be wonderful to have you there. And I'm sure Tony will be happy to see you there too."

"I've always tried to watch him, and participate if possible, whether it was sports or music. He's great at both. I just wonder who he'll turn out to be."

"He'll turn out to be a good man, like his dad," said Anne.

John paused, embarrassed at the compliment—or maybe it was the butterflies he felt.

"Thanks," he said quietly. "Well, great!" he perked up. "I'll see you Friday at seven!"

Anne was excited at the prospect of seeing John in the flesh and one-on-one... surrounded by about a hundred teenagers. She mentally ran through her closet, choosing and discarding one outfit after another. "Maybe I can squeeze in a quick shopping trip before Friday," sighed Anne.

She returned home to find the usual chaos. Richard's shoes were closest to the front door, then his backpack, and then, last, his jacket. He was sprawled out on the couch with an empty soda can and a package of cookies, only the last two remaining. His favorite video game blared from the TV, and he was oblivious to Anne's entrance.

"Hi, Richard," said Anne.

No answer.

"Hello, Richard, dear son of mine," said Anne, louder this time.

Richard grunted, "Hmphmf."

"Hello, Mother dear," said Anne.

"Hello, Mother dear," Richard mumbled.

Maggie was in her room, door closed, music loud enough to compete with the game.

"Richard, turn that down to a dull roar, please," asked Anne.

"Only if Maggie turns hers down. Otherwise I can't hear," complained Richard.

"Maggie, turn down the music, please," said Anne, knocking on her door.

Once things were quieter, Anne began to read her students' responses while she prepared dinner. The first one was from Keosha.

Dear Mrs. English,

Well, it's been a busy time for me. I was there when Li'l Joe was shot and I know who did it. Well, I don't know exactly who did it but I know who was there. I've talked to the police a bunch and now all those guys are going away, for a little while anyway. No one knows it was me, so it's gotta stay between you and me. It's been hard, especially since Tamika's my best friend. Did you know she had her baby? It was a girl and she named her Takeesha—kind of a mix of our two names. Cool, huh? But I feel kind of guilty since I was the one who told the police all about BD. I know he got into the business all on his own—and I participated too—but he still did a lot of harm all by himself.

I guess I should get on to the subject. Once again, Mrs. English, you are making me think about stuff.

I think you're right. People say "I love you" too much and too easily. Guys say it to get a girl in bed, girls say it to guys so they'll take them out and buy them things, maybe even get them pregnant. Believe it or not, some girls get pregnant on purpose so they can get the guy. Crazy, huh?

Anyways, I tried your suggestion the other day. Instead of telling Tamika that I loved her (in a definitely non-lesbian way! LOL), I told her that I thought she was a great mom. She was surprised that I told her that, but I think she liked it better too. I'm gonna try it with other people too, like my mom, and see how many ways I can say "I love you" without actually saying it.

And for you, I think you're a great teacher because you make me think and look at things in a new way. You know what that means, right? ;)

Anne was surprised at the final comment, and pleased with Keosha's progress. Her grades had returned to A's and B's, and truancy was no longer a problem. She had even had a brighter smile and a lighter step over the past few weeks. It was gratifying to see the positive changes in someone with so much potential.

Chapter 36

Anne hurried home after school on Friday for a quick break and a change of clothes. There was never a spare moment for shopping, so she resorted to her old standby: jeans and a sweater. She flipped through the mail—bills and solicitations—trying to act nonchalant while her insides did flip-flops at the thought of seeing John in a couple of hours. After fluffing her hair and adjusting her makeup, Anne zipped back to the school to help with the setup for the dance.

When she arrived, there were a dozen or so teenagers in the cafeteria, arranging balloons and streamers, setting up tables and chairs, and organizing refreshments. A couple of the kids were in theater and had borrowed stage lights, a disco ball, and strobes. Pairs of hearts hung from the ceiling, promoting the theme of the dance. There was a buzz of excitement in the air, with Kim in the middle, shouting directions and praise.

"You are all doing a great job! This looks fantastic! James, a little higher on the left, please. Sally, the food looks wonderful! Looks like we'll have plenty. I'm so excited—I can't wait to see how this all turns out. Yay! The band is here!"

Tony and the rest of his crew walked in, lugging gear. Bringing up the rear, rolling a box full of equipment, was John. Anne's heart skipped a beat. As soon as he deposited the equipment, his eyes searched for Anne. He spotted her and strolled over.

"Hey! Everything looks great!" he said.

"Thanks. The kids have worked really hard. I know Tony is excited about you being here."

"Yeah, it's been a while since I saw him play. You look very pretty tonight."

"Well, thank you!" Anne blushed.

John leaned over and said, "I know it's not really a date, but I'm going to pretend like it's one. May I get you something to drink?"

"I would love a diet soda. There's a machine in the teachers' lounge."

"It would be my pleasure. Be right back."

"Thanks, John," said Anne as she watched him walk away. "I like the view!"

After John delivered her drink, it wasn't long before both of them were helping with various projects: filling the punch bowl, stringing red and white twinkle lights, and setting up band equipment. As they worked, they would look surreptitiously for the other, smile, and look away, but neither one caught the other's glances.

"Ooh, look, Angela," said Kim. "Mrs. English keeps checking out Tony's dad. Isn't that cute?"

"He's checking her out too. I saw him."

"Maybe they'll fall in love. She deserves someone nice," added Sally.

"And Tony's a nice guy; I bet his dad is too. Doesn't he fix motorcycles or something?" asked Angela.

"Yeah, he's got a shop or something. And Mrs. English rides. They'd be perfect for each other!" said Sally. "I have an idea. Hey, Tony! C'mere!"

Tony looked up when he heard his name and trotted over at Sally's request.

"What's up?" he asked.

"We were thinking that your dad and Mrs. English would make a cute couple. What do you think?" Sally's eyes shined at the prospect.

"They're already practically dating. They go on rides together, talk on the phone, email…" said Tony.

"Well, what do you think about it?" asked Angela. "Are you okay with it?"

"Yeah, she's great and he seems really happy. He talks about her all the time, whistles when no one's around, stuff like that. I don't know why they don't just date. I don't think they've ever, like, been out to dinner or a movie."

"Maybe your dad thinks you don't approve or something," offered Sally. "After my parents split up and my mom wanted to date again, she was scared to because she didn't think I'd want her to. But I wanted her to be happy again. My dad was an asshole, and she deserved better. It sounds dumb, but once I gave her my 'permission' to date, she met Matt and has been really happy ever since. Maybe you should talk to your dad, Tony. Tell him it's okay."

"Maybe. Hey, I gotta get back. I'm sure my dad's got this all figured out," he laughed.

Nothing could be further from the truth. John felt like he was back in high school—metaphorically as well as literally. He felt gawky and tongue-tied. He was trying to think of an amusing story he could share from his week at the shop, but it had just been a regular week. He tried to recall some interesting news item he could mention, but he had been too busy to read much. He racked his brain for something—anything—to talk to Anne about, but his mind was blank. For a moment he wanted to go home, run away, so that he wouldn't make a fool out of himself in front of the woman he loved. He chuckled at his adolescent anxiety and thought, *If she's the right one, it won't matter, and if it does, she ain't the right one.*

But his fears were dashed as soon as the dance started. Anne motioned for him to join her at the punch bowl. She leaned over to him and said with a wink, "Make sure no one spikes the punch. We don't want any lovebirds going crazy in a broom closet."

Throughout the dance, John and Anne chatted like old friends about their own high school days and other pleasant memories, and shared reading and travel recommendations. Time flew by as they laughed together; soon, Tony announced the last dance.

"We want to thank you for coming out tonight. I think the first Hearts United dance has been a big success. Let's give Kim Le a round of applause for heading this up."

Kim basked in the cheers and applause.

"And how about a round of applause for the GSA sponsor, Mrs. English?"

Anne waved and gave Kim a thumbs-up.

"All right, everybody, this is the last dance, so grab a partner! And since it's a Valentine's dance, we're making it a slow one," said Tony.

John turned to Anne and offered his hand. "How about it?"

Anne blushed. "I'd love to."

John took her hand and led her to the dance floor. He pulled her close and put his hand on her waist. He could smell her intoxicating perfume. Wisps of hair brushed his cheek as he closed his eyes.

Anne had dreamed of being this close to John. His hand was warm on her waist, and he held her hand confidently yet gently. She could see how his hair flipped up in soft curls around his neck and ear. She inhaled his manly fragrance, drinking in as much as she could so she could remember it later. She was falling in love, no doubt about it. She had thought the idea would frighten her, but she felt oddly calm and at peace.

Both were disappointed when the song ended, but were grateful for the brief opportunity to stand close together.

"Thanks so much for coming and helping," said Anne.

"It was my pleasure. Speaking of which, I better help Tony break everything down."

"Yeah, I need to help clean up. At least it doesn't take as long to clean up as it does to set up!"

"That's true. Well, I'll talk to you soon. I really had a good time tonight," said John, wanting to stay.

"Me too. I'd better get to work."

"Yeah, I know. Me too. I just don't want this to end," said John.

Anne looked into his dreamy green eyes. "It won't." She smiled, squeezed his hand, and walked off to help take down streamers.

"Man, I love that woman!" John said as he watched her walk away.

Chapter 37

The dance was a huge success. The club made about $200, but more importantly there was a good turnout and everyone got along. Kim and Anne couldn't have been more pleased. They had a wrap-up meeting with the other committee members after school on Monday. Kim led the meeting.

"I'm so proud of all of you for the hard work you put in for this dance. I had a great time and hope you did too. We made about $200, so we can add that to our treasury. I want to talk about anything you liked or didn't like or think we should do differently next year."

"I really liked the disco ball and twinkle lights, but I think the strobes were too much," said Sally.

"I think we needed more food," said James. "And other stuff besides cookies, like chips and dip. I got really hungry!"

"You're always hungry!" said Becky.

"I'm a teenage guy. We're supposed to be hungry. It's part of the job description," laughed James.

"I can vouch for that," said Anne. "My son inhales food the minute I get it home from the store. It absolutely amazes me. And he's as skinny as a rail!"

Tony walked in late. "Did I miss anything?"

"We're talking about how you guys can pack it away," answered Sally.

"Yeah, I'll pretty much eat anything that doesn't eat me first," said Tony.

"Great job with the music, Tony! You guys got everyone up and dancing right away, and they stayed on the floor all night," said Kim.

"Thank you, thank you ver' much," said Tony, doing his best Elvis imitation.

"Mrs. English," teased Sally, "I saw you and Tony's dad dancing. What's the story there?"

"No story, just friends," smiled Anne.

"That's not what Tony says. He says his dad talks about you all the time, and that y'all go on motorcycle rides together and talk on the phone. Sounds like you're dating to me," Sally continued.

"*Dating*? No, we're not dating!" exclaimed Anne, fearful that they had become too obvious.

"It's okay, Mrs. English. I don't care if you date my dad," said Tony. "In fact, he's been really happy since he met you. He talks about you all the time."

"Really?" asked Anne, trying to hide her excitement.

"Oh, yeah. I think y'all should just go out. I told my dad the same thing last night."

"Okay, well, enough about my love life! Let's finish this meeting so we can go home!"

Later that night, while rinsing the dinner dishes, Anne smiled as she recalled Tony's words: *He's been really happy since he met you. He talks about you all the time.*

She was jolted out of her memory by a familiar ringtone.

"Hi, John!" she smiled.

"And hello to you, Twinkle Toes!"

"Twinkle Toes? Where did that come from?" she asked.

"We lit up the dance floor, don't you think? At least, according to Tony we did."

"Oh, my! Yes, the kids were talking about it this afternoon at our meeting. I'm so sorry!"

"What for? I had a great time!" he said.

"I just hate that I made you the topic of conversation at the high school."

"I believe there were *two* of us dancing, so I don't think *you* did anything at all. Besides, I thoroughly enjoyed myself."

"So did I," said Anne. She felt her blush would travel along the phone lines to John.

"It seems to me that the cat is out of the bag," began John.

"So it would appear," said Anne.

"On top of that, Tony not only gave me permission to date you, but encouraged it. Something about how happy I've been lately," said John, pretending to brush it off.

"You've been happy lately?" asked Anne coyly.

"Silly woman, surely you know how I feel. I don't think I've been all that good at hiding it."

"No, not really," agreed Anne.

"So let's just do it. Let's go on a real date. Before June. Like, Saturday night."

Anne hesitated long enough to make him nervous. There wasn't anything in the Teacher Code of Conduct about parents and teachers, but she didn't want to create any unnecessary hardships for Tony or herself. On the other hand, their attraction for each other certainly wasn't a secret anymore. And apparently Tony was all right with it. She knew Maggie and Richard would approve. Maggie had practically forced her to call him, just to talk. Not a hard sell, admittedly, and it eliminated any remaining fears Anne might have had about her children's feelings.

"Okay, Saturday it is."

"Really? You'll really go out with me?"

"Yes, John, I will," Anne laughed. The excitement in his voice thrilled and amazed her.

"Great! How about I pick you up at seven?"

"Sounds good. See you then!"

As if coordinated by Venus herself, immediately after John and Anne ended the call, they both punched a fist in the air and shouted, "Yes!"

Anne's fingers could not find Karen's number fast enough.

"Ohmygod, John and I are going out on a real date Saturday night!"

"What? That's awesome! But I thought you were going to wait until June," said Karen.

"We were, but we hung out at the dance, and the kids were talking about us after school, and Tony approves, and you know Maggie and Richard are fine with it."

"They're beyond 'fine'!" laughed Karen.

"So, since the cat's out of the bag anyway, we're going out. On Saturday. Now, how can I lose thirty pounds by then?"

"Anne, you're beautiful. Stop that! Listen, let's go shopping and pick out something new for you to wear. My treat," suggested Karen.

"You don't have to do that. I can buy clothes… as long as we go to the thrift store. I find great stuff there."

"No thrift store! Something new and pretty and feminine. I insist!"

"All right, we'll go shopping. What's good for you?"

"Probably Thursday, if that's okay. We can hit the mall about six, snag some dinner, and find a fabulous dress for you, and some killer shoes!"

"Not shoes too! I have plenty of shoes," Anne protested.

"Dammit, Anne! I make twice as much as you, and I have no kids and a very generous boyfriend. We are going to find you a sexy, glamorous ensemble, head to toe, no arguments. And I'm giving you cash for a cut and blow-dry, and a mani-pedi, on Saturday so you can get some pampering before your date. Period. End of discussion."

"Yes, ma'am." Anne's heart swelled with love for her sister. "Thank you, Karen."

"You deserve it. You always put yourself last. So, even if it's for one night, I'm going to make sure you put yourself first. Thursday at six. I'll pick you up. Love ya!"

CLASS LETTERS

"Love you too!"

Anne busied herself with grading, hoping the week would pass quickly. All of the February responses were in, and she had about seventy-five to go. As usual, she recognized Tiffany's handwriting immediately.

Dear Mrs. English:

Wow! It's like you're reading my mind or something. LOL! This letter really hit home this time and I've done a lot of thinking about it.

I'm pretty confused about love these days. You know my history with David, so that's one part of love that's weird to me. After all the lies, and the abuse, and, of course, the baby, I know better about what love isn't. It isn't about hurting the one you supposedly love. And it isn't about abandoning them either. It's about being kind and supportive.

I also know from my dad what love isn't. It isn't drinking all the time and getting angry about stuff that doesn't matter. It isn't about yelling at my mom until she's so scared she doesn't know what to do. She says she loves him and that he loves her but it doesn't look like love to me. I know he's not acting like it when he yells and she doesn't either when she lets it slide. She thinks she's helping him and us by not confronting him, but I think she's wrong. I'm trying to help her see what he's really doing to our family, but I don't think she wants help. She always makes excuses for my dad's drinking, like it's no big deal. But I started going to Alateen and it IS a big deal. I've only been to a couple of meetings but I really like it. It's kinda confusing too because they laugh at stuff that doesn't seem real funny but they also listen and support each other. Even though I haven't been going long, I feel like I belong. They all told me to come back and that they understood. To me, that's more what love is supposed to be like.

I really hope that one day I'll find true love out there. Right now, I'm just trying to learn how to love me.

Love,

Tiffany

Anne's eyes got misty. She felt sad that Tiffany and her family were dealing with addiction, but she was so proud of Tiffany for taking that all-important first step of attending an Alateen meeting. Anne understood through experience that, just as the disease of alcoholism and codependence was a family problem, getting into recovery would be a family solution, even if it started with just Tiffany. If she continued to attend meetings, her thinking and behavior would change, and these changes would spill over to the rest of the family. It might take months or even years, but change was possible. Anne added a note to the grade: *I am so very proud of you. Keep going to Alateen. I really think it will help. Let me know if I can help in any way.*

The next letter in the stack was from Ray. Anne had watched Ray and Isabel whispering happily together recently and wondered what was behind it. She hoped the answer would be in his letter.

Miss—

It seems like I've been getting big lessons on love lately. You know that Isabel and me are engaged. We're moving the wedding up because she's pregnant. It's twins! We're getting married on Saturday and I hope you'll come. I moved in with Isa and Jessie last weekend. To me, that's what love is all about. Family. I know you may be disappointed that we are already pregnant, but believe me when I say that we're really happy about it. I know we're young but we love each other and can handle anything together. I'm going to try my best to be a good husband and father. I know I already love the babies, so I guess that's a good start.

CLASS LETTERS

The wedding is at five at St. Mary's Catholic Church and cake after. Just family and a few friends, but I'd like you to come.

Ray

Anne wrote: *Congratulations! I'd be honored to attend. May I bring a guest?*

David's letter appeared behind Ray's. As usual, it contained a reference to football.

Dear Mrs. English:

I love football like you love chocolate! LOL! Like I talked about in my last letter, I get things like wants and needs and love all messed up. It all goes too far. But I'm working on it. That's all I have to say.

David

"Hmm... mighty succinct, Mr. Spears. Makes me wonder if something's going on with you," Anne muttered.

She was able to knock out the majority of the papers by 11:00 p.m., but her eyes became too drowsy to continue. At least if she was this tired, she might be able to sleep instead of thinking about Saturday night. Once she got the okay from Ray, she would ask John if he'd like to have their first date be a wedding. The combination made her giggle.

Chapter 38

The week passed slowly for Anne, but it was a quick one by school standards. There were some minor adjustments to the schedule, such as ordering graduation caps and gowns and invitations, in addition to a monthly faculty meeting. On Thursday, Karen and Anne shopped as planned. They went to several stores, ranging from the ones for twentysomethings to high-end designer boutiques. Karen pushed for something slinky and sexy, while Anne leaned toward a more conservative look. Finally, Anne found a beautiful long-sleeved burgundy knit dress that hugged her curves in just the right way. They added a pair of black heels, a little black clutch, and a lovely, chunky necklace-and-earring set that matched perfectly. Anne was ready!

John had no qualms about going to the wedding before their date. He simply looked at it as an additional ninety minutes he would be able to spend with Anne. He arrived promptly at four thirty, carrying a large bouquet of her favorite lilies.

"Oh my goodness! They're gorgeous!" exclaimed Anne as she greeted him at the door.

"Wow. Not nearly as gorgeous as you," said John. He looked her over in wonder and appreciation. He always thought she was pretty, but the hip-hugging dress and heels caused him to regard her in an entirely different light. Her soft, glowing beauty and feminine curves affected him in ways he hadn't felt in years.

"Thank you," Anne blushed. She was unaccustomed to receiving such sincere compliments and longing looks.

"Wow," he repeated. "Sorry, but you've got me all tongue-tied."

"And you look very handsome, I must say." She had never seen John in a suit, but he wore one very well.

"I'm about to gag, Mom," called Richard from the living room.

"Richard! Don't say that. It's sweet," cooed Maggie.

"Okay, time to go!" Anne handed the flowers to Maggie. "Put these in water, please. I'll arrange them later, but I don't want them to get all wilted."

"No problem, Mom! Have fun! I'll try not to kill the squirt."

"Not if I kill you first!" yelled Richard.

Anne grabbed John's arm and said, "Let's get while the gettin's good!"

"I'm all for that," he laughed.

The evening passed quickly for both of them. Ray and Isabel had a sweet ceremony and looked very happy. Ray grinned when he saw Anne enter the chapel and nodded at her, grateful for her presence and support. Anne and John stayed through the cutting of the cake and were about to leave for dinner.

"Wait, Mrs. English!" called Isabel. "I'm about to throw the bouquet!"

Anne laughed. "That's for girls, not an old lady like me!"

"It's for single females," Ray corrected her.

"I certainly fit in *that* category!" she sighed. "All right, Mrs. Martinez, toss that bouquet!"

Anne lined up with the other two "single females" and waited for the big moment.

"One… two… three!" called Isabel, lobbing the flowers over her head.

In spite of all her efforts, Anne couldn't help but catch the bouquet. It was as if Venus once again stepped in to spur her and John's budding relationship along. The bouquet flew about five feet in the air, away from Anne, then hooked to the left into her waiting hands. She held it up victoriously while everyone clapped. She hugged the bride and groom and ventured off to dinner—and her first date—with John.

John had selected a small, quiet Italian restaurant for their dinner. Grapevines hung from the ceiling, wax-covered Orvieto wine bottles served as candleholders on each table, and Italian opera played unobtrusively in the background. They were tucked into a booth in a dark corner. The waiter approached them for drink orders.

"Good evening. I am Mario, and I will be your waiter this evening. May I get you something from the bar?"

"Would you like to share a bottle of wine?" John asked Anne.

"That sounds great."

"Red or white?" asked Mario.

"White, please. A Chablis would be nice," suggested John.

"Yes, sir." Mario scurried away to retrieve the wine.

A basket of warm, garlicky rolls appeared on the table, courtesy of a passing busboy. Anne placed the wedding bouquet on the table.

"Now we have candlelight *and* flowers!"

John lifted the basket of rolls. "Would you like one?"

"Yes, please," said Anne, choosing a small one.

They each buttered a roll and nibbled for a minute in that awkward silence that permeates many first dates.

"The wedding was nice, don't you think?" asked Anne.

"Yes, it was. Ray and Isabel looked very happy."

Mario arrived with the wine. He uncorked it and poured a taste for John's approval.

"That's fine, thank you," agreed John, and Mario filled the wineglasses and took their food orders.

"Do you know what you want?" John asked Anne.

"The pasta with grilled vegetables sounds wonderful. I'll have that."

"Pasta with grilled vegetables for the lady, and I'll have the spaghetti with meatballs. Thank you."

"This is a cute place. Have you been here before?" asked Anne.

"Just once with Tony a few months ago. He was itching for some lasagna, and it's not one of my specialties. I tend to prefer these little hole-in-the-wall restaurants over the big chains."

"I agree. You usually get better food and atmosphere." Anne studied the flowers for a moment. "I hope Maggie put your flowers in water. They won't last more than a couple of days if she didn't."

"I bet she did. She's a great girl. I noticed her walking cast is off now. Has her leg healed?"

"Yes, thankfully. She needs to exercise it to get her strength back, but other than that, she's just fine."

They each took a sip of wine and nibbled on bread for a moment longer.

John broke the silence. "Why is it that I can talk to you so easily on the phone but I'm all tongue-tied sitting right here in front of you?"

Anne laughed. "I don't know, but I'm having the same trouble."

"Okay. How about this?" John picked up his cell phone and put it to his ear. "Ring, ring."

Anne placed her phone next to her ear.

"Hello?"

"Hello, Anne, this is John."

"Well, hello, John. And how are you this evening?"

"I'm great. I'm sitting in a romantic Italian restaurant with a beautiful woman, sipping wine."

"That sounds nice. Are you having fun?"

"Oh, yes! It's just a little weird because it's our first date and I'm so dazzled by her, I'm speechless. I'm afraid she's going to think I'm a boring guy and never want to see me again. Do you have any advice for me?"

"Hmm… I had a similar problem very recently myself. I finally got to go out with this really great guy and was tongue-tied. I took a deep breath and decided to be myself, and that if he was the right one, it wouldn't matter. I was still nervous, but it helped."

"Good advice. I think I'll try it. Thanks! I'll call again soon!" John ended the make-believe phone call, and they both laughed at their silly antics.

"I really didn't think I'd be this nervous," John confided. "But then you opened the door, and you looked so amazing, and I was so blown away by the fact that we were really going on a date, and… well, it all threw me for a loop!"

"I completely understand. I bet we'll manage to muddle through."

John was especially fond of hearing the word *we* come out of Anne's mouth. "Yes, I believe we will."

Mario arrived with their dinner shortly thereafter, and they chatted happily throughout the rest of the evening, completely at ease.

After a three-hour dinner, they returned to Anne's home, and John walked her slowly to the door.

"I had a wonderful time tonight," said Anne. "Thank you for dinner—and for going to the wedding. I know it was sort of last-minute, but I appreciate your flexibility and willingness to attend."

"It was my pleasure. I hope they have a long, happy life together."

"I hope so too! But, oh my goodness, they're so young, and then there are the twins, and…"

John scooped Anne into his arms, pulling her close.

"And the twins…" Anne tried to continue to the conversation but was overcome by his nearness.

"Shut up and kiss me," smiled John. He put his hand on the side of her face and looked into her eyes as he came nearer. Once their lips touched, he closed his eyes and was catapulted into a different dimension. He had kissed a few women in his life, but none had kissed him with the tenderness and caring that Anne did.

"Wow. Let's do that again!" said John, holding her tightly. He was experiencing feelings that, long dead, had been awakened by her sweet kisses, and he was overwhelmed with desire.

"It's late. I'd better go in," said Anne, reluctant to leave his warm embrace.

"I guess you're right. I hope we can go out again soon."

"Absolutely! I think we'd have some people upset with us if we *didn't*!" Anne laughed. "Good night." She opened the front door.

"'Night," said John. He watched her until the door was almost closed. "Wait!"

"What is it?" she asked.

He cupped her face in his hands and kissed her again. "I just had to do that one more time."

Anne smiled. "'Night," she said, as she disappeared behind the door.

Anne walked through the living room, reliving the kisses.

"Hey, Mom. Have a good time?" asked Maggie.

Anne walked into the kitchen and filled a glass with juice.

"Have a good time, Mom?" Maggie asked again.

Anne stood at the counter near the kitchen sink, looking off into the distance.

"*Mom!*"

"Hi, Maggie. It's really not necessary to yell."

"Wanna bet?" Maggie laughed. "I tried to get your attention, like, fifteen times, and you're off in some kind of la-la land. I'm guessing that means you had a good time."

"Yes, honey, I sure did. Time for bed. See you tomorrow!"

Maggie smiled as Anne practically floated into the bedroom.

Chapter 39

When Anne arrived at school Monday morning there was a note on the front door directing all faculty and staff to go to the library for a meeting. Anne stopped by her room briefly to drop off her things and walked quickly to the library. Mr. Wallace, the chemistry teacher, called to her from the stairs as she passed.

"Hey, Anne!"

"Hi, Herb. Do you have any idea what this meeting is about?"

"I was about to ask you the same thing. I guess we'll find out when we get there."

As they walked in, teachers were talking in hushed tones, huddled together in small groups, some dabbing their eyes with tissue.

"C'mon in and find a seat, folks. I know your time is valuable," said Mr. Henderson, the principal. He paused while everyone found a seat; then he continued.

"I have some sad news to report. One of our seniors, David Spears, was involved in a fatal accident last night. Apparently, he was driving down the highway at great speed and crashed into an abutment. His parents found a note later, after they were notified of the accident. Although David is—was—assigned to the alternative school, he spent most of his high school career here. He was involved in football, basketball, and track. In spite of all our efforts, he seemed to have lost his way a bit in the past few months, and I'm sure you will join me in sending his family our deepest condolences. Funeral arrangements are pending. Our counselors will be available for any faculty or students who are distraught over his passing. I'm sorry to begin your morning with such tragic news. Thank you for your time. You may go to class."

Anne sat in stunned silence while her colleagues jostled around her toward their classrooms. David was gone? *Suicide?* He had certainly had a rough year, but she had never anticipated this. Her mind whirled. What could she have done differently? She had felt something was wrong after his last letter. Should she have said something? Notified someone? She shook her head. It was always dreadful when a student died, but suicide was heartbreaking. It was a permanent solution to a temporary problem—a solution that was really no solution at all. She felt anger, compassion, and grief simultaneously. She plodded back to her room. She knew this would affect her students, and tried to concoct a plan that would help them cope while busying their minds.

As she approached her class, she found Tiffany sitting on the floor in the hall. She looked up at Anne with a red nose and tearstained cheeks. She stood up to hug Anne.

"Isn't it awful? I just can't believe he's gone."

"Yes, it is awful. I'm so sorry," said Anne, handing her a tissue and helping her into a desk. "Is there anything I can do for you?"

"Bring him back?" asked Tiffany. "I mean, I didn't want to be with him as a boyfriend anymore, but I've known David since kindergarten! He can't be gone. He just can't!" Tiffany broke into sobs.

"Oh, honey. I wish there was something I could do. Are you sure you need to be at school today?"

"I wanted to stay home, but my dad wouldn't let me."

"Maybe it's good to have the distraction."

"I guess. Can I just stay in your room today?"

"My room? All day? No, honey, you need to go to class. Or speak to a counselor if you're having a tough time. I'll see you during third

CLASS LETTERS

period, though." Anne smiled at Tiffany and held up the trash can for her tissues. "I know it doesn't seem like it now, but you'll get through this. I have faith in you."

Tiffany smiled weakly, picked up her backpack, and turned toward the door.

"Thanks, Mrs. E. I'll see you later."

Students began to file in and take their seats. There were more whispers, more exclamations of distress and disbelief. Anne took roll and started class.

"Good morning. I'm afraid I have some distressing news for you."

"Yeah," said Josh, one of her more challenging students. "I heard Spears offed himself."

"Josh, I'd appreciate it if you wouldn't interrupt. Sadly, it's true. David Spears drove into a concrete abutment last night and died as a result of the accident."

"I heard his parents found a note," said Naomi.

"Yes, that's what I understand, although I don't know the contents. Does anyone have any thoughts about David that they'd like to share?"

"Yeah, I do," Josh spoke up again. "I think David's a real chicken-shit for taking the easy way out. He shoulda been a man and faced his problems."

"You sound a little angry, Josh, although I agree that it's better to face problems. And please watch your language."

"Hell yeah, I'm angry. I've known David since third grade. Hell, we even played on the same Pee Wee football team. We've been through a lot together. And then he started with those damn steroids. I told him to leave 'em alone, but he wouldn't listen. That's when I think things started going downhill for him. If only he'd come to me. Maybe I could have helped." Josh's voice reflected a quiet desolation instead of anger.

"'If only' I had said something. 'If only' I had done something. We are all survivors of this tragedy. We are the ones left behind to figure out what went wrong, or what we could have done, and it's natural to feel guilty. And angry. In a few days or weeks, you may find yourself feeling depressed, about either David or your own life. This is all normal behavior after a suicide. You might even find yourself contemplating a similar option. After all, it 'worked' for David. However, in my opinion, suicide is a permanent solution to a temporary problem. Situations and circumstances will always change. In fact, the only real constant is change; it's one thing we can really count on. But you can't 'take back' suicide." Anne paused to let her comments sink in.

"I know this is a difficult and complicated subject. I'd like you to take some time to reflect quietly, and then write about what you're thinking and feeling. If you want to share it with me, I'd be honored to read it. If not, feel free to tear it up and throw it away. These thoughts and feelings don't need to be shared with anyone else—it's up to you. I'll play some music in the background. And, of course, if anyone needs to see the counselor, please let me know."

Anne played Vivaldi's *Four Seasons,* one of her favorites. She needed a breather as much as her students.

Bzzzz. Bzzzz. A text message vibrated her phone. It was from John: *Heard about David. I'm so sorry. Anything I can do for you?*

Her eyes grew misty. It was so tempting to lean on John. It seemed like forever since she had depended on anyone but herself. Of course, she had Karen and their parents, but she longed for the comforting strength of a man. A man who radiated love for her, who could hold her while she cried and celebrate her victories with her. She felt that John could be that man. The hope for a good man outweighed her fear of disappointment if he turned out otherwise.

How about two pepperoni and black olive pizzas and a six-pack? My place. Six. Tony too. She held her breath.

Bzzzz. Bzzzz. It would be our pleasure. I'll bring three pizzas. See you then. Hang in there.

She smiled slightly, able to breathe again.

The rest of the day passed in a similar manner. She discussed David and his death with each class, then allowed them to write. She read through the thoughts of previous classes while students wrote. Some of her students expressed their sadness at the event and some meditated on mortality, while others debated the sanctity of life in general and, in some cases, David's life in particular.

A few students hung around after school, reluctant to go home, afraid to begin the grieving process. For some, the normalcy of home was the type of environment to force their thoughts and mood outward. It was a safe, secure place where they were able to share themselves without fear of reprisal or ridicule. Others found it necessary to turn to people outside of their family, and sometimes—the least desirable option—they, like David, lost their way with the help of drugs, alcohol, sex, or some other escape. Anne often wondered what they went home to, especially on days like this. Did they have the support they needed? Or were their parents unreliable, even dangerous? Through their letters and confidential talks, she knew that many of her students were unhappy at home. How much of that was gospel, and how much was stretched a bit, she couldn't know. She had contacted Child Protective Services on more than one occasion in her career; she had a legal obligation to report any suspected or authenticated cases of abuse. But her kids were smart; they knew how to work the system, and said just enough to get the message across but not enough for a call to CPS. *This was a hard day at a hard job*, she thought. *Time for a long soak in a hot tub.*

Maggie knew her mother well and realized that she would take David's death to heart. In anticipation of John and Tony's arrival, she arranged chips and dip on the coffee table and turned the TV to the History Channel. Although John and Tony arrived promptly at six, as Maggie had predicted, Anne was simply not ready for company. She soaked in the lavender-scented tub, as planned, but after only ten minutes sobbed uncontrollably. She wept for David, and for all the kids who were confused or disoriented by life's twists and turns. She wept for David's parents; she couldn't imagine the loss of either of her children. Maggie's accident was as close as she had ever come, and it was emotionally devastating. Anne's heart broke at the thought of what the Spearses were going through. And, for a little while, she wept for herself—for all the times she had ignored or become unreasonably frustrated with Maggie and Richard. She wept angry tears over Charlie—the drugs, the women, and, finally, his abandonment of her and their children. She also wept tears of fear at the thought of somehow losing John. She knew she was falling in love with him, and the idea of a life without him was unbearable. When she had exhausted her deep reservoir of tears, she added more hot water to the tub and soaked for another ten minutes.

Anne decided that John might as well see her "as is." After drying and powdering herself, she slipped into red flannel pajama bottoms peppered with penguins and polar bears, a long-sleeved T-shirt emblazoned with Karma's Only a Bitch If You Are, and her favorite pink fuzzy slippers. Her hair remained up in a messy bun, and ringlets created by the steam in the tub framed her face. She hadn't reapplied her makeup, and her skin glowed with fresh radiance. John thought she looked adorable—and decidedly sexy.

The five of them gathered around the dining table in the living area to claim their piece of pizza. Maggie suggested they watch a DVD of one of her favorite comedians—a ventriloquist who had an interesting array of puppets. It proved to be hilarious, and everyone was enjoying the humor and camaraderie. John stole glances at Anne periodically, checking to see if her smile and happiness were authentic or a show for company. Each time, she seemed to be genuinely enjoying herself, and he hoped that he was at least partially responsible.

Once the stand-up routine was over, John and Tony gathered their hats and coats, preparing to leave. There was a collision of people in the small entry hall, pulling on coats, shaking hands, saying their good-byes. John focused on Anne, pulling her close for a hug and whispering, "Let me know if you need anything. I'm just a phone call away." She nodded and smiled. If she allowed herself to speak, she wasn't sure if "Thank you" or "I love you more than life itself and I'm dying to rip your clothes off" would come out of her mouth, so she remained silent but smiling.

She heard the truck motor engage and whispered, "Good night, John." A moment later, she called the children back into the living room.

"I'd like you to both sit down," she said.

"What'd we do?" asked Richard.

"Nothing, my sweet boy. I just wanted to talk to you for a minute."

"It's about Spears, isn't it?" asked Richard.

"Yes... sort of."

"Awwww, Mom, I'm sick of talking about it and thinking about it. It's sad and all, but can we just drop it?" pleaded Richard.

"Hear me out, okay? Yes, David's death has gotten me thinking about some things, and I wanted to... touch base with you. I know that sometimes you may think I don't understand or remember what it's like to be a teenager, and I know that I get frustrated with you sometimes over the choices you make, but I want you both to know that there's *nothing* you can tell me that would make me stop loving you. I may not always like what you *do,* but I always love *you.* I don't want you to be afraid to come to me and talk things out. Richard, I know that it may feel a bit more... awkward for you, but I still want you to know that I'm here."

"I know that, Mom. Yeah, there's guy stuff that would be too weird to talk about with you. But one of my coaches is really cool, and I talk to him sometimes."

"That's great, Richard. I'm so grateful you have an adult in your life whom you trust. You can always go to another adult if you can't talk to me—teacher, coach, counselor, or even Dr. Jonas."

"My *pediatrician*? He treats *children,* Mom. I need an *adult* doctor."

Anne successfully suppressed a smile.

"Of course, son! What was I thinking? What about you, Maggie? You've been pretty quiet."

"I was just thinking about you. It didn't occur to me until right now that it can't have been easy for you to raise us alone. Geez, I was, like, seven or eight when Dad left, so the squirt was only, like, four or five. But we've always had everything we needed. I think you've done a great job. Don't worry—we know you love us and are there for us. And we're not going to do something stupid like David did."

"You thought I was going to kill myself?" asked Richard.

"Of course not, son. Don't be silly! I only wanted to let you know that I love you, and I'm here for you, and if there's ever anything you need, you can come to me. You two are the best things that ever happened to me, and I thank God for you every day."

"Awwww, thanks, Mom," said Maggie, leaning over to hug her mother.

"Yeah, Mom, thanks. Love you too," added Richard.

"Okay, guys, it's a school night and it's late. It's been a long day. I suggest we hit the sack." Anne was back in "strict mom" mode. "Scoot!"

Maggie and Richard scurried to their rooms, yelling, "'Night, Mom!" simultaneously.

Anne's head was on the pillow a scant five minutes before she was sound asleep.

Chapter 40

Anne stopped by the funeral home the following evening after school. This was not the first time she had lost a student, but the experience didn't make it any easier. The family had reserved the largest parlor for the visitation, yet mourners lined the hall, all a tribute to David's popularity and a show of compassion for the family. Anne saw many of her students, including Tiffany and her parents. As she shook hands with Mr. Wallace, the sweet-sick smell of liquor assaulted her nose. She understood that he wanted an escape; Tom Wallace and David had been very close. In many ways, he was the son that Tom wished Tiffany had been… until the steroids. Still, when Tiffany turned up pregnant, Tom was willing to forgive and forget. But then David pushed her—and caused the miscarriage—and now this. Too much. It was all too much. Too much sadness and disappointment. Too much was beginning too unravel, which made him want to drink more. The invisible irony, the vicious cycle: alcohol was the problem, and yet Tom continued to rely on alcohol for the solution.

Anne continued around the room toward David's parents, nodding and smiling at faculty, students, and parents. Although the casket was closed, there were pictures and mementos around it amid the plants and flowers. He smiled out through his gilt-framed senior picture. He looked rough and ready, game face on, in his football uniform. A laptop played looped pictures of David over the course of his life, accompanied by his favorite songs. Anne finally reached the Spearses.

"Mrs. Spears, I'm Anne English, David's English teacher. I wanted to tell you how sorry I am for your loss. We will miss David very much."

"Thank you for coming, Mrs. English," said Mrs. Spears.

David's father was in a corner with his pastor and other congregants from his church, praying. Anne smiled again at Mrs. Spears and slipped out into the night.

The kids were back to normal the following day at school. Anne liked teaching seniors, for the most part. The real challenge came after spring break, when "senioritis" set in. It was a chronic pandemic that affected the entire senior class. Symptoms included apathy mixed with a sense of mischief—a deadly combination. If her students weren't complaining about the work, they were concocting senior pranks to pull on classmates and faculty members. They were usually innocent enough—the occasional whoopee cushion or hand buzzer—but sometimes they were more extreme, like a food fight. They weren't fully infected with senioritis yet, but she could smell it coming, so she provided as many antidotes as possible. She always planned her year so that she saved the best for last. Still, classroom management was a daily struggle in April and May.

Maggie's focus was also toward the future, but slightly further down the road. She had worked diligently throughout high school and made it into the top 5 percent in her class. This achievement secured a place for her at any public university in the state. Her dream was to be a writer—a novelist—and she had kept a daily journal since she was ten years old. In it were novel ideas, character sketches, and detailed settings, as well as her adolescent thoughts and feelings. She loved reading every type of literature she could find, particularly women writers, from Austen to Woolf. She dreamed of long hours by the fire in her cozy loft, tucked away, putting words together in a way that no one had ever considered before or ever would again. To her, this idea was as awe-inspiring and incomprehensible as quantum physics, but it was the source of her passion. Imagery that could come alive only through her vision; characters who could say only her words; motifs and nuances so subtle, yet so precise, that only the most intuitive readers would understand. This was the cancer and the cure. Throw in a little perfectionism for good measure, and you had the right combination for a novelist: innate creativity coupled with a deep yearning to tell a memorable story.

Anne watched her with great admiration—mixed with jealousy and intimidation. Maggie was sitting cross-legged on her bed, laptop in front of her, headphones on. She would type furiously for a while, then stop in desperation, waiting for the right word, pluck it out of the ether, and begin typing again, completely oblivious to her mother's presence. Anne never said a word to Maggie, but she secretly hoped to be just like her one day.

Maggie approached her mother after dinner.

"Hey, Mom. Can we talk about college for a minute?"

"You betcha! Come on in." Anne was propped up in bed, reading essays. "I would love a break!"

"Well, you know that I made it into the top 5 percent, which means I can automatically get into any state university."

"I know, and I'm so proud of you! I know how hard you've worked and all the sacrifices you've made to get here. I truly believe it will all pay off!"

"I'm sure it will. But high school hasn't been all about hard work. I've had some fun along the way," Maggie winked.

"Margaret Anne English, is there something you need to tell me?" said Anne in mock severity.

"Yes, Mom, I've been waitressing part-time at a gentlemen's club and have decided to drop out of school and become a stripper full-time!" laughed Maggie, playing along.

"Cool! Can I get half-price drinks? Or maybe we could do a mother-daughter show!"

"Ewwwwwwww! You took that tooooo far!"

"Probably!" chuckled Anne. "All silliness aside, what about college?"

"Well, I've narrowed it down to two schools: UT in Austin, of course, and Texas State University in San Marcos. I like UT and their writing program, but it's just so big. TSU has Tim O'Brien on their faculty. He's the guy who wrote *The Things They Carried,* that book I read in class last year. I love the way he writes! So maybe I should go there. And San Marcos is a cool little town. Remember when we went through there and had lunch on the river on the way to San Antonio to see the Alamo?"

"Sure do! There was that ginormous live-oak tree that provided shade for the whole deck at the restaurant. It was gorgeous! So majestic! You know, it sounds to me like you've already made up your mind. Frankly, I'd rather you went to TSU than UT. You're right, UT is huge, and it's easy to get lost and just feel like a number. It was already like that way back in the Stone Ages when I went there. TSU is smaller, and I think you'd have a better opportunity to meet other kids and get to know your professors. I'm sure there are clubs, maybe even a sorority, you could join. Have you finished your application?"

"Yep, right after school. I wanted you to look it over."

"I'd be happy to. I'm at a good stopping point and could do it now if you like."

"That would be awesome. I'll go get it."

Anne enjoyed reading through her children's applications and essays. It gave her a glimpse into their lives, and she loved discovering heretofore-unknown facts and accomplishments. There were simply parts of their everyday lives that Richard and Maggie deemed too inconsequential to share with their mother, but it was those little hints and nuances about her children that Anne craved, all the tiny colors that wove a beautiful tapestry of their attitudes and beliefs.

Anne proofed the application.

"I didn't know you were in Key Club!"

"Yeah, we adopted some residents of a nursing home and visit them once a month. We curl their hair, do their nails, or just talk. In my case, it's listen. Mrs. Pfister just loves to talk! She's told me stories about her life all the way back to her childhood. She grew up on a farm. She said they 'got up with the chickens' every day—even on the weekends! She had chores, like milking the cow or feeding the chickens, before *and* after school. And, of course, she had homework, and she made her own clothes, and she had her boyfriend, who became her husband the day after they graduated. Her parents died shortly afterward in a car wreck, so she and her husband just stayed. They had six kids, and everyone is gone but her. It makes me sad to think of her not having anybody."

"She has you."

"Sorta, but it's not like I'm family or anything. Still, I guess it's better than nothing."

"I think it's a lovely, selfless act, and I have no doubt that your sweet smile and cheerful attitude bring her more joy than she's had in years. Have you considered continuing your relationship with her after you graduate?"

"I plan on it. In fact, I was hoping that maybe we could pick her up sometime and bring her over here for dinner and a change of scenery. It's got to be depressing to look at the same old walls and faces day in and day out."

"I would be delighted to have her over anytime you like."

"Thanks, Mom. What did you think of the application?"

"I think you did a great job and that Texas State University will be thrilled to have you." Tears sprang into Anne's eyes unexpectedly.

"What's wrong, Mom?"

"Ohmygod. I guess it really just hit me that you're going away next year." Anne's tears were unstoppable at the thought of her firstborn, her only daughter, going off to college. Their relationship would never be the same.

"Oh, Mom!" Maggie laughed. "San Marcos is only about four

hours away. Besides, I figured you'd be glad to get rid of me. No one stealing your favorite shoes anymore, no one rummaging through your belts and scarves… unless, of course, there's something you're not telling me about Richard!"

"Maggie! Shame on you!" Anne couldn't help but howl at the imaginary picture of Richard attempting to walk in heels, with a plethora of scarves around his head and neck. "Can you see him in those hot-pink stilettos I got at the thrift store for that New Year's party last year? Trying to walk on those skinny, hairy legs? And scarves placed just so?" She swirled her hand around her neck and head to show their placement.

"And what about that floppy hat you have? Maybe with some pink flowers in the brim? Hello, I'm heah to see the Queen," Maggie quipped in her best English accent.

Maggie and Anne held their sides and cheeks as they continued making jokes at Richard's expense, rolling on Anne's bed at the hilarity of it all. Richard poked his head in the door.

"What's so funny?" he asked.

"Nothing, son, just some silly girl talk," said Anne, punching Maggie surreptitiously in the leg.

"Whatever. Hey, did you know the English say 'fish and chips' instead of 'fish and French fries'? Weird, huh?"

At that point, Anne and Maggie collapsed in roaring laughter, leaving Richard to shake his head as he returned to the safety of the living room, muttering, "What have you two been smoking?"

Chapter 41

The world opened up and came alive over the next few weeks. Quince and forsythia bloomed happily in their role as the first greeters of spring. Overnight, the tight buds of the flowering pear tree burst open like bowls of freshly popped corn. The outside air, warm and breezy, beckoned the denizens of North Texas to come out and play. Everyone felt it. Birds sang in the trees and hovered near the eggs that would hatch any day. Insects were brought to life with the warmth of the sun and lengthening days. The energy surge that was happening outside influenced the students as well. There was a decided increase in behavioral problems, and a decrease in the quality and quantity of work. It was time for Anne's seniors-close-to-the-end speech.

She put on her best "teacher face" and began:

"Okay, guys, it's that time of year again. Spring break is around the corner, everything is gorgeous outside, and you'd rather be anywhere but here. I get that. The end is in sight! You have to keep working. You have to stay focused and attentive until the end of May. Trust me, I have seen kids who thought they had everything under control. They were passing with a reasonable average, but once spring came along, they quit. It was more fun to play and procrastinate than to work. Some of those kids had to work very diligently in order to graduate. And I've even had a couple that didn't graduate, simply because they stopped working. Can you imagine going to school for thirteen years but not getting a diploma because it was more fun to skip school and blow off homework for a couple of months? Over the course of your state-required education, K through twelve, you attend school for about two thousand, three hundred and fifty days. So don't lose two thousand, three hundred and fifty days by blowing off ten or twelve. Make sense? Okay, time to get to work. I know this is coming quickly on the heels of the February letter, but in order to avoid giving you homework over spring break, I want to hand out your March letter now."

A collection of groans radiated around the room.

"Let me put it this way," Anne continued. "One of us will be working over spring break. Is it going to be you or me?"

They made their choice and worked diligently the rest of the period, first reading the letter, then writing their response.

March

Dear Class:

I've been thinking about coping mechanisms when faced with a crisis. There are really only two ways: face it or run from it—that "fight or flight" response you've no doubt heard of in science class. As far as survival goes, much depends on the crisis to determine which is the right choice. If you are faced with an angry mother bear protecting her cubs, "flight" is definitely the way to go! But we encounter situations every day that aren't a matter of survival. And, except for literally keeping yourself out of harm's way, it seems to me that most situations should be faced head-on in some aspects.

First, what does it mean to face something? It means you have to at least begin looking at it. Some things can be very difficult to even think about looking at. Maybe it has to do with coming to some sort of truth about yourself or someone else in your life. And I'll give you a hint about this one: it's way easier to see things in someone else! I've heard that everyone is a mirror or a teacher, and I can learn something about myself from everyone in my life. For example, you may see a friend behaving selfishly and find their attitude unbecoming or possibly reprehensible. And then, a few days later, you find yourself acting the same way. They can be a mirror in that they reflect your behavior back to you. They act like a teacher because you get to see and feel how that type of behavior impacts another person. You can gain great insight into your own psyche by watching how others interact and how their actions impact those around them.

It may be that you have other things in your life, such as your past or choices you have made, that will require the help of a counselor, priest, or trusted friend or family member in order for you to make sense of them. But they need to be faced nonetheless. When I was in my mid-twenties, my boyfriend at the time decided he needed to end his own life. We talked on the phone before he died, and he blamed me for his death. I needed the help of a counselor to sort through my feelings of guilt and sadness. It was very helpful, and I managed to move on, but I'm not sure I could have done it without professional help. Objective people can help you get to the bottom of an issue because they aren't emotionally involved. Even though it was painful, I faced it and worked through it.

Another thing that I think helps me cope with unpleasantness is to try to stay in the present moment, without regretting my past or worrying about the future. I cope better if I look at the present day as the gift it is and enjoy it! If I'm always living in the past in guilt or shame, I'm not free to enjoy today because I don't think I deserve to. If I'm living in fear of what tomorrow brings, I've wasted all the glorious things that today brought me. You live life on life's terms, taking each day as it comes, grateful for the opportunities and experiences that come your way. This isn't so much a specific action as it is a general attitude.

Some events require that we do some kind of grieving. We

touched on this in the fall semester. There are five stages of grief: denial, anger, bargaining, depression, and acceptance. Obviously, a death would require this process, but there are other things too, such as the loss of a job, home, or long-term boyfriend or girlfriend. I hope that many of you haven't had to cope with big losses at such a young age, but I know that some of you have. Walking through the stages is not a linear process; you may jump from one to another, out of order, and then find yourself back at the beginning. But if you persevere, you will reach acceptance and, with it, peace.

What about the "flight" aspects of coping? This is common—especially when the things you are coping with are emotionally painful. Sometimes it's much easier to bury those feelings than to face them. This is really at the heart of addiction. Addicts, alcoholics, and overeaters all run from their feelings, through taking drugs, drinking, or eating. But people can get addicted to anything: money, sex, work, religion, and rage are probably the most common. The sad thing about this way of life is that it doesn't solve anything. It becomes an endless cycle: you do or experience something that brings up unpleasant feelings, so you drink over it, for example, feel badly about your drinking, feel a need to bury the feelings, and the cycle starts all over again. Of course, this is the worst way to deal with a situation, because it isn't really "dealing" at all.

If all else fails, you can at least hold on and remember, "This too shall pass." There is rarely anything that causes permanent damage in our lives anymore. If you had a bad day or week at school, it'll pass, and a new day will dawn. You don't have to feel hopeless and helpless. And if you do, please, please, please talk to someone. Nothing is worth taking your life over. Suicide is a permanent solution to a temporary problem.

This month, I want you to think about your coping skills. Are *they healthy or unhealthy? Do you lean more toward "fight" or "flight"? Did you read anything in this letter that you think might help you cope? Talk to your friends—see how they deal with difficult situations. Maybe they have useful tools that you can add to your toolbox. Not every solution is going to work for every problem, so it's good to have a variety of "tools," or coping mechanisms, that will help you walk through life's trials and tribulations. Do you have any tools you want to share with me? Just because I'm an adult doesn't mean that everything goes smoothly all the time. I have my own "stuff" to work through!*

You guys know the drill: You have a week to read and respond. Your letter will remain between you and me, unless you reveal something that forces me to take it to a higher authority.

Anne stayed at her desk, grading as the papers came in. Tiffany's was first. Anne initially thought she had rushed through it, but quickly realized that she had written from her heart.

Dear Mrs. English,

I really like this topic because I have learned so many tools since I have been in Alateen. Some of it still kind of confuses me because I haven't been going all that long. Like the steps and traditions, but my sponsor is helping me understand them. The first one is about being powerless. What that means is that I can't do anything about my dad's drinking. Then step two is about a power greater than myself and me being insane. I'm not really insane (LOL) but my sponsor showed me that trying to talk to Dad when he's drunk, or trying to change him, IS crazy. So I have to turn to a power greater than myself (God) to help with all of it, since I can't do it alone. That's really all I understand so far, but just this little bit of knowledge has helped a lot. It's taken a lot of pressure off me because I always thought if I was a better daughter, he wouldn't drink. Now I know that he's going to drink no matter what kind of a daughter I am.

I've learned some other tools too. More like sayings. They are called the slogans. Some of them are One Day at a Time, How Important Is It, Live and Let Live, and Think. The first one means that you're supposed to just live one day at a time. Sometimes when things get hard, you think you can't go on if you have to do it forever. But, really, you just have to do things one day at a time, so that it's not so overwhelming. How Important Is It just means that there are lots of things that seem important but really aren't. For example, there's no reason to get real upset if you spill something on your new outfit. It can be washed or cleaned so it can be fixed. Therefore, there's no point in getting mad, because it's really not that important. The next one, Live and Let Live, is about letting other people be who they are. Like, if someone bugs you because they're really loud and you're quiet, you just accept them as they are. You can't change them. The last one is Think. This means that you need to think something through before you do it. Like if I try to talk to my dad when he's drunk or mad. There's no point in it and I have to think about that and remember it before I try.

Thanks for sharing your tips. I think all of mine could help you too... or anyone else. I think they're really good and a lot of people would benefit from them, especially my mother, but she refuses to go to Al-Anon. So, that's another area where I have to live and let live. I hope she comes someday but I can't make her. All I can do is take care of myself.

And one more thing... I'm still really sad and angry about David. I just think it's such a waste. Like you said, a permanent solution to a temporary problem. I figured that's who you were talking about.

Have a great spring break and get lots of grading done! ;)

Love,

Tiffany

CLASS LETTERS

Anne smiled as she read the letter. She had watched Tiffany talk to Ray about Isabel, the wedding, and the baby. Her eyes sparkled and her face had a peace about it that was a new, and welcome, addition. It was obvious to Anne that Alateen was helping Tiffany; it was too bad her mother was so resistant. Hopefully, she would eventually take Tiffany's lead and join her.

Kim walked up to Anne's desk to deliver her paper. She, too, possessed an air of confidence and serenity that had been absent at the beginning of the school year. It was gratifying for Anne to see "her" kids grow, change, and mature.

"I hope you have a fun spring break, Mrs. English."

"You too! Do you have any plans?" asked Anne.

"Part of it's in the letter, but mainly hang out with friends—and sleep!" Kim laughed. "What about you?"

"Nope. No plans. My children will be on a mission trip for most of the break, so I'll be alllll alone," said Anne, feigning despair.

"Poor Mrs. English! Maybe you can ride your motorcycle to help with your, uh, anguish."

"That *is* part of my plan. Other than that, I'll just cry myself to sleep every night."

"Aw, Mrs. English… what are you going to do when they are both off at college?" asked Kim.

"I've got to get through the next three years before that happens. Maggie has decided to go down to San Marcos. And Richard? Well… let's just hope he lives that long," said Anne with a wink.

"Okay, Mrs. English," laughed Kim, "I'll watch *Cops* to see if they catch up with you!"

"Good plan!"

Anne really *wasn't* quite sure what she would do over the break. Maggie and Richard had heard about the mission trip during Sunday school in December, and they had proposed to earn half the money if she provided the other half. Maggie had found more babysitting jobs, and Richard had been raking neighbors' leaves, disassembling Christmas lights, running errands, spring cleaning… anything to make a buck. He reminded Anne of her cousin Phillip, an entrepreneur always looking for a deal. And finding them. He was very successful and was beginning to mentor Richard in business. Apparently, it was rubbing off; Anne had never seen Richard so industrious. In addition to their endeavors, the family had eaten a lot of hamburger and macaroni, enabling Anne to scrape together her share of the money for the trip.

Anne didn't have much alone time as a single mom. The kids had weekends with Karen, and they spent two weeks with their grandparents in the summer, but the rest of the time, they belonged solely to Anne. Still, she always looked forward to being on her own and found new things to try, even if she had to force herself. Once, she heard about a regular jam session at her church and decided to show up alone. There were only a few regulars, and they all welcomed her. It was an enjoyable, laid-back evening, but not one she revisited. Still, Anne had to walk through her fear of trying something new, and single, and alone. She always felt like Steve Martin in *Lonely Guy* when he walked into a restaurant alone and a spotlight and fifty pairs of eyes followed him to his table, where he sat alone. Anne knew it was no crime, but she was determined to overcome her fear of doing things by herself. She was well aware that she would be one of those "empty nesters" in a few years, and she had mixed feelings: excitement at watching her children grow and mature, anxiety about which paths they would follow, curiosity about what her life would look like, and sadness at "losing" them. It felt like an impending death to her. Regardless of what they did or where they went, once Maggie and Richard left home, her relationship with each of them would be forever changed.

Ray walked up, smiling.

"Here's my paper. Hey, I have a new picture of the babies. Wanna see?"

"Of course! Have you found out the sex yet?"

"No, Isabel doesn't want to know. But I'm sure they are both boys," said Ray, handing Anne the sonogram.

"Boys, huh? Got any names picked out?"

"Ray Junior. We'll call him RJ. Actually, Raymundo Jesus, so we can include Jessie. So, technically, he won't be a junior, but we can't call him Ray or Jessie, so that's what we figured out. Ernesto Guillermo, for Isa's grandfather. We'll probably call him Ernie."

"Wonderful names. You may want to come up with a girl's name—just in case. And, Ray, you are going to be a great dad."

Ray blushed, still unaccustomed to compliments. "Thanks. And thanks for coming to the wedding and for the set of dishes and the diapers. It'll all come in real handy. Isabel wrote you a note, but I left it at home."

"You are more than welcome, Ray. I'm very happy for you and Isabel, and I was honored to be invited to the wedding."

"And you caught the bouquet," teased Ray. "Who's the lucky guy?"

"No guy," sighed Anne.

"What about the guy from the dance? Tony's dad, right?"

"We're just friends," said Anne. She harbored a glimmer of hope that something more might come of their friendship. He seemed interested. Who was she kidding? She knew he was interested, and she was fairly certain he knew she was interested. Her plan: relax, enjoy, and wait. John was definitely worth waiting for.

"Mrs. English? I asked if you have any plans for the break."

Ray's voice brought her back to the classroom.

"Uh... no, not really. I'm hoping to do some riding."

"It should be great weather for it! Me and Isa have to work."

"Isa and I," Anne stated automatically.

"Isa and I have to work. Kinda sucks, but we need money for the babies. We feel pretty good about it, though. We see lots of cribs and other baby stuff at garage sales and at the flea market. We'll find what we need."

"I'm sure you will. If I hear of anything, I'll let you know."

"Thanks, Mrs. English. Have a good break."

The rest of the day passed quickly, although she didn't get as much grading done as she would have liked. The kids were chatty and wanted to visit with her, sharing their spring break plans. She enjoyed the rapport she had with her students, more so this year than usual.

She attributed it to the letters. The letters had opened an avenue for dialogue, one that the students clearly enjoyed and, in some cases, needed. It showed up in her classroom too. Her students seemed generally calmer and easier to manage. Maybe it was just this class. She would need to compare results over several years, but she believed that simply by establishing private communication with her students, their overall behavior and work ethic improved.

Anne managed to read a few more letters before leaving for the day. Keosha's was on the top of the stack.

Hey Miss,

I read a lot of good stuff in your letter. I'm so sorry about your boyfriend. That must have been a hard thing to deal with. I've been dealing with some of my stuff too. I hear people all the time ask if anyone knows who turned in BD. It makes me scared and want to run off (the flight part). It's just Mama and me that know (and you, but I trust you), so I think we'll be okay. I've had to face the things I've done in my past—like the way I hurt Mama and how I got into all that stuff to begin with. I talk to a police officer 'bout that stuff. I met her behind all this mess with BD and she's really cool. She grew up a lot like me so she can relate to what's been going on with me. It's good to have someone to talk to that understands. She wants me to do good from now on and I'm really trying. I have an interview over spring break for a job at a clothes store. I hope I get it! Have a great break!

Anne scribbled a note at the bottom of the letter: *I hope you get it too. Keeping fingers and toes crossed!*

Kim's letter was next on the pile.

Dear Mrs. English:

I'm so excited about spring break and I have to tell you about that first! I'm volunteering to help with a gay-rights parade in

Dallas. I'll be helping at the refreshments area. After the parade, everyone gathers for snacks and drinks. That's where I'll be working. It's so exciting to be able to help and I hope to have a bigger role next year.

My biggest fear, until a few months ago, was telling people I was gay. It made me act really shy most of the time. To me, that was the "flight" part. It's like I was flying away from my true self because of fear. So, I told people—even my parents. My life has been so much better since then, with one or two exceptions (like the assault). There are some people who don't accept me, but I have come to believe that it's their loss. I'm not a bad person, or an immoral person. But they consider me different. I can accept their non-acceptance, if that makes sense. I'm so grateful for your support through all this. It's awesome to have a teacher like you.

Love,

Kim[Q]

Anne decided she had time for one more letter, and she chose to read Ray's.

Please don't tell Isabel this. I'm really excited about the babies, and I love Isa with all my heart, but when she told me she was pregnant, I was really scared. I acted happy, but on the inside, I thought I was going to throw up. It's a big responsibility—that's what scares me, not the babies. It's all the stuff a baby stands for like college and diapers and doctor bills. After she told me, that night I woke up in a panic and thought about running away. But I knew Jessie would kill me and Isabel would hate me. And that would be horrible. So I stayed and I made a promise to God that night to try to be the best dad I could be. And a good husband, 'cause I knew we would get married. Now I'm okay with it, but it was scary at first.

Anne wrote: *I'm so proud of you for overcoming your fear. You are going to be a great dad!*

On the way home, she received a plea for one last run to the store to pick up forgotten but necessary items, like mascara for Maggie and snacks for Richard.

"Mascara and snacks? Seriously?" demanded Anne.

"Please, Mom. If you do this one thing, I promise we won't ask for anything else for about… five days."

"Maggie, you're leaving in the morning and will be back in five days. How exactly does this benefit me?"

"Uhhh… it'll add about twenty minutes to your trip, so… that's twenty less minutes you'll have to spend with us?"

"Twenty fewer minutes. Use *fewer* with quantifiable things, things you can count, and *less* with abstracts, like frustration. The mother had less frustration before the daughter's phone call."

"I know what *quantifiable* means, Mother. C'mon. Please." The *Mother* part of her statement indicated Maggie's current frustration level.

"Begging is so unbecoming, and I'm so tired."

"Mom, you know you love us. You can't help it!" crooned Maggie.

Anne smiled at their family phrase. "You're right. I do love you and I can't help it. I'll get your stuff and be home shortly thereafter, k? Love you."

"Wait, Mom! I didn't tell you what kind yet."

"Maggie," said Anne slowly, "It's late. I'm tired. Stopping by the store is about the last thing I want to do, but I'm willing to do it. However, I'm ready to leave, so I want to get off the phone so I can drive. I'll get mascara and snacks. If you want specifics, text me. Got it? Love you. Bye." Anne disconnected before Maggie could get in another word.

Shortly, Anne received four text messages, all in a row.

"That's quite a list," growled Anne.

Chapter 42

Anne arrived home, grocery bags in hand, to a flurry of activity. Maggie and Richard had bags out and were packing in the middle of the living room.

"What are you doing out here? Aren't you doing a lot of running back and forth?" asked Anne.

"Yeah, but I have so much stuff all over my room, trying to decide what to take, that it's easier to bring the stuff I'm actually taking out here," explained Maggie.

"Me too," added Richard.

"Okay, here are the snacks and mascara and sunscreen and toothpaste and all the other things you texted to me," said Anne, setting down the bags. "How about pizza and salad for dinner?"

Anne turned on the oven and retrieved a pizza and a bag of mixed greens from the fridge. She watched her children interact; Maggie shared packing tips with Richard while he extolled the virtues of throwing seaweed and half-eaten fish on girls in bikinis.

"Richard, don't you dare!" yelled Anne and Maggie simultaneously.

"Sheesh, guys, I'm not gonna actually do it. I just think it would be funny."

"See that you don't," warned Anne. The buzzer rang. "Let the feasting begin!"

As they ate, Richard and Maggie filled Anne in on the details of their trip. Anne had a packet, including an hour-by-hour itinerary, but she was enthralled by their enthusiasm. They were traveling to South Texas, and their primary objective was to rebuild a school that had been destroyed by a hurricane, but the trip also included downtime at the beach and an aquarium. Neither child had worked on such a project before, and Anne hoped it would provide them with a new perspective on and awareness of the way others live.

"I want to tell you how proud I am of both of you," Anne began. "Not only are you giving up your free time to help others, but you earned half the money for the trip. I think you're both beyond awesome! Now, once you're done with dinner, please finish your packing and get ready for bed. We all have an early day tomorrow."

The bus was leaving at 6:00 a.m. Anne wore a big T-shirt and pajama bottoms to bed; she could roll out of bed to drive them, come home, and fall *back* into bed. Bags were ready to go and in the trunk. Donuts would be their breakfast fare. The alarm was set. All was well as Anne settled under the covers.

I'm sexy and I know it / Wiggle, wiggle, wiggle, wiggle, wiggle, yeah.

LMFAO woke Anne up at five fifteen. She could hear Maggie and Richard talking in the living room.

"Good, they're up," mumbled Anne, and closed her eyes. "Just five more minut—"

"Mom!" Richard burst into the room. "Geez, get up! We need to leave now!"

Anne glanced at the clock. "Ohmygod! It's five forty-five. Let's go!"

Anne threw on a hoodie and the three of them raced out the door—grabbing the bag of donuts—into the car, and toward the church. The bus driver loaded the last of the luggage while parents and children hugged their good-byes.

"Made it," sighed Maggie.

"Yes, we did! Whew! Richard, get the luggage out of the trunk, please. Lean in here and give me a hug and kiss. I'm in my pajamas."

"But, Mom, you went to the drugstore in those once," objected Maggie.

"Only because I was on my deathbed," said Anne. "Better get on the bus. And have fun!"

Anne watched as the driver loaded the luggage and Richard and Maggie found their seats. Both had made a pact with a friend—first one there grabs the seats. She watched from the heated car as the bus pulled out of the driveway. She was about to drive off when she noticed a dark figure with a ball cap on approaching the car. Instinctively, she locked the doors and placed her hand on the gearshift in case she had to take off in a hurry.

The person bent over to look in the driver's seat.

"Hi, Anne!" said John.

"Awww, shit," she muttered, rolling down the window. "Hi, John. What are you doing here?"

"Uhhh... same reason you are, I s'pose. Tony's going on the mission trip."

Anne tried to pull her hoodie tighter over her T-shirt and SpongeBob pajamas. "I didn't know he was going."

"Nice pajamas," he smiled.

"Well... the alarm went off, and I snoozed... and here I am!" Anne laughed.

"How about a cup of coffee? There's a Starbucks around the corner," John suggested.

"I can't go in there! Besides, SpongeBob doesn't drink coffee. He's too young," Anne protested.

"He lives in a pineapple with a snail. No parents. No supervision. He can drink coffee. Besides, no one cares, except me, and I think you're gorgeous."

"In SpongeBob SquarePants... uh... pants?" said Anne.

"Yes, in SpongeBob SquarePants pants," agreed John.

"What the heck? Let's go," said Anne. "Quick, before I change my mind."

"Okay. It's just around the corner. I'll follow you there—and head you off at the pass if you try to escape."

"I have lost my ever-lovin' mind," said Anne as she pulled into the parking lot.

They waited in line—of course there would be a line—and placed their order. Anne selected a small table in the dimmest corner she could find while John waited for the coffee and pastries.

"Here we go: one *mucho muy grande* black coffee with sweetener, and one very, uh, healthy-looking bran muffin. And I will enjoy this wonderful white chocolate macchiato and gooey cinnamon roll." John placed the treats on the table with a smile and stopped for a minute.

"You are truly lovely in the morning. Hey, I've got an idea. Let's go out of town this week."

"*What?*" Anne choked on her coffee.

"Why not? All our kids are gone. You're off work. And I've got a store manager that I've babied for six months. It's time I let him fly on his own for a while."

"You're serious."

"Absolutely! I'd like nothing better than to sneak off with you for a few days."

"Oh, John, I don't know," Anne stammered.

"When are we going to get an opportunity like this again? I mean, really, when?" John took her hand. "Look, babe, no pressure. Separate rooms. I just want to spend time with you, k?"

"What did you have in mind?" asked Anne.

"Well, we have a couple of options. One, we could hit the road on the bikes, or in the truck, I guess, check out some little towns in the area. Stay in a centralized motel, take day trips. Or we could camp. I've got lots of equipment; Tony and I go camping all the time. We could fish, maybe swim if it's warm enough."

"Honestly, John, it took a lot for me to send the kids on this trip. I just don't think I can handle a trip financially."

"Yeah, I get that. I have some money stashed away. I could foot the bill."

"I can't let you do that, John. It just wouldn't be right. I couldn't…"

"Yeah, I get that too. I figured you'd say that. Okay, camping it is! I've got two tents, two sleeping bags, two chairs… whatever you need. And I know some great spots. C'mon, it'll be fun!"

Anne looked into the green eyes she had seen so many times in her dreams. She weighed the pros and cons, closed her eyes for a moment, and said, "When do we leave?"

"That's my girl! How about… noon?"

"*Today?* Holy cow! I've got to go to the grocery store, talk to my sister about taking Rocky, and do some laundry. How about Monday? We can come back Thursday, since the kids will be back on Friday."

"You are a clever negotiator. Monday noon. I'll have all the gear, meat, and drinks. How about you bring sides? Bread, potato salad, eggs, stuff like that. I have pans and a stove, so we can cook skillet dishes at breakfast and dinner and make sandwiches for lunch. Maybe you could make some brownies?" John asked with a wink.

"Sounds good. Any idea where we'll go?" asked Anne.

"There's a beautiful park near Meridian, another one outside of Mineral Wells, or we could go to the one with the dinosaur tracks. I'll have to see what's available, since it's spring break. Hopefully it won't be full in the middle of the week."

"This is going to be fun. I'll bring Richard's telescope too. I think a comet will be flying overhead this next week. Maybe we'll see it."

"I'll bring some deer corn so we can feed the deer. It's one of Tony's favorite things to do, even still."

Anne and John talked excitedly about their upcoming trip, heads together, like two thieves conspiring about a heist. After an hour of busy chatter, they hugged and went their separate ways.

Anne fell back into bed exhausted. Her vacation had started off with a bang, and she needed some time to take it all in. Her mind whirled with visions of green eyes, lying under the stars, sitting quietly and watching deer graze. She thought of easy dishes to take or cook there. And she mentally scoured her pantry to see if she had all the brownie ingredients. Maggie and Richard both loved them, so it was a frequent treat at their house. One night, Richard had gotten a brownie craving and made a batch all by himself. Anne had been as thrilled by his accomplishment as she'd been surprised. She finally fell asleep, waking around noon.

It was a beautiful day: seventy-five degrees, breezy, and sunny. Anne felt rested and a lightness in her step as she pranced around the house, picking up and doing laundry. Once everything was straight and loads were in the washer and dryer, she donned her helmet and sunglasses, fired up her bike, and sped down the road. Anne breathed in the clean, fragrant spring air and felt freedom and peace flow over her. She truly loved to ride and hoped to make a cross-country trip. She knew of a woman at her church who had made the trip with her husband. Maybe someday… But right now, she was simply enjoying the ride.

Chapter 43

"Let's see, I have snacks, potatoes, cheese, salad stuff... maybe some bug spray? Or one of those mosquito candles? Oohhh, maybe some vanilla candles... but maybe that sends the wrong message? Maybe just *going* sends a message... or maybe I shouldn't worry about messages or candles or anything.... Too many 'maybes,'" Anne mumbled to herself as she strolled through Walmart, wondering if she had lost her mind.

"It was his idea—but I agreed. Two tents should be okay. Ugh, this all makes me so nervous. What have I done?"

"Excuse me?" asked a passing customer.

"Nothing... sorry... just talking to myself," answered Anne, embarrassed.

Anne snagged a few more items before heading to check out, then home to make brownies, as requested. It was only eight thirty, and she had been up since six, buzzing nervously around the house, packing, unpacking, and repacking. Hopefully, cooking would keep her hands occupied and her mind would follow. Anne snapped on the radio in the kitchen. Stevie Ray Vaughan serenaded her as she cooked.

She's my sweet little baby
I'm her little lover boy

Two hours later, Anne had a batch of brownies, potato salad, chicken salad, and fruit salad ready to go. She hopped in the shower for what might be the last time over the next couple of days. After drying off, she debated curling her hair.

"Should I or shouldn't I? Hmm… it would give me something to do; I've got plenty of time.… Oh, what the hell!"

For the next hour, Anne curled and primped and waited. When the doorbell finally rang, Anne almost jumped out of her skin.

"He's here!" she squealed. Excitement and nerves seemed to boost her voice up an octave.

"Are we off to the prom or going camping?" smiled John as she opened the door.

"Well, I had some extra time, and…" stammered Anne.

"Hey, I think it's great. You'll be the prettiest camper out there!"

"Thanks. Where are we going?"

"Meridian State Park. It's small but pretty, and it was the only park within a hundred miles that had available campsites. Ready to roll?"

"You betcha. I've just got a bag and a cooler."

"You pack light! I thought most women took three times more stuff than they needed—just in case."

"I have a hard time finding the right balance. I usually either over-pack and bring home tons of clothes I never wear or underpack and end up wearing the same things over and over."

"You just need more practice! We should take trips every weekend, just so you can refine your packing techniques!"

"Great idea! And once I get better at it, you can test me with different kinds of trips. Like a week in Paris versus a month on the Congo." Anne relaxed with the banter.

"And when you get really good at it, the notice I give you could get shorter and shorter, like, six hours to get ready for three months in Italy. Skiing in the north, and tropics in the south. See how long *that* takes you!"

"Your challenges may be my undoing, but I'm willing!" Anne laughed.

"Well, it seems like you passed your first packing test. Unless, of course, we get there and you realize you've forgotten something!" John winked. "Let's get the truck loaded and on the road!"

Anne and John chatted about their kids, wondering about their trip. They stopped in a small-town gas station/Laundromat/taxidermy/gift shop for drinks and gas. Anne bought a small jackalope for Richard and a wildflower T-shirt for Maggie. She wondered what they would think if they knew what she was up to.

The campsite was small but cozy, surrounded by trees and rock outcroppings. There were three other groups of campers in their immediate area: an older couple, a group of four twentysomethings, and another couple about their age. Anne was secretly grateful there were no children in their alcove. She loved her children and students but craved adult conversations.

The weather was glorious. Soft, warm breezes stirred the leaves in the oak trees to an erotic dance, accompanied by bobwhites' cooing, punctuated by insects buzzing by. Bright puffy clouds, swirls of rich whipped cream, floated overhead through the azure sky. Anne breathed in the fluffy softness and exhaled a prayer of gratitude.

"Okay, here are the tents and sleeping bags. And the egg-crate foam—you don't want to forget that. Have you ever put up a tent before? Oh, wait, never mind. Of course you have! You've been camping before," said John. "This looks like the smoothest and flattest part of our site. Set up your tent here."

"You should get that spot," protested Anne. "It's your gear, your idea. I'm just along for the ride."

"Anne, do you seriously think I'm going to take that spot? Let me explain my philosophy on male-female relationships. You are the woman. My job, as the man, is to make sure that you, the woman, are as happy and comfortable as humanly possible. Chauvinistic? Absolutely! Politically correct? No way! But, I'm a Southern gentleman, through and through. Your wants and needs will always come before mine, and you will be treated like the lady you are. That's not to say that when we're camping or whatever that I won't ask for and expect your help with things. But I will still insist that you get the best of everything. Now, let's put your tent up."

Anne was speechless and processed his words while they worked. Her wants and needs came first? Treated like a lady? So far, John had acted in such a manner, but so had Charlie at first… until she slept with him, when it became all about him. And once his addiction took hold, Anne and the children weren't first, or second, or even third—they weren't even on the list.

She wanted to believe John. Still, experience had taught her skepticism. Time would tell. It always did.

After setting up camp, John and Anne took a walk around the park. There was a beautiful lake sparkling under the spring sun, alive with turtles and fish. Wildflowers bloomed in brilliant clumps, lizards skittered among the grasses, and bees zipped about from flower to flower, as if all were participating in a joyous ode to Flora, the goddess of spring.

As the day closed, the sunset added to the peace and serenity that surrounded them. John had brought some Christmas lights that he strung up in the trees around their campsite. Country-Western music floated on the air from the older couple's picnic table. Fireflies blinked to their lovers, flirting in the dark recesses of the surrounding brush. The smell of campfires and various grilled meats filled the air, bringing with it a party atmosphere.

"Hey, you two!" called a bright-eyed, gray-haired woman. "I'm Bertie and that's my husband, Boone. All of us in our little area here are getting together at the RV and hoped you'd come over. Bring your dinner and a couple of chairs and join the party!"

John looked at Anne the way couples do, in unspoken questions and answers.

After a smile from her, he said, "We'd love to!" They quickly gathered their dinner and chairs and moved into the circle around the campfire. Introductions were already in progress. In addition to Bertie and Boone, the quartet included Kayla, Blake, Mario, and Sasha, and the other couple were Tim and Catherine. The troupe shared stories and jokes, and everyone enjoyed the camaraderie. After several hours of laughter, the revelers returned to their respective sites, full of good food and the warmth of friendship.

Anne went to the ladies' shower/bathroom, or casita, as it had been called back in her high school summer camp days, to take care of her nightly duties and change into pajamas. She was grateful for a separate tent, but it was a small one, even for her five-foot frame. She had nightmarish visions of trying to change clothes, tripping, and bringing the tent down with her. The casita was definitely the safer option. Besides, her SpongeBob pj's were no longer a secret.

By the time she returned to the site, John had built a fire and was toasting marshmallows.

"Well, hey there, SpongeBob. I thought it would be nice to have a little something sweet and watch the stars for a bit," he said.

"Sounds lovely!" said Anne, settling into the canvas chair next to his. "It's gotten chilly. Glad I have old Bob here to keep me warm."

"I hope to apply for that position someday. But for the moment, I am happy and content to sit here with you."

Anne enjoyed this not-so-subtle reference to the future as much as she had his relationship philosophy earlier. These were the things she was looking for, and he was demonstrating them over and over again. His actions matched his words—very important—and he was respectful of her requests. He knew the camping idea pushed the envelope just a bit, hence the two-tent concession. He was willing to wait; he knew she was a prize worth waiting for.

"I love looking at the stars," sighed Anne. "My father and I used to go out late at night during meteor showers, and he knew lots of constellations. I can't remember any of them except the dippers and Orion." She paused in contemplation. "I wonder what's out there, or if we'll meet any aliens during my lifetime. There has to be something out there. *A lot* of somethings, when you think about it. I find it really hard to believe that we are the only sentient beings in this ginormous universe. Think about it: we are just one small speck in one small galaxy. It just amazes me."

John watched her gaze at the stars with the wonder of a child. Her eyes sparkled at the possibilities that might exist, and the firelight lit up her face, revealing her delighted smile. He ached to hold her close and drink in her perfume. He took her hand, kissed it, and enfolded it in his.

"Oh, look! A shooting star! Did you see it?" Anne asked.

"Yeah! I saw it just before it burned out. Caught the last little bit of the tail."

"Did you make a wish?"

"Was I supposed to?"

"Lordy, John, don't you know anything? Shooting-star wishes always come true. Better watch closely, in case there's another one. You don't want to miss another wish, do you?"

"No way, Jose! And I know exactly what I want to wish for."

"What?" asked Anne.

"I can't tell you that! My wish won't come true. And this is one wish I really, really want to come true!"

"Hmm… a new motorcycle?"

"Not sayin.'"

"A winning lottery ticket?" she asked, poking him in the side.

"My lips are sealed."

"How about a trip around the world?" The poking turned to tickling.

"I told you, I'm not telling. Now, if you don't leave me alone, I'll be forced to take drastic action."

"Hmph. Drastic action? You don't scare me! I bet you wished for a boat!" Anne exclaimed, trying to tickle with both hands.

"Now you've done it! You have no one to blame but yourself." He grabbed her leg above her kneecap, one of Anne's most sensitive tickle spots.

Try as she might, Anne couldn't keep from laughing. He had her in just the right spot, and she was helpless to resist.

"I give, I give!" she said, holding her side. "Ohmygod, that knee thing just kills me."

"Told ya. Maybe next time you'll listen."

"No, I think next time I will have a supersecret plan that will defeat you!"

"Oh, really? How 'bout now?" he asked, grabbing her knee again.

"Enough! I can't take any more," laughed Anne, wiping away a tear.

"Better work on that plan," winked John.

"Apparently! Actually, I think I'm going to do that in the quiet and comfort of my tent. I'm pretty pooped."

"Me too," said John, standing up. He pulled her close for a hug and whispered, "Good night and sweet dreams."

"'Night," said Anne, and disappeared into the tent.

John took one more look at the sky. Just then, a meteor streaked overhead.

"Make her mine," he breathed.

Chapter 44

Anne and John spent the next morning hiking through the park; they went back to the campsite for lunch, and then fished the afternoon away. John was an easy man to talk to. He was about as transparent as a man could be. He didn't spill his entire life story all at once but let out details here and there, in accordance with Anne's questions, honestly and with integrity. The more she knew him, the more he impressed her. He was a pretty simple guy; he loved his faith, his son, and his bike, in that order. He was kind and gentle, without being a pushover. Anne always knew what was on his mind because he voiced his wants and needs—gently but firmly—yet was flexible enough to go with the flow. He was knowledgeable in the ways of nature, pointing out medicinal plants and interesting wildlife as they hiked and fished. Anne could tell that he wasn't just on his "good behavior." John presented himself exactly as he was with no qualms, regrets, or hesitation, regardless of how his actions or words were perceived. It took Anne aback at first—she had never met anyone so forthright—but she soon found it refreshing and even inspirational.

Anne could be shy in asking for what she needed. In her childhood, her mother, especially, had tended to discount her requests; then, later, Charlie had quashed that part of her until there was nothing left. Anne had learned, through therapy, how to state her truth in addition to setting boundaries. Attempting one without the other didn't work very well, so she had had to learn and practice both. Although inconsistent, especially in the beginning, Anne had continued practicing. Now she had a role model to learn from and practice with. She knew instinctively that regardless of how graceless her attempts were, John would honor them and encourage the behavior.

The afternoon was drawing to a close; John was cleaning the bass they had caught while Anne busied herself with the rest of the dinner. They worked well together as a team and innately knew how to jump in and help the other at the right time. In no time, the fire was burning and the fish were frying. And, as they had the night before, they joined the rest of their group for dinner, conversation, and laughs. They all had a wonderful time and talked until midnight, when the party broke up and all the participants strolled to their respective tents.

Around 2:00 a.m., Anne awoke to the sound of thunder. The wind had picked up and rattled the sides of the tent. Flashes of light surrounded her. She could hear the rain falling in sheets around her tent. Suddenly, her tent flap unzipped and a soaked John poked his head in.

"My tent is leaking. There's water everywhere!"

"C'mon in, then! I had no idea we were in for a storm."

"Me either, but it's here!"

Anne and John tried maneuvering in the small tent, hunched over by lamplight, shifting clothes and sleeping bags around so they could both lie down. They ran into each other constantly, like bumper cars, and laughed at their antics. Finally, the close quarters were arranged and Anne and John crawled into their respective sleeping bags.

"You know, we could zip these together and be all nice and toasty," suggested John with a wink.

"Oh, now I get it! You ordered this storm just so you could get into my tent!"

"Damn! You found me out! Worked, though, didn't it?" laughed John.

"Apparently it did. You just stay in your sleeping bag, mister!"

"No problem. I'm just worried that you'll come over here and have your way with me."

"I think you're safe," said Anne. "But if I feel that the urge is too much for me to handle, I'll let you know."

"Whew! I was worried there for a minute."

John paused and rolled over to look at her.

"I just want you to know that this has been the best time I've had in a long time. Thank you for coming."

"Oh, John, I've had a wonderful time being outside, meeting these crazy people, and getting to know you better."

"Getting to know me better, huh? What have you learned?"

"All kinds of things: how smart and kind and funny you are, how sweet and considerate you are, how much honesty and integrity you have…"

"Wow! I must be a pretty good guy for you to see all that stuff."

"You *are* a good guy. In fact, you're the best guy I've ever known."

"Well, Miss Anne, it sounds like you might like me… just a little."

"A little, yes," Anne smiled.

John gazed at her for a moment. He wanted so badly to tell her how he felt, but he wasn't sure if it was the right time. He didn't want to scare her off, but he also wanted her to know. He wasn't sure if he was prepared, though, if she should deny his feelings. He knew he had found the love of his life, and he didn't want to jeopardize the future of the relationship. Best to wait until summer, he decided reluctantly. At that point, there would be nothing to stand in their way—assuming she felt as he did. John quickly pushed that thought away.

Anne broke the silence. "Are you ready to turn the light off and get some sleep?"

"Yes, ma'am. Good night."

"Good night," answered Anne as she rolled over to face away from him.

After the light was out, she could feel him inching closer to her.

He wrapped his arm around her protectively and whispered, "Sweet dreams."

Anne snuggled into his warm body. "You too," she answered, and fell promptly and comfortably asleep in his arms.

Chapter 45

Anne and John awoke to bright sunshine and singing birds. Once they stepped out of the tent, it was a different story. The storm had been as vicious as it was unexpected. Debris littered the ground—leaves and sticks, mostly, but a tree limb had fallen on top of John's tent.

"Good thing you came over to visit last night," said Anne, indicating the limb.

"Yeah, that might have hurt," agreed John.

Other articles were scattered about as well. Towels, fishing gear, overturned chairs, and some of their food had all been strewn around the campsite.

"I hate to say it, but I think our camping trip is over," said John after scrutinizing his tent. "Unless, of course, you want to bunk with me again tonight."

"It looks like your tent got pretty well crunched last night."

"Yeah, the center pole is broken. I might as well toss it."

"Well, I hate to cut our trip short, but I believe we'd both be more comfortable in our own beds tonight instead of that tiny tent," agreed Anne.

"Okay, let's clean this place up. I believe our best bet for breakfast will be in town," said John, holding up a broken carton of eggs.

Cleaning up the camp wasn't quite as difficult as it looked at first; much of what they had brought ended up in the trash. Within thirty minutes, they were packed up and on the road. After a welcome cup of coffee and a hot breakfast, they headed home.

When she got home, Anne unpacked and started a load of laundry. She wondered what Maggie and Richard were doing; she missed them terribly. Then she laughed at herself.

"They drive me crazy when they're here, and I miss 'em when they're gone. The mother's plight!" she muttered.

Anne cleared the kitchen sink of the dirty dishes she had left before the camping trip, picked up the clothes she had contemplated taking and rejected, and tossed the junk mail and old newspapers. With her chores done, she wanted a reward—a ride.

It was cool-ish, so she added another layer. She knew that once she got on the road, the wind would bring the temperature down a bit, and riding wasn't nearly as much fun when she was chilly. She grabbed her leather gloves and helmet as she headed to the door.

Riding helped her clear her head. She loved going out of town to the two-lane country roads. Everything was bursting with life. Baby lambs and goats ran alongside their mothers. The buds on the trees waited for just the right moment to open—when the mix of sun and water was perfect. Wildflowers bloomed along the roadside in swaths of yellow, blue, and pink. Anne wanted to cut some to take home, but knew they would wither in her saddlebags. A visual bouquet would have to do.

She thought about John as she rode. They had had a wonderful time camping together, in spite of the downpour. They had bantered and joked as if they had known each other since the diaper days. Although she had been nervous in the beginning, his easy ways and personable style of interaction had calmed her. Irritations and complications slid away like water from a duck's back. She had never known anyone so calm and centered. It was a very attractive trait; she had noticed it in Tony as well. It made her wonder if her life contained too much drama for him. It wasn't like her kids were bad, but they had their moments.

Would their families mesh? Maybe she should just end it altogether and forgo any future issues. But she loved him. And she didn't know whether or not to tell him. How would he react? She was always going back and forth, weighing all the sides in her mind—so exhausting.

Shit!

Anne pulled the motorcycle off the road and parked at a rest stop. She needed to stomp around and vent.

"Shit!" she yelled at the clouds.

She began one of her conversations with herself, out loud (her kids called this persona the Crazy Lady).

"Do you hear yourself? You sound like some whiny, angsty teenager. You remind me of Bella Swan, possibly the most annoying character in fiction today." Anne screwed up her face, and in her best whiny voice, she chastised: "Oh, you're not sure if he likes you? Poor little girl."

Anne kicked a rock.

"Seriously," she countered in her normal voice, "you are a grown woman. You *know*—and you know you know. He loves you and you love him. It's as simple as that. Be a woman, not a teenager. Is it a risk? Maybe, but probably not, at least as far as the beginning. The rest of it? You know he's a good guy. It will all work out. Shit, there's no drugs, no other women, no lies; he's got a business; and he's a great dad—even if you start with that, you're way ahead of the curve. And you don't even know what kind of a lover he is… yet. He's an awesome kisser, though, so maybe…"

Anne closed her eyes, tilted her head toward the sun, stretched out her arms, and breathed. She slowly turned in a circle, gathering strength from her surroundings. Peace engulfed her, and she knew what to do.

The ride back to town was exhilarating. It amazed her that a little clarity could make such a difference.

She pulled into John's motorcycle shop parking lot a little after five o'clock. He was walking to the door to lock up.

"Hey there! Been out riding?" he asked, locking the door behind her.

"Yes. It's a fabulous day. Maybe you should have taken this as a vacation day, like you originally planned; you could have enjoyed it firsthand."

"It was a good thing I came back early. The truck carrying some special-order parts got into a wreck and won't be here till tomorrow at the earliest, Monday at the latest, or anytime in between. Which puts a kink in some delivery dates for a few customers. Ah, the joys of being a small-business owner. Kevin did a great job, but I know he would have freaked out if this had happened while I was gone. So it's all good."

"All's well that ends well," chimed Anne.

"So, whatcha up to? Wanna go grab some dinner and a movie?" asked John. "The kids don't come back till tomorrow. You could probably even stay out past midnight."

"Okay… actually, I've been thinking…" Anne began.

"Uh-oh, conversations that start like that usually don't end well," sighed John.

"Well, this one ain't over yet," said Anne, grabbing his shirt with both hands, pulling him close. "Kiss me like you mean it."

"With pleasure, my love," agreed John.

The next few minutes looked like so many romantic comedies—kissing, groping, knocking into walls, clothes shedding, back to the small office-turned-boudoir. John threw down a foam mat, quickly unrolled some sleeping bags, and lit some mosquito candles, and the kissing and groping recommenced.

They made love well into the night, eating snacks out of the machine, drinking warm sodas, talking, laughing, and simply enjoying each other… and the scent of citronella.

Just before dawn, they gazed and touched, as if to create an indelible memory of their night together. Anne stroked his face and said what was in her heart.

"I love you, John. It has scared the shit outta me, but I can't deny it any longer. I'm a goner." Anne held her breath and watched him for a sign. She watched him smile, and his eyes crinkled and sparkled like they did when he talked about Tony. She knew.

"Oh, Anne, I love you too. I swear, I think it started with your damn emails," John laughed. "I thought, *How can you fall in love with an email?* But I did. Then, once I got to know you, even with all your rules and boundaries," he chuckled, "my love has done nothing but grow bigger and stronger. I've wanted to tell you so bad, but I was afraid it would scare you away. Whew! Glad you're still here."

"I'm here and I'm not going anywhere." She kissed his nose, then looked at her cell phone. "Except maybe home. Shit! Do you know what time it is? Holy crap. I need to get some sleep and a shower before the kids get home."

"Damn. I know you're right, but I don't want to let you go," said John, pulling her to him. Anne laid her head on his chest, breathing in his scent. Another ten minutes passed before they were willing to separate.

"If I don't leave now, I'll be a wreck." Anne dressed and gathered her belongings. John pulled on his jeans and walked her to the shop door. The sky was turning from black to purple, with hints of orange and pink on the eastern horizon.

"I'll call you later," John whispered. "I love you. So very much."

"I love you too," she said, squeezing him one last time.

By the time she reached home, birds were singing and the sky was lightening. As soon as she entered the house, she stripped off her clothes, threw them in the washer, and jumped in the shower. She checked the clock as she dried herself; she'd manage four or five hours of sleep before the kids were ready to be picked up. She slipped on a sleep shirt and crawled into bed, with one name on her lips: *John*.

Chapter 46

Anne arrived at the church just as the bus pulled in. She was excited about seeing Maggie and Richard, and still reeling from the events of the night before. She spied John across the parking lot and walked toward him. The smile on his face negated the irrational fears that had filled her head. It wasn't just some one-night stand; he truly cared for her.

"You almost missed them," smiled John.

"I know! I had a hard time waking up. I wonder why," she winked.

"I dunno. Insomnia? Late-night movies? Infomercials?"

"No, I think it was more along the lines of hanging out with a certain someone all night."

"Do I know him?"

"I believe you do. He's a wonderful man… and very sexy."

"Naw, I don't know anyone like that!"

"Just look in the mirror. You'll see him," Anne smiled.

Tony, Maggie, and Richard waved and joined their parents.

"How was it?" asked Anne. "I can't wait to hear all about it!"

"Hi, Mom," said Richard, giving her a hug.

"Hi, Mom! I missed you!" said Maggie.

"I missed you too! Both of you, believe it or not!" joked Anne.

"Hey, Dad," said Tony.

"Tony! I've missed you, kiddo!" said John, hugging his son.

"What did you do while I was gone? Hang out at the shop?" asked Tony.

"Um... yeah... mostly," said John, smiling at Anne. "Let's get you home and you can tell me about your trip."

"Mom, basically everything I have is dirty. Looks like you've got some laundry to do," said Richard.

"No, dear heart, it looks like *you've* got some laundry to do. We better get moving. Do you have everything? Ready to go home?"

Maggie and Richard answered in unison, "Yes!"

It had been a fun but exhausting trip for the kids. Lots of hard work, new friends, a long bus ride, and a late-night, impromptu "going home" party had worn them out.

Back at home, with the washing machine running nonstop, Maggie and Richard were glad to be back among familiar surroundings. They spent the rest of the weekend online or on the phone, reconnecting with the friends they hadn't seen in a week, catching up on their rest, and preparing to return to school.

Although Anne was grateful to get back into a routine, she dreaded her morning alarm. It was the time of year when students were tired of school. Spring beckoned to them, pulling them away from their studies, sending them outdoors to play. The seniors, with graduation in their sights, were especially rambunctious. Anne understood their restlessness, but she still had two months of her curriculum to teach. First, the classes would break into small groups, choose a novel to read together, and complete a series of assignments related to it. The students had a laundry list to choose from, from vocabulary to artistic assignments, allowing them to be as creative as they wanted to be. They would end the year with *The Importance of Being Earnest*, a perennial favorite.

In truth, Anne was just as distracted from her work as they were from their studies. In spite of her efforts, John remained the focal point of her attention. They talked on the phone daily, first thing in the morning and last thing at night. It became a cherished routine for them both. The morning call was simply to touch base and wish each other a good day. The evening call was much longer, sometimes going further into the night than planned. They would talk about their day and their kids, and occasionally about their future. No specific plans were made, but they were certain they would be together. Even their children were in agreement, after competing together at a track meet.

All three were involved in the spring sport. Maggie was the runner, Tony was the jumper, and Richard excelled in javelin and shot put. It was the only sport where parents sat on hard bleachers all day, waiting for their child to perform for a few minutes. Likewise, the athletes endured long intervals between events. Maggie, Tony, and Richard found themselves together during these lulls.

"Hey, Tony! Great jump. Bet you win a medal," said Maggie.

"We'll see when all the results are in. Didn't you set a new time in the relay?" asked Tony.

"I think so, but that girl from Austin High may have beat me."

"When do you throw, Richard?" asked Tony.

"I still gotta wait an hour or two. Ugh. Track meets last forever."

"But you get lots of time to hang with your buddies," said Maggie.

"I'd rather be home playing video games," answered Richard.

"Or out riding motorcycles," said Tony.

"Do you ride too?" asked Maggie. "You know, my mom rides. I think it's cool."

"Why don't you learn how? My dad taught me. I bet your mom could teach you," suggested Tony.

Maggie paused.

"Uh... what do you think about my mom and your dad?" she asked.

"I think it's great. My mom wasn't so great, to be honest. I mean, I loved her and all that, 'cause she was my mom, but she was an addict, and then she died."

"That sucks, Tony," said Richard.

"Yeah. I hadn't seen her in a long time, so I don't remember that much. Where's your dad?"

"He's off being a musician, I guess. We never see him," said Maggie. "I like your dad. He seems really nice."

"He's great. He's always been there for me, even when times were tough."

"Hey, do you think we'll end up all being related? Like, if my mom marries your dad?" asked Richard. "I'd like having a brother. Sisters suck, dude!"

"Trust me, little brothers are pretty sucky too, if you ask me. But I'd be okay with it if our parents got married. What about you, Tony?"

"It might be weird at first, just because it's been my dad and me for so long, but it'd be cool."

"Do you think we ought to tell them we approve?" asked Maggie, ever the matchmaker. "Maybe they're worried about it. Maybe that's why they keep their relationship so quiet. You know they talk every day, right?"

"I guess. I don't pay that much attention to my dad's phone calls."

"Yeah, they talk in the morning and at night before they go to bed. I hear Mom giggling and sounding kind of flirty. I think it's cute," sighed Maggie.

"Yeah, whatever, Mags. Do you think they're doin' it?" asked Richard.

"Oh, gross!" said Maggie. "You *would* bring that up. I swear, all boys think about is sex."

"All you think about is love and stuff," said Richard. "I think it's cute," he mimicked.

"Well, I do! And I like seeing Mama happy. He gives her flowers and brought her soup that time she was sick. She deserves someone nice."

"So does my dad," added Tony.

"So, we're in agreement? If our parents get married, we're okay with it, right?" Maggie polled the boys.

"Absolutely," said Tony.

"Yeah, I guess," said Richard.

"Cool. It's settled. I'll figure out a way to let Mom know, in case she's worried about it."

Anne wasn't worried about it—much. She was in love with a good man who was also a good father to Tony. Richard, especially, needed a strong man in his life. She tried to be both mother and father to her children; Maggie did well, but Richard required someone masculine to relate to.

That night at dinner, the three of them discussed the track meet.

"I think you both did a great job today. Did you have a good time?" asked Anne.

"Yeah. Me and Tony and Maggie decided that it's okay if you marry Tony's dad."

"Richard! I was going to find a *subtle* way to tell Mom. Thanks for blowing it."

"What? Wait a minute. You think we're getting *married*?" asked Anne.

"No, Mom, we just said it was okay if you did. You don't have to," said Richard.

"Gee, thanks! Right now, John and I are just good friends," said Anne.

"I bet they're doin' it," Richard whispered to Maggie, who simply rolled her eyes in reply.

"This is new territory for all of us, and I don't know how it will all turn out," said Anne, "but I'm glad I have your approval. Who wants dessert?"

Later that night, Anne shared the news with John.

"Did you know that we have been a topic of conversation with our kids?"

"Yep. Tony told me about their consensus at the track meet. Apparently, they like us as a couple."

"Not just as a couple—they talked about us getting married!" said Anne.

"Is that so bad?" asked John.

"I'm not saying it's bad—just kinda… weird. *We* haven't even talked about it yet."

"Maybe we should," suggested John.

"I don't want to have this conversation over the phone, do you?"

"No, I really don't. Wanna meet?"

"*Now?* It's almost nine, John."

"C'mon. Put on your leathers, get on your bike, and meet me at Summit Park—you know, the one that looks over the lake."

"Yeah, right. I know where it is. But—" Anne began.

"No 'buts,' Anne. I have something I need to say to you."

Anne's heart stopped for a moment.

"Okay. I need to talk to the kids, and leather up, of course. How about thirty minutes?"

"Great. See you then."

Anne's mind raced as she changed clothes. On cue, the negative thoughts rushed in. She thought things were going well. Was he going to end it? Had he met someone else or just decided he didn't want to be with *her*? Anne tried to push them aside, but the negative still outweighed the positive.

"Maggie, I'm going out for a while," said Anne, poking her head in Maggie's room.

"A nighttime bike ride? Sounds great, Mom! Have fun!"

"K. Thanks," answered Anne, surprised at her daughter's nonchalance.

"Richard, I'm going out for a while."

"Heard you tell Mags," he replied, absorbed in his video game.

"Okay, I'll be back in an hour or so. You'd better be in bed."

"Uh-huh," Richard grunted.

Anne strapped on her helmet and rode toward the park. She saw the outline of John's bike against the sparkling lake. John was sitting on the picnic table nearby. As she sputtered down the road, she saw a glow on the table. John had brought candles, flowers, drinks, and snacks, arranging them beautifully on the table. Anne hooked her helmet on the handlebar.

"What's all this?" she asked, relieved. Surely he wouldn't have planned an impromptu picnic to break up with her.

"I thought a moonlight picnic might be nice. How about some fake champagne? Can't let you drink and drive!"

"Champagne? Even fake champagne signifies a celebration. Are we celebrating something?"

"I hope so. Please, have a seat. Help yourself. There's some Chex Mix and string cheese. And the fake champagne. I forgot napkins."

"It's lovely, John. And the celebration is for… ?"

"If you would, please, let me say this in my own way. I've been practicing," he blushed.

"Okeydoke. You'll hear nothing from me until you tell me it's okay," promised Anne.

John stood in front of her and took a deep breath.

"I've been in love with you since the first email you ever sent me. I already knew Tony liked you, but I fell in love with you from day one and haven't stopped since. I think you are the most wonderful woman I have ever met, and I can't imagine my life without you."

John sat next to Anne on the bench, taking her hands in his.

"I think about you all the time—holding you, touching you, loving you… You are my best friend, my lover, my riding buddy all in one. I never dreamed I'd meet anyone like you. But here you are, and I am so very grateful we met."

He cleared his throat.

"I know you've wanted to take things slow, and I've tried to respect that. But, to be honest, the kids are the only ones I care about, and since they're okay with our relationship, I'd like to become more public—uh, not hide it or anything." He paused. "That's not what I want to say. What I want is to marry you—to spend the rest of my life with you, to be one family, us and the kids, to love and cherish till death do us part. Whaddaya say?"

Anne waited a minute before speaking. "May I talk now?"
"Please do! All I need is one three-letter word."
"Y. E. S."

Chapter 47

Monday morning arrived way too early. Sleep had eluded Anne after the surprise proposal—and her equally surprising answer. They had known each other only six months and hadn't spent much time together. And yet her gut told her she had done the right thing. And she always trusted her gut. Still, it remained a shared secret between them for the time being.

Anne smiled as her students shared stories of their break. Ray told the class about hearing the babies' heartbeats, and proudly displayed the black-and-white sonogram for everyone to see. Tiffany continued creating art, in spite of her father's objections. Alateen was creating huge shifts in her thinking and actions. She had always appeared confident, but now it was a reality. She was living her life according to her dreams, not her father's, and the change was remarkable. Kim had volunteered to help with a gay-rights parade in Dallas, making new friends and contacts. She was involved in the movement on a local level but aspired to bigger challenges. Like Tiffany, Kim beamed with a newfound confidence and sense of self, sustained by Anne's encouragement. Keosha shared details of her new job. She worked in a women's clothing store and had found she had a talent for putting cute outfits and accessories together.

Anne loved seeing her students' enthusiasm about their lives and futures. As with her own children, her aspirations for her students included health and happiness, and she was always gratified to see sparks of both in their eyes.

At lunch, she received a text from Karen. *Call me ASAP!* Fearing the worst, Anne called immediately.

"Is everything okay?" she asked.

"Everything is wonderful! I'm getting married!"

"*What?* To Lorenzo?"

"Of course to Lorenzo! My handsome Italian doctor."

"Tell me about it! When did he ask you? What did he say?" pumped Anne.

"Ohmygod, it was so romantic. He took me to that little French bistro. You know, the one with the great steaks. There were flowers on the table, and chilled champagne, and he even hired a string quartet. Right there in the middle of the restaurant, he got down on one knee, told me I was the most wonderful woman on Earth, and popped the question. And you should see the ring! Ohmygod, it's gorgeous. It was his grandmother's ring, and it has a huge round sapphire in the middle, surrounded by diamonds, with two other diamonds on the side. I can't wait for you to see it. I'll text you a picture, but it doesn't do it justice. And the absolute best part (besides marrying Superman) is that we are going to get married at his family's estate in Italy in June. And you and the kids are coming, our treat. No arguments!"

"Karen! Are you kidding? Italy? You can't pay for us. It would be too expensive."

"Like I said, no arguments. Besides, you have to be my maid of honor. And Maggie is going to be a bridesmaid, and Richard is going to be a groomsman. Period."

As much as she wanted to, Anne didn't divulge her news for two reasons. She didn't want to steal Karen's thunder. After all, Karen was thirty-six and it was her first marriage. And Anne had promised John she would keep their secret until they had a chance to tell the children together. Besides, she believed they should lie low until the end of the school year. But she was excited too and wanted to share their news. Still…

"Well, what do you think?" asked Karen.

Anne snapped back to the conversation.

"I'm sorry. I got distracted. Think about what?"

"Blue and gray for my colors."

"Don't you think that's a little Civil War-ish?" asked Anne.

"Do you really think they give a shit about the American Civil War in Italy? A war that happened over two hundred years ago? Seriously?"

"I dunno. It was the first thing that came to mind. Sorry."

"Maybe you're right. But it's not like a dark blue; it's a silvery blue."

"I'm sure it will be gorgeous."

"Crap! Now I don't know what to do."

"Karen, don't worry about it. I'm sorry I said anything. I have no doubt it will be beautiful. I think you should choose what you like. It's your day. Don't listen to me!"

"Okay, I won't!" laughed Karen. "Are you free on Saturday? I have a two o'clock appointment to try on dresses, and you have to be there. And bring Mags too."

"What about… Mother?" asked Anne.

"Have you lost your mind? I want this to be fun, not Momzilla!"

"I guess you're right. Aren't you afraid she'll be hurt?"

"Believe it or not, we've had this conversation. We decided a few years ago that choosing a dress together would *not* be a good idea."

"How adult! Both of you, amazingly enough! I'm stunned. Well, I can't wait! And, Karen… I'm so happy for you. You totally deserve a good man who makes you happy."

"And he does. But I have one more thing to tell you. After the wedding, I won't come back to the States. We're moving to Italy. Permanently."

Anne felt like she had been kicked in the gut. It hadn't occurred to her they would live there.

"Permanently? As in, forever and ever, amen?"

"I'm afraid so. Lorenzo is going to set up a medical practice with his brother. And he's needed in the family business too. But we're going to get a house with lots of bedrooms, and you can stay as often and as long as you like."

"Oh, honey, that's wonderful. What an adventure! You'll learn Italian, and travel all over Europe, and have the best time! I'm so happy for you."

"I know it'll be hard, but we'll see each other a bunch, I promise."

"Oh, my! Will you look at the time? The kids'll be back in a minute. Better run!" said Anne.

"Okay, sis. We'll talk later. And tell Maggie about our appointment. But not before I break the news to her. I want to tell her myself."

"No problem. See you Saturday. Love you!"

"Love you too."

Anne needed a minute to compose herself. Karen in Italy? What would she do without Karen close by? Even though they were both busy with their jobs, they always found time to get together, even for a few minutes. They lived only a mile or two apart and dropped by each other's home frequently. Her relationship with Karen was special, unique. They had a bond beyond blood. They were more than sisters; they were best friends. Anne knew she would eventually accept the idea, but at present she was devastated. She quickly texted John before the bell. *Can I stop by after work? Need to talk.* After Karen, he was next in line when she needed a shoulder. She snapped to the implication of the text and added: *Not about us. Love you.*

She smiled as she realized it was her first "Love you" text to her… fiancé.

Brrrring. Anne sighed. "Not much of a lunch," she muttered, and put on her game face.

The rest of the day passed surprisingly quickly. The kids kept her busy; if she slowed down too long, she thought of Karen and felt that knot well up. She headed toward the shop as soon as her school day was over. Luckily, the shop was empty when she arrived. John looked up from the computer.

"Surfing for porn again?" joked Anne.

"Yeah, you know how it is. A guy's gotta do what a guy's gotta do. What's up, babe? Your first text had me worried about us… till I got the second one. After that, I was just worried."

"I guess it's silly, in a way. The good news is that Karen and Lorenzo are getting married. She's thrilled, needless to say. And I'm thrilled for her. We're going to pick out the dress on Saturday." Anne's eyes were teary.

"So what's the problem?"

"After the wedding, they're going to stay… in Italy… permanently!" Anne's tears gave way to sobs, and she cried on his shoulder.

"But that's great! I think living in Italy would be awesome. Maybe not forever…" John tried to console her.

"I know it's wonderful. It's the chance of a lifetime, and I really am happy for her. I just wasn't expecting… this. I pictured us growing old together, spoiling her children like she does mine. I never thought she'd be half a world away. John, she's my best friend! How am I going to get along without her? And, of course, I can't talk to her about it, even though she's the person I always go to for crap like this."

"Sweet, sweet woman. I'm so sorry you're sad. I understand how you're feeling, though. I feel that way sometimes when I think about Tony going off to school. It's been just the two of us for so long. But the good news is that I'll have you. And you'll have me. We can get through anything together—even when our best friends are miles away. It'll be okay, hon."

Anne stood there for a moment, comforted within his strong arms. She pulled away from him.

"It's like a little death, ya know? I have to give myself time to grieve it. I'll try to do most of it on my own, but some of it may spill out onto you. Forewarned is forearmed," winked Anne, trying to be brave.

"I doubt I'll need to be armed," John laughed, "but I will be here when you need me, day or night."

"I know that. Even before you said it, I knew it. But thank you for saying it anyway. It's just one of the reasons why I love you."

"It sure is nice to hear you say that."

"What?" asked Anne.

"'I love you.' It seems like I waited forever to say it—and to hear it. Definitely worth the wait."

"I'd better get home. The kids will think I got abducted by aliens or something."

"Tell 'em hi for me. I'll call you later. Love ya, darlin.'"

"Bye, John."

It felt good to be able to depend on someone, to lean on someone. Of course, she had Karen, but Charlie had never been any help. Even before he left, she had always been the strong one. Then add teenagers to the mix, and the responsibility she felt flew to a higher level. They would both be on their own in about four years. Were they properly prepared? Had she done a good job of raising them, teaching them morals and values? Would they be able to not only deal with the disappointments that inevitably came with adulthood, but succeed in spite of them? She would know that answer only in hindsight. But she wouldn't be alone in the process. Now she had someone she loved and trusted to talk to, confide in, and rely on. Someone to bounce ideas off of, someone who had her back. Finally.

On Saturday, Anne and Maggie met Karen at the bridal salon. Maggie was so excited that she found it difficult to sleep the night before. Luckily for Anne, her daughter's enthusiasm was infectious. Anne had had a few days to get used to the idea, and with the help of writing and grieving, she was genuinely happy for her sister. She and Maggie talked excitedly while waiting to see the first choice.

"Oh, Mom, I can't believe we're going to Italy! I'm so excited! Can we stay a few extra days and look around? Or maybe go to another country? I mean, we'll already be in Europe. Let's take advantage of it and go to France or Spain. Can you imagine? Being on the Champs-Élysées, by the Seine, where all those writers have walked: D. H. Lawrence, Marcel Proust, Henry Miller, Scott and Zelda… Could we, Mom?"

CLASS LETTERS

"We'll see, honey. Oh, look! Here she comes!"

Karen emerged in a very fluffy dress, with lots of tulle and ruffles. Anne thought she looked like one of those bride cakes where there's a doll stuck in the top of a cake dome, frosted to look like a dress. *Ugh*, thought Anne.

"Too much?" asked Karen.

Anne smiled and nodded. "I'd say so. Maybe something a little more sophisticated—and less Little Bo Peep."

"Does a stick come with that one? You know, those things that herd the sheep," giggled Maggie.

"Crook. Or staff. Either works. Shh…" said Anne.

"Hey, Mom, isn't Karen gonna, like, live in a five-hundred-year-old vineyard or something? How cool is that?"

"I think it's only, like, three hundred years old, but still very cool. Hey, I think she's coming back out."

Dress numbers two, three, four, and five were all equally disastrous. Karen was getting frustrated.

"Hey, Karen, I have an idea. Let me pick out your dress. And close your eyes while we put it on you. Whaddaya think?" Anne offered. "I have a theory…"

"What do I have to lose? Couldn't hurt; might help."

Anne rustled through the dresses, quickly discarding anything that looked like it belonged on a Southern belle. Likewise, anything with ruffles, lots of lace or beading, or a long train was the next to go.

"This one," she smiled. "Got one, Karen. Close your eyes!"

"Yes, ma'am," said Karen, standing dutifully in front of the three-sided mirror.

Karen felt the fabric slide over her skin. It was cool, silky… satin? Sleeveless, that was obvious. The back was laced? Awesome! Way tighter than she had planned. She felt vulnerable.

"Ready, Karen? Open your eyes!"

Karen gasped at the beauty in the mirror. Anne had always been envious of Karen's body, sleek and lean, nice bust (like all the women in the family), and long legs—all from her father's side of the family. Anne, on the other hand, was the dumpy one—short, overweight—like her mother. Her father loved his wife and wasn't ashamed to show it. He grabbed at her playfully, kissing her neck as he snuggled up to her. When he was feeling especially frisky, he would slap her rear and exclaim, "I love your body, honey! You give me a little something extra to hold on to. Sexy mama!" When she had first heard Maya Angelou's poem "Phenomenal Woman," Anne had felt it was written about her mother. Anne was certain that her father's attention fueled her mother's self-confidence and sassy attitude.

Anne envied that too. Not just the attitude, but having a man who loved her no matter what. Charlie was always affectionate—until Anne started carrying extra weight when she was pregnant with Maggie. After that, sex was so rare that it surprised her when she became pregnant with Richard. Part of Anne's frustration with Karen was due to Karen's body issues. Karen always talked about "losing five pounds" when she was already perfect. She had a great physique but hid it under scrubs or sweats and T-shirts. Anne knew the reason, but hoped she had resolved it: Karen (and Anne too, for that matter) had developed breasts early. She'd thought the girls would understand, but they had ostracized her because she received so much attention from the boys. The boys had been fascinated but intimidated, and flirted with her constantly, but only in front of their friends, ignoring her the rest of the time, and never calling. Their family moved to a different part of town by high school, and all was forgotten, but Karen had had a couple of rough years in middle school. Anne wanted her to show off her best features, not hide them.

Karen's eyes filled with tears. She had a great body. With her hair and makeup done, she thought, she would be really pretty—maybe even beautiful. She looked to Anne for confirmation. Anne's tears revealed her answer.

"Ohmygod, Anne! This is the most beautiful dress I've ever seen. I would *never* have picked this out." Karen felt the material as she slid her hands up and down the dress. It hugged her voluptuous curves and wrapped her waist and hips with diagonal swaths of satin. It flowed luxuriously over her body, barely touching her skin yet accenting every aspect of her silhouette. She guessed most things about the dress correctly. It was satin and strapless, and laced in the back. What she had missed with her eyes closed was the delicate beading—silver bugle beads that shimmered across her body in line with the fabric. It was elegant and sophisticated—and she *felt* gorgeous!

"I know. Contrary to what your wardrobe suggests, you have a great body. Great boobs. Great legs. Show 'em off. Dress for your body, not your fears." Anne grabbed her hands. "You are a beautiful woman. I see it, the kids see it, Lorenzo sees it… Everyone sees it but you. I wanted to open your eyes, figuratively and literally."

"I hear ya, sis. Thanks for the nudge. You're absolutely right. It's perfect!"

Karen turned to view herself from all sides. "I guess I *do* have a pretty nice butt. And the girls are relatively perky." She paused a minute before emitting a shriek that could shatter glass. "Ohmygod, I'm getting *married!*"

Chapter 48

After the initial wedding flurry, life resumed some normalcy. Still, it was the primary topic of conversation whenever Anne spoke to Karen or Maggie. They were both caught up in the excitement and planning, while Anne was content to let them whirl. She had two and a half months of school to plan, execute, and grade; she left the wedding arrangements to Karen and Maggie, primarily, along with some help from their mother. As with the dress, all concerned knew that the mother of the bride needed limited input in order to keep the peace.

Unfortunately, the ban on input didn't extend to Anne. Jane called Anne daily to discuss the wedding, her feelings about Karen's choices, Lorenzo, their move to Italy, and any other facet of Karen's life she could think of.

Anne, the peacemaker, tolerated it for a couple of weeks, knowing that her mother needed some kind of outlet. Then Anne was gradually sucked in, relegating more and more of her life to her mother and the wedding. After all, she was the one who never said no, even when it was in her best interest. In spite of the work she had done with the therapist, old habits died hard, and this one was practically immortal.

Then it hit her.

One evening, she was talking to her mother, cooking dinner, grading papers, and doing laundry simultaneously. She was behind on everything and felt overwhelmed. And then she really listened to her mother's diatribe, realizing that they had had this same conversation about Karen's choice of colors umpteen times.

"Mom, I've got to go," said Anne, interrupting the monologue.

"Is everything all right?"

"Yes. I just need to get off the phone. And, Mom, I love you, but the constant discussions about Karen's colors, or anything else wedding-related, have to stop. I can't continue to spend all my time on the phone with you. Either talk to Karen directly, or talk to Dad or one of your friends, but you can't call me all day every day anymore. Okay?"

"Well, you know I can't talk to Karen. She set up one of her laws about it."

"It's called a boundary, Mom. That's what I'm doing: setting a boundary. I love you, but I just can't continue to spend all my time on the phone with you."

"I guess it's been a little excessive. I'll try."

"Thanks, Mom. I really do have to go. I have work to do. I'll talk to you in a few days, okay?"

"All right, sweetheart. I love you too."

Anne hung up and sighed. She had definitely been in victim mode: Mom would call, Anne would either multitask or drop everything to accommodate her, and then she would become resentful at the intrusion and yet participate anyway, without standing up for herself. Old behavior that Anne knew well.

Anne had played the victim for years, but it had reached new heights—or lows, as the case may be—when she was married to Charlie. All their problems were his fault; she was simply trying to hold their small family together as best she could. She felt powerless and hopeless. She saw a similar pattern when dealing with her mother: the way she took the criticism and "help" her mother offered about her weight, her life, her relationships, without saying a word. Her life was all about taking blame and making excuses. And it gave her the subject of her next letter.

When the kids were quietly tucked away in their rooms, she began to write.

April

Dear Class:

There's a phrase I relate to; maybe you can too. It goes like this: "First you're a victim, then a volunteer."

A victim and a volunteer? For what?

My sister is getting married. It's an exciting time, and there's lots to do and, apparently, talk about. As a result, my mother has been calling me several times a day to discuss various aspects of the wedding. There are several problems with this. One is that my mother really needs to discuss this with my sister, not me. It's her wedding, after all. Another problem is that my mother tends to call often—like, eight or ten times a day. And we generally discuss the same things we did the last time she called. She's not senile, just needy! And I have played right into that. I've answered all her calls and talked about every part of the wedding you can imagine. It took way too much time, but I did it anyway.

I knew from the first phone call that it would be like this. And I did it anyway.

Why? Because it's hard to say no to my mother. But it leaves me feeling like a victim. Like I'm powerless to stop her or to set any kind of boundary. So I continued to take her calls, which made me feel angry and resentful. It's really not a fun way to live your life.

I was a victim the first time she called on this topic; the other fifty million times she's called, I have been a volunteer. It had to stop.

First, I had to become aware of my actions. I could see how I was making more time for her calls than for anything else. I needed to find some balance. I had to take responsibility for my actions. My mother was not going to stop calling until I asked her to. So when I allowed her to call over and over, even though I didn't like it, I essentially encouraged her to continue.

Once I saw that I was back into my old victim-behavior patterns, I knew it was time for a change. I had to set a boundary. I can't blame her for disrupting my day when I'm allowing it. As a result, I told her I can't talk to her several times daily, and that I would call her in a few days. It wasn't too hard telling her. Trust me, we've had lots of practice at this.

But sometimes, when a behavior is new (like, if you're setting a boundary with someone for the first time), the others involved may rebel. It's not like the way it "used to be": comfortable and familiar. Change is hard, but it can be done, even when you have opposition. You just have to stand your ground. Sometimes you may have to reset the same boundary over and over. Just because you want to change doesn't mean everyone wants to! And sometimes you may have to be assertive and stick up for yourself. That can be tough too, especially when you're not used to doing it, but it's better than being a victim your whole life.

The trick is to add a little detachment in with your request to protect yourself, in case there's a negative response, or backlash later on. Many times we don't stand up for ourselves because we are afraid of the reaction. Do not be afraid! Ask for what you need! Take responsibility for your life! The ball is entirely in your court. Do nothing, and all behaviors will continue. Speak up, and you take yourself out of victim mode. It's your choice. Setting a boundary is simply a limit: You can do this, but not that. This is okay; that is too far. When you take care of yourself and then detach from the outcome, you are no longer a victim. It's no longer "someone else's fault" if you are unhappy with your life.

One way to detach is to keep the conversation "businesslike." In other words, be concise, reasonable, and specific. You don't have to go into a long explanation; just ask for what you need (concise). For example, I told my mother that we could talk again in a few days (specific), just not daily, as we had been. I didn't tell her we could never, ever talk about the wedding again (unreasonable). And remember, "no" is a complete sentence.

Sometimes you have to set boundaries over and over again until the other person "gets" it. It can be frustrating, but they aren't doing it to make you angry; they are simply acting out of old behavior patterns that need to be rerouted. Even if you have to say the same thing over and over ("I can only talk to you once every other day," for example), then say it over and over—and stick to it. It will eventually sink in.

You are the one who determines the course your life takes. If you don't, I promise someone else will. Don't gripe about it (i.e., be a victim); take action and do something. As my grandmother used to say, "Fish or cut bait."

Have you found yourself playing the victim? Did you like being a victim? If not, what did you do to change it? Could you find ways to set reasonable, specific, concise boundaries with the other person? How did it go?

You know the drill. You have a week to write a response for a quiz grade. Think about this behavior and search your life for it; it can be hard to spot if it's deeply embedded, but well worth the effort if you no longer wish to be a victim. Good luck!

On Monday morning, Anne stood in the workroom, making copies for class. She was pleased with the letter and grateful to be able to share solutions with her students. She had had a difficult time with this concept and hoped a few of her students could see themselves in this letter. Lord knew, Anne had seen evidence of victimhood in their lives; now it was up to them. But this was usually the case with her letters: her goal was to make them aware of her foibles and challenges so they could see them in their own lives, and to offer solutions so they wouldn't have to suffer like she had. Just as she did with her own children, she hoped that the kids who really needed it would grab on to some tidbit—even if only to store it away for a few years until the time was ripe for its resurrection. Even though she received great feedback from her students about the letters, she wondered if they really did any good, or if the kids looked at them like platitudes from a well-meaning teacher. That part was out of her hands. Still, she felt a little nudge inside her to continue the letters, so she did.

Chapter 49

The last couple of months of the school year were a flurry of activity, especially for the seniors. There were multiple meetings related to graduation and counselor visits to determine the students' next course of action. The ones who vied for the top spots in the class continually checked their class rank. On the other end of the spectrum, some students were simply trying to accrue enough credits to graduate. The athletes were keeping busy as well. Track meets, tennis and golf tournaments, and spring soccer meant that most classes were smaller on Fridays. With so many students in and out of class on a daily basis, Anne's goal was to simply keep the ones in class engaged and keep the ones out of class caught up. It required organization and lots of sticky-note reminders on her part.

This year was more challenging than those of the past because of the addition of Karen's wedding preparations. Since Jane had limited input by mutual agreement, Karen relied on Anne for help, direction, insight, and approval. Decisions had to be made regarding colors, fonts, flowers, invitations, monograms… the list was endless. Even though the wedding itself would be a relatively small affair—around one hundred guests—the trappings were extensive. The wedding and reception were going to take place at the family's three-hundred-year-old estate. The ceremony itself would be in the family's chapel and the reception in the garden. Karen and Lorenzo would be married on a Sunday, the luckiest day for weddings, in the Italian tradition. A meal with several courses would follow the ceremony, with dancing afterward. Anne enjoyed her involvement, in spite of the addition to her full workload.

Today was one of the days when several students would be missing from each class because of counselor conferences. Anne passed out the April letter and assigned the next chapter in the novel they were reading, allowing her students to choose the assignment they wanted to complete. Since the majority of her students were ahead in the novel, they focused on the letter.

Keosha was the first one to finish the letter. She walked up to Anne's desk with a smile on her face.

"I think you're going to like this one," she smiled at Anne.

"I'm sure I will," Anne replied.

"You can read it now, if you want."

"I think I will," said Anne, smiling at Keosha's enthusiasm. Keosha sat down and waited quietly while Anne read.

Dear Mrs. E:

I have learned a lot about being a victim and a volunteer this year. I got sucked into BD's crap and stayed there too long. I thought I had it bad, but I didn't know how good my life really was. I felt sorry for myself cuz I didn't have a dad and cuz my mama had to work so hard. I tried to help out and got involved with the wrong people. I didn't see that there was any other way. I felt stuck. Even though I knew it was wrong. Like you said, I didn't know how to say no. Then all that stuff with Li'l Joe happened. I thought it was going to make my life terrible, but it really helped me a lot. It made me be honest with my mama for the first time in a long time. And it made me be honest with myself. Once I could see everything the way it really was, it helped a lot. Then I got my job, which I love. I get to help women look their best, which makes them feel their best.

You said in your letter that I am the one that's in charge of my life. That's part of what I learned when I got honest with myself. I saw that I had put my life in the hands of a drug dealer. That was crazy! I didn't like myself much then either. Then I got my job. I was talking to my manager the other day. She told me how good I was doing and how good I was with the customers. She told me that I have a talent for putting cute stuff together that she would never think of. She thinks I should go to that design school that has ads on TV. I didn't really know what she was talking about so I googled it and learned all kinds of things about being a clothing designer. It sounds like so much fun! Do you think I'd be good at it? I haven't signed up or anything, but I really think I'd like it. What do you think?

Wow! This is probably the longest letter I wrote! LOL. Things are looking good!

Keosha

Anne couldn't stop the tears that welled in her eyes. To be witness to the changes in this young woman's life astounded her. The strength, the courage, the perseverance… she was as proud of Keosha as she was of her own daughter. She glanced at the clock and realized there were about fifteen minutes left of class; she motioned to Keosha to come to her desk.

Anne whispered, "I'm so stinkin' proud of you! Look at how you've taken back control of your life, and found an occupation you love in the process. That's awesome, Keosha!"

"I know! I mean, thank you. I can't believe it. My manager really said all those things."

"Have you talked to your counselor about a design school?"

"Nah. You know, my grades weren't so good the past coupla years."

"Let me tell you a little story: When I was in college, I had the opportunity to spend a semester in Europe. I was lucky; I had been before and knew how cool it would be to spend several months there. But my grades weren't so good either. I *assumed* they wouldn't be good enough, so I didn't even try. I heard later that grades really weren't even that big a deal, and I could have easily gotten in. So I missed out on that experience because I just assumed my grades weren't high enough. I didn't even check. I have always regretted that. Do yourself a favor, Keosha. At least check before you give up on your dream. I don't want you to have regrets in thirty years, like I do."

"Wow," said Keosha, in awe. "You've done dumb sh… stuff too."

"Trust me, I've done more dumb stuff than you can imagine," laughed Anne. She paused, then looked Keosha in the eye. "But I don't give up."

"Yes, ma'am. I'll stop by and put in a request right after class."

"Here's a pass. Class will be over in two minutes. Get ahead of the masses in the halls."

"K! Thanks, Ms. E. I'll let you know how it goes," said Keosha with a wave.

"You better!"

The rest of the day was predictable and relatively easy. Anne talked with Karen throughout lunch about wedding details and decisions, as she usually did three or four times a week. It was fun, exciting, and draining. Anne was looking forward to June 15, the day *after* the wedding. She also took time to do a little dreaming about her own. Something small; family and close friends; not real dressy but not real casual; something sweet; smelly flowers. Anne's favorite fresh-cut flowers were any with a lovely fragrance. Richard had called them "smelly flowers" as a child, and the name had stuck.

Anne gathered the papers she needed to grade and clipped them together; she was putting them in her satchel when something caught her eye. She was surprised at how worn the satchel was, especially since it was only a year old. No, wait. It was *five* years old. She couldn't believe it had been that long. She remembered buying it as a present to herself in honor of her fifth year of teaching. Now it was *ten*. Had she really been so preoccupied with her life that the last ten years had blurred together? If she really focused, she *might* be able to put it all together. So many kids, and parents, and drama, plus her own family.

Twenty minutes later, she walked into her living room to find Richard and Joe completely absorbed in playing video games, surrounded by snacks and drinks.

"Richard, I swear, you're going to eat me out of house and home."

"We're teenagers, Mom—we tend to eat a lot."

"I can see that. Be sure to clean up after yourselves."

"Uh-huh... will do."

Anne checked on Maggie, who was sitting on the floor by her bed, talking on the phone. Yet another scene of these wild inhabitants in their natural surroundings.

Since Anne had had the foresight to put together a Crock-Pot before she left for work, dinner was done. *Whew!* she thought. She was free to read more letters.

After changing into shorts and a T-shirt, Anne settled in on her bed—out of earshot of the murder and mayhem that continued in the living room—and pulled the papers out of her satchel. Tiffany's was on top:

Dear Mrs. English:

I'm beginning to wonder if you haven't been to Alateen cuz lots of the stuff you talk about is stuff that I hear in meetings. Like this letter about change. We talk about change a lot but not so we can change other people, but so we can change ourselves. That part about detachment works great. I have to detach from my father all the time. I used to be angry at him, and sometimes I still am, but I'm getting better at just leaving him alone. I don't ignore him, but I don't talk to him much when he's been drinking. It's really helped too. I don't feel so angry all the time anymore. And I've learned how to ignore his mean comments about my art. I've been painting a lot and have entered a painting in the city art show. I'm so excited! It's called Lost Soul Rescued and it's based on David. I really like it. I'll have to show you a picture of it.

Anyway, like you said, change can be hard. When I first started going to Alateen and tried some of the stuff I was learning at home, it almost made things worse. I thought I was doing it wrong, but my sponsor told me that that's how stuff happens a lot of the time. One person starts to change and other people don't like it. Like you said about boundaries, sometimes you have to do it over and over. I hate that! I wish I could just say it or act a certain way once and that he'd get it. I guess I have to be persistent. It's hard, but it's worth it when it works.

I'm still looking into art schools. And my dad is still bugging me about law school. I guess some things never change! LOL.

So lots of things in my life are changing, but for the better, I think. At least I'm happier than I've been in a long time. Even through all the things that have happened. I'm learning new ways to deal with my problems. I'm so grateful for Alateen and I'm so grateful to you for telling me about it!

Love,

Tiffany

Anne always smiled when she knew she had made a difference.

Chapter 50

Anne was almost through grading papers for the night. It was late, almost eleven. She was exhausted; she began her evening routine of brushing her teeth and applying the antiwrinkle cream she had recently begun using. Then the phone rang.

"Hello?"

"May I speak with Anne English?"

"This is she. Who's this?"

"My name is Gloria Jimenez; I'm a nurse in the emergency room at Mercy Hospital. We have one of your students here, Kim, and she asked me to call you."

"Kim? What happened to her?"

"It looks like she was attacked and beaten. Bruises, mostly, but she needed a few stitches too. Would you be able to come to the hospital?"

"I'm on my way."

Both kids were asleep, so she left a note on her pillow in case one of them came in looking for her. Anne jumped in her car and raced downtown.

Kim was asleep when she arrived. A knot above her eye was stitched, and the entire area showed various shades of black and blue. There were cuts and bruises on her arms. Her lip was swollen. Kim stirred and opened her "good" eye.

"Oh, Mrs. English. Thank you for coming," Kim said.

"What happened, honey?"

"Three guys came up behind me and just started hitting me for no reason. They called me a dyke lesbo cunt." Kim began to cry.

"Did you recognize any of them?"

"No, it was dark and I tried to protect myself with my arms. But one of the voices sounded familiar."

"Did they take anything? Do you think it was someone from school? Do you think you'd recognize their voices if you heard them again?"

"They just kept hitting me. And laughing. That was the worst part. I might be able to if I heard them, but I don't know for sure. Did they do this just because I'm gay? How can anyone have so much hate in their life?"

"I don't know, honey. I don't get it either," said Anne. "The police took your statement, right?"

"Yeah, but there wasn't much I could tell them. They said they would look into it, but I doubt they'll find much. They said they would see if there were any witnesses and would contact me in a few days. And I probably won't be at school tomorrow."

"Of course not! You need to stay home and rest. Let those injuries heal. Kim, I'm just so sorry this happened. I can't imagine how awful it must have been for you. I don't understand why they would target you. I know you're active at school and in the gay community, but you're not radical."

"You don't have to be radical. You just have to be gay," said Kim. "But Mrs. English…"

"Yes, Kim?"

"Please don't tell my parents, but this just makes me want to fight harder for gay rights."

"I don't blame you, Kim. You make me so proud! But I'd hate for this to happen again."

"It's *because* of this that I have to fight."

Kim's parents arrived, horrified and angry at the injuries to their daughter. Anne couldn't understand their conversation in Korean, but it was clear they were very upset and worried. After they talked with the doctor, they left with Kim and her prescriptions and care instructions.

Anne returned home around 1:00 a.m., exhausted, saddened, and angry about the scene at the hospital. She didn't understand such hate and ignorance, especially when it was displayed against Kim. She had done nothing to deserve this. She was a good student who was kind to everyone. Her only "sin" was her sexual orientation. She didn't promote anything except acceptance and tolerance. Anne turned off the light and cried herself to sleep.

The next day, she spent her conference period talking with the principal, Mr. Henderson, about Kim. They brainstormed ways to promote tolerance and create a safe campus for all students. Nothing was officially resolved, but Anne hoped they would make some headway. There probably wasn't much they could do this year, especially since there were only another six weeks of school left, but they could strive to improve things for the next year.

During their daily lunch call, Anne shared the incident with John. In the middle of it, Maggie texted: *Mom, two guys in my math class are laughing about Kim Le and how she got hurt last night. What happened?*

What guys? Anne texted back.

I don't know their names. They've only been here a couple of months. I think they're brothers or cousins or something. Did something happen to Kim?

I'll tell you about it later. Find out their names and let me know, okay?

K.

A few minutes later, Anne received another text from Maggie: *Josh Maxwell and Justin Haynes. And they're posting about it on Facebook.*

Bingo! Maybe they were ignorant *and* stupid. After school, she went back to Mr. Henderson with the new information. After digging into the boys' records, they found similar instances at their previous school. Nothing was proved, but it was noted nonetheless. Mr. Henderson made plans to investigate the following day.

Kim stayed home from school the rest of the week, but the administrators were busy in her absence. They obtained records of the postings and called in students for additional information. The suspects were sent to the office and questioned. Ultimately, the administrators got the information they needed. Parents were called. The boys were first suspended, then sent to the alternative school for the rest of the school year. Kim's parents declined to press formal charges, out of fear of retaliation. They had too many fears about authority from their lives in North Korea, and old habits were hard to break. At least the boys were off campus for the remainder of the year, and Kim could enjoy the rest of her senior year in peace.

Chapter 51

The following Monday, before school started, Ray walked into the classroom with a black eye and a split lip.

"Ray, what happened?"

"It's here in my letter. Sorry it's late."

"It's not like you to be late with an assignment."

"I know. It's all in the letter. I gotta go find Isabel before school starts. See ya later!"

Anne was confused. He seemed pretty chipper, almost proud, considering he was black and blue. Anne glanced at the clock. Luckily, she had her lesson ready for the day and had plenty of time to read his letter.

Dear Mrs. E:

I know this is late. Sorry. I hope it'll be worth it anyway.

I grew up being a part of a gang. My father was in a gang, which is why he's in prison now. So it seemed like the normal thing to do. I stole, did drugs, sold drugs, and other stuff. It was all I knew. They were my homies....mi familia. I pledged to put them above all others. Until I met Isabel and Jessie. Jessie was part of a gang too for a long time. He helped me see that the gang life isn't a good life. And he showed me that there is another way to live. I already knew alot about fixing cars, but he's taught me alot about that too. Isabel taught me what love is. The gang doesn't really love me. They say we're familia but they don't act like it. They just want me to do stuff for them. After I read your letter, I knew what I had to do. I felt like a victim. Like they were taking my life in a direction I didn't want to go. Like I didn't have a choice. I wanted out. I wanted out for a long time but I didn't know how. They know about Isabel and the babies. They know I'm doing good with Jessie. So Jessie and I talked to them so I could get out. Outta respect for my father, and after talking to Jessie, they said I could get out if they gave me a beatdown. It's when they beat you up and you just have to stand there and take it. So, that was Friday night. And now I'm out. And I can just live my life, work for Jessie, and be a good man to Isabel and the babies. This is something I wanted for a long time, but it wasn't until I read your letter that I knew what I had to do. There was that one line that made me sure. If I don't plan my life, someone else will (or something like that). I had to get control of my life. I have too many responsibilities now. And I don't want to end up like my father. I want to be there when the babies grow up. The only thing that's left for me to do is tell my father. He may be mad at me, but that's okay. I can deal with that.

Wow! This is like the longest letter I wrote all year. I want you to know that you helped with this decision. You've been my favorite teacher in high school.

Love,

Ray

Anne sat in amazement, more so at Ray than at the impact of her letter. It must have taken a great deal of strength and courage to endure the beating. The desire to be different, to take care of his family, to live his life his way, these were the things that impressed Anne. She was so proud of Ray, she thought she might burst. The letter, and his obvious pride in himself, kept Anne smiling all day long.

The weekend ahead would be a busy one. Now that John and Anne's relationship was kid-approved, they wanted to spend time together as a couple and as a "family." This weekend, they planned to take a trip to Dinosaur Valley near Glen Rose. It was a wonderful state park on the Paluxy River. Remnants of the ancient beasts were everywhere in the form of visible tracks along the river. The Paluxy itself varied from ankle- to knee-high in most places, depending on the location, time of year, and rainfall. They took a picnic lunch, bathing suits, and towels and planned to spend the day hanging out on the river. Anne and John lounged at their chosen spot and watched the kids and Rocky play in the river.

"They all seem to be getting along just fine, don't you think?" asked John.

"I love it! Especially for Richard. He's been surrounded by estrogen for way too long!" laughed Anne.

"Wait 'til hunting season in the fall. He's going to love going out with Tony and me."

"He's never shot a gun in his life. I hope he doesn't shoot one of you."

"No problem. We can take him to the shooting range and get him up to speed. Hey, I forgot to tell you. A customer came in wanting to sell a two-fifty. I thought I'd get it for Richard to learn on. What do you think?"

"Richard on a motorcycle? I don't know..."

"He'll be fine. All he needs is a little instruction and practice."

"Someone's getting a motorcycle?" asked Maggie as she approached the couple.

"Yeah, there's a two-fifty for sale that I thought Richard might like to learn on," said John.

"Richard? What about me? I want to learn to ride!"

"I didn't know that," said Anne.

"You ride. Why can't I?"

"You can; I just didn't know you wanted to. What about it, John?" asked Anne.

"Absolutely! I'll teach you both. We'll just be one big motorcycle-riding family!" laughed John.

"So when are you two getting married?" asked Maggie.

"Yeah, I was wondering that too," said Tony, joining the group.

Anne and John glanced at each other with a silent *What do we do now?* look.

"Hey, Richard! Come over here for a minute, okay?" called John.

As Richard walked up, John said, "Have a seat. I guess it's time for a talk."

"Whatever it is, I didn't do it," said Richard.

"Guilty dog barks first," teased Maggie.

"I'm not a dog and I'm not guilty, Miss Perfect."

"You're usually guilty!" said Maggie.

"Maybe, but not this time… whatever it is," countered Richard.

"No one's in trouble. We just wanted to talk to you for a minute," said Anne, looking to John to take over.

"You guys know that we've been seeing each other for a while. And, much to our surprise, we fell in love. I don't think either of us was expecting it, but it has made us both very happy." John took Anne's hand, kissed it, and smiled at his beloved. "And, amazingly enough, this wonderful woman has agreed to marry me."

"Finally! When? Can I be the maid of honor?" Maggie asked.

"Of course you can," said Anne. "We haven't picked a date or anything. We thought we'd even wait to announce it until after Karen's wedding. I guess we blew that!"

"Now we can tell everyone!" gushed Maggie. "Oh, this is so exciting! C'mon, guys, don't you think this is cool?" She looked to Richard and Tony for confirmation.

"Of course it's cool! I was just waiting to get a word in! You're all,

'Oh, goody! How wonderful! I want to be the maid of honor!'" said Richard, aping Maggie.

"Well, it *is* wonderful. What do you think, Tony?" said Maggie.

"Sounds good to me!"

"Well, when you figure everything out, lemme know," said Richard, heading back to the river.

"Yeah, me too," added Tony, following Richard.

"I'm sure you two want to bask in all this love stuff now. I think I'll hang with the guys," Maggie said.

Anne and John watched the three teens wade in the river.

"I guess they're okay with it," John laughed, breaking the silence. "So whaddaya think? When should we tie the knot?"

"I don't want to steal Karen's thunder. On the other hand, after the wedding, she'll be off on her honeymoon, and then living in Italy; it might be too much to have them come back to the States so soon…" Anne wrestled with the time frame.

"How about this? We just want something small anyway. I'd really be okay with our family and a couple of friends at the courthouse or a JP somewhere, and out to lunch or dinner to celebrate. I don't think we'd be stepping on toes if we kept it small—and got married sooner rather than later," suggested John.

"Hmm… you may be right. Would you want to move into my house? Tony and Richard could share a room. Maggie will be gone next year, Tony the year after that, and Richard the year after that. It would be a little tight for a while, but we could make it work, don't you think? We'll have to find a way to make all our stuff fit."

"Honestly, I could give all that furniture away. Or toss it. It's cheap stuff we got after Katrina, and most of it's falling apart. How about next weekend?"

"Can't. Karen's shower. Besides, I'd like a little time to plan something. It may be small, but it's my last wedding, so I'd like it to be nice. Let me look at the calendar when I get home, and we can go from there."

"All right. Sounds good. Just tell me when and where, and I'll be there with a big ol' smile on my face."

"That's what I like to hear!" said Anne. Her head whirled with ideas. She leaned into John, smiling.

Anne was getting married.

Chapter 52

The next couple of weeks were a blur for Anne. Spring fever and senioritis were in full bloom. Anne spoke with the minister from her church, who suggested the small prayer chapel for her 11:00 a.m. wedding. They would then head over to the tearoom at the botanical gardens nearby for lunch and cake and flowers—smelly ones, of course! After Karen's shower, Anne, Karen, and Maggie went dress shopping and found a beautiful ecru shantung suit for Anne, plus some gorgeous shoes to match and cute little chiffon numbers for Maggie and Karen, all on sale. John bought his groomsmen new suits, also on sale. Later, John and Anne visited a local craftsman who created unique bands and found a matching pair they both loved. The whirlwind of activity made for a wonderful, albeit hectic, day.

Anne's excitement robbed her of sleep until around 5:00 a.m., when she fell into a deep slumber. So deep, in fact, that she slept through her nine o'clock alarm.

"Ohmygod, Mom! I can't believe you're still in bed. Get up! We have to get you gorgeous! It's your wedding day, remember?" Maggie roused her mother.

"Crap! Okay... shower first, right? Coffee... can someone please bring me coffee?" asked Anne.

"It's going to be okay, Mom. Just breathe," Maggie reminded her.

Anne jumped in the shower and began scrubbing furiously. She stopped and chuckled at her panic. *Breathe... Maggie told me to just breathe.* She leaned against the shower wall and allowed the water to run over her, soothing her. She thought about John—how they had met and fallen in love, what a good man he was, how safe and loved he made her feel. Maybe their courtship had been a bit short, but she knew it was the right thing, for her as well as the children. They needed a man in their lives, especially Richard. Tony was a bonus. What a great kid! She hoped they would become a real family. No steps—just Mom, Dad, brothers, sister.

"Mom? Did you drown?" Maggie called.

"No, honey, just taking my time."

"Well, I think you should take *less* time in there and *more* time out here so we can do your hair."

"Yes, dear," sighed Anne.

With Maggie and Karen both barking orders, Anne did as she was told. She sat while the two buzzed around her, applying makeup, rolling hair, and securing jewelry. Meanwhile, the groom and his helpers were eating pancakes, drinking coffee, and watching cartoons, waiting for Pinky and the Brain to complete their mission of world domination.

At ten thirty, the three women jumped into the limo Karen had hired to go to the church. In spite of their lackadaisical attitude, all the guys were at the church on time, showered, shaved, and dressed. The groomsmen seated a number of family members and friends.

The couple opted for the simplest ceremony possible. Short and sweet, but meaningful. They ended with lines from *The Prophet*:

You were born together, and together you shall be forevermore.

You shall be together when the white wings of death scatter your days.

They said their "I do's," exchanged rings, and kissed as husband and wife. Just the way they wanted it.

The small congregation clapped, and pictures were snapped before the trek to the tearoom was made. John and Anne smiled continuously, thrilled with their partnership and joyful at the thought of the life ahead of them. Their wedding luncheon was filled with the sound of laughter, clinking glasses, funny stories, and loving toasts. There was no doubt that everyone was happy about the union. After cake and more toasts, Anne and John slipped off to their suite at the new luxury hotel downtown, with plans to stay holed up in their room, order room service, and make love until checkout time the next day. They were grateful for the alone time, in spite of the short duration. Besides, they were taking a family honeymoon to Italy in June. And no one was complaining about that.

News spread quickly among students and faculty at the high school. Anne had told only a few people, and yet virtual strangers were congratulating her. The English department surprised her with a thirty-minute lunchtime shower midweek. But more important to Anne was the news she received from two of her students.

Before school started that Friday, Anne found Tiffany and Keosha sitting in front of her door, awaiting her arrival. Both were beaming.

"Hi, Mrs. E! 'Scuse me—Mrs. Rogers. It's so weird calling you that!" said Tiffany.

"It's kinda weird hearing it too!" chuckled Anne.

"We have news! Keosha, you go first."

"Naw, you were here first."

"Well, one of you has to go first! I'll pick a number between one and ten, okay?" suggested Anne.

"Five," said Keosha.

"Seven," said Tiffany.

"It was three. Keosha wins! Now tell me what's going on before we all bust!"

"Okay, so remember how I told you that the manager at my work said I was good with putting outfits together? Well, Mama and me talked, and with me working too, she says I can go to design school, so I applied and I got in! Even with my grades! Can you believe it? Man, I never thought I'd be going to college. And doing design? This is the best sh… stuff that's happened to me in a long time. Anyway, I know Tiffany has news too, so I don't wanna take up any more of your time. Go on, Tiff."

"K. Well, first, I found out last night that I won the city art competition. First place in high school and first place overall! There's gonna be, like, some ceremony where they announce the winners. Can you come?"

"Can you tell me when and where?"

"I'll have to find out from my mom, but I'll let you know. It's no big deal if you can't. You may be busy with your new husband and stuff. But if you can, it would be awesome. And, on top of that, my dad has agreed to let me go to art school since I won. I guess he figures all those judges can't be wrong. So we're going to look into schools this weekend. I'm so excited. Oh yeah, he went to AA too. And my mom finally went with me to Al-Anon while Dad was in the AA room. Dunno if he'll stay, but at least he's giving it a shot."

"Wow! Both you girls have such great news! Congratulations to you both! Keosha, I'll look for you in *Vogue*, and Tiffany, I'll look for you in some museum somewhere," Anne laughed. "Really and truly, that is awesome news! I'm so proud of both of you! Good job!"

Anne spent the rest of the day on cloud nine. She thought about Keosha and Tiffany and how far they had come. She thought about Ray and all the positive changes he had made. She thought about Kim, her courage, and her determination to promote tolerance and equality. And she thought about David—how confused and angry he had become—and her sadness at a life cut so short.

It was time to write the May letter.

Chapter 53

The weekend was a busy one. John and Tony had a yard sale to dispose of the things they didn't need—which was almost everything except their clothes and a few treasures. It wasn't a "sale" in the traditional sense, but they didn't know what else to call it. They didn't want to throw everything away, and John deemed their belongings not worth enough to make any real money on, so they gave it all away. It was gone by noon. Afterward, they cleaned their apartment, packed their remaining belongings, and moved permanently into Anne's house.

It was an adjustment for all of them. Neither John nor Anne was used to having a roommate, and both bent over backward to be accommodating. Richard had to learn to share his room as well. And although Maggie didn't have to share a room, she had to share everything else, including the bathroom—formerly her oasis. Still, with all the changes in their lives, they enjoyed the togetherness and the company.

By Sunday afternoon, everything John and Tony owned had been moved, given away, or stored, and the two of them, with Richard in tow, went fishing as a reward for their hard work. Maggie spent the day with Lauren, and Anne was completely and blissfully alone. It was a good time to write.

May

Dear Class:

Can you believe the year is almost over? Pretty soon, you'll be out of high school and ready to move into the next phase of your life. I hope you don't forget your (favorite) old English teacher along the way. But you can always come by and visit. I probably won't be going anywhere… unless I win the lottery or write a Pulitzer Prize-winning novel.

So in this, my last letter to you all, I want you to know how proud I am of you. Throughout the year, I have been amazed at your courage in the face of adversity. I've been impressed with changes you've made and the different ways you have grown. You all have an inner strength that is undeniable—one that will carry you into your twenties and beyond. You may not recognize it now, but, trust me, it's there. Trust your gut. There is a wisdom deep inside you that has all the answers. All you have to do is listen quietly for the still, small voice.

Now, think about the person you want to be. Where do you see yourself in two, five, or ten years? What can you do to ensure that you will reach that goal? Keep doing these things! They will help you. What are you doing today that will ensure you do not reach that goal? Stop doing these things; they will only hurt you.

Maybe you've already made some big mistakes in your life. Real whoppers! But guess what? Those mistakes don't have to define the rest of your life. You can overcome them and move forward. Even if you take baby steps, you're still moving in a positive direction. Problems arise when you take a step backward into old behavior or remain at a standstill. When that happens, it's easy to stagnate and get stuck. Just keep moving forward, little by little, and you will succeed.

You may be a little nervous, even scared, about leaving high school. You may be unsure of your path, or uncertain about which way to go. Even if you lack confidence in yourself and your decisions right now, I believe you are completely prepared and ready to take on the world. Will you make mistakes along the way? Absolutely! I've made plenty, but I've tried to learn from them. Will you have doubts and reservations about the decisions you need to make? You betcha! But I trust and believe that you will make the best decision for you at that time.

Remember that you are doing the best you can with what you have at that moment. And so is everyone else. Have kindness and compassion for those you meet along the way. No one's perfect, and we all make mistakes. Help people up instead of putting them down.

Finally, remember that you are special and unique. You have talents and gifts that are yours and yours alone. There is a story that only you can tell, a dress that only you can design, or a painting that only you can create. Don't rob the world of your talents because of fear or uncertainty. Share your gifts! You may think your talents are mediocre and not very special. If you are a street cleaner, be the best street cleaner you can be. Take pride in what you do. Improve your skills. Add to your knowledge base. Above all, have fun!

Again, let me say that I am proud of each and every one of you. I think you are all awesome, and it has been a privilege to teach you and know you. Now... go make your life the best it can be!

I want to end with two quotes (why is it that other people say things more eloquently than I do? LOL):

"You are never given a wish without also being given the power to make it come true. You may have to work for it, however."
—Richard Bach

"If one advances confidently in the direction of his dreams, and endeavors to live the life which he has imagined, he will meet with success unexpected in common hours." —Henry David Thoreau

Surely you know the drill by now, so I'll forgo the assignment part (yes, you still have to turn it in!). 'Til we meet again...

Anne reread the letter through misty eyes. The end of the school year was always a mixed bag of emotions. She was usually glad to see some kids go, like the ones who provided the most frustration over the year. But this year was different. The letters had provided an insight into her students' lives as they shared their dreams or frustrations, and Anne realized that there was something about each of them that she would miss. Then there were the ones who had truly embraced the letters and shared their souls with her. It was an honor she hadn't expected when she began the assignment. After all, she had written the first letter only because she was angry at them. But, through the letters, they had revealed themselves to each other—she to her students and they to her. They had built a connection. And, hopefully, she had instilled in them a working knowledge of some of the intangibles they would face: honesty and integrity, boundaries, self-worth, gratitude, and love. She hoped she had made a difference in their lives; she felt she had impacted a few of them. She closed her eyes, offering silent gratitude to the universe for this school year, these kids, and the inspiration of the letters.

Chapter 54

There was a lull in Anne's activity in all areas of her life. She knew it would be temporary, but she enjoyed the relative peace. Senior exams were in two weeks, followed by another week until graduation. John and Tony settled in comfortably and seamlessly, as if they had always been there. Karen's wedding planning was done: invitations sent, cakes and flowers ordered, dress altered. There was nothing to do but wait for the big day.

All five of them had passports and tickets in hand, excited for the trip to Italy. The wedding festivities constituted three days of their ten-day adventure. None of them had been abroad, and they couldn't wait to explore all that Italy had to offer. Anne charged them with doing a little research on their own, with the purpose of finding something specific they wanted to do. Maggie, a *Twilight* fan, wanted to visit Volterra, the setting for the übervampire group known as the Volturi. Richard wanted to climb to the top of the Tower of Pisa so he could jump up and down in an attempt to finally make it topple over. John and Tony knew their fantasy destination immediately: the Ducati factory in Bologna. They had heard stories about it for years and couldn't wait to go. John frequently teased Anne that he had married her only so they could go to Italy… and the Ducati factory. Anne's dream was to spend the day at the Villa d'Este, a magnificent garden in Tivoli.

Once they had their destinations in mind, they planned their post-wedding itinerary.

Anne had wanted to visit Italy all her life. Miroslav Sasek's books *This Is Rome* and *This Is Venice* were a part of her childhood library and had ignited her interest. Later, *Roman Holiday* became her favorite movie, and *Under the Tuscan Sun* her favorite novel. She was thrilled about the trip, and so very grateful to Karen for falling in love with a handsome, wealthy Italian. Karen and Lorenzo were gifting the entire trip to Anne and John as part wedding present, part thank-you for their help and support. Anne was so overwhelmed by their generosity that she almost couldn't accept it, but thought better of it and agreed. It would be the trip of a lifetime, and she didn't want to deprive the kids, John, or herself of the opportunity.

The students were prompt in delivering their last letter. No one wanted to have to play catch-up at the end of school. John was still at the shop, and all the kids were with friends. Anne used the quiet time to read some responses.

Dear Mrs. E:

I can't wait to get out of high school. I'm tired of the reading and writing (sorry). I'm smart, and I can do the work, but I like to work with my hands. I like being a mechanic. Jessie has taught me everything he knows and I'm getting to be a pretty good mechanic, if I do say so myself. LOL. You should bring your car in. I'll give you a discount. ;) I'm also ready for the babies to be born. Just another three months. I can't wait to be a dad. I want to be the best dad I can be. Isabel is going to be a great mom. She's so sweet to everyone. I know the babies are going to love her. My plan is to work hard, save money for a house, and be the best husband, father, and mechanic I can be.

So that's about it for my future. But I also wanted to say thank you. You have been a great teacher this year. You've really been

CLASS LETTERS

my favorite teacher in high school. I hated these letters at first, but they made alot of sense. They helped me see that being in a gang was no good. And they helped me think about the man I want to be for Isabel and the babies. And myself.

Have a great summer. And come see the babies after they are born.

Your student,

Ray

Anne couldn't help but smile. Ray and Isabel were going to be great parents. She felt very good about their future. She found Keosha's letter next.

Miss,

I'M GOING TO DESIGN SCHOOL! I know I've already told you in person, but I'm excited, so I thought I'd tell you again. LOL. I get to start in July and I'm gonna work about 20 hours a week to take some cost out of my tuition. But I'll be working in the fashion department so it'll help me with school too. I hope. But I'm really excited. It's like all I can think about. And I keep getting all these design ideas and drawing pictures of them so I don't forget. I also like going to the mall and watching people to see what they're wearing. Some people got crazy ideas about what looks good. I wanna stop them and tell them what they're doing wrong but I don't cuz I don't want no trouble. LOL. That will have to wait till I'm famous. Maybe I can be on that reality show. I guess you can tell I'm excited.

Anyways, I wanted to say thanks for this year. You've been a great teacher and role model for me. You helped me see what I was doing wrong and supported me through it all. It's been a crazy year, but I guess I made it thru it okay. And, like I said, alot of that is because of you. And my mama. It really helped me to get things straight.

I hope you have a great life with your new husband. He's lucky. I'll come back and visit. And don't forget to look for me in fashion magazines. It's gonna happen. I know it! Thanks for everything!

Keosha

Just as she was finishing Keosha's letter, John sent her a text: *Be home in an hour. Want me to pick up dinner? Love you.*

Anne marveled at the changes in her life over the past nine months. A new husband-helpmate and a great stepson were wonderful, but there was also the relief that she didn't have to do it alone anymore. She loved her kids and her life (before John), and it hadn't been as bad as some folks had it. Her kids were good kids, in spite of the fact that they were currently teenagers—an acute "condition" in and of itself. They made good grades, had nice friends, and weren't out doing drugs or causing trouble. Still, she was grateful for John's part in her life—even for something as simple as his offering to pick up dinner. Teenagers were notoriously self-centered, and she felt safe and secure in the fact that someone thought about her and took her into consideration.

She texted him back: *I love you and I'm so grateful to have you in my life. Dinner's covered. Thx. See you soon!*

Ahhhhh… another hour to read and grade. Anne attempted to help herself in that area as much as possible. Of course, as an English teacher, she was required to assign, read, and grade essays, which took an inordinate amount of time. Some, like the letters, were graded on content only; others required a closer inspection to review grammar, paragraph construction, or transitions. There were many times in her teaching career when she wished she had been better at math—very little reading required.

Tiffany's letter was on top of the pile.

CLASS LETTERS

Dear Mrs. R:

It's still so weird calling you that! LOL. Welp, I have good news and bad news. I'll save the good news for last.

My dad drank again. My sponsor says that it's normal. Lots of alcoholics go back. It made me mad though. I guess I got my hopes too high. I'm okay now but it really hurt for awhile. Now the good news, he felt so bad about getting drunk again, he got me into the art school I wanted to go to. It's called Pratt Institute and it's in NEW YORK CITY! Eeeeeeeeeeee!! I can't wait! First, I'll be able to do what I love, which is art. And next, I'll be far away from Texas and my parents. I know that sounds mean, but it's going to be a relief to be away from the drinking and arguing. But I'll miss you! It's been awesome having you this year. Thanks for all your help. I know alot of kids say that to their teachers at the end of the year, but I really mean it. Oh yeah! Thanks for coming to the art competition awards. It was so nice of you to take your time to do that.

Anyways, have a great marriage. Good luck next year! You're gonna need it. You thought we were bad! LOL. And keep writing these letters. Kids need to read this stuff.

Love ya!

Tiffany

"'Kids need to read this stuff,' huh? Thanks for the recommendation, Tiffany," Anne chuckled. She checked the time on her phone and laughed at herself again. She hadn't worn a watch since she'd started carrying a cell phone. If she lost her phone, she'd have no idea what time it was.

"We do some weird stuff sometimes, don't we, Rocky?" she asked her dog. John should be home in another fifteen or twenty minutes. Enough time for one more letter. It belonged to Kim.

Dear Mrs. Rogers,

I can't believe this year has gone by so fast either. So much has happened! I've gone from a shy, quiet, closeted lesbian to a fully out activist. LOL. I've been hurt twice, but I wouldn't change anything. Not even that. I have had a weight taken off my shoulders. It was hard being gay and not saying anything. It was like I wasn't being real. I've known since I was five and that's a long time to not be the real me. Remember the October letter about masks? It hit me hard. I knew I was living a lie. That letter gave me the start I needed to come out. Then we started the GSA. It has helped me and so many others here. We owe that to you for helping us get started. I even think that some kids don't think they can "catch" being gay anymore. ♥ And I also wanted to thank you for coming that night at the hospital. I was scared and I knew you would help calm me down. I love my parents, but I knew they would be worried. And it stresses me out when they worry. Especially about me. I know I've added to their worries since I came out but I have to be me. They are okay with it and have been great with everything. I want to go to college and be an accountant. I'm good with numbers. Better than English! LOL. It will take a long time because I can only go part time right now. But I will do it. I know that because I believe in myself. And I believe in myself because of you. Thank you, Mrs. Rogers.

Kim

Anne sobbed. She couldn't help herself. Feelings of joy, sadness, grief, and gratitude welled up inside and spilled out. The emotions acknowledged the culmination of a year of change, worry, fear, elation, victory, and tragedy. Rocky nudged Anne's hand, a little concerned about his human. She knelt down beside him, wrapped her arms around him, and sobbed into his coat. Rocky leaned into her a bit and rested his head on her shoulder, as if to say, *Let it out. I'm here as long as you need me.* She held Rocky for a bit longer, calming herself, and remembered Browning's words: *God's in his Heaven / All's right with the world.*

Chapter 55

Anne put away the ironing board and iron after pressing her graduation ensemble. Faculty members, administrators, and board members were to file in before the graduates while the band played "Pomp and Circumstance." They would all be wearing the requisite black robes, but had other accoutrements determined by their degree and alma mater. Anne's happened to be burnt orange. Not her favorite color, but she was grateful for the degree.

Maggie had had her cap and gown ready to go days earlier. The gown hung from her closet door so it wouldn't wrinkle. She had received her acceptance letter from Texas State University the previous week and was beside herself with anticipation. Anne had cried when the letter arrived, sharing her daughter's joy. The other tears, the grieving ones, she reserved for John, or those moments in the shower when the idea of her baby's leaving overwhelmed her. She accepted them as part of a parent's process of letting go, but they came nonetheless.

The graduates were in the back halls of the coliseum where the ceremony was held, theoretically in alphabetical order. Some were hugging and congratulating; others were putting the finishing touches on their makeup and hair. One boy flew through the crowd, late as usual, to claim his spot in line just before the processional began.

Teachers, like students, had assigned seats, all facing the stage.

The band and choir were assembled to one side, and behind them were rows of families and friends. There were claps and whistles, along with the occasional blast from an air horn. The band repeated the famous song until everyone was seated and the ceremony began. Anne looked around until she found her crew. She spied Karen, Lorenzo, and her parents, grateful they had made the trip to watch their granddaughter's graduation.

There were all the normal prayers, anecdotes, and advice. Just before giving out diplomas, the president of the student class walked to the podium.

"Our class has had many successes, but we have also endured some loss. This year, we lost one of our own. David Spears was a good friend, a talented athlete, and a caring person. The senior class voted a couple of months ago to begin a fund in memory of David. Part of it will go to the counseling department for ongoing education regarding teen issues and suicide. The rest of it will go to the athletic department's summer football program for tuition for those who can't afford it. In addition, we wanted to honor a teacher with a plaque in memory of David. It is called the David Spears Award of Excellence and is for a teacher who exhibits a caring and helpful attitude toward students, one who actively tries to make the students have the best high school experience they can, in and out of the classroom. Several names were submitted and then voted on by the senior class and the administrators. The David Spears Award of Excellence goes to Anne English—I mean, Anne Rogers!"

Anne was perusing the program when she heard her name called. Students were looking around at her, urging her to claim the award. She blushed as she strolled toward the stage. Now it made sense: Karen and Lorenzo; her parents. The sneaks!

She crossed the stage and accepted her award, hugging the student before returning to her seat. She hadn't heard anything about this—unusual, considering the normal high school gossip mill—and if she had, she would never have thought that she'd win it. She

CLASS LETTERS

remained composed, in spite of the tears and butterflies that plagued her. Students and teachers whispered their congratulations as she passed. By the time she returned to her seat, the list of names had begun.

She watched them file up to the stage, and memories of the year flooded in.

"Antonia Marie Del Rio."

Such a pretty girl. I think she's going to UTA... Anne began an inner monologue.

"Trevor Wayne Elliott."

Ohmygod, she's next! Look at how grown up she is. I can't believe she's graduating...

"Margaret Renee English." Anne clapped and tried to wipe away tears simultaneously, without much success at either task. She wanted to be with John and the boys for this moment, but Maggie wanted her on the floor with her. Although they weren't seated next to each other, they were sitting in the same row, and Anne gave her hand a squeeze as Maggie and the rest of the row moved into place. They had always been close, but Anne knew from experience that their relationship would never be the same. Some things, like the questions Maggie posed when she was confused, would be replaced with confidence and self-assurance. Others changes, like their growing friendship, were peeking over the horizon, ready to appear when the time was right.

"LaQuandra Collette Ferguson."

She's doing such a good job with that baby...

"Keosha Raquel Jones."

Wooohooo! Look at her go. What a pistol! I still can't believe she designed the dress she's wearing under that gown. It's amazing!

"Christina Joann Kozlowski."

I'd swear I've never seen that child before in my life... weird!

"Kim Le."

Wow, she amazes me...

"Carolyn Sue Lomax."

Red hair? That girl has a different color every week.
"Isabel Perez Martinez."
Oooooohh... she's starting to show...
Anne watched the glowing mother-to-be waddle across the stage, followed by an ecstatic Ray.
"Raymundo Manuel Martinez." Ray raised his arms in triumph.
Doesn't he look handsome, and so proud. I just love that boy...
"Pablo Luis Munoz."
Another one I've never seen.
"Ricardo Raul Ramirez."
Ha! My cousin is 'R cubed' too!
"Tiffany Diane Wallace."
Lord, I hope her dad is here and sober. She's such a smart, talented girl...

The master of ceremonies called the last few names, ending with Lila Zazamorro; the final congratulations were made; prayers were spoken; and, with a whoop, mortarboards flew through the air. Following the recessional, students, parents, and friends tried to locate each other in the crowd. Hands waved in the air, people whistled across the throng, and groups gathered for pictures. Anne searched for Maggie, John, and the rest of her crew. She clutched her award, afraid to drop such a treasure in the clamor. She spotted Lorenzo, the tallest in the group, and headed in their direction. Once she joined them, there were hugs and congratulations for both Maggie and Anne. As the group headed to their cars, ready for a celebratory dinner, Anne heard her name.

"Mrs. English! I mean, Mrs. Rogers!" Ray and Isabel waved her over.

"Could we get a picture with you?" Ray asked.

"Absolutely!" grinned Anne.

"Look, there's Tiffany and Keosha! Hey!" Ray yelled for their attention. "Come get a picture with us an' Mrs. Eng... Rogers!"

CLASS LETTERS

The two girls snagged Kim along the way, saying, "You need to be in this too. We're getting a picture with Mrs. Rogers. C'mon!"

Ray, Isabel, Kim, Anne, Tiffany, and Keosha stood together, grinning and posing as John, Karen, and anyone else with a camera or a cell phone snapped pictures. The next day, a framed picture of the six of them took up residence on Anne's bedside table until the following fall, when it made the permanent move to her classroom. It reminded her of Kim's courage to be herself, Keosha's and Tiffany's hopes for a better life, Ray's enthusiasm and love for his new family, and David's struggles. And it confirmed and validated her prayer that the letters had made a difference. Like Tiffany had said, kids need to read this stuff.

Acknowledgments

I'd like to thank three wise, wonderful women at She Writes Press: Brooke Warner, Krissa Lagos, and Trudy Catterfeld. With patience and expertise, they helped this neophyte maneuver through the publishing process. Thank you for taking me on and for growing my baby into a real book!

To my husband, John. Thank you for being patient when I disappeared into my writing. I'm so grateful that you support my hopes and dreams.

Finally, I'd like to thank all the students who participated in our monthly letters. It was a joy to get to know you through the letters. You made this all possible!

About the Author

Claire Chilton Lopez is a writer, blogger, and former high school English teacher. She has written two novels, several spiritual fables, and a number of poems. The inspiration for her novel, *Class Letters*, originated during her years of teaching and her desire to encourage other teachers to connect with their students through the power of letters.

Claire enjoys travel, reading, and riding motorcycles. She lives with her husband and three dogs.